WOLF

Book 1 of the Wolfslayer Series

Mark Fleming

WOLF WARRIORS
Book 1 of the Wolfslayer series

Copyright © 2015 Mark Fleming

The right of M J Fleming to be identified as the Author of the Work has been asserted by him in accordance with the Copyright, Designs and Patents Act 1988.
Apart from use permitted under UK copyright law, this publication may only be reproduced, stored, or transmitted, in any form, or by any means, with prior permission in writing of the Author or, in the case of reprographic production, in accordance with the terms of licenses issued by the Copyright Licensing Agency.

First published as an Ebook by Kindle Direct Publishing
(April 21 2014)
This edition published by CreateSpace Independent Publishing Platform (October 31 2015)

ISBN-13: 978-1519101617
ISBN-10: 1519101619

All characters in this publication are fictitious and any resemblance to real persons, living or dead, is purely coincidental.

Edited by Anne Duffy

Cover illustration © Mark Drummond Johnson

CHAPTER ONE

Wessex, 584 A.D.

A whip lashed across Telor's face, jolting him back to consciousness. Blinking into the dank cell, he noticed a bucket: he had actually been doused in icy water. He was also aware of rope coiled around his wrists and ankles. As his dripping hair matted to his bruised cheeks, a voice sneered.

"Awake, Celtic dog!"

He winced at the alien words: English. Water soaked into his rags, stinging numerous cuts, then a boot materialised from the shadows and stamped his kidneys. Hissing in agony, he doubled up. A heel connected with the bridge of his nose, the crack magnifying in the darkness. Blood seeped into a sticky necklace. He braced himself when the feet approached, only this time his antagonist grunted and hauled Telor by his ponytail onto his trembling feet. He was shoved towards a doorway.

"Quicker, you fat bastard, quicker!" Had he been able to understand, the taunt might have smarted. Telor was a bard, his stoutness testament to years of long winter evenings entertaining his clan with mead-fuelled songs and sagas. During his manhandling he was aware of other dejected Celts pleading for mercy in varying accents: Atrebates from the forests to the north, Durotriges from beyond the Mendip Hills. Telor could only guess at their current location: when the raiders took slaves rather than heads they often transported their human booty for miles. A fist smashed into his jaw. "Hurry!"

Telor glimpsed malevolent eyes, obscured by a helm's nose-guard then fingers tightened in his scalp. He was dragged over pulverised earth and scattered straw to a point where flames curled from a large log fire. In the background many eyes twinkled against the glare.

"Bow before your masters, Celts," the guard spat, and before Telor had time to comply he was shoved forwards, his knees impacting the ground. Rocking unsteadily, his glance wavered towards beams high above the long hut's floor. There was a brief commotion as another prisoner was forced into position. Telor dared not turn towards him but noticed the man was white haired and also very corpulent. When the English enslaved Celtic males it was invariably for manual roles: miners, foresters, or soldiers. Did their barbarism allow for the modest indulgence of sparing entertainers? Further captives were heaved into line, all bulky: Telor counted they now numbered five. There were possibilities of harmonies to delight this audience who would be more familiar with Germanic dirges.

Silence descended. Telor listened to the crackling flames. Outside, horses whinnied, then some beast bellowed, giving the impression of monstrous lungs emptying: an ox? He had heard fanciful tales of the livestock the English tribes had brought with them from Germania and his imagination conjured a colossal bull. A heavy-set warrior separating himself from the gathering distracted him.

As Telor returned to full consciousness, tears welled. He blinked them away, determined not to give this barbarian the satisfaction of gloating at his despair. Glowering at the one who approached, he observed scars along muscular forearms, mementoes of many brutal skirmishes. A Celtic torc gleamed at his neck, undoubtedly wrenched from a decapitated victim during those battles. Sinister of all was a patch obscuring his left eye.

The warrior snorted, his expression growing with disdain as he studied each captive in turn. After the scornful gaze had dismissed him, Telor recalled the events that had led him to this hell. He had been gathering blackberries, had dropped the basket in order to mop his sweating brow again. Shrill peals carried from the sentry post. Short blasts meant a Norse longship on the horizon; those elongated tones warned of a Saxon warband. Waddling towards the village he halted: smoke was already billowing from thatched roofs, people were scattering, and soldiers were lunging with bloodied swords and axes. Turning back into the trees, he roared as branches tore at him: more to mask the screams of his kin being slaughtered. His frantic breathing obscured the jeers of the hunting men until they were almost upon him. Betrayed by the undergrowth, his feet caught in weeds and he crashed to the forest floor. His dazed eyes wavered towards a young Saxon, drawn to a crimson birthmark on the boy's neck, shaped like a skull. A raised sword had winked in the sunlight before its hilt crashed into his skull, opening a trapdoor into a void.

"I am Modig of the West Saxons, and you are guests at my son Oxa's wedding, Celts," boomed the one-eyed warrior. Telor detected a mocking tone, but when the Saxon clapped his hands together, he instigated a curious procession that begun winding through the congregation towards a table. Saxon women were carrying plates laden with roasted game, the succulent aroma mouth-watering to captive and captor alike. Behind, two guards dragged another shackled man, mottled with bruises yet defiant. The food was positioned on the table, then the serving wenches bowed to Modig and stepped aside. The prisoner was hauled before Modig, cursing in a tongue that reminded Telor of English, but courser. Telor observed his forked beard and tattoos swirling over his lacerated torso and arms; not the random blue patterns favoured by the Celts, but designs intricately etched: wolf heads, a serpentine dragon, an eagle plunging at prey. A Norseman, crazed as a cornered wildcat. When he cursed Modig, the Saxon kicked him squarely in the balls.

Modig glared at the man writhing, his wrath reduced to whimpers. His features softening, he returned his attention to the five. "These fucking Vikings are the only Germanic people more savage than we English. They drink weird brews that send most of them mad. Lucky for all of us in these islands, they live at the edge of the world, and restrict their visits to one or two longships every other month. But this Norse dog is going to help me provide some sport before today's proceedings. Actually, more of a lesson, especially for all the children gathered here ... the next generation of our brave warriors. Before this lesson begins, you Celts must fill your bellies. You've been fed nought but scraps since you were each brought here. And all of you look as if you enjoy your food.

You must be starving. Now you will gorge yourselves. Anyone who does not clear his plate will lose his fucking head."

The captives stared blankly. Modig resorted to miming the action. Glancing hesitantly at one another, Telor and the others were prodded towards the table by spear shafts, before sitting at a long bench. Nodding to one of his men, Modig murmured a command. The soldier drew a knife and hacked through each wrist bind. Having endured days of beatings and meagre rations, the prisoners needed no further prompting. Each fell upon the feast like wolves around a deer.

Telor spotted a furtive youth stepping beside Modig, his features a less-haggard version. He also scrutinised the attractive maiden standing submissively by the young man's side, her shoulders draped in flowers, as were many of the others he could now distinguish. He felt a weight lifting. The partridge was roasted to perfection. Despite their initial rough treatment, the Celts had apparently been hauled here, not to lose their heads, but to sing at a marriage.

"Enjoy your feast. The game was trapped on moors you natives could once call your hunting ground. It is ours now, and the animals we chase there speak Celtic." He paused while the Saxons watching in the background cackled. "Eat well, in honour of Oxa and Mildgyd. You must clear all those plates and bowls." Turning to the lone prisoner, still squirming before him, Modig grinned. "As for you? I want your help in a demonstration to my wedding guests. Many are the Saxon thanes – chieftains – present this day. I wish you to put on a fine show for them, before the ceremony and the hard drinking to follow." Hearty roars reverberated. Modig joined in their cheering before his expression darkened. "Weddings are such a special occasion. As well as looking to the future, we celebrate our past, our achievements. I want everyone here to see the fate of this island."

Telor balked when Modig unsheathed his sword. The chieftain dug its tip into the compacted earth at his feet, working it into what the bard eventually deciphered to be a map. Those watching from the rear craned for a better view. Although rudimentary, Telor recognised the jutting Cornish peninsula with

Cymru looming over it. The blade traced a jagged south coast, adding a small circle for the Isle of Wight, before heading eastwards to Kent, carving the rump of Anglia, then proceeding in a line up the eastern seaboard that stopped short of Caledonia. To the left a simple circle denoted Hibernia, a larger one the European mainland.

Modig gestured to part of his handiwork. "Children ... the Romans once called these lands Britannia. The native Celtic tribes, the Britons, bowed down before the Romans, bowed until their miserable bellies crawled along the ground, like fucking slugs. The British became lazy. They stopped sharpening their swords ... stopped tattooing their skins. They got a taste for Roman food and Roman wine. The Brits became fat, like these five greedy pigs ... and started wearing fine Roman clothes ... their menfolk would wear togas and sandals and soak in scented baths."

Between mouthfuls, Telor noticed many of the audience casting disdainful looks in his direction. Puzzled, he continued chewing into a bird breast, juices roving into his beard.

"All of this was the price they were happy to pay for their loss of freedom. The Brits have spent generations learning how to be servile. The Romans never colonised Germania. *Never*. Germania was soaked with the blood of too many legionnaires." The remark provoked gruff approval. "To be fair, some of the natives fought harder than others." Modig thrust his sword into Anglia. "Here, the Iceni, ruled by their warrior queen, Boudica, allied with other tribes. Their army of one hundred thousand sacked Roman cities. Camulodunum, Verulamium and Londinium. Such was the scale of destruction, Emperor Nero even considered abandoning Britannia. But his general, Suetonius, regrouped the remnants of the garrisons, before attacking Boudica on the Roman road, Wattling Street. Despite being outnumbered ten to one, the Romans chose their battleground carefully, at the head of a valley. The stupid blueskins simply charged at them in one mass, not realising they were being funnelled into a narrow point. Their army became a rabble that could not move, soldiers advancing from the rear merely adding to the crush. Then the Romans launched volley after volley of javelins and arrows until men were knee deep in blood. The British retreated in panic. The legionnaires harried the fleeing warriors, whose escape was blocked by wagons. There followed a massacre. None were spared, not even the women and children among the camp followers, not even the pack animals.

Unlike these southern lap dogs, the tribes in Caledonia - the Dalriati, the Caledonii, the Picts - were so hostile the Romans were forced to build a vast wall to keep them at bay, all the way from the German Sea to the Solway Firth." Modig sliced a line between the rugged coasts. "But two hundred years ago, the mighty Roman Empire fell. Their colony of Britannia was abandoned. All the Celts enjoyed freedom. That did not last."

Modig hacked a mouthful of phlegm from his throat and dropped it into the channel between Britannia and Europe. Spitting again, his globule splattered by the east coast. "The fucking Norse," he gibed, forcibly smacking the tattooed captive across the back of his head. "The pirates from the frozen wastelands were next to show an interest in these islands. Their longships continue plundering the shores and estuaries, sacking villages at will, whether English or British."

He dragged his sword back to the portion of ground far to the right. "Germania. Jutland." He hacked several lines towards Britannia. "We cast our greedy eyes on this fertile island to the west, its inhabitants mostly farmers now, rather than fighters. Fleets of warships were launched by Saxons, Angles and Jutes."

Modig grasped the Norseman's right arm and held it towards the map. "Behold, how our English nation was forged in our enemy's blood!" The chieftain's blade winked, severing the right hand. While he shrieked, Modig maintained a tight grasp of his hair and tugged the stump, directing the spurting blood over his crude map. "The land once occupied by those rebellious Iceni was conquered by the Angles. They settled here, where they became known as the North Folk and the South Folk, and gave birth to a new English kingdom, East Anglia."

Modig seized the bleeding man and dragged him until he was above the centre of the map. While the Norseman whimpered, Modig dug his sword into his left thigh, aiming the fountaining blood. "The heartlands of Britannia became awash with dead Celts ... so much blood staining the earth ... red for the territories now ruled by the Middle English and the Mercians, whose kingdoms now stretch up to the River Humber." His blade struck again, removing the Viking's right leg from below the knee. The Saxon ensured the blood seeped towards the north of his gory montage.

"Above the Humber, more Angle tribes, Bernicians, Deirans ... their territories now form the kingdom of North Humberland." Peering over his enthralled audience, he winked when Oxa caught his eye. "But I am far from finished. There is so much more land where the spilling of enemy blood has given birth to our new England." The thane ensured blood splattered over Kent, then the Isle of Wight. "The Jutes now rule these parts of the south coast." Modig kept the man suspended, the gruesome stains welling into an puddle that crept towards the south and west. "From the fringes of Kent to the borders of Cymru ... all is ours ... all is Saxon land." This was acknowledged with thunderous acclaim, sword hilts crashing against shields. "Where the Thames meets the German Sea is Essex, kingdom of the East Saxons. Westwards to the kingdoms of the Middle Saxons and South Saxons." Thrusting his sword deep into the lurid quagmire, he left it embedded there. "And right here, the greatest realm in England ... Wessex." A roar boomed from the onlookers. "Home of the proud tribes of West Saxons: Dorseatas, Hwiccas, Wilseatas, and my own people, the Somorsaetas. Our sworn aim is to drive the blueskins into the sea."

Telor nibbled at the moist meat around a leg. While he felt guilty sating his hunger during all this, it perturbed him more to notice the Saxon children poking their way through the forest of adult legs for a better view of the torture. They were gawking at the horrid crimson pools that twisted and merged, but with a terrible pride rather than the disgust he felt.

Modig merely leered at his handiwork. "Those areas of bare soil you see ... Cornwall ... Cymru ... Cumbria ... Caledonia ... the English are driving the British ever westwards, ever northwards, into those far corners of this island, until they will have nowhere else to run. Soon *all* the land will be stained red with the blood of the blueskins, and the blood of any of these Viking vermin daring to raid our shores." That statement was the cue to extract his sword and hack it across the Norseman's neck. The body splashed onto the floor, spraying the five diners. "Oxa. It is time for the ceremony."

The younger warrior elbowed his way to the front of the throng of Saxons, leading his intended bride by the hand. When he stepped into the firelight, Telor recognised the skull birthmark.

"At your service, thane." Oxa stepped over to the Celts. "You oafs have filled your bellies enough. Now drink."

His words were met with blank expressions. Oxa snapped his fingers and a woman approached, clutching ox horns brimming with mead. Thrusting one into each of the captives' grips, he smashed a fist onto the table to provoke them all into generous gulping. When Telor had drained his horn, he belched. Oxa seized his tunic. "With me, you British dogs. With me." The force he applied hauling Telor to his feet was ample translation.

The bard's eyes locked on the grisly map as he was shoved across it, his bare feet swishing through the swill. The foul picture symbolised the extent to which the English tribes had conquered the east and south of the country. He glanced at the small patch of exposed ground at the frontier of the Cornish peninsula, his own realm, Dumnonia, languishing next to the deep red of Wessex. Symbolically, maroon tendrils were already weaving deep inside his tribe's ancient territories.

He accepted the torture of the Norseman had also served as intimidation. If the Celts were literally singing for their lives, the melodies were bound to be particularly acute. He was aware of the Saxons laughing as all the captives were bundled by, the women casting flowers towards them, their children giggling. Telor caught the eye of twin Saxon toddlers and he exchanged smiles with them. Breathing harshly, he realised he was seeing double, the hastily downed mead having gone straight to his head. The sensation became dreamlike and for an instant he indulged the notion that he was about to awake from this nightmare.

The unlikely wedding guests were escorted from Modig's chambers into a courtyard. While the bemused Celts blinked at the sunlight and shuffled onwards, encouraging cries echoed from Saxon villagers clustered on all sides of the open space. More flowers cascaded over the prisoners, the fragrant petals of pansies and roses sweetening the breeze. Oxa stalked alongside the five men, then raised his right hand aloft. At this signal the crowds parted. The chieftain's son paced forward, beckoning his captives to follow. Telor glanced around as more villagers gathered in the background, jostling closer to the action.

Assuming the wedding party would follow to take advantage of the glorious summer afternoon, Telor cleared his throat. Obviously none present would appreciate the lyrics to the celebratory songs these five men might chose to entertain them with, but the melodies would transcend ethnic division.

Oxa jabbed a finger at a point just beyond where he was standing. Only when Telor and the others stepped towards this did they identify the obstacle before them: the ground plunged into the maw of a cave. The stench emanating from its shadows was a vile meld of blood, rotting meat, shit and piss. One of the other captives vomited and Telor heard the splatter seconds later.

Closing his eyes, he sang the introductory bars of a Dumnonii marriage aria. Oxa fired an inquisitive look at him before cupping his free hand to his mouth and giving a piercing whistle. A moment later a growling seemed to reverberate from the very bowels of the earth. The surrounding Saxons cheered in delight. Still singing, Telor stared downwards. As his eyes accustomed to this fissure, he could make out numerous clusters of bones, partially stripped of flesh. He gaped back over his shoulder.

Modig had joined his son by the cavern. He bellowed to his audience: "Behold the fate of the native Brits. Our new English kingdoms are being forged in their blood. Their women make fine slaves for our warriors. Their men are but meat. And these five blueskins, spared death when we sacked their villages due to their generous girths, will make an excellent sacrifice to our god of war, Tiw ... and fine entertainment for the wedding of Oxa and Mildgyd."

Oxa grasped his father's proffered fist. "Thank you, my thane. Bee-Wolf will welcome these fat oafs."

Without further ceremony, the young Saxon warrior lunged at the captives, one by one, tipping them over the edge of the pit. Telor landed heavily, crumpling to the rubble-strewn ground, limbs snapping, his fingers clawing into stinking sludge. High above, torches were brandished, casting fitful glares over the charnel house, shining against pools of congealing blood and glistening mounds of tissue and body fat. He saw another prisoner attempting to stand, his overweight body dyed crimson from head to foot. Telor focused on him reaching to the cave wall to steady his faltering steps. A vast shape disengaged from the shadows with a horrifying roar. Excitable gasps sounded above, and children squealed with glee. A gargantuan bear fell on the hapless man. Telor was riveted to its jaws grinding into flesh, its haunches heaving from side to side, tearing the head from the shoulders. Transfixed by the brutal killing through his woozy vision, he tried squirming backwards but his arms and legs were molten with agony. He had been fattened for this monster and now his shattered bones were presenting his body on a platter. The beast chewed at a trailing ribbon of intestines. Telor gasped. The tiny sound was enough to draw the bear's attention. Still masticating, it bounded through the viscera, its snorting breath hot and putrid. The bard thought of transforming his last lungfuls of air into a song for all the loved ones he had lost but what else could he do but scream?

CHAPTER TWO

Cyneheard was irritated his view was being hampered by so many skittish brats. A chieftain of the Dorseatas tribe, his entourage had ridden to Modig's village from the southern coast, where Saxon Wessex encroached furthest into Celtic Dumnonia. While he would much rather have been leading raiding parties westwards, this bear bating was proving to be an excellent distraction.

"As uneven a contest as when our hounds are set on rabbits, my thane?" his companion ventured. Resting on a stave, the older man was wrapped in a sheepskin cloak. Necklaces were draped around his scrawny neck, thick twine threaded through a motley collection of animal bones and teeth.

"Indeed, Paega," Cyneheard agreed, just as the bear swung an enormous paw, striking a Celt so forcefully his neck splintered before it chewed at the flesh around the throat. "Or a Saxon warband overrunning a Brit village?"

"The better analogy."

Cyneheard watched an overweight native's pitiful demise. "As Modig said, some of the Brits have fought back before now. When they choose to make a stand, even when they are about to be vanquished to a man, at least you can respect that. But what warrior could withstand such an onslaught of teeth and claw, Paega?"

Paega turned away from the butchery, his eyes roving to the dead Norseman that two burly soldiers were now dragging towards the cave. After a nod from Oxa, the dismembered corpse was toppled overboard to add to the bear's macabre feast, the severed parts following. Shutting his eyes, Paega murmured an incantation. Cyneheard observed the older man's lips moving silently against the snarls and screams from below. He knew Paega was reciting a spell. Shamen existed in many of the English tribes, and among their Norse enemies: the equivalent of the Celtic druids who practiced ancient magic.

Paega's eyes snapped open. "I sensed the Norseman was from a longship that ran aground on the Severn. A band of Somersaetas came across the wreck, killing the survivors. On Modig's orders, one was captured and ridden back here to be dissected for his ... history lesson."

"Lingering deaths are fine for sport, Paega, but too drawn out for battle. Think how swiftly my warriors could overcome our Celtic enemies if they had teeth and claws like Oxa's bear?"

"That is exactly what I am thinking, my thane."

"What do you mean?"

"There are many stories about the Norse."

"Stories?"

"They say some fighters drink potions before battle which give them the viciousness and strength of cave bears. In a trance, they assume themselves wild animals. In battle, none withstand them. Other potions make their warriors imagine they are wolves."

Blood flecked the onlookers, provoking intakes of breath. The beast had struck a prisoner so forcefully his detached head had launched into the air. Tracking its motion, the bear rose on its hind legs then opened its jaws to snatch the spinning skull.

"Wolves, Paega? That would be something. If I had a dozen men who believed themselves to be wolves, we could drive all the Celts from Cornwall."

"There are other stories about the Norse, told only by shamen."

"Only by shamen? Why?"

"Because they refer to dark magic."

"Isn't *all* your magic dark, Paega?"

"This is *especially* dark magic, my thane. *Black* magic. Magic that saps the strength of those who would tamper with it. It is said some of the Norse shamen concoct potions so evil, whoever drinks them actually shapeshifts. They *transform* into wolf demons. Werewolves."

Cyneheard guffawed at this, slapping Paega's shoulders. "Would that there was any truth in *those* stories." He gazed into the cave again. "The feast appears to be over. The fat Celts and the Norse pirate are all torn to shreds and the bear's belly is full. He waddles into the shadows to snore. Our one-eyed host will shortly be ushering everyone back into the main chamber for the ceremony. The human feasting will soon begin."

"I fear we may have to forgo our share of Modig's boar and mead."

"*Why?*"

Paega's brow furrowed. "I had a vision, of another Norse vessel. Its sails are taking it on course for our village. There is a strong offshore current, but the pirates will make landfall in the early morning."

"In that case we must bid farewell to Modig and wish Oxa good fortune. Then we ride south to bloody our swords."

CHAPTER THREE

Camouflaged by the undergrowth, the warriors watched the longship gliding into the inlet, its rowers gathering momentum in anticipation of the imminent plundering. It was time to spring the trap. Cyneheard bellowed: "Destroy them!"

All along the headland, the bracken stirred and men rose, bows primed. Arrows scythed, embedding in wood, or meat. The seasoned pirates were swift to react, raising a wall of shields, while oars pitched the vessel away from the cliff-face. Cyneheard had known the Norse boat would only be taken by hand-to-hand combat. "Let's send these dogs to their Valhalla! With me, Saxons!"

Leaping from the cliff, he plunged into the waves twenty feet below, thrashing to the surface. As he stroked towards the dragon figurehead the sea exploded around him, hundreds of his men following his lead. The enemy screamed taunts and a storm of javelins rained on the swimmers, staining the water red. Cyneheard braced himself when a raven-haired Norseman raised a spear. But an arrow pierced his left temple, its momentum pitching him overboard. Covering fire continued while more Saxons neared the barnacle-encrusted hull.

Norse ships were built with a shallow draft for speed and maneuverability: the defenders were only feet away. Cyneheard noticed his soldiers already clambering aboard from the stern and the starboard side. There were clashes of sword against sword, and the air grew thick with sparks and curses. When the Saxon chieftain climbed over the gunwale, unsheathing his sword, an axe whistled through the air. Jolting his head, its razor-sharp blade brushed his beard. Although his antagonist wielded a second axe, he was already badly wounded, bloodied arrows puncturing his rib cage. He could only manage a sluggish defence when Cyneheard cracked his broadsword against the axe hilt with an ear-splitting ring. When the Norseman raised his weapon again, groaning with the effort, the chieftain thrust his blade deep into the exposed gut before kicking the corpse away.

While the pirates were making a ferocious stand, the accuracy of the archers on the cliffs tipped the scales of the one-sided battle. More Saxons swarmed over the deck. Swirling blood rendered swordsmanship impossible and the melee degenerated into a brutal scrum. Cyneheard's warriors gradually funnelled their remaining adversaries into the prow. The Norsemen's impending demise made for desperate lunges and parries with their bloodstained weapons. One by one their legs were hacked away. When they toppled to the deck, their helmets were kicked off, their skulls mashed open.

Battle roars gave way to the agonised wailing of the injured, until a lone Norseman faced the Saxons clustering inside the longship, knee-deep in human detritus. His breath rasped and blood was streaming down his forked beard, but his face was contorted with hatred. He pointed his wavering blade towards the Saxon chieftain's neck. Cyneheard gave a wry smile, lowering his own sword. The cornered man hissed in his guttural tongue, spittle flecking his lips. Cyneheard stepped closer, so the metal point was pressing into his skin. Then he lifted his right hand. The Norseman squinted curiously at the blood forming crimson bracelets around the Saxon's wrist. Deliberately, the chieftain opened his fist, all the while fixing the bewildered man in his sights. Then he took one step backwards, touching the flat of his hand to his throat, slicing it across. At his signal scores of arrows struck their target, pinning the slain Norseman to the curved neck of his dragon.

* * *

"Thane! This one still breathes!"

Cyneheard remained focused on the ox horn, raising it to his blood-matted face then gulping the mead. "Killing Norse is even thirstier work than killing Brits, Edwig," he winked at the soldier. "They put up much more of a fight. Now. What were you saying?"

"This one lives." Edwig spat into the face of the Norseman he was dragging towards the mound of corpses. The pirate's mail was hacked to shreds, the leather undershirt perforated with stab wounds. Cyneheard observed a flicker of movement around the eyelids. The man struggled to move, his features red as the surrounding timbers, delving into his garments.

"Perhaps he hides a blade, my lord?"

Cyneheard frowned. "I doubt the duel would be entertaining, Edwig. Our beards will be white by the time he manages to present his hidden blade."

Crouching, Cyneheard helped the doomed man with his task, ripping a ragged hole across his shirt. "Nought but a small flask." He addressed him. "They say you Viking dogs ferment the fiercest of ales in your frozen villages? What else is there for you to do up there aside from get drunk and fuck reindeer? I'll grant you a last few mouthfuls before your journey to Woden." Cyneheard tugged the vessel from the bloodied clothes then removed the cork stopper. Instantly he recoiled. The surrounding warriors also reacted to the stench. "I thought *I* had a strong stomach, lads … his brew is only fit for drowning ticks in a sheep-dip!"

Unperturbed, the man reached out quivering fingers. Cyneheard touched the decanter's neck to his quivering mouth. Closing his eyes the Norseman sipped, his face grimacing with the agony of propping up his body while struggling to swallow. When the stink became too unbearable, Cyneheard snatched the flask and tossed it into the sea.

"Oswald! Chop down the dragon figurehead. If any Brits roam too close to our villages, it'll scare the fucking hell out of them. Bring kindling, men. Stack it all over the deck." Standing up again he kicked the Norseman's side. "We'll see if your ale has given you the strength to scream when we set your ship alight."

* * *

The boat reminded Cyneheard of some monstrous boar that had been hunted; the broken and blood-drenched beams its ribcage, smoke seeping over its carcass while it cooked. From their vantage point on the cliffs, the Saxons watched the flames weaving around the kindling, engulfing the stacked bodies, filling the air with a pungent aroma of blistering skin and sizzling hair.

Cyneheard focused on the dying man uppermost on the pyre, who remained twitching even as the fiery arrows hissed across the deck. When his eyes wavered upwards and locked on his own, they were dripping with contempt. The Norseman attempted to raise himself from the mound of his mutilated comrades. The chieftain muttered: "The Viking has left it late for an escape attempt." Presently the conflagration became so intense the warriors had to draw back from its searing heat. A moment before Cyneheard tore his gaze away from the inferno he got the impression the Norseman had somehow managed to roll away from the pyramid of cadavers, his clothes in flames, his blood-curdling screams smothered by the raging fires surrounding him. Cyneheard's men backed off further, cursing at the clouds of ash flakes clogging the air. Throwing himself to the ground, he crawled towards the cliff face, his fists digging into grassy clumps, blindly pawing at the ground ahead lest he pitched over the edge. Reaching the lip, he glared down, blinking furiously as the world dissolved into a putrid, all-enveloping black fog.

As he was about to retreat, a blast of wind tore a fissure in the smoke. The entire deck was incandescent, and sparks danced through the churning eddies. But a figure suddenly emerged, wreathed in red and golden flames, howling in agony. The chieftain's heart quickened when he observed this apparition diving overboard.

CHAPTER FOUR

The chieftain's brow furrowed. "This headland is honeycombed with caves. The raider swam towards the tunnels in the cliffs. Oswald, Godric, Edwig, I want you as archers; you remain up here to cut off his escape. The rest of you, with me. We'll climb into the caves and root him out. Tread carefully. The natives believe trolls mine for tin in these caves, who are clumsy oafs, who hack at the rocks with great picks that are forever causing the tunnels to collapse on top of them."

His mocking tone was not identified by many of his entourage, who exchanged fearful glances. "But we are Saxon men of war, are we not?" Irritation had crept into his booming voice. "We can tell the difference between tales the idiot Brits tell their brats at night, and what we can see with our own eyes, can't we? These tunnels are ancient. And they open to the sea. The god of the sea, Wade, is jealous of this beautiful land, and sends his waves to attack the cliffs. There are sometimes cave-ins. Watch your step."

Cyneheard about turned. The warriors stomped behind their chieftain's torch as he clambered into the dingy tunnel opening, stooping beneath overhanging lichen that dripped with rainwater. Although battle-scarred weapons were grasped with the familiar enthusiasm of the hunt, heading into these unstable underground chambers was a challenge. They formed an extended line, skulking down the cramped passageway, the scuffing of their boots mimicked by the limestone walls. Far below, there was a constant roar of the sea boring into the cliff face. Their progress was arduous, the tunnel occasionally narrowing to a point where the men had to twist sideways or stoop down; at one juncture Cyneheard slithered through an opening on his belly, his torchlight dancing crazily before him. While he wriggled along, feeling more maggot than warrior, he spied archaic runes decorating the quartz-encrusted chamber. The indecipherable script merely emphasised whichever primitive tribe had rendered them was long extinct. Even more ancient markings lurked beneath the dead language: sketches of hunters surrounding some beast with great curling tusks. Cyneheard dismissed the distraction and cast his torch ever onward, probing this underworld for his own quarry.

Twenty minutes into the labyrinth, the meandering tunnel forked. Cyneheard cast his flickering flame towards each entrance. "When we first built the settlement, we chased the natives into the forests. We came down here, to make sure none had hidden. Both passages lead down to the sea, and at high tide the caves fill with water. Whichever cave the Norseman swam to, he is trapped." Groans reverberated from the gloom. "Listen ... the dog was almost burned alive. Hear how he wails. He must be put out his misery." It was impossible to tell which direction the cries were emanating from. Cyneheard cocked his head for a while then tired of straining into the darkness. "Leofwine. Wigmund. Take the tunnel on the left."

Wigmund, a rotund and ill-tempered warrior, barged past his comrades. For all his bluster, the others noted the extent to which the light thrown by his torch jerked in his unsteady grip. "Move yer fuckin' arse, Leofwine," he growled over his shoulder.

While their hesitant footfall faded, the others listened. A bat darted overhead, squeaking; many among the patrol gasped. But moments later even more frightening noises resounded from the dark: an anguished yelp, followed by a succession of prolonged screams. Cyneheard immediately bounded in that direction. This passageway was far narrower, and eventually the walls tapered. Rivulets trickled around his boots; while he was concentrating on working his way around a large buttress, his right foot slithered away, almost making him lose his balance. Impatiently he flashed his torch downwards. Instead of an underground spring, the floor of the cave was running with blood. A few tentative steps further on he came across a Saxon sword. Its owner's severed hand still gripped the handle. When he squinted into the murk, he could make out the rest of the body sprawled among scree. He knew it was Leofwine, because the lad's blond curls were being splashed with blood gushing from the point where his throat had been torn out.

He gazed beyond Leofwine's body. His torchlight was reflected in gleaming orange eyes. He was transfixed, but finally murmured: "Back, men." When none took heed, it took a great deal of composure to mask the rising hysteria in his voice. "Back, I say. Let's get the fuck away from these cursed caves."

A hellish roar echoed around the warriors. The Saxons steeled themselves, weapons thrusting into the darkness. While torches carved grotesque patterns on the glistening walls, Cyneheard lunged his blade. "Show yourself, Norse cur."

Below his torch's fluttering aura, a shadow ghosted towards him. His legs were swept away and he tumbled backwards, his sword clattering to one side. He watched aghast as a huge wolf lunged at the soldier behind, its jaws clamping on the man's head, then wrenching it free. The victim crumpled, blood splattering the walls. Before the next warrior could defend himself, the beast had wrested his sword arm from its socket, then buried its muzzle into his midriff, its incisors boring into his abdomen, snatching at entrails. During the mayhem, a rumble came from lower in the caves. The ground trembled and stalactites dislodged, crashing among the Saxons. Cyneheard could only gawk as his men fought to retreat in the confines of the collapsing tunnel, their squirming bodies wedging into the chamber mouth leading to the main shaft in a screaming mass of chain mail and flesh. The frenzied creature hurled itself towards the human blockage, its jaws and massive claws hacking and tearing. When it tossed another severed head over its shoulder as casually as a fox with a rabbit, its vivid eyes focused on Cyneheard. The chieftain tried to move, only to discover his legs pinned by a limestone slab. He reached for his sword, so tantalizingly close. As he stretched, his fingertips inches short, he noticed the wolf in the corner of his vision, its hackles rising. It was preparing to pounce. The sound of a momentous wave reverberated through the maze of tunnels. The aftershock gathered momentum; more fragments dashed against the cave floor, larger boulders splitting, filling the air with choking clouds of dust.

* * *

When Cyneheard's eyelids flickered open, it made no difference: he was immersed in blackness. He tried moving his fingers but found no feeling in the muscles. He visualised the Saxon war god. "Tiw. I beseech you. I don't want to die here in this cave, like a fucking worm. Grant me strength again."

Summoning the last of his sapped energy, his lungs bellowed and he squirmed, inching his battered legs free of the heaped rocks. Pushing other stones away, he fumbled for the walls then heaved himself upright. For a long while he swayed, flexing his sinews, willing the customary brawn to return to his bruised limbs. But when he pawed around, he felt only the tunnel's serrated walls pressing on all sides. His heart sank. "For the sake of one fucking Viking," he spat. Crouching, he groped among the fragments, searching for his sword. Rather than slow asphyxiation, he resolved to expedite his journey to the feast table of Tiw by slicing into his wrists.

It was impossible to gauge the passage of time, but it was becoming an effort to breathe. Dust invaded his throat, clogging his airways: he coughed furiously. A dull ache formed in his chest like a fist opening, the fingertips clawing agonisingly inside his ribs. His knees buckled and he collapsed, his forehead cracking a boulder. Fighting against the remorseless pain, his hand brushed a metal shaft. He sought the handle, his fingers closing around the grip. The sword that had sliced through skulls so recently he could feel hair meshed to its grain, was embedded, its tip stuck fast in ancient stone. Tears streamed while he fought for his weapon. As his arm muscles ached and he felt his lungs expiring, another tremor shook the foundations of the headland. The sword was released. With his final gasps, he pressed the blade to his left wrist. There was a further quaking. Stalactites rained. He sliced down the full length of his forearm.

CHAPTER FIVE

The man's face was caked with blood, emphasising his unrelenting white-eyed stare. Cyneheard knew he was one of Tiw's slaves, come to escort him to the great feast. All sensation had seeped from his left arm but he knew Tiw would be pleased to welcome this particular Saxon warrior, who had similarly sacrificed an arm to prove his fearlessness, just as the god had done when he had fed his arm to Fenrir, the giant wolf. Picturing Fenrir stirred the confusing images swirling in his mind. Had a nightmarish wolf killed him? Perhaps this celestial guardian could provide answers?

"Was Fenrir here?" he whispered. His diaphragm stung with the effort. "He attacked us ... in the troll caves. Take me to Tiw ... I crave to discover the taste of a god's mead."

"Cyneheard?"

The voice was familiar. "Paega? Is that you? Do you also dine with Tiw?"

Paega crouched to the chieftain. "Thank the gods. You live, my lord!"

Cyneheard remained focused on the face looking straight at him. As lucidity filtered back, he recognised he was staring at a corpse. When his bleary gaze roved beyond, he realised the bloodied man lay foremost in a long row of mangled bodies. Most were so viciously dismembered it appeared as if they had been trampled underfoot by some giant, the way his own boots might squash slugs.

"Where am I, Paega?"

"On the headland, above the caves."

"What happened? How did I get here?"

"You led a search party into the tunnels to capture the Viking."

"I remember. Leofwine. Wigmund. They went ahead. They were slaughtered by a monster. Was it Fenrir?"

Paega frowned. "Fenrir? The tunnels collapsed, my lord. The earth has swallowed Leofwine and Wigmund. We could find no trace of them. We spent hours shifting rocks and managed to recover all the others. When we found you, you were near death, bleeding from a cut on your arm. I bandaged the wound, applied a poultice made from magical herbs."

"Magical herbs?"

"Yes. The wound will be healed in hours rather than days."

"I'm grateful. But it fucking smells. What of the Viking?"

"We found his body, close by you. He is over there."

Cyneheard raised his head laboriously. Propped against a rocky outcrop lay the man they had hunted in the dank caverns, naked, his bones crushed by rocks, his skin black.

"And Fenrir?"

"My lord?"

"The giant wolf that butchered so many of my soldiers?"

Paega turned to all the men who had been retrieved from the carnage. Their injuries were so brutal it was understandable his chieftain's concussed imagination had conjured Fenrir, the mythical wolf.

"We found no wolves among the boulders, my lord. Only Saxons. And one Norseman."

"But that one Norseman was *superhuman*, Paega. To have survived a funeral pyre? I think it might well have been his secret brew!"

"Secret brew?"

"It comes back to me. He had a hidden flask. He drank from it, just before we torched the longship. The cur was at death's door, yet I watched him rise from the fire, jump overboard, and swim to the caves. Almost as if he had the strength of Fenrir!"

"The strength of Fenrir?" Paega repeated, his eyes darting from Cyneheard to the fallen Saxons then locking on the Norseman. His eyebrows telegraphed long moments of intense contemplation before he hissed: "By all the gods."

"What, Paega?"

"Rest, now, my lord. Men are bringing carts. You'll be taken back to the fort, to rest. Our fallen will be consigned to barrows. I have something else planned for the Norseman."

CHAPTER SIX

After the warriors had placed the charred body onto the floor, Paega's eyes impatiently followed them exiting his hut. Once he was alone he set candles around the perimeter of the corpse, their flickering glow highlighting its gnarled and corrupt flesh. Delving into a bowl containing a noxious solution of toad entrails, swamp weeds and the bobbing skulls of cats, hedgehogs and weasels, he scooped out spoonfuls, sprinkling them over the dead Viking. Closing his eyes, he began reciting an ancient shamanic chant, his tongue relishing the old Germanic words. His spell reached a crescendo, after which he smacked his wizened hands, the sharp crack extinguishing the tiny fires. Acrid smoke drifted over the cadaver. Stooping to his knees, he turned the horridly emaciated head towards him. Aiming two spindly fingers, he touched the eyes. Gritting his sparse teeth, he applied pressure with his talon-like nails until the balls ruptured, oozing jelly. He continued forcing his fingertips inside the soft matter beneath the skull.

Visions flooded his mind. Arrows showered, their lethal barbs glinting. Next he was staring into the cruel eyes of the Saxon warlord whose forces had butchered the rest of the crew. He felt a flask; drank its precious fluid. Then his body was cloaked in fire, his flesh peeling in black slices. Clutching the rim of a boat, he plunged into the sea, the relief of ice-cold water against skin orgasmic. Now he was swimming towards the maw of a cave, before clambering over slimy rocks and on into twisting tunnels. When the English dogs pursued him, he would lurk down here in the blackness. He would be invincible. He knew he would be invincible because he could already feel his body yielding to the dark magic. His flesh and muscles were so raw from the punishment of fire that this transformation would be much less traumatic. His limbs lengthened and his spine twisted around to accommodate his quadrupedal stance. Coarse hair sprouted all over his body and he relished the exuberant liberation of this wild animal nature taking over. The sensation of vicious teeth expanding inside his huge muzzle was so satisfying he could not resist the triumphalism of filling his lungs. When he howled the noise echoed around myriad hidden chambers, startling bats that swirled and chirruped all around. There was torchlight ahead. He homed in on the shivering amber flares, his claws grating along the cave floor. A Saxon appeared around a corner, his expression locking in terror as he stared up at the towering creature. He swiped with a powerful paw, tearing his prey's throat. As the warm blood gushed into his mouth, he sucked greedily, the tunnel magnifying the slurping.

Paega delved deeper, fluids seeping around his digits. A montage of older memories flickered by: leaping from the longship to the shore, rampaging through villages, slaying Angles and Saxons and Celts during pitiless pillaging; swigging mead while baying bawdy songs with his comrades, their longship in full sail, the salt of the German Sea spraying their beards. Then Paega concentrated until his whole body was trembling, the head shaking violently in his grip. Now he was with the tribal medicine man, guarding him while he gathered the ingredients for the shapeshifting potion: an evil cocktail that had been passed down over countless generations. He studied this process intently, watching every ingredient that was plucked, unearthed, or snared. He observed the components of the age-old Nordic recipe being consigned to a cooking pot. He inhaled this fetid soup. As soon as the elixir was ready, he travelled back in time again, escorting the shaman as he entered the forest to commence hunting the additives. Paega relived the key moments, over and over, before surrendering to a self-induced trance to lock the sensitive information into the recesses of his own mind. Only when the recipe was mastered did he snap out of it and relinquish his grip, his fingers sucking free of the skull.

"Paega? Cyneheard awakens. He requests your presence," Osgar, his guard, called from the entrance. When Paega noticed the congealing stains beneath his nails, a crooked smile smeared his gnarled features. Like a cook relishing a fine dish, he touched the fingertips to his lips, his tongue roving around them.

"Enter, Osgar. I have cast a spell and drained the Norseman of his memories. It only remains for you to cast his useless carcass into the sea."

CHAPTER SEVEN

Under the full moon, the lumbering procession made its way along the old Roman road, two oxen heaving a cart. Warriors paced either side, torchlight revealing anxious eyes beneath helms. Each time the wheels snagged on crumbling flagstones, curt voices harangued the twin beasts, and the night thickened with curses. The men's glances wavered between the oxen, the ominous darkness surrounding them, and their cargo: a large cage with a prisoner shackled inside.

When the road crossed a low bridge, Cyneheard tugged a leather leash to halt the oxen. Through the jerking flames the others watched him raise his right arm towards the swollen moon and scattering of stars. "The druid's village lies ahead, no more than five miles distant. If we venture closer their sentries will spy our torches. It is time."

Grasping the rusting bars, the others lifted the cage from the cart onto the road. The manacled man reached towards them, his fingers straining. One by one, the men went over to envelop his hand with lingering handshakes, the thick chains secured to his wrists jangling.

"Good luck, Godric. May Tiw be with you."

"Tiw is watching over you, Godric."

"Bring back some Brit heads to decorate our fences."

Cyneheard faced Paega, who had been shadowing the warriors. The moon had turned the hair brushing his shoulders in greasy strands even more silver than usual. Although his back was hunched and the stick supporting his wiry frame was trembling, his expression was intense as he inspected the incarcerated man.

"You really think this will work, shaman?" asked Cyneheard.

"I am *sure*, my thane. I used potent magic to extract the information. Reading the mind of a dead man requires wicked necromancy. I feel weakened by it. But it was worth it."

Cyneheard thought the price the shaman had paid to cast his spell had clearly gone beyond weakening. Balancing on his crutch in the half-light, Paega seemed to have aged a decade. "I'll stick to interrogating prisoners while they're still alive," the chieftain smiled, flashing his decaying teeth. "A sword placed in a forge till the blade is hotter than the bowels of Hell inspires the most obstinate captive."

Paega drew a phial from his rope belt. It winked against the torchlight. Cyneheard grimaced. "That looks like blood."

"Part of it *is* blood, my lord. *Wolf* blood. Among many other ingredients."

Nodding, Cyneheard grasped at the cage's thick bars. "And what savage animal was this rusting crate built for?"

Paega regarded the sturdy metal construction. "Prior to your men discovering it abandoned among the trees, I'd say it once belonged to a Roman circus. But a timely discovery, given its new purpose. Where Godric now awaits his fate, I'd say all manner of exotic beasts once skulked. Large cats from Africa. Lions. Leopards. All set upon slaves for entertainment."

Rather than be repulsed by the ghoulish vision, the chieftain clapped his hands. "Excellent. Did you hear that, Godric? You are following in noble footsteps, indeed. A ferocious killer, held inside a cage, then unleashed on slaves."

Matching his chieftain's gallows humour, Godric guffawed. "Just let me at the Brit bastards."

"Paega, you think your potion will have our friend seeing red before the night is done?" Cyneheard enquired. "My champion warrior already champs at the bit."

"I can see that, my lord," the shaman agreed. "I could have just fed him the potion, then let him head off into the forest on his own. But I need to see for myself that I have mastered the ancient recipe. I need to watch how Godric ... *changes*. I need to see how his shape shifts."

"Good," concurred Cyneheard, his voice intense. "If he wasn't inside that cage, when he *does* change, he might attack his thane?"

"He would try to kill us *all*. You saw yourself what these werewolves are capable of. Legend has it afflicted warriors are just as likely to attack their comrades such are the delirious levels of bloodlust incited by the magic."

The thane stepped over to the warrior inside the cage. "You hear that, Godric? A magical brew has been concocted for you. You may well have a headache in the morning."

Paega passed the phial through the bars. Godric grasped it, tugging out the cork. The others winced at the toxic aroma. Godric looked to the thane, the shaman, then to his comrades. "To Tiw, our god of war. I will seek out our enemy. And slaughter him."

With that, he touched the glass to his lips. Jerking his head back, he gulped the fetid solution. For a moment his knuckles whitened against the bars and he breathed urgently, fighting the impulse to cough up the repugnant mixture. Eventually he sighed. "It is done."

"How long?" asked Cyneheard.

The shaman studied Godric's features, his forehead furrowed in trepidation. "I can't say for definite, sire. With the Norseman in the tunnels, it was within the hour. For the moment, we wait."

The Saxons drew back, nervously clutching pommels. The thane checked the extravagant chains securing the cage door, glancing anxiously at Godric. For these witnesses the following moments seemed the longest of their lives. Godric sat at the centre of the cage, restlessly flexing his fingers. The other warriors remained cross-legged on the ground, fidgeting with their weapons, the torches they had set into hollows in tree trunks casting fitful light. Owls punctuated the tense silence.

Suddenly Godric doubled up in agony, clutching his stomach. Writhing to the cage floor, his body trembled. The onlookers jumped to their feet as one, unsheathing swords.

"Godric?" shouted Cyneheard.

Ignoring his chief, the young man was immersed in a private world of agony, his features contorted, eyes screwed shut. When they snapped open again the whites had transformed to a fierce orange. The spectating warriors gasped.

"Godric?" repeated Cyneheard. "What is happening?"

Godric glared back, his expression dripping with venom. His torso appeared to be growing more muscular and his beard seemed wilder. When he shook his head, his lank hair tumbled down his fringe until only the terrible eyes remained visible.

"It begins," exclaimed Paega. "I would draw back, my thane. Swiftly. In his altered state there is no way of predicting what Godric will be capable of. He will have the strength of ten. Moments from now, we will no longer be his friends. We will be his foes. Take your soldiers away from this place. I will follow."

Without needing further persuasion the thane ushered his warriors from the clearing, tugging the oxen, those behind urging the animals on with their spear shafts. Paega watched the glow from their torches until they had seeped into the gloom, like dying embers. He turned his attention to the cage. Horrified, he stumbled backwards. What he glimpsed inside defied explanation. Trying to make sense of the fleeting impression, he squinted into the gloom. Lurid eyes glared back. Large claws clutched the bars and the entire metal frame rattled furiously.

Paega raised the torch, steeling himself, pacing closer. Godric tracked his approach, his harsh snarls coughing sprays of putrid saliva. The shaman waved the flame towards the distant trees.

"Seek out our enemies."

Stepping backwards, he cast the torch to the ground with enough force to extinguish it. As the flames persisted, he delved under his robes, his breath panting while he unleashed a meagre stream of piss until the smouldering fire spat and steamed. The caustic scent provoked snarls from within the cage then a furious rattling of the bars.

As Godric's strength grew, Paega felt his own draining. The past few days had been fraught, the stresses interminable. Not only had he been forced to gather the potion's many ingredients –

including plant roots from barely accessible crevices, weeds from the murkiest depths of stagnant ponds, the blood of a wolf – he had been wary of Cyneheard's warning. If this magic failed and Godric, one of the tribe's fiercest fighters, was poisoned, then the chieftain would have his head. Paega appreciated the line between the thane's hot-tempered bluster and actually enacting threats was as thin as his rigorously sharpened blade.

Twenty yards away, the roaring rose to an alarming crescendo. The shackles broke, the chain's links clattering against the bars so violently they sparked. Paega held his breath, unable to open his eyes. Mustering the courage to look, he could make out the cage, the moonlight winking from cloud cover turning its bars silver. Within its shadows, a darker shape moved from side to side. This seemed to grow in stature until it launched itself at the door, the impact wrenching it from its hinges. Paega strained to see the shadowy being but clouds were cloaking the moon again. There was heavy footfall as it hurtled into freedom.

"What have I done?" he whispered, listening as branches thrashed in the wake of Godric; or what had once been Godric.

"May your gods grant you a swift end, whoever lies in its path ... may the gods protect us all."

A shrill howling pierced the night. To Paega, it was the sound of the doors of hell being prised open.

CHAPTER EIGHT

Kady woke with a gasp, sucking lungfuls of musty air. Rivulets of sweat soaked her shirt to her skin. The intensity of the nightmare was like none she had ever experienced. It had been more vivid than any dream; more like a vision. For drawn-out moments she remained rigid, anticipating the caged creature crashing into the hut.

Eventually her laboured breathing relaxed. Her heavy eyes flickered towards the hearth. The fire shimmered, drawing tears. As she blinked the glow intensified, the shifting pattern becoming hypnotic. There was movement beyond. Among the shadows on the far side, she could make out her father, wrapping a blanket around his shoulders. Moments later he was lifting a sack from the floor. The flames diverted her attention. Their quivering shapes altered into twin orbs that detached from the upward flow to remain in a fixed position, hovering like lurid eyes. The more she stared, the more the impression grew of being scrutinised by some supernatural entity within the fire. These light patterns evolved into perfect almond shapes, with cruel black slits for pupils. Any questions about why her father should be skulking around at this hour faded as the sense of terror increased. Every sinew in her body tautened.

The door creaked; a chill wind seeped inside. The spell was broken but only because the eyes released her from scrutiny, instead switching their attention towards the draught that stirred eddies of smoke. They burned in intensity then faded. For moments she could only peer into the flickering red tongues, fearful of their return. But this sense of dread became compounded. Somehow she could sense her father was heading into danger.

They were all used to his coming and going at unsociable hours. This was only to be expected: druid recipes required meticulous attention to detail. Sometimes he roamed deep into the forests to collect herbs at the precise moment of their maturity; or to capture the pure waters from streams before they were tarnished by rainfall. Tonight was different. Whether or not the hateful eyes had been optical illusions prompted by fatigue, her panic was real. Notions of sinking back into sleep vanished.

Tugging the covers away, she clambered out of her nightshirt and donned her clothes. She was aware of being examined again. The eldest of her two younger sisters, Tara, was fixing her with a concerned expression. Kady stepped towards her, ruffling her tousled hair.

"What is it, Kady?" the twelve-year-old's voice quavered.

"Quiet now, Tara. Just go back to sleep. Father has to run an errand. And I must answer a call of nature. Sleep, now. Cuddle into Gwynn."

Tentatively, she stroked the younger sister, her fingers lingering on Gwynn's unruly red curls. She was the precious one, their mother having died in the moments after Gwynn's birth. Kady grasped the furs from where they had ruffled around the child's torso, tugging them towards her neck. She cast an anxious glance towards her younger brother, Brice. Although aged fourteen, he was sprawled across his feather mattress, snoring like a warrior who had collapsed on some tavern's beer-soaked flooring. She headed towards the exit, pausing only to seize her sword from its resting place on the wooden dining table.

Outside the moon was full but veiled by clouds, bathing the Celtic village in a cold light. Her attention swept over the clustered huts, each leaking faint smoke trails towards the imminent dawn. Further motion caught her eye. A shadow had slipped into the nearest trees.

* * *

Crouching in the dark, she waited until ragged clouds drifted by. She murmured a thankful prayer to Rhiannon, the moon goddess, for offering her face again. Light dappled the undergrowth.

Grasping at the twisting fibres of plants she sped onwards, her heart fluttering like a trapped sparrow.

Every so often the fleeting illumination cut out. She appreciated Rhiannon's gifts could not be taken for granted. As she froze, her breaths became ghostly clouds. Suddenly amplified owls, nightjars and more unsettling sounds surrounded her. After an hour scrabbling through tangled bushes she drew close to a great clearing. Wary of being spotted, she squinted ahead. A torch's flame danced like a firefly. She hurried on, watching this beacon brightening until she could also make out a silhouette.

She reached the immense oak that guarded this secluded corner of the woodland. Druantia, mythical druid Queen, ruled over these trees and this tower of thickly knotted wood was one of her most impressive subjects. Digging her toes into the bark, Kady clambered up the branches. She disturbed a bat, its beady eyes wary of these strangers trespassing in its realm. It screeched into the canopy. Waiting anxious seconds, she pressed her body to the trunk. Continuing, she reached a majestic bough that stretched like the muscular arm of some spear-bearing bodyguard. Inching along, she peered below. There was movement. The flickering torchlight revealed her father bending to the ground, digging out fungi. At this time of year she appreciated his magical harvest would be in homage to Brighid, Queen of the Heavens, and he would be praying for protection from the oncoming winter storms. But there had been more ominous portents than the weather. His voice drifted within earshot.

"Mighty Brighid. It has been two hundred years since the Romans departed your islands. The cult of the druids has emerged, after the relentless persecution by their legions. Yet more conquerors plague us. They come from Europe again, but this time from further east, from the lands the Romans called Germania. At least the Romans brought culture, trade, housing and roads. These barbarians simply raze our Celtic homesteads to make way for their own. Those who resist are killed; those who do not are enslaved. These Jutes and Angles and Saxons, these English tribes, they will also scour the land for druids. Our magic is a threat to their occupation. Oh, mighty Brighid, I accept these tokens from your bountiful forest. I will feast on your delicacies, and my incantation will allow me to enter the trance immediately. I know you will show me what I can do to protect my people, especially Kady, the one who will follow me."

Hearing her name she started, but she appreciated the need to remain silent. While it was tempting to call her father, to appeal to his sense of humour and let him know his eldest daughter was spying, his status as a druid was far more important. He would be furious to discover she had trailed him to this sacred place. Worse than that, were non-druids to intrude on such strict ceremony the magic would be diminished. She watched his silhouette shifting before the flames and delving inside the sack. Seizing palmfuls of his crop he chewed greedily.

Further words drifted towards her, but he was now murmuring in the ancient druidic tongue, the language the builders of the great stone circles would have used. This filled her with immense pride in her heritage. Her father impressed upon everyone in the village that in order to maintain the druid bloodline, his firstborn would have to be tutored in the age-old ways. He had demonstrated basic tricks to her, a hint of the power of certain potions; involved her in the preparation of secret recipes. While she had gleaned much for someone not yet in her eighteenth year, she appreciated she still had a long way to go on the journey of harnessing the skills. Much of the knowledge had already been planted in her mind, her father having explained how he had sown many of his secrets telepathically; the true extent of this would only ever become apparent on the occasion of his death. The passing of his spirit to the underworld would be the catalyst that invoked her latent powers. Only then would she become a fully-fledged druid.

Kady felt ridiculous clinging like a furtive squirrel halfway up a tree in the middle of the night. The sense of foreboding had diminished, replaced by guilt. She was also conscious of being regarded herself. The glowing eyes of nocturnal creatures reprimanded her for intruding in their habitat. By regarding each set of eyes she could identify the lifeform lurking beyond. To her right she pinpointed a tawny owl, its head swivelling before it fixated on her trembling frame. There was a rustling on the forest floor and a barely perceptible hint of plants being stripped of their succulent berries. Without seeing them she knew a doe and her speckled fawn were satiating their hunger. The deer panicked. Kady glimpsed their white rumps vanishing into the trees. Something had startled them. Her father remained hunched, now in deep communion. There was heavy footfall, close by. Wolves? No, they were never solitary hunters; besides this was bipedal. But this realisation was even more alarming. Who else would be stalking through the trees at this hour? No one from the village would approach these sacred glades if they saw the druid here. Someone from a neighbouring village? All the tribes in the valley respected the sanctity of this place. A stranger? Why was he creeping around the forest in the dark? The most perturbing aspect was that, unlike the owl and deer, she could gain no sense of this intruder, almost as if the identity was being shielded. But that notion was preposterous. Surely there was another possibility: a bandit. Parts of the West Country had become lawless, with brigands and slavers stalking the crumbling Roman roads. It was this suspicion that raised her hackles. She had to warn her father. One of the earliest wiles she had mastered from him was the ability to impersonate a range of creatures. She knew he would react to the alarm call of a nightingale: a harsh frog-like croak. Cupping her hands, her abrupt cough rasped across the tree canopy.

    Her father reacted, dropping the sack. For seconds he gawked, still locked in his trance, but also troubled by the signal. Kady glanced downwards: someone was moving right below her vantage point; branches snapped. There was a primeval growling, a stench reminiscent of the village dog pound but grossly magnified. The hairs rose on the back of her neck. Her father remained sluggish but eventually lifted his staff. This walking stick could also be deployed as a weapon: Kady had witnessed him unsaddle a horse-thief by wielding it towards him from twenty yards away. Fear paralysed her as he raised the rod.

    What happened next was a confusing blur. Kady was aware of her father aiming the staff, barking an incantation. But the weapon immediately caught fire. As he dropped it, the wood disintegrated into ash. Then a shape was leaping towards him. She got the impression of an animal until it rose, hind legs stretching its lithe body to tower over him. As torchlight bathed this creature she froze. It was a wolf, its fur matted and black. From snout to tail it was at least double her father's height. A scream rose in Kady's throat. At that moment her father gazed beyond this monster and looked straight into her eyes. She watched his lips moving. A cry struggled from her throat only to escape as a muted gasp. This was her final impression of her father, his spell striking her dumb to spare her life after what was about to happen. The wolf fell on him, its arched back sparing her the grisly visuals that accompanied its snarling jaws tearing from side to side. Blood fountained across the clearing.

A flicker of gold winked over the skyline to the east. The enormous wolf howled. Kady had one terrible glimpse of its reddened muzzle as it sped below, crashing through the undergrowth. Immediately she scurried down the tree trunk, launching herself to the ground when she was still ten feet away. Landing nimbly, she covered the distance to her father. Although his chest was lacerated with claw marks, blood oozing from the exposed ribs and steaming in the cold air, he breathed faintly. Kady tried to speak but discovered she remained mute.

Kady?

His lips remained quivering: he was projecting his thoughts by telepathy.

In seconds, all my powers will be your powers ... we are in great peril ... if our enemies have learnt how to shapeshift ... we are all in danger ... great great danger ... you ... you must protect our village and our people ... Brighid awaits ... I love ... I love ... you.

His eyes rolled inwards and the wisp of his final breath evaporated into her face. Blotting out the enormity of what she had just witnessed, she was driven by a compelling force. She knew she had to commit her father's body to the earth. Within minutes she had gathered twigs, stacking them together. She dragged his butchered corpse into the midst of the kindling, then applied the torch he had dug into the earth during his foraging. As the fire took hold she transmitted her thoughts.

Brighid, Queen of all the Heavens. Welcome my father, Kai, of the Dumnonii. He was one of your loyal druid servants, who served his gods and his clan with equal dedication. Grant me the strength to carry on his centuries-old duties.

Her eyes bored into the fire's darting tongues. The smoke smarted her eyes, exacerbating the flowing tears. She glowered towards the lightening skies to the east, where the ancient Celtic territories had been swallowed by Wessex.

Grant me the courage to avenge my father, Brighid.

The flames devoured clothing, skin, muscle and hair. Kady bowed to the ground and grasped a bundle of dock leaves, thrusting them over her mouth to spare herself from the stench. She marched from the clearing, the light from the pyre illuminating her journey through the wolf's escape route, past trunks flecked with blood. The horror of what she had witnessed was tempered by a growing awareness of her environment. Her senses had been re-born to a fantastical extent. All around she was becoming aware of the components of this ancient forest. Where she had remained blissfully ignorant of any such phenomenon on the way here, she could now filter the nasal kaleidoscope, identifying where particular scents were emanating: the shapes of the leaves they signified, the colours of the flowers. She appreciated it would take considerable time to reach her father's level of knowledge but at least she had a sense of having commenced this journey.

Kady ... although my spirit has passed, I will remain your guide.

The shock and sadness of hearing her father's voice emanating from the underworld faded. It emphasised the latent power of the druid magic and she knew she was ready to embrace it. She had never been surer of anything. As if reading her mind he continued.

... but the druid magic is never to be taken for granted, my beloved, and your teaching will remain a strict learning curve ... I have already implanted much of the knowledge which you will be able to tap into as your skills grow ... but always remember these ancient powers can ebb and flow ... when you are stressed or panicked you will find it much harder to recall the spells, the incantations ... but with experience you will learn to focus on your abilities ... never drop your guard, not for a moment ... I

was so lost to my communion with Brighid that I failed to sense the evil presence until it was too late ... know this, Kady ... the half-man half-wolf was conjured by a terrible sorcerer who aims to drive our people into the sea ... your powers have never been more vital to our people ... but take heed ... this sorcerer will be hunting you now ...

The beast's putrid scent remained strong. Although its flight had already taken it a mile away, she could hear its paws crunching through the brush. Now she sensed it splashing across the ford near their village, skulking to avoid the sentries, making for the hills to the east: Saxon territory. Kady had an impression of one final dismissive backwards glance; glaring red eyes a haunting mirror of those her imagination had conjured earlier. She also appreciated this creature had reverted to human form.

CHAPTER NINE

A pale sunrise doused the landscape in fragile grey; each time Kady grasped a branch she imagined it might splinter in her trembling grip. A bullfinch darted from her path, its alarm call piercing the silence. As its rose-red breast vanished into the undergrowth, her heart pounded. She stopped to get her bearings.

Using her newfound druid senses she concentrated, visualising the werewolf. He was naked, his shoulders hunched, his skin florid with bruises and lacerations from thorns, as if generously tattooed in purples and reds. This gaunt figure was now limping over the rolling highlands that marked the current boundary of West Saxon encroachment into Dumnonia. Every so often his legs buckled and he would slump to the ground. The blond hair she knew would have been tied into a resplendent ponytail had transformed to lank tatters. He spent the final yards towards his destination crawling on all-fours. Presently guards at the entrance to a hill fort challenged him. One grasped his hair, wrenching him upright, while another drew a sword. Assuming him some native vagabond, they would despatch him as casually as the rats that burrowed beneath their huts. Except a voice carried from the stockade walls. "Godric returns!" With recognition, the sentries' impassive features gave way to shock. The vision faded.

Ahead of her the trees were thinning. Soon her own village beckoned; she almost wept at the sight of its welcoming squares of light and the scent of breakfasts wafting over the ploughed fields. Then she thought of Brice rousing, demanding to know their father's whereabouts. It would annoy him that Kady had slunk out at the same time, as if he had deliberately been excluded from some mission. Then a new dread struck her. Until now she had been concentrating on fleeing the forest's horrors. She steeled herself at the thought of having to explain to little Gwynn that she was an orphan. If inheriting her father's druid skills was a journey, it was going to be an arduous one, with few opportunities for respite. Facing Saxon warriors and werewolves or any other demons their shamen might conjure were certainly the most dangerous aspects she could imagine. But as well as becoming the tribal druid she was now head of her own family. She would have to summon words of comfort for her siblings, while dealing with Brice's constant resentment.

In the growing sunlight, something caught her eye. During the frantic retreat through the trees her eyes had scanned her surroundings. Now she focused on herself. Her tunic's patchwork of greens and blues was unrecognisable: her garments were caked in her father's blood. At the sight of it she sunk to her knees and stared into the heavens. The druid's final spell had waned, because all the pent up terror and fear of the last few hours were unleashed in a prolonged, terrifying scream. The moment her lungs were emptied she keeled over.

CHAPTER TEN

The rain had been lashing without respite since mid-day and as the village elders took their places inside their chieftain Torean's hut, the ceiling drummed. Rolling claps of thunder did nothing to soften the grim expressions surrounding Kady; most were directed towards her. Gazing towards the timbered roof she toyed with her necklace. When stressed her fingers invariably sought its links. It had belonged to her mother and although its bronze had become discoloured over the years since her father had passed it on to her, she did not mind the green tarnish it left on her fingertips. Kady remembered her mother as someone who spent too much time on the practicalities of rearing free-spirited children, not to mention her role as a druid's wife, to expend much effort polishing jewellery.

Brice stood by Torean's chair, accentuating the sombre atmosphere by strumming a lament on his lyre. Against the storm he was plucking the strings with such vigour she imagined his plaintive melody drawing blood from his deft strokes. Her eyes were drawn to sporadic drips from the ceiling spitting against a cauldron.

Torean bowed to Brice, eyes glistening. For one whose battle skills had earned him a formidable reputation as a younger man, Kady had often watched the chieftain moved to tears by beautiful music; or whenever his grandchildren proudly presented him with the results of painstaking sketching. She also knew how devastated he would have been to receive the news from the forest. He turned to his peers. "Brothers and sisters of the Dumnonii, we convene." Adjusting his cloak, he settled into his seat. His rings captured the fire's glow to wink unnervingly like the demon eyes from the previous night. While his stare hovered over the figures crammed into the long hut, his own fingers went to the silver torc at his neck.

The muted conversation that had been filtering across the benches and straw flooring dwindled. Her sister Tara and cousin Jana, who had been serving ox horns brimming with Cornish mead, curtsied towards Torean then peered towards her. Smiling, Kady indicated the door. They flitted outside, bracing themselves against the deluge before exiting.

"To Kai," Torean announced, raising his horn. As if on cue, lightning flashed beyond the windows; seconds later the thunder rumbled directly overhead. "Dagda himself is welcoming our beloved druid into his kingdom with all this heavenly fanfare!"

Appreciative cheers rang through the crowd and drinking vessels were raised; generous swigs were taken. Torean's gaze sought Kady. Lifting his free hand, he beckoned her to take her position before the gathering. "The druid's heir will address us."

Clearing her throat, she heaved herself from the warmth of the bench she had been seated on by the fire. Taking a stance before the adults, she nodded at the chieftain. Heads craned on all sides. She could not help noticing Brice's surliness.

Torean continued: "Kady. By our ancient and sacred laws, you have inherited your father's position. I can only assume he has prepared you in the druid ways, as his father did before him?"

"Yes, Torean. My father has implanted the basic skills."

"Good. Now, Kady. We will be mourning your father's untimely death for the days to come. However, in the meantime, the village council would care to be enlightened about the manner of his passing?"

The weather's relentless barrage was unnerving enough. As her eyes danced over the sea of faces, she felt her throat drying. Coughing, she took a deep breath. "I'll tell you exactly what I saw. My father had left the hut at dead of night. I woke just as he was leaving. I sensed he was in danger." Appreciating the puzzled expressions, she decided not to elaborate about the eyes in the fire. "I followed."

"Why?" Brice jumped to his feet, voicing the question that had been burning inside him since another youth from the village,

Ardal, had discovered her body and carried her to safety. "Why did *you* follow, instead of waking *me?*"

Torean aimed a finger towards him. "*Brice.* All will have the floor who wish it, in good time. For now, none but the druid speaks here."

"Thank-you, Torean. I followed my father, tracked him for many miles, deep into the forests. He was gathering the ingredients to send him into a trance, before he recited verses in the old tongue while communing with Brighid. I didn't want him to see me until he had finished, so I watched, hidden in a tree. From that vantage point." Here she faltered.

"Please, Kady. Take courage," Torean prompted, his tone soothing.

"I saw ... I saw my father ... I saw my father ... *slaughtered.*"

This announcement provoked uproar. Torean smacked his palms against the armrests. "Silence!" The hubbub subsided. "Continue, Kady."

"It was dark. *Very* dark. There was a full moon but there was also cloud. And father was in a narrow glade, surrounded by overhanging branches."

"Slaughtered?" repeated Torean's wife, Greer, seated to their chieftain's left, her voice faltering.

"Yes, Greer," affirmed Kady. "All I can say, with any certainty, is this. I saw something ... a figure ... rush from the trees. It fell on my father so quickly he had no time to defend himself, even with his staff."

"*Who?*" This time is was Tannus, the blacksmith, who interrupted. A towering man aptly named after the god of thunder, his broad arms crossed over his chest.

"Not *who. What.* It was a *wolf*, Tannus. A huge wolf."

"*One* wolf?" Tannus snorted.

"Yes, Tannus," she carried on, closing her eyes, picturing the scene destined to remain seared in her memory, "and the moment this monster struck, it rose onto its hind legs, like a man."

Voices clamoured for Kady's attention. Raising his drinking horn over his head as if its pointed curve was a weapon, Torean shouted loudest of all. "*Listen to me, Dumnonii!* This much I already suspected. Brothers and sisters, Kady is sharing information she confided in me earlier, after Ardal had brought her back to the village. While you were tucking into your soups and stews, Kady was describing how she built a funeral pyre for her father, lest any lingering unearthly forces infest his body. How many of you would have had the courage to perform such a task when you were of such tender years?"

"*I* would have," Brice exclaimed, his youthful voice cracking with the strain of projecting into the din. All eyes swivelled onto him.

"Well?" demanded Torean.

"If *I* had been present, I would have protected our druid from attack. You took your sword with you, Kady. Why didn't you use it? What wolf can withstand steel?"

Kady glared into her brother's accusatory eyes. But annoyance swiftly overcame her surprise. "A *blade*, Brice? This was no ordinary wolf."

"A wolf is a wolf, Kady. It is a large dog. Had it been *me* who had followed our druid to the sacred glades last night, our chieftain would have had a fine pelt to decorate the wall over there."

"Well said, young lad," Tannus concurred.

"A wolf is a wolf, yes, Brice. But when it is twelve feet tall and can charge on its hind legs and can change back into a man, it is *not* a wolf, Brice. It is a shapeshifter. It is a werewolf." Again, voices became a tumult. Kady projected: "You might as well stand before the sea and demand the waves stop, Brice! If you had faced that werewolf, yelling your proudest Dumnonii war cry, *you* would have joined our father, butchered among the trees. Father saw me, hiding. With his last breath he cast a spell that struck me dumb so I would not scream, so the demon would not notice me. The last action of our father's life was saving mine."

"Brice," Torean concluded, "your courage is in no doubt. When you gain a few more years your swordsmanship will be invaluable to the Dumnonii. But, believe me, lad, this was no wolf attack."

In the shocked silence that followed, even the rain's steady percussion appeared to become more subdued. "I had a vision," Kady persisted, controlling the wavering in her voice. "I saw a Saxon war party leading one of their number inside a cage. Their shaman gave him an elixir. He transformed into a wolf, smashed the cage bars and prowled into the forest."

Faces glanced at one another, some shifting their fearful expressions towards Torean. The chieftain nodded grimly. "We are all aware of the stories about the Norse raiders, whose longships plunder the English kingdoms to the east and south, and the Celtic lands around the Hibernian Sea. There are tales of their so-called *berserker* warriors, their fighting men who take potions that make them think they really *are* wolves, capable of tearing enemies limb from limb." Illustrating this, he delved into the bowl before him and wrenched apart a hunk of bread. Chewing on a morsel, he continued. "Kai once confided in me that one of his greatest fears was that our enemies would develop the ability to shapeshift. Facing an army of berserkers would be bad enough. But an army of werewolves?"

"Surely not, my love," Greer gasped, her pained features glancing to the door, as if this manifestation was imminent.

Tannus bellowed: "But if this is *Norse* magic, Kady, how has it been mastered by Saxons?"

"As we have our druids, the Saxons have their medicine men, their shamen. In my dreams my father has warned me of a shaman from the land the German invaders now call Wessex. This man is powerful ... dangerous. My father granted me a most disturbing vision of him ... a terrible one."

Torean smiled sympathetically. "Courage, Kady. Your father would wish you to share it."

Kady nodded. "This Saxon sorcerer cast a black spell ... it allowed him to read the mind of a Norse shapeshifter *after* his death ... to extract the ingredients for the magic."

Torean stood abruptly, his expression grave. "The druid cult has always been our strength. That is why the Romans went to such lengths to try and root out every last druid. And the English will never conquer this land until they finish the task. That is why

Kady here is so precious to our people. As a druid's firstborn, her latent powers will become a powerful force to defend us. Kady. I appreciate you will have to learn your craft quickly if you are to protect the Celtic tribes from evil. But I trust you with all my heart."

Brice remained agitated, standing up himself. Kady noticed the extent to which her fourteen-year-old brother now towered over her. "This is a heavy burden, for a girl. These Saxons might one day make their way here, into Dumnonia. If their soldiers can shapeshift, we need a *strong* druid." Swivelling on his heel, he addressed the company: "Does it not worry anyone else that this Saxon *wolf man* was able to overcome an experienced druid? How can we rely on a novice? Kady couldn't possibly defend us against a similar attack."

Torean frowned. "Kady *will* be that druid."

"I don't doubt that she will, chieftain. In time. But I am a druid's son. If anyone should be granted the powers to defend us with the old magic, it is surely me?"

"I agree with Brice," roared Tannus. "We need a druid who is also a warrior. Kady, your father taught you the basic recipes. Could you not simply pass them on to your brother? I think I can speak for most of us here when I say this would be the better solution. The druidic magic is potent. It would be *less* so in the hands of a girl, younger even than my own daughter."

Brice stepped over to Tannus, thrusting a hand out. The puffed-up blacksmith enveloped her brother's fist. "After all, can you even tell us what powers your father might have *bequeathed* you?" Tannus scorned the word and many in the company chuckled, colluding with his scepticism. "Tell us what you think you can do, Kady, apart from the occasional vision after taking a sleeping potion?"

"I hear my father's voice. I hear him reciting spells and incantations, sometimes in the language our ancestors used when they first settled in these islands. In my vision last night, I could even understand the Saxon tongue. My father will still be guiding me from the underworld."

Tannus sputtered a mouthful of mead. "Childsplay! You think imagining voices will thwart a Saxon warband? Will your little petal stews stop a *werewolf* next time it comes visiting?"

Even Torean's withering glance had switched from Tannus to herself. As her eyes flitted around the faces, she sensed the mood altering.

"Teach me the recipes, *big sister*," boomed Brice. He only ever addressed Kady that way when he was being superior. In their younger days it had invariably preceded him striking her. She shut her eyes. Embarrassment and doubt twisted into frustration. That, too, ebbed. Her temper rose. Brice's disdain had sparked her fury.

Kady, my beloved ... the power is in you, now ... do not fear it ... embrace it ... surrender to the ancient druidic ways, for they are yours now, just as they were once mine ... follow this path, as you were always destined to do, and you will never have cause to fear anyone, or anything ... I did not have time to prepare for the dark one ... but you must always make sure you are prepared ... for now, trust in yourself ... trust in your abilities, my beloved ... and play with fire!

Her father's voice faded, leaving her with an adamant sense of what had to be done. Immediately she raised both arms to the ceiling and shrieked. Startled into silence, the arguing died out once more. All eyes fixated on her. Slivers of sweat trickled down the small of her back. An unpleasant prickling sensation flowed over her. Her knees trembled. Brice snorted derisively. Tannus conspired with this, mocking Kady's stance by lifting his own arms high. This game became infectious, as other got up from their seats, mockingly stretching their hands. Although Torean's brow furrowed, he held back from admonishing them all. He suspected what was coming.

Kady yelled again, sweeping her hands down and up. The fire erupted, huge flames leaping towards the ceiling vent in fountains of brilliant orange that crashed into the beams, splitting into twin bird-shaped entities that flashed to either side, their lurid wings cascading sparks over everyone. There were gasps before the fireballs receded, leaving clouds of curling steam below the eaves.

"I am Kady, Kai the druid's firstborn. I and I alone have inherited my father's powers. I swear on my father's life and on the lives of all my brothers and sisters of the Dumnonii that I will devote my life to defending my people and avenging my father. Death to the Saxons."

Awestruck eyes trained on her. She noticed a tear trickling down Brice's ruddy cheeks. At that moment she also appreciated another power she now possessed. She could read minds and, unbelievably, her brother's was bursting with admiration.

CHAPTER ELEVEN

The howling was closer this time; an eerie sound that sent shivers coursing down her spine. Kady listened intently, her senses filtering out the birdsong, the gurgling stream and the breeze hissing through the tree canopy. Sunlight pierced the dense foliage. Aside from its welcome warmth, it was also a reassurance. Her father had explained the shapeshifters would only ever come under cover of darkness, and that they were tied to the lunar cycle, a full moon being a paramount influence on the potency of the shamanic potions. Yet there was a menacing quality in the distant clamour. There were few actual wolves this far south, but hunger would give any wild beasts the audacity to roam far from their normal habitats.

Bracing herself, she leapt over a meandering stream, making her way through shoulder-high bracken and wincing as each frond seemed determined to spar. Fraught minutes later the wild landscape gave way to undergrowth peppered with anemones. Brushing their petals, the dew moistened her skin. The Romans had described these white flowers as tears from their goddess of love, Venus. They swirled around trees like snowdrifts; to her right, the snaking waterway bubbled over rocks.

In the hours since sunrise her sack had already become crammed with toadstools and mushrooms, fragrant herbs and blooms. By considering this bountiful harvest she realised she could instinctively sort them into the various recipes that had come as second nature to her father. Kady appreciated how poppy roots could be mushed to create a painkilling medicine. She knew how the sap weeping from certain trees could be boiled into a soup for a strong sedative: if the mixture was too diluted it would have little effect; too strong and it would cause a catatonic trance lasting for months. That her father had posthumously imprinted all this knowledge in her mind meant wherever she glanced in this seemingly limitless wild garden she felt a connection to him.

Stepping through the anemones her boots alighted on stone. Although clogged with weeds, she could make out the remains of the Roman road that had cut across this part of the landscape. Before the forest had become so overgrown, legions had marched through these trees, heading from the garrison at Exeter whenever clans of the Dumnonii and Cornovii had grown rebellious. At the height of the Roman occupation fifty thousand soldiers had been deployed across Britannia – one eighth of the total Imperial army – and the tribes of Dumnonia and Cornwall had been particularly volatile.

She followed the route for half a mile, the sensation of its even surface a pleasant contrast to the unkempt paths she had been trailing. Eventually the road led to a clearing. Pausing, she watched the sunshine cleaving upper branches. Looking more intently she could make out symmetrical shapes among the trunks and twisting vines. She had discovered a long-abandoned Roman villa. Pacing further along the stone slabs, another path broke off, leading towards the building's entrance. Framed by pockmarked columns, this edifice now yawned at the encroaching wilderness, the main door's rotting wood splintered and tarnished with moss. Light streaming through smashed roof tiles had an inviting affect.

Positioning her sack on a flight of steps leading to the entrance, she trod across the threshold, ducking inside the ruin. There was an all-pervading stench of decay and greenfinches flitted among the ceiling timbers. But she got the impression of how this building must have appeared in its heyday, more than two hundred years before. A vast hallway opened before her, statues of various deities lining the walls on either side. Where these characters would once have basked in gleaming white marble, they were now suffering the incongruity of being frames for climbing plants. A figure she recognised as the Roman gods' messenger, Mercury, retained his winged feet, but his laurel wreath appeared to have been generously coated in bat droppings.

As she progressed further into the derelict villa, she noted vast tapestries to either side, their woodland scenes given an extra dimension of authenticity by weeds sprouting through the stained fabric. She entered a side room: the light cast by shattered windows revealed this had once housed a library. Volumes were arranged along shelving in varying states of collapse. Selecting a journal, she flipped it open. Damp had long wormed its way inside and even as she focused on the painstakingly rendered Latin inscriptions, a miniature cavalry charge of woodlice and centipedes prompted her to cast the book aside. It pulped across the tarnished floor tiles.

An object lying on the floor caught her eye. It was cylindrical, made of bronze, with glass circles at either end. She plucked it up, shaking it free of cobwebs. Stepping into the hall again, she rubbed away the years of grit and dust. She held it closer. Instantly she could see the nearest tapestry transformed so vividly she felt she could have reached out and touched it. She spent several moments getting a taste of this fantastical device, studying the swallows jostling in their nests in the eaves; marvelling at the fading but ornate patterns of a distant fresco.

Shoving the looking glass into her hood, Kady carried on with her exploration. Rounding a corner she became aware of an overpowering stench. She had arrived at a flight of stairs leading down to a bathing pool clogged with algae. In the centre of the stagnant water she could make out the decomposing form of a boar, arrow shafts jutting from its neck. Escaping a hunt, it appeared the wounded beast had taken refuge inside the ruin, sinking into the pool then drowning. When she gazed at the bloodstained fur she could see it tugging: rats were feasting on the bloated corpse.

Making her way outside she savoured the forest air. Scanning the statuary that had been engulfed by the wilderness, she felt a tinge of regret. Her great great grandparents would have known the Romans as benign rulers who had introduced civilization to this wild country. Many Celts had married into Roman families, enjoying aspects of their culture: food, fine wines, recreational activities, education, fashionable clothing. Some had become rich with the lucrative trading opportunities that had come with living in an imperial province. But the principal reason for that Empire's decline had been barbarian invasion from the east. These delicate marble figures, smashed to pieces and scattered among the ferns, were a metaphor for that decay. And Celtic Britain was shrinking all the time, its forests, meadows and farmland engulfed by English kingdoms. "What will become of the Britons?" she articulated her thoughts, her voice echoing between cracked columns. "Norse pirates attack the coasts. Our ancient clan territories have become Wessex, Sussex, East Anglia, Mercia, North Humberland. Their very language sounds hateful. We could live with the Romans. We die with the English."

Heading for her sack, something caught her eye among the fronds, glinting as it captured filtered sunbeams. Parting stems she gasped in wonder. Here was a mound of plunder from the villa: goblets, plates, jewellery, urns, cups; all fashioned from gold and silver. Some of the objects were inset with gemstones in a rainbow of colours. A ceramic vase was glazed with hunting scenes, featuring what looked like a giant striped cat, ferocious enough to have pounced on one of its antagonists.

These items would have travelled along the trade routes from distant Syria or Carthage, providing glimpses of more exotic worlds. Whoever had gathered this together had been disturbed, had abandoned their booty here, perhaps in the hope of retrieving it later. Returning to her village with this treasure would cause great excitement. She could picture her sisters gleefully trying on the burnished necklaces.

Bending over the bracken, digging her hands into the prize, she did wonder why everything was so polished. While pondering this, she dismissed the shining surfaces as evidence of exposure to rainfall. Leaning further forward, she stretched into the trinkets, licking her lips as if she was about to select the choicest morsels from a feast. Just as her fingers touched a slender golden figurine, the entire trove fell away from her. In seconds, she was hauled upwards while her body twisted into impossible angles. When her screams faded, she squirmed, trying to make sense of what had just happened. Twisting around she could see the hoard far below, its sheen now cruelly taunting her. Her immediate predicament became plain. She was secured inside netting: the countersunk force of a boar trap had launched her into the air. Swaying among the canopy, she desperately contemplated her next move as blood rushed to her head. The twine had begun gnawing into her skin so she tried to relax, breathing steadily. There was movement below. Squinting downwards she saw the vegetation parting. There were men down there, Celts, their tunics camouflaged with branches. Sighing with relief, she worked her head around within the confines of the trap, counting seventeen, armed with spears, swords and longbows. The sight of her dangling inspired ribald laughter.

"I'm not a boar, you oafs! Cut me down!"

Their ringleader, a towering man with a torso broad as an oak, removed his cap, revealing matted red hair that tumbled to his shoulders. "I can see as you in't a fuckin' boar," he barked in the thick accent of the Cornovii. "We in't been livin' in the forests for so long we's forgot what a fair maiden looks like."

"Good for you, Cornishman. Now. Cut me down! Please."

Another slapped the redhead about the shoulders. "Thing is, already had us breakfast, in't we, boys? Cooked w'selves a nice couple o' fawns s'mornin', in't we? So we's glad you in't no fuckin' boar."

"Good," she gasped. "Cut me down."

"Boars we catches all the fuckin' time," persisted the giant. "But we gets fed up with 'em, we does. So we uses a *different* bait. Every so often we checks who's been after stealin' us treasure. S'how we catches us *two legged* pigs for us cooking pot. Or, dependin' on what we catches, our *beds*."

"You ... you're Cornovii ... I'm Dumnonii ... when the English come to take our land, we're *all* Britons."

"Not a Cornishman no more, I fuckin' in't," he spat. "Brethren to no men, aside from wursel's. We's from all over. Once were Dematae. Ordovices. Iceni. Parisii. Manx. Couple o' the lads back in the camp is from other side o' Roman wall. We's all had us families wiped out, by Vikings in my case ... or by the Germans ... or Dalriati or Caledonii. We in't from any tribe anymore. We's men of these forests. We takes whatever we wants from it, and from anyone foolish enough to fuckin' trespass in it."

"My people are close by. A search party will be here soon. If you cut me down now, I'll say no more. Your lives will be spared."

"Oh, hear that, lads? This pretty little piglet trussed up for a fuckin' roastin' is goin' to spare *our* lives! Oh, cut you down, I will, in a minute. First, we's got to throw dice."

"*What?* What are you talking about ... *dice?*" In her exasperation Kady wriggled, furious that the more she exerted herself, the greater the constriction became.

"We's glad you in't a boar," their leader concluded. "We don't fuck boars, we doesn't. Well, not *all* of us." He aimed a roguish glance at a cock-eyed youth clutching a bloodstained wood-axe. "Eh, Gethin?" Jerking a thumb in his direction, he added: "That cunt'd fuck a hole in a tree."

Ugly sniggers spread through their motley ranks. Kady's eyes darted around their toothless grins, their lascivious stares. The ringleader goaded her further by rubbing his crotch. "Fresh Dumnonii meat for us to share, eh lads?"

Dumbstruck, she watched them huddle together, the redheaded hulk producing dice from his pockets. Moments later, they began rolling these cubes across a moss-mottled paving stone. As their game proceeded there were chuckles and sly glances towards her. The notion of employing her father's magic grew ever stronger, but his spiritual guidance had momentarily deserted her: the shock and the disconcerting effect of the blood pulsating around her scalp merely inspired panic.

"Easy, piglet," yelled the redhead. "Count the men you see rollin' us dice. We's all expectin' to 'ave us passions matched. You needs to keep up your strength, don't you? Best be hungry for us cocks. Cause that way you's comin' with us, as us slave. You *does* have a choice, mind, pretty one." He paused, a single tooth flashing in his bruised mouth's dark maw. "You doesn't give the lads the fuck of us lives, each and every one of us, then Gethen here takes his axe to your fuckin' throat. We'll fuck your corpse, then roast it on a spit, then we feasts on you, then we leaves what's left for the crows, then shit out what's left of you for the fuckin' flies."

Kady screamed until her throat ached but ceased when she realised it merely bolstered their sick amusement. She glared down as they returned to their game. Presently there was more bellicose hilarity and she could only gape at their leader shoving the dice into his tunic.

"Fane it is, then. You goes first, you ugly Iceni cunt. And don't take all fuckin' day, either, or you'll feel me boot at your fat spotty fuckin' arse while you's humping up an' down like a good 'un!"

The redheaded bandit reached for the rope securing the trap. Kady felt the tension slackening as he took the weight then began lowering her. While she descended towards the forest floor, she struggled, watching the hunch-backed brigand named Fane leering while he unbuckled his belt. Closing her eyes she felt a calm settling over her at last.

Kady ... beloved ... this is what you must do ... never let your enemies sense your fear as that will only empower them ... let my words linger inside your mind until the age-old powers they invoke take hold of your present ... these forests are host to many creatures, some ancient and benign ... as well as more recent interlopers who are evil ... we can never control the evil ones but we can channel them for short spells ... use the ancient druidic language of our forefathers for this invocation ... listen closely ... duibh a-steannach am tarduchillin a thu a'lorggabh ...

As the undergrowth inched closer her hysteria sparked again. This made her lose concentration, unable to focus on the ancient words. Their meaning seeped from her grasp, like the memory of a vivid dream fading upon awakening. Fane's breeches were around his ankles, while his comrades smacked his arse cheeks, sniggering along with him. Kady thought of a spider inexorably reeling in a fly.

When she was still suspended ten feet above them, their leader caught her eye, winked then let the rope go. She crashed to the ground to a chorus of jeers and roars. Winded, she groaned, squirming to one side. Fane stood over her. Except instead of contemplating his prize, his features were gripped with terror.

From her restricted vantage point she could see the bandits backing off, knuckles white around their weapons. Even the ringleader's bravado had evaporated. There was a sudden bark, echoed by several, then scores more. The hellish sound stiffened the hairs on her neck. Abandoning their trap, the vagabonds turned tail. Lithe bodies flashed over her and missiles of fur erupted all around: a pack of feral dogs that snarled as they chased down their quarry.

Jerking around, she observed her captors being hauled down, multiple jaws fastening around ankles. Some tumbled as larger beasts threw themselves onto their backs. One man backed against a trunk, lashing with his sword. There was a sickening yelp as one dog was bundled aside, blood spurting from its chest. Another was nearly decapitated, its head whipping to one side to hang by a sliver of muscle; other dogs quickly fell upon this maimed beast, tearing its lifeless pelt to shreds. As the bandit continued his desperate last stand, a sturdy mastiff seized his forearm, its jaw locking. The man's weapon slipped from his quivering fingers. Holding the dog aloft, his features contorting with agony, he tugged a dagger from his belt and plunged it into his assailant's muzzle. Others eagerly took its place, dogs climbing over his body until they seemed to merge into some unearthly creature comprised of quivering and bloodied brown, white and black pelts. His final scream was drowned in a horrid vomiting of blood. When a gap appeared in the writhing fur, Kady saw his chest had been chewed open. A tiny mongrel burrowed its head into the gore, seizing a strand of gut. Hungrily turning away, it hauled this slithering cord between its teeth, unfurling it from the twitching corpse, dragging it into the undergrowth.

Once the fury of the initial hunt had subsided, the dogs bickered over leftovers, and the crunching of bones and slurping of innards sounded across the clearing. Eventually the frenzied barking died down. Kady continued her unsuccessful attempt to extricate herself, until she was aware of heavy breathing. Turning over, she came face to face with an immense mastiff, its snout soaked with blood, thick strands of human hair matted to its bared teeth. Its breath was rancid. As it hyperventilated, saliva slithered from its mouth in silver globules. Kady was transfixed. Suddenly it thrust its head straight towards her abdomen, grasping the net in its bloodied jaws, twisting from side to side. She shrieked as its rows of teeth shredded the thin material. Closing her eyes, she waited for its evil mouth to lock onto her flesh. When she opened them again she caught sight of the creature's rump as it sped off. The pack's barking receded, the mastiff halting, peering over its immense shoulders at her. For a moment she suspected it was about to return. Instead it disappeared in the dense undergrowth, branches thrashing in its wake.

Freeing herself from the torn netting, she stood up, her breathing frantic, her whole body trembling. Those mastiffs had originally been bred by the Romans as guard dogs, and in the hands of careful owners had been loyal and loving. But with the departure of the legions many had escaped. After centuries of living off the land, the baying of these feral dogs signposted forest tracts to be avoided.

The stench of blood assailed her nostrils. Butterflies hovered in the shafts of sunlight, their azure and purple wings incongruous against the carnage strewn across the forest floor. She glimpsed a body, garments ripped to shreds, the flesh beneath lacerated to reveal the rib cage, the bones snapped, its symmetry twisted. Body parts lurked beneath flowers or were splattered against bark. One corpse lay face down, its neck partially devoured so the pulped face was angled towards the skies. Where its eyes had been were clotted holes. She hoped this had been Fane. Creeping from the scene of annihilation, she heard the harsh caw of crows. Drawn by the aroma of death, hundreds were gathering overhead. She sought a vantage point to determine the direction the pack had taken.

Searching among the trees, her eyes alighted on a sturdy oak. Scampering up its trunk, she heaved herself up to a thick bough then squirmed up through its layers of branches. Pausing after fifteen minutes, she stared down through the nodding leaves, catching sight of the massacre, the verdant undergrowth awash with red. There was an occasional yelping but she was relieved to note this was now coming from some distance. Resuming her climb, she crept ever closer to the summit, eventually reaching a point where the branches became precariously thin.

After resting, she parted the foliage, gazing at the powdery clouds drifting by. The treetops marched into the distance like a tempestuous green sea. Delving into her hood she produced the eyeglass. She trained it towards the east. At first the sight was too blurred to make sense. Then, as she stared with bated breath, the scene cohered. Twenty miles away the forest gave way to rolling meadows and farmsteads that stretched as far as the Mendip Hills. As well as the countless villages scattered across the landscape, there were several former Roman towns: she could make out the regimented rooftops of the largest, Venta Belgarum. But the magnifying lens revealed many of these dwelling places were being consumed by fire. Flames were engulfing huts, barns, and haystacks, and black smoke was twisting towards the clouds. When she focused, the image became more nightmarish. Figures were fleeing from homes, a swarm of ants desperately making for the forests. Behind these refugees were riders, some brandishing torches, others spurring horses forwards, swinging swords and axes.

"Saxon *devils*," she hissed.

Twisting in the other direction, she trained her glass on the western skies. At first she saw only clouds. Then she noticed darker smears. Villages were burning towards Exmoor. Enemy soldiers had already outflanked the Dumnonii territory. Clambering down the oak, she was oblivious to the certain death lurking beyond any ill-judged manoeuvre. She could think only of Gwynn, Tara and Brice, and the murderous savages who were coming for them. When the ground beckoned ten feet below she grasped a bough, then swung herself outwards, her feet kicking briefly before the juddering impact. Hauling herself up, she spied the sack she had abandoned, snatching it up. But that tiny moment of triumph was destroyed. Far closer than she had anticipated, a chorus of dogs began howling.

CHAPTER TWELVE

The cries of the hounds swirled all around again. Heart thumping, she drew the sword that had remained lodged in her belt throughout her ordeals, heading back towards the Roman road. While the hair-raising barks drew closer, her escape route was strewn with human remains. Slithering through the carnage, she struggled to keep her balance. When she inadvertently kicked a bloodied head, its eyes seemed to fix her in an evil stare.

A roar pierced the gloom. Focussing on its source, she was confronted by the monstrous mastiff again, its reddened snout testing the air. Kady sprinted on through the dense foliage, her panicked footfall provoking an abrupt yelp. This signal was transmitted throughout the pack. As her feet pounded the uneven ground, scores of the feral beasts trailed her, scenting fresh meat. She lunged deeper into the forest, her frantic flight taking her down paths she had never ventured along. Although she was stumbling blindly through this wilderness, blundering into nettles and thicker weeds that were spiky claws trying to ensnare her, she found herself drawn to particular turnings, heading past trees that were mysteriously familiar. She realised she was being guided.

These forests have been our realm for centuries, the routes through them mapped by druids for a thousand sunsets, my beloved ... we druids know these ancient pathways like the backs of our hands ... surrender to the old magic and sense your way through the labyrinth of wood and leaf ... your feet will leap over furrows and streams seconds before your eyes see them ... you will soon lose these four legged vermin ...

But her savage pursuers were gaining, their breaths panting. A spritely terrier broke cover to her right. The animals were outflanking their prey, as they would a deer or a boar. Her grip tightened on her sword. A glance over her shoulder revealed the mastiff bearing down. Its shoulder muscles stiffening, it prepared to leap. Then the world opened. The ground fell away, leaving her feet lashing into thin air. Her arms flailed, her sword spinning out of her grasp. Seconds later she plunged into ice-cold water. This fresh danger banished all thoughts of the dogs. Now she was immersed in swirling torrents of darkness, struggling to keep her airway clamped. Seized by remorseless currents, her limbs battered against the force, attempting to gain some purchase so she could swim to freedom. But she was being buffeted, her shoulders dragging against submerged rocks, weeds wrapping around her feet. There was a moment when she was engulfed by an overpowering sense of calm. She felt her panic seeping away, fading among the myriad streams of bubbles. No longer aware of being underwater, her eyes closed. She imagined herself on horseback, riding a beautiful white mare, its mane trailing with the wind, its thunderous hooves carrying her towards a glorious sunset where her father awaited her. Then his voice intruded into the fantasy.

Fear not ... your powers grow, Kady ... the forest is home to secretive beings more powerful than anything you have ever known ... you will learn how to harness them ... the kelpies are fearsome things who will destroy those who do not respect their ancient waterways but we druids have always been their allies ...

Her eyes snapped open. Through the murk she was aware of contrasting shadows: boulders, vegetation, darting fish. Her fingers were indeed locked in the mane of a fantastical horse, its shape defined by silver bubbles. She felt exhilaration as this creature suddenly reared, altering direction to speed upwards. Sparkling light grew in intensity. They exploded through the surface, waves cascading all around and sweet air rushed into her lungs. Inhaling greedily, she coughed water. The gleaming horse trotted through shallows to the bank. Kady eased onto the grass, gratefully smoothing its glistening hide, wondering at the glowing sensation that transmitted to her fingers. When she tried making sense of it, its equine shape was indistinct. Instantly it spun around and leapt back into its domain.

Kady listened until its splashing had faded into the babbling waterway. The noise of the hounds had also vanished. She considered the cost of her flight. She had lost her sword, the one her father had presented to her to mark her sixteenth year, as well as her painstaking morning's harvest. But there were even more pressing concerns. When she gazed westwards, she could see columns of smoke smearing the low-drifting clouds. The Saxons were closer than she had first anticipated from her lookout point. They were only miles from her loved ones.

CHAPTER THIRTEEN

Making her way home, Kady weaved around the trees, stooping in case enemy scouts were near. She also kept listening out for dogs, either the feral pack, or the huge hounds the Saxons often unleashed when hunting Celts. Eventually she came to the point where tribal cooking pots sent innocuous smoke plumes skywards. It was Tannus who noticed her breaking cover. He recognised her alarm, as well the garments leaving puddles in her wake.

"Kady? What has happened?"

Gasping air, she pondered which to mention first: being captured by cannibals, witnessing them torn apart by dogs, or the kelpie saving her from drowning. Tannus would only assume such lurid tales were down to hysteria. Instead she focussed on their immediate predicament: "Tannus. Please. You must sound the alarm."

"What is the danger, Kady?"

"Smoke rises from the valleys to the east."

"I noticed earlier, before the wind changed. Is it a forest fire?"

"While I was foraging I climbed a large oak. I saw. The Saxons from Wessex wage all-out war on British land. Already they've struck what's left of the Durotriges' territory. Now they're heading towards Dumnonia, their war parties scarcely an hour's ride away. If we're lucky."

The burly man lifted his forge hammer and turned towards the battered cauldron suspended from chains towards the rear of his forge. Kady winced as each ominous clang resonated across the meadows, fearful they might also draw Saxon attention. Figures emerged from far-flung locations, whether they had been gathering wood, or tending to livestock. Others scurried into view from the direction of the river, laden with glistening fish. Soon all were assembled in front of the forge.

Torean blustered forth, wrapping his cloak about himself, drawing his right forearm across his beard. Although he was clearly irritated that an afternoon nap had been curtailed, he was well aware of the gravity of being summoned by the blacksmith's bell.

"Tannus? Why have you sounded the alarm?"

"Kady is back. She will explain."

The chieftain's intense gaze sought her out from the expectant throng. Kady stepped forward. "Back from your harvesting, Kady. Have you been swimming, too?"

"I fell into the river, in my haste to return. I needed to warn you all."

"About what?"

"I saw smoke, to the east."

"Smoke?" queried Brice, elbowing his way forwards. "Is that all? That's why you had Tannus ringing his bell? You've got ants in your breeches, Kady."

"Brice, enough," Torean interjected.

"There was smoke near the Dorset Hills," Kady insisted. "But also to the west." Frustrated, she paced up the steps to stand beside Torean. "My people," she began, peering over them, "while I was out in the forests, I saw columns of smoke rising. Clambering up a tree to get a closer look, I could see the countryside stretching to the horizon. Celtic villages were in flames. Among them, Saxons, on foot, on horseback, with war dogs, sacking the villages, driving our kinfolk before them, hunting them down. The invaders are sweeping through the valleys. And they're outflanking us. The English aim to drive us out of Britannia."

Commotion broke out; Torean had to shout several times over the clamour, something he had grown wearily accustomed to. "*Please*. You must listen. *Everybody*. We've feared this moment would come. The English have rebuffed all attempts to live peaceably beside us, or to trade with us. They reply to our offers of peace talks with raiding parties. We knew they would not be content to remain in the lands they robbed from our brethren and renamed Wessex in their harsh tongue. We knew the Durotriges would be attacked and then the Dumnonii. More fool us for expecting Celt and Saxon could co-exist. Kady?"

"This is no raiding party. They've launched an invasion of the West Country. And they've us cut off. They'll be here within the hour. This time tomorrow, those of us who haven't been shackled as their slaves will have lost our heads."

"If we are cut off, then what can we do?" protested Greer.

"We must fortify the village," Brice bleated. "Sharpened stakes on the perimeters. We could hold them off, for days if need be." At this, many of the warriors in the village voiced their approval, digging their spear shafts into the ground.

Torean frowned. "How many Saxon warriors approach Dumnonia, Kady?"

"Hundreds and hundreds. And these will just be the vanguard. We cannot possibly fight. Well, of course we could fight, but we could never win."

Greer's voice was despairing. "Is there no hope, druid?"

"They have only cut us off by land. There is one escape route left to us. We must take our coracles and head out to sea."

Tannus' voice thundered across the gathering. "Head out to sea? Have you lost your mind, girl? You only have to cast your eyes towards the horizon to see how wild it is, especially at this time of year. The currents are way too dangerous for anything other than the short trips to our lobster creels. If we fled by boat, where would we head? Cymru remains a Celtic stronghold, but between Dumnonia and Cymru there is nowt but Saxon land, their longships patrolling the Severn. Hibernia? How many do you honestly believe would survive *that* journey, Kady? I've heard even the Roman galley captains feared the great seas to the west."

"Not Hibernia, Tannus. There is an island much closer than that."

"Where?" Tannus roared.

"My father showed me, in a vision, as I was fleeing from the forest. It's only four miles offshore, just beyond the horizon. A small isle, but riddled with underground caves. It would be an ideal sanctuary. As you say, Tannus, surrounded by treacherous currents. And also screened by haar. But that will work in our favour. We can set up camp there while we make longer-term plans."

"Do you mean the isle of mists?" demanded Tannus. "Where seal people are supposed to live? That's only for children's stories. If there really was an island out there, how come we've never heard about it until now? Why didn't Kai ever mention it before?"

"You said so yourself, Tannus. The seal people live there. It is sacred to them, so the fewer prying eyes that ever venture there, the better. But that has all changed. They will welcome us."

"Half men half wolves, now half men half seals? Has the world gone mad?" Tannus growled in exasperation. "Torean? Sacred islands? Seals that can change into people? Do we listen to fairy tales, or do we stand *here* and fight?"

Brice fisted the air. "I'm with our brave blacksmith. Ignore my sister and her *visions*."

Torean remained pragmatic. "Anyone who thinks going into battle against an enemy who outnumbers you by hundreds to one might well think themselves foolhardy warriors." Brice accepted this compliment, grinning ear to ear. Torean continued. "But they are also fools. While I admire your courage, young Brice, in suggesting we build a stronghold, I fear we would only be delaying the agony."

Although she regarded the all-too-familiar sight of Brice's pride deflating, she derived no pleasure from it. "We have but little time before their scouts will come near our village," she noted. "From the attack on our father it's clear the enemy already have an idea of our location. The night of the shapeshifter's visit was no random attack. The Saxons must have known where to unleash their werewolf warrior."

"What if they send a score of these beasts, or more?" Torean asked. "Why do they even bother sending war parties to root us out when they could simply conjure their demons?"

"I've seen visions of the aftermath of the shapeshifting. The process is fatal to whoever takes the potion. The transformation turns Saxon or Viking warriors into old men, who die very soon after resuming human form. We have *that*, at least, that the shapeshifting magic can only be used sparingly, and only at night, and only then when the moon is full."

"Yes, we can be thankful for that," Torean murmured.

"I'm not sure whether they think the wolf attack killed the last remaining druid in Dumnonia, and that is what has given them the resolve to start this invasion ... but as I said before, I can sense there is a medicine man, a shaman, in Wessex, who suspects there may still be druids standing in their path. Whichever it is, their thousands of foot soldiers outnumber us, druid or not."

"Then we must place our faith in our druid," concluded Torean. "It's what we have done for centuries."

Kady nodded. "There's just one more thing," she added. "We should torch all our homes."

CHAPTER FOURTEEN

After several vigorous smites from Torean's sword, Kady skulked through the gap in the entanglement of thorns, cursing as tiny spikes still sought her skin. Squirming through she entered a dank tunnel and paced inside until the only sounds were her harsh breaths, and the steady dripping of water from the ceiling. Presently Torean edged his way into the space behind her, his darting eyes scanning the myriad creatures scuttling across the wet scree.

"The old passageway to the abandoned tin mine," he murmured. "You really think this will lead us to safety, Kady?"

"I *know* it will, Torean," she insisted. "My father is guiding me ... guiding *all* of us. This is actually the safest route to the shore. Has Tannus set to work?"

"He has. The brushwood has been stacked around our homes. The Saxons may be fooled into thinking an advance party has already attacked the village. Whatever happens, it might give us precious time."

At that point his resolve faded. To make a stand against a foe outnumbering them by hundreds to one was impossible, but the chieftain was clearly dubious about this alternative. "Lead the way, Kady, with your father's eyes," he said, his voice quavering. "Kai's spirit will preserve his people."

She smiled at him then accepted the flickering torch he passed to her. About turning, she stooped into the tunnel, Torean falling into position behind. Negotiating the first turn in the path, she heard more villagers joining the single-file procession. The tense silence was interrupted by the awkward footfall of boots negotiating the rugged terrain and the relentless drips cascading from the roughly hewn rock to splatter against the tunnel floor. The torchlight revealed the encroaching walls, glistening with quartz. Although there was little change in the landscape on either side, Kady got the impression of the ground falling away. With each step it was also growing noticeably colder. When someone stumbled in the darkness behind, this provoked screams from a child. She decided the strained atmosphere needed to be lightened.

"We don't really have to go too far, Torean. This tunnel leads to the seams where our forefathers used to dig out tin. At this point we're probably as far out of sight of any Saxon scouts as it's possible to be. I'd say we're currently heading about fifty yards beneath the sea bed."

She decided that drawing this fact to the chieftain's attention might not be the best way to soothe his claustrophobia. "Torean."

"Kady?"

"Why not entertain us with one of your battle stories?"

"My *battle* stories?" he replied, warming to the suggestion. "Of course." His voice projected, echoing in the subterranean walkway. "People ... did I ever tell you about the time I was invited to a Carvetii chieftain's wedding, in Cumbria? En route, my party were attacked by Picts. They were all as naked as the day they were born, plastered in blue woad from top to toe, and every one of them so drunk on home brew they kept falling over as they tried to charge at us ..."

Having heard this tale many times before Kady switched off, a wry smile fixed as she held the torch ahead of her. After some time the ground began rising. Eventually light shone in the distance. There was also a sound of waves crashing.

"Look, Torean. The end of the tunnel."

"Excellent. We're nearly there," he announced over his shoulder. "Pass it on."

The message was relayed back down the line. This lifted everyone's spirits, in as much as it was possible to lift the spirits of an entire community who had just abandoned the homes they had known for generations. Kady approached the exit. After twisting for a mile under the bay, the old tin mine's main tunnel had emerged below the headland on the far side, opening into a secluded inlet. This was the point where the earth's valuable spoils were once loaded into cargo vessels for transportation to distant corners of the Roman Empire. During those days the Britons in this part of the West Country would have been handsomely rewarded. Stepping outside she took in the unfamiliar surroundings. The rocky shore was screened on both sides by towering cliffs. The battered remains of a jetty jutted above the churning sea like decaying teeth. For sailors unfamiliar with this horseshoe-shaped bay and the turbulent channel beyond, these would indeed be treacherous waters.

Torean was by her side. He took in the cliffs, then the hostile shoreline. "Now what?"

"We launch the coracles."

CHAPTER FIFTEEN

Tannus' powerful forearms plunged into the grey sea, carving great swathes through the waves. As the craft lurched to and fro, Kady fought against a rising sense of nausea. Every so often she would cast a nervous glance over her shoulder. This was the most perilous aspect of their flight. All it would take would be for some eagle-eyed Saxon to spy the flotilla of rickety crafts from the headland and they would be finished. The trip was undertaken in a fraught silence. Tannus stared resolutely ahead, making it obvious he was scanning the horizon but seeing nothing. Finally his frown grew even more intense.

"Do you see the island?" she asked him, shielding her eyes against the sun's dappling reflection.

"No. But, to be honest, I don't know what I'm supposed to see. The sea is grey. The sky is grey. At some point in the distance, they merge in a fucking blur of ... grey. Beyond that blur somewhere, I suppose, is Hibernia. Between us and Hibernia there is only this sea, where the only other vessels are Viking pirates."

Pursing her lips, tired of arguing, Kady peered into the distance. A mile to the northwest, the waves melted into a bank of mist. The closer they drew to this, the vaster it became, until the shifting eddies of haar were poised to envelop them.

"Kady! This is madness. We can't navigate through *this*. The seas are growing ever more choppy. Manannan is showing his displeasure at our intrusion. We can't go back, either. We're fucked."

"Listen, Tannus. Did you hear that shriek?"

"I did. A seagull. So what?"

"Not a seagull, Tannus. That was a rabbit. Are rabbits in the habit of swimming through the seas?"

Tannus chose not to respond to her sarcasm. "How can you be so sure it was a rabbit?"

"My druidic intuition. I can identify the occasional squeal of a young rabbit, just as I can differentiate between the cries of great and lesser black backed gulls, black-headed gulls, herring gulls and kittiwakes. I can also tell the difference between seals and seal people. We are entering the realm of the latter. They will help us steer past the rock formations lurking below us."

Tannus glanced nervously overboard.

"Wait here, Tannus. Until the other coracles have caught up."

"But what of these ... rock formations?"

"Ships struggle to navigate these waters because there are miles of hidden reefs and shoals below us."

"That's what bothers me, Kady."

"Tannus. I can assure you, any Roman vessels that ever headed this far out, on this course, were hopelessly lost. The same will go for any Saxons. They will tend to skirt along the shore, always within eyeshot of land. But our light coracles are perfect for the task. Once our fleet is gathered, I'll summon the selkies. We'll cross this misty wall together.

"Selkies? Werewolves? I am but a humble blacksmith. I truly believe this world has gone fucking mad."

* * *

At times the currents seemed ferocious enough to drag the convoy towards the vast ocean to the west. But as each rower continued the dogged journey they noticed sleek seals darting through the waters nearby, sometimes gently buffeting the coracles to steer them in a particular direction. After bunching up then following Kady's vessel through the mist, the welcome sight of a sizeable island greeted salt-stung eyes. Their sanctuary was a mile long, topped with a dense wood of weather-beaten trees; a haven pitifully small compared to their previous territory. Several hundred seals basked on its shores, wary of their approach. Among the unlikely armada, relieved chatter was punctuated by the agitated grunts of livestock.

Tannus steered the lead craft towards a sandy portion of the beach among the seaweed-mottled rocks. "You'll have to jump from here, Kady, I can't risk taking her in any further."

"*Her*? Beneath that gruff exterior I do believe you've developed a fondness for your little boat. Have you decided on a name for *her*?"

"Just get out! Druid or no druid, you're still an impudent teenage girl, Kady!"

Grinning, she ducked his playful lunge towards her ear. Bracing herself, she gripped the side and launched into the waves. Again she felt the sea's chilly embrace, rising to chest height. She pushed her full weight against the tide's onslaught, forcing her legs towards the shore. Tannus clambered out and began hauling the coracle, his colourful language drowned by the crashing surf. She smiled. While they had their differences, she had nothing but admiration for his strength and determination, especially at this difficult hour. Right now, the reliability of this humble blacksmith was one of the few pluses in their community's dire predicament.

CHAPTER SIXTEEN

Mochan edged his way along the precipitous ledge. Despite the imploring of the onlookers not to look down, his fearful gaze kept wavering to the swell frothing over rocks hundreds of feet below. Each monstrous wave mustered momentum before racing headlong to smash against the cliffs, like an army mounting a relentless siege.

Torean was at the forefront of the knot of tribespeople keeping the rope taught, allowing him just enough slack to continue his precarious journey towards the kittiwake nests. The nearest gathering of twisted twigs was almost close enough for Mochan to reach for its precious eggs. This also meant he was at the point where the adult birds were at their most hysterical; screeching overhead, their frantic wings brushing against him as he cowered into the guano-crusted crag. Gasping with the effort he dropped to one knee, stretching his trembling fingers towards the fragile ovals. Sighing with relief, he clutched an egg.

"Still warm," he noted, failing to disguise the nerves in his voice. Ignoring the squealing gulls, he tenderly placed his prize into the sack attached to his waist. Moments later he had secured two more. He was reaching for the final egg when a beak struck a glancing blow to his head. Caught off-guard, he lost his balance. Without having enough time to fill his lungs to cry out, his body pitched backwards, his feet kicking towards the ledge. As he jolted against the rockface, Kady watched the rope tighten around his waist.

Torean and the others called in alarm while they battled with the other end. Mochan's sack opened and his morning's plunder dashed against the rocks far below. As skuas pounced on this unexpected feast, Mochan crashed into the crag again, his head and shoulders impacting. Kady could only watch as the others struggled to reel him in, as if they had caught some monstrous fish.

"Mochan? Mochan ... are you all right?" Torean bawled, his voice echoing against the towering cliffs.

"The rope!" Kady cried, her finger stabbing towards him. As Mochan's limp body draped from the rock, the precious lifeline had snagged into a jagged crack; the rope's weight was beginning to serrate the chord.

"Kady, look!" Brice grasped her shoulder, heaving her away from the cliffs.

"Brice! Mochan needs me!"

"Look. Everyone ... *look!*"

His shrill voice seemed a wholly unnecessary distraction to Mochan's demise. Yet they were all drawn to the way his wavering finger was pointing towards the sea.

"What the fuck is it, Brice?" Tannus snarled at him, peering in that direction before returning to Mochan's silent form.

"What is it you young idiot? Can't it wait?" Torean barked.

"I see it, too," Kady said, similarly aiming her finger.

Her voice carried greater authority. Tannus shielded his eyes, staring towards the horizon. The irritation faded from his features, replaced by shock.

"What is it?" Torean blustered.

Kady glared outwards. A change in wind direction had created a momentary fissure in the thick mists that normally screened the island. Beyond, she could glimpse tempestuous seas. There, riding the wave crests, then plunging into the troughs, was a longboat. It was close enough that she could make out its oars thrusting into the unruly waters as it desperately cleaved a northwards path, and a red boar emblazoned across its sail.

"A Saxon emblem," Torean gasped. "Everyone take cover. If they spot us we're done for."

They all hunkered down, pressing into the grass at the cliff edge. Save for the pressure maintaining the whites of their knuckles at their end of the rope, Mochan was almost forgotten, until Kady spoke. "They must not even see this island. But if we can see its insignia, Torean, then it is close enough for its crew to spy someone wearing a plaid tunic, dangling against these white cliffs."

* * *

While her fingers ached and trembled against the rope, Kady's feet struggled to find toeholds in the uneven rockface. Despite Brice's boasts that his grip would remain sure, she had convinced Torean that she was much lighter. Gradually she was lowered down the rockface.

At one point the momentum of her painstaking descent twisted her whole body around. Straight ahead, the Saxon ship seemed to have sailed even closer. She could make out a figure at the prow, his helm silvery against the green swell. Wriggling around she saw Mochan, six feet below. The rope that was the only thing preventing him from crashing into the maelstrom had worn to thin tendrils. "Lower! *Hurry*!" she shrieked towards the concerned faces, now so tiny as they peered over the cliff.

Eventually she was close enough to touch Mochan. Although he had appeared to be out cold, she could hear feeble groans. She did not want him coming to, jerking and finishing the rock's work against that umbilical cord. Raising her hand, she signalled Torean to feed a third rope down. Keeping an eye on the loose end, she lunged for it. Missing, her momentum carried her into Mochan, jolting him. As another fragment of his rope sheared away, his body sagged, slipping further down the cliff. Panicking, she glanced over her shoulder, watching the spray cascading over the longship's prow. She could discern the boar's curled tusks. Its cruel eyes appeared to be glaring at her. She imagined it about to expose them all with a shrill porcine squeal.

At a command from Torean, her rope was lowered further. When the third rope dangled enticingly before her again, she seized it, wrapping it around Mochan's waist. Securing it with a sturdy knot she sighed with relief, flashing a thumb at the others just as the original rope snapped. Mochan's body juddered as the fresh rope took his weight. Roosting guillemots watched the frayed end flapping around the rock.

As they were both heaved up, she caught sight of the Saxon vessel again, its sleek bow rising. She heard her father's voice.

You are naturally panicked, daughter, but remember how strong your mind is now that I have sown it with druid magic ... if you can see your enemy you can get into his mind ... if you can get into his mind you can control him ... if you concentrate hard enough you can ensure the German sailors see nothing but sea and mist and gulls ... sea and mist and gulls ...

The helmsman tugged the rudder, the muscles in his broad arms flexing. He followed the directions of the lookout, thrusting his arms to port or starboard, depending on the proximity of the rugged reefs. The vessel's captain shuddered, drawing his sodden furs closer, staring at fulmars wheeling over the spume. He noticed a gaggle of serpentine cormorants cowering against the wind on a large outcrop. His eyes drifted upwards. More seabirds struggled against the furious eddies of the wind. Beyond, veils of mist seemed to seal out the rest of the world. He turned his attention to the prow cleaving the waves. "Guide us past these cursed rocks, Wade, god of the sea," he roared, the harsh Germanic tone apt for such a wild backdrop. "They're only fit for gull shit."

* * *

Kady touched Mochan's forehead. "The fever has him now."

Torean considered his contorted features. "What about the wound?"

She turned to the shattered arm. Although she had managed to re-connect the dislocated bone and bind the wound, infection was spoiling the exposed flesh. She had applied a poultice to the deep gash running down the side of his head.

"He needs medicine, Torean."

"Well. Make up one of father's potions, Kady," Brice insisted.

"That's *exactly* what I must do, brother. There's only one thing."

"What, Kady?" Torean asked. "Just *hurry*, whatever it is?"

Her eyes wavered around all the concerned faces watching Mochan shivering beneath his deer hide covers. "I need monkswood. I've been all over the island. There isn't any growing here. I've scoured every inch. But I know where it is abundant. I heard the druid's voice telling me. There's a glade … near our old village."

"You mean you must return to the mainland?" Torean's eyebrows arched. His glance flitted around the others.

"I have no choice."

"Nonsense, Kady. There are *always* choices," protested Torean. "One of the warriors can go. Angus. Or Fedlimid. I would even go myself. Just describe this *monkwood* and one of us will fetch it."

"*Monkswood*. And what if you brought back the wrong plant? They look similar to several other flowers. It is a *vital* ingredient, and if the wrong plant is used, in his weakened state Mochan could be poisoned. I must go."

"Kady. *Please.*"

"I am going to my coracle."

CHAPTER SEVENTEEN

With minimal paddling the current was still propelling the boat at an even pace. Kady merely had to use the oar as a rudder, guiding the coracle towards the smudge of land on the horizon. The closer she got she could pick out the ragged outlines of trees jutting from the pre-dawn shadows. The more this definition grew, the greater the sense of foreboding. She realised this venture was not just reckless; it was suicidal. The invaders had swept across this part of the West Country weeks before, driving the remaining Britons before them. Whole Saxon farming communities were being established beyond the forests that marched to the coast.

Remaining undetected beyond the cusp of the horizon, Kady's people were relying on a harvest of fish, and seabirds and their eggs for survival. But Mochan's accident had underlined how fragile their predicament was. During their flight from the mainland, Kady had tried to grasp as many of the more precious woodland plants as she could, especially those bearing seeds. She had hoped to begin cultivating a herb garden, but was only too aware how pitifully sparse this would be compared to the wilderness where her father had foraged.

While he could still assist her with knowledge sown in her sub-conscious, at times this seemed sorely tested by the practicalities presented by real dilemmas. But the image of Mochan's fever-drenched brow had been enough to steel her resolve.

Beloved daughter, the monkswood you seek is only two miles distant ... if we were playing one of the games you used to love as a child, I would soon be telling you how warm you were getting ... the glade is a mile from the abandoned village ... I used to harvest the flowers myself ... near a copse by the dolmens ... they bloom in abundance ...

Land was fast approaching. Thrusting the paddle into the icy surf she steadied herself as the coracle rode the crashing waves, bucking like an unruly colt before pitching onto the shore. After hauling herself out, she allowed herself moments to catch her breath then scowled towards the threatening shadows in the trees. Hurriedly she dragged the vessel over shingle. She came across a thick carpet of dried seaweed, deposited by the high tides the previous week. Upturning her little vessel, she hauled a covering of the stinking plants over it, blinking at the blizzard of disturbed sand flies.

Satisfied with her handiwork, she sped onwards into the forest. The trees enveloped her. As she created distance from the rolling waves she became immersed in an eerie silence, punctuated by the occasional trills of secretive birds. Presently she came across a stream. Ducking into the hollow, she followed its winding course for a mile then slithered up the muddy bank to get her bearings. The boughs of tall beeches enveloped her and as the sun crept upwards, the dawn chorus soared into a fabulous choir all around. Kady could identify each enthusiastic chorister: the sharp clicking of hawfinches, the fluid chaffinch songs, and the excitable chirps of blue tits. She loved how all this knowledge of the environment had been implanted by her father; had been passed through the druid bloodline for countless centuries. Recognising bird cries reinforced her sense of the potential depth of her untapped powers and gave her some resolve. But as she skulked through ferns, eventually coming towards a clearing, a deep sense of foreboding returned.

She noted footprints that had disturbed a nettle patch to one side. Heavy Saxon boots had passed here recently, weighed down with weaponry. Possessing the ability to differentiate between the mating cries of willow warblers and chiffchaffs suddenly seemed a peculiar irrelevance. As she inadvertently grasped a thick nettle stalk, managing to stifle her instinctive yelp, she also yearned for a champion warrior's broadsword. Lifting a long twig she parted the clumps of bristling nettles, gazing beyond their barbed leaves. A faint hint of charcoal lingered in the air where what had been left of the original huts had been removed to make way for Saxon abodes.

There was movement among the freshly hewn timber structures. Freezing, Kady's knuckles whitened around the stick. A Saxon had emerged from a log cabin, drawing on a clay pipe. Lifting a leg he farted generously then made his way towards a latrine pit.

Kady about turned. Retracing her steps, she stooped back down the hollow to the stream. She listened intently. Dragonflies buzzed over the surface. A fish flipped just below, flicking a ripple that sped towards her. Far to her right she could make out the white flash of a dipper's underbelly as it hopped from rock to rock, searching for insects. She could hear a more urgent water flow in the other direction.

Stealthily she crept this way, sighing with relief as she eventually spied clouds of vapour rising above water cascading over a six feet dip. Looming over this vista were the great stone slabs that marked the final resting places of her clan of the Dumnonii. The English never disturbed these dolmens when they came across them, although it seemed an unfathomable irony that they respected the Britons in death as much as they despised them in life.

All around the banks at the base of the waterfall were clumps of the prized monkswood, the sunlight filtering through the treetops transforming their petals to brilliant blue. Vigilance tempering her triumph, she bowed to them, realising that even as she broke each stem to thrust them into her basket she was diminishing their potential strength. Every second counted. Rising from the hollow, she gave another glance towards the village. That prosaic final impression of the fate of their former homes had been so cruelly apt: a Saxon oaf going for his morning shit. Her stomach churning, she faced in the direction of the sea.

Half an hour later she was approaching the hidden boat. Stepping towards it to flip it over, a startled crow exploded at her feet, interrupted from its meal of rotting crabs. Her heart pounded and she cursed the ragged black shape wheeling towards the trees. She found her attention rooting on it until the bird settled high in the canopy, cawing at her. The grating cry grew in intensity until it drowned out the crashing surf. Her eyes wavered shut.

My beloved Kady ... I sense danger approaching ... the crows may be black, with ugly voices, and bellies full of carrion but they often serve the druids ... concentrate ... see the world as the crow sees the world ...

Kady was aware of gazing down at herself, a tiny figure silhouetted against the grey sea. Switching her attention to the right, treetops gave way to a haphazard patchwork of farmland that sprawled for miles, fading towards rolling hills. Smoke trails snaked into the brittle skies. To the west, a roadway wound across the countryside, hewn by slaves during the Roman occupation. Intricately paved with stone layers, in the decades since the legions had abandoned Rome's northwestern frontier this road network had succumbed to weeds. Nevertheless the crow flinched nervously at the sound of hooves clattering along the surface.

Kady's eyes snapped open. The crow rose from its perch and wheeled out of sight. Alarmed, she scampered back towards the trees. Grasping the looking glass from her pocket she scanned the woods. She discerned two riders, vanishing then re-appearing through the ranks of moss-encrusted beeches. They were clad in ragged sheepskin blankets, continually scanning their surroundings as they progressed. She knew exactly what these warriors were scouring the countryside for. They were not hunting boars.

Kady returned to the coracle. The horsemen were drawing closer; she could feel their passage reverberating under her soles. There was no time to drag the boat into the sea. Just as the first rider emerged from the treeline, his steed whinnying as the reins were tugged abruptly, she squirmed under her makeshift hide. Her heart was pummelling her ribcage so furiously she wondered if the sound might echo within this shell and betray her. Calming herself, she took steady breaths. Although her heartbeat slowed from a gallop to a canter, her hands were quivering when she reached for her scabbard. She clutched the handle but imagined the thugs belly-laughing at a teenage girl's attempts to defend herself against battle-hardened butchers.

The horses were stamping across the shingle, the scree shifting beneath their weight. Their faltering steps drew ever closer. Deftly withdrawing the sword from its sheath, she waited. Muted by the wooden wall, a horse snorted. There were voices;

she focussed on the harsh, guttural tones. The Germanic language was full of consonants that grated across their tongues like flints grinding stone. Kady heard her father's tones translating the speech.

This hunt is tiring me, Torr. If there are any more fucking Brits left out here, I say let them hide away in their caves, eating worms until they starve.

Can't you think of anything other than killing Brits for five minutes, Oxa? Just enjoy this scenery. Britannia is beautiful, isn't it?

Fuck Britannia, Torr, and all the pigs who used to call it home.

Oxa. Look at the sea. After living in the middle of the Black Forest, where the only sight of water was lakes, the sea never ceases to amaze me, my friend.

The blueskins can stick their scenery up their arses. We are the hunting dogs, Torr. Britannia is one giant fucking rabbit warren.

Kady could also picture them clearly. Celtic villagers dismayed at the sight of the English invaders. Unlike the native tribes who took great pride in their appearance, fashioning clothes from colourful fabrics, finding time to decorate them with finely woven facings, these plunderers who had leapt from their ships to steal their land invariably appeared to have merely thrown on random animal hides. The horses stepping from foot to foot on this uneven ground were unlike the sturdy working beasts familiar to the British farming communities. These animals were lean, constantly snorting and champing at the bit; bred for the speed required for combat, or leaving ransacked homesteads in their wake. The men themselves appeared vigilant, one hand white-knuckled to the reins, the other poised by their scabbards.

The way their swarthy eyes probed the landscape reminded her of hawks looking-out for prey. Securing the conquered territories remained a drawn-out process. Just as in the Roman times, some local tribesmen had refused to submit to foreign occupation - although most of these renegades would end up decorating English villages as severed heads impaled upon fences.

Kady pictured the one called Oxa. Younger and leaner, he was a foul-mouthed teenager with a red birthmark on his neck, shaped like a small skull: appropriate for one who relished butchery. He also kept on spitting, his saliva splattering against the stones around his horse's hooves. Torr had greying hair and a matted beard. His speech was slurred. This older soldier had developed a taste for wine and mead that was being well satiated in this former Roman colony, with its derelict villas hiding well-preserved cellars. And when the Celts fled their homesteads they tended to seize sackfuls of food for the flight, abandoning any heavy caskets of beer and cider. He much preferred plundering, whereas Oxa's chief passions lay in killing and raping.

Oxa was ruffling his horse's mane affectionately; an incongruous action given his fingers were matted with the blood of a spotty-faced teenager who had emerged from a cave in the woods an hour beforehand, and whose severed head was currently being relieved of its eyeballs by chuckling magpies.

Torr.

What is it?

Towards the shore. Those tracks. It looks like a boat has landed.

Kady's heart skipped.

I see it, Oxa. One of the little Celtic tubs. See where it has been dragged. All the way to ...

What do you think, Torr? More fucking blueskins with blood for us to spill.

Her throat was dry. Tensing, she prepared to launch herself against the hull, gambling that the element of surprise would give her precious moments to drag the coracle back towards the sea. Bracing herself, she suddenly heaved herself to her feet, thrusting the coracle high into the air. The nearest horse reared onto its hind legs, its rider barely managing to grasp hold of the reins before it wheeled around and cantered in the direction of the trees. Its companion neighed in alarm, following close behind. As the warriors bellowed at their mounts, she grasped the coracle and hauled it towards the sea.

The tide was almost fully in, so the distance between the shingle and the waves had been reduced to a mere ten yards. As she watched the Saxons gaining control of their charges, heels digging into the beasts' flanks, jerking at their reins to bring them about, she heaved the boat. She was close enough to feel spray against her face. Now the cold water was rushing around her ankles. Staring backwards, she caught sight of the nearest Saxon as he bellowed to his colleague. Her father translated his rasping voice.

Head him off, Torr!

Torr urged his horse away to the left, steadying himself as the shingle led to more substantial rocks. He steered his horse onwards until it was knee-deep in the surf, blocking her escape route. Kady turned to watch Oxa's horse slowing to a purposeful canter, closing in. The younger Saxon drew his long, bloodied sword. Ahead of her, Torr jolted his reins, bringing his beast to a halt.

Her father's voice brought Oxa's words.

I will enjoy toying with this cur. Where do you think this miserable Brit came from, Torr? How has he been evading our patrols? We should torture this bastard first, let him betray any comrades he might have, before we take his fucking head back to the camp.

The older Saxon, rocking against the motion of the sea, drew his sword. He gestured towards Kady's head, made a sweeping movement. As the offshore breeze whipped across the bay, scattering sand like wisps of smoke, her long locks dislodged from her hood and fanned like flame around her shoulders. Torr's lips bared with a grim satisfaction.

Look at this, Oxa!

The young hunter grinned.

No native boy to decorate our blades. Not at all. A fair young maiden who'll make a fine new bride for one of our elders! Look at her, Torr. Isn't she stunning? We'll be handsomely rewarded for returning with this prize.

Yes. This hunk of meat is worth more to us if we preserve its pulse. Bonds, Oxa! This is one prime piece of Celtic plunder to guard with our lives!

Oxa dismounted, while Kady stared at the blade poised over her, a single tear slithering down her freckled cheek. Delving behind his saddle, the Saxon extracted a leather whip. Normally used for administering harsh punishments to wayward horses or prisoners, it would function just as well as a means of securing her limbs before shackling her across his horse's neck.

At that moment an oystercatcher erupted from a dip in the ground, its black and white plumage streaking into the air, its piping cry echoing across the vast bay. Torr's mount, momentarily startled again, reared high, forelegs kicking, whinnying as its warrior master roared in exasperation. Distracted, Oxa gazed as his partner brought the beast under control, jerking the reins. The Saxons regarded her again. Torr plunged his heels into his horse's shanks, steered the animal closer. Leaning down, he indicated her sword.

Be a good girl and drop your little bread knife.

Fear prised it from her grip. Leaning from his horse, he heaved the coracle away from her fingers. Leering at her, Torr winked at his mate.

Oxa. The whip.

As the burly Saxon climbed from his mount, her father's voice continued. He began speaking undecipherable phrases she recognised from spells she had heard him recite. The words began issuing from her lips.

Listen to her, Torr ... praying to your pagan gods will not help you, now, whore.

Closing her eyes, the words of the old tongue flowed. The temperature dipped. Opening her eyes again, she noticed Oxa unfurling the cruel lash, but before he could bring it towards her, he was swathed in a shifting grey curtain. Haar was enveloping them in its cold embrace. Disorientated, Torr drew his horse closer. His frantic eyes sought his prey. Turning towards the shore, he searched for Oxa. Finally he held his right hand before his own eyes and was dismayed to find the mist had grown so dense he could hardly discern his trembling fingers. But despite this fog, Kady could study his every move.

Torr! Where the fuck are you? I'm fucking blinded!

Over here, Oxa! I see her red hair ... I think.

Keep talking, Torr. I'm guiding my horse towards your voice ... Keep talking! Stay where you are, Celtic virgin. No fog will keep you from your destiny. To become a Saxon slave. To be used and abused and to give our tribe fine Saxon babies until your cunt is as worn as my fucking saddle. Then you'll end up like so many of your native brethren, your pretty head on a spike.

You know what I'm thinking, Torr? She's led us such a merry dance she needs to be punished. I think you and I should break her in. The elders will be happy we're bringing a beautiful bride for them to fight over. What the fuck do they expect? We're in fucking Britannia! There are no virgins here over the age of twelve!

Oxa clambered from his horse, the tip of his broadsword thrusting into the dense mist.

No escape this time ... if you want to keep your head, Celtic wench, you lose your garments.

Torr also dismounted, plunging into the waves.

You're wasting your breath, Oxa. This blueskin won't understand a word we're saying, you fool.

They all understand the language of steel.

Through the sifting currents of haar, she watched the two warriors closing in on her position. But Oxa bristled. Torr was still scanning the fog, so he failed to appreciate his comrade's sudden stance until a moment later. He swivelled towards Oxa, only to be distracted by their horses. Both animals had retreated some yards away and were nervously stepping further back. Raising, her arms, she felt herself rising, her feet lifting from the sand until they were being lapped by the waves.

What trickery is this? I see her, Torr! She stands on a rock! Down from there, you fucking wench!

Oxa, your whip! Lash her up and let's get away from this accursed place.

She looked down at Oxa unfurling the yards of leather, gripping the handle, testing the strength of the weapon by pulling it tightly. The leather hissed into the breeze, cracking. Oxa's anger had been replaced by an incongruous expression of dread. He lunged forwards.

Torr! She's right here! She's holding my legs, the fucking vixen!
Impossible! She's got my legs!

Torr swivelled around. As the patterns of mist shifted momentarily, he caught sight of Oxa, several yards away.

This cannot be!

Dropping the whip, Torr unsheathed his sword and lunged between his legs, anticipating a shrill cry. He heaved the blade out again, holding it close to his face to study any blood. Instead there was only sand: muddy sand, slithering along the shaft. He screamed in frustration and growing terror. This startled turnstones somewhere in the murk, which wheeled overhead, their alarm calls taunting his despairing cry.

Oxa lunged at his unseen assailant attacker, stabbing repeatedly. But each frantic motion seemed only to increase his rigid stance.

Torr! I need help! She's got me in a lock like a fucking Slav wrestler!

Your horn, Oxa. Call for reinforcements!

It's too late!

What?

It's not the girl that has us trapped, Torr, you idiot!

Torr looked down again. Kady knew what he was seeing. She realised he could now make out the ground, through the mist. There was certainly no Celtic girl's arms wrapped tightly around him. Only quicksand. And this had already worked its inexorable way to his thighs. Oxa whistled towards the horses.

Here, you cursed dogs! Here!

There was no sign of the creatures. Instinctively sensing the change in terrain beneath their hooves, they had backed off. No amount of threats or brandishing whips would bring them any closer. Torr cried towards the skies.

Woden! Save us!

The sludge had worked its death grip around his waist. Gazing over at Oxa, he saw his comrade had been sucked down as far as his beard. Torr threw himself forward, trying to ease the sinking by repositioning his weight. But his torso was embedded too far. His horror was replaced by a warrior's sense of the inevitability. Kady felt the noble calm descending on him as he shut his eyes and waited for the quicksand's kiss to greet his parted lips. In that moment of peace, he twisted his body for his final glance of the world.

Kady swam to the coracle, clambering inside. The paddle was strapped to the hull with twine. Retrieving it, she dug it into the sea. She heaved forcefully, the splashes obscuring the moment their screams became horrible splutters. She watched all that remained of the existence of these hunters, their twin helms projecting above the mud for seconds until they disappeared.

CHAPTER EIGHTEEN

Pushing out to sea, she studied the receding shoreline, wary in case the unfortunate wretches had been scouting for a larger party. The beach remained deserted, save for their horses that were trotting back towards the woods. Facing the horizon, she dug the paddle into the water with renewed vigour. Ominous clouds were mustering, heading inland, laden with rain. Within the hour the seas would transform into heavy squalls and her return to the island would become even more hazardous.

She focussed on the relentless process of plunging the oar into the water, dragging it back, watching the bubbles vanishing. Soon her arms ached. Each thrust with her white-knuckled grip sent agonising shock waves through her frame. She was determined to reach the island before the storm broke, but equally desperate to rest. Placing the oar across her lap, she closed her eyes for precious moments. Feeling the boat rocking more insistently, she patted the sack that had remained tucked into her belt. Pleasingly, she could feel the bunched outline of her precious flowers.

Kady's mind drifted and she thought of her father. Her childhood was crammed with fond memories of their time together. She now appreciated that the magical tricks he had performed for his children's amusement, which they had taken for granted, had been so much more than fun. They had hinted at the gateway into a secret realm. Kady had always accepted the bulk of his expertise would be transferred upon his death. But exactly how this would manifest itself had always been something of a mystery. Now she understood the true potency of the druidic forces she had inherited. As a druid, she possessed a rare gift. Her father had once explained the druids held the destiny of their people and their country in their hands. She realised the emphatic truth of this.

The coracle jolted. Her eyes snapping open, she stared at her surroundings, alarmed at the speed of the transformation. Dark clouds were billowing directly overhead, rain falling in vast veils. The swell was rising, buffeting her fragile vessel like a child's toy. Staring to either side she could see the coracle was being dragged way off-course. The land was rushing to her right, trees giving way to open meadows and rolling hills. Saxon dwellings were drifting by. She could make out figures darting around their huts, fearful of the impending storm, dragging children inside and ushering livestock to shelter.

There was a shuddering impact. She stared at the jagged sliver of barnacle-encrusted rock that had ruptured the hull. Icy water fountained upwards, blinding her. The coracle spun, briefly righting itself before foamy water engulfed the stricken vessel.

CHAPTER NINETEEN

Inside Tannus' forge, Kady was dancing clear of sparks as he dashed his brutal hammer against a fiery shaft. Every so often he would pause and mop his sweat-drenched brow with a rag. He would beam at her then proceed honing the lurid strip into the desired shape. The rhythm of the metallic crashing remained but its noise evolved, lightening, gaining octaves, transforming into a piercing staccato. Kady's eyes flickered. Knuckling sleep from the sockets, she listened intently. A nearby stream gargled. The chiffchaff, whose relentless song had woken her, fluttered out of earshot.

Tentatively she raised herself, wincing when her joints stretched. Hours curled in this hollowed tree in soaking garments, combined with the biting dawn cold, had left her entire body aching. This was exacerbated by a gnawing hunger. Peering over the rim of the trunk she took in her immediate surrounds. The tide had washed debris up the shingle beach; a hundred yards further on she could see the husk of the coracle, its leather skin frayed to expose its wooden beams, like the carcass of some beached whale.

Kady had spent fraught hours clinging onto to its sides as it had listed and had eventually been carried shoreward by the waves. Eventually she had thrown herself into the frothing shallows, pushing for the shore, succumbing to fatigue when she had made it to this landfall. Her final conscious action had been to slither inside this refuge, lest more Saxons were prowling. Immediately she had lapsed into a fatigued sleep.

Wary of the dangers lurking beyond every headland, she clambered out of her makeshift shelter, moving laboriously as her sodden clothes weighed her down. She headed into the woods that fringed the beach. After fifteen minutes skulking from tree to tree, she halted. Glancing down, her eyes were drawn to another clump of monkswood. Having lost her earlier crop, she plucked a generous fistful of these vital flowers, securing them under her cuff. For Mochan's sake, she hoped she would avoid becoming immersed in water yet again. She also spied a mushroom crop. Without thinking, almost as if she was watching someone else, her fingers dug into the soil surrounding their gnarled stems. Uprooting several, she whipped them against leaves, dashing away the black earth and clinging woodlice. Drawing the meat closer she blew forcefully. Eagerly she launched the mushrooms into her jaws, chewing the damp flesh, swallowing chunks. Only when her fingers had been licked free of any lingering morsels did she start, gazing down at the remainder. The only mushrooms she had eaten previously had been browned and served on wooden platters, often with a sprinkling of mouth-watering herbs, or spices purloined from derelict Roman homesteads. Her favourite way to gorge on them was as an adornment to sizzling boar steaks.

But from playing among forest glades as a child she knew mushrooms well. Her father had often stressed the fine line between the many wild variants and their relatives, the toadstools. Fungi should be given a wide berth, let alone sampled. Unfamiliarity with the subtle shades or textures distinguishing the species would mean stomach pains at best; at worst, days of relentless vomiting spasms and hallucinations, terminated by an agonising death. Only druids knew the subtle differences among the spores lurking in Britannia's dense woodlands.

Her fist clawed into the mushrooms again. That she had developed such reckless indifference to any potential side effects of wolfing them down was something she no longer dwelt on. The meat was sweet. It had stopped her gut from grumbling. And now she was a druid herself, she had nothing to fear from the natural bounties the forests had to offer.

The trees thinned. Sunlight was bathing the landscape, the rolling hills ahead assuming definition. Haar drifting from the coast coated the swaying grass with silver beads. A westerly wind carried the nearby surf's relentless tumult. Against that backdrop, Kady heard a scream. Jumping to her feet, she peered through the murk. Again, a piercing shriek sounded. This time she gained more of a bearing: it was closer than she had first assumed. A third scream surely came from a mere thirty yards distant, just beyond a hill rising over a copse of ragged elms.

At the hill's summit, she threw herself to the ground and peered over. The slope dipped towards a rocky inlet. There was a shack down there, a stone hut with a wooden roof, typical of the abodes favoured by the Dobunni tribe. Their villages had once proliferated around this stretch of the coast; most of them had fled the invasion. Any stragglers lived an isolated life, eking a living from meagre sea harvests. The hut's walls were inset with shells: intended to ward-off evil spirits. On this occasion its supernatural defences had been no match for a physical enemy. The source of the terrified voice was a girl, sprawled near the high tide mark. Surrounding her was a gang of riders, their horses tethered among rocks close by. The horsemen were also Celtic: Iceni.

Iceni were a savage eastern tribe whose reputation had been sealed several centuries before by the exploits of their warrior queen, Boudica. After being flogged by Romans and seeing her daughters raped, she had led a confederation of Celtic tribes against the legions, sacking cities and temples. But these descendants of Boudica's brave rebels had soiled that legacy. The Iceni had fled the English swarms, but rather than seeking solidarity with their Celtic brethren in the hinterland, they were leaving a trail of ransacked homesteads.

Now Kady noticed a body lolling in the waves, the skull bludgeoned. An Iceni was brandishing a crimson axe. The girl bayed as the surf toyed with the corpse then flowed beneath her soaking garments. Kady's initial guess was of a youngster, barely into her teens. But as she was pawed by three of the thugs, a hand suddenly wrenched at her tunic, tearing at the material. Her skin was pale as a netted fish, but the topless figure revealed was a young woman's. The axeman handed his weapon to an underling. Nausea uncoiled in the druid's stomach. The barbarians were jostling, eager to take their pleasure lest their predecessors' over-exuberance either damaged her, or silenced the pathetic mewling that was stoking their sadism. Their coarse laughter was the ugliest sound Kady could imagine.

Their leader dragged the girl to the shore, forcing her down and straddling her, almost as if he had fished her from the waves and was about to breathe life into her little lungs. So fiercely was she quivering with terror, he bowed closer and twisted his grubby fingers into her dark curls.

"Be still. The less you wriggle, the quicker this will all be over for you, my beauty."

Another roughly grasped his shoulder. "Nay, my friend. Let her fucking wriggle. Let us drag this out for as long as possible, afore she meets Judoc's axe."

Kady scanned her surroundings. Tugging a cord coiled inside her tunic's front pocket, she unfurled her sling. She had become expert at targeting the vermin that had scurried around her village, which was exactly how she viewed these cowards. Reaching to her right she clasped a fist-sized pebble, deftly feeding it into the weapon's pouch. Easing herself into a crouching position, she focused on the piebald rump of the nearest grazing horse. Her father's voice seeped into her mind.

Remain calm, beloved one ... you are unseen ... use stealth, surprise and the advantage of height ... draw on every second of the hours we spent honing the skills of the slingshot ... harness the abilities you know you have ... never ever doubt them ... you will strike these barbarians like lightning ...

Taking the strain, she whirled the device around before unleashing her projectile. Flashing through the air, the stone smacked flesh. The horse whinnied, rose on its hind legs, buffeting others in shock. Panic lanced through the beasts and they broke into an ungainly gallop along the shore.

The bandit leader had already heaved his breeches to his knees. In the pause between his victim gazing in horror at his exposed dick, and his own eyes following the panicked animals, another shot was primed. The second stone cracked against the rear of his head, pitching him into the rocks with a spray of blood. Kady ducked; when she glanced back into the bay, the Iceni were scampering into defensive positions among the boulders.

Seizing another stone, she launched it into the inlet. It struck a rock and showered the cowering men with shards. A futile salvo of arrows sailed overhead. Kady counted four bandits slithering for cover like lizards. Again and again she raised her sling, the lethal missiles striking home. An Iceni raised his hunting horn to unleash a shrill blast. Kady's next stone slammed into that raised hand, splintering the instrument, before another whacked against his neck. Among the seaweed and sandflies, he curled into a foetal position, spluttering as blood fountained up his throat. Kady mused that his gargling sounded as if the bastard was appreciating a fine wine.

The remaining bandits broke cover, scampering off in the direction their horses had bolted. Empowered, Kady took to her feet, launching stones in quick succession, dropping two more Iceni before their comrades scrambled over a headland. She hurried to the girl.

"Those bastards," she gasped. "They killed my father ... why?"

Kady's eyes darted towards the stragglers vanishing beyond a headland. "These are hard times. The east and south are now German kingdoms. These bandits roam freely, helping themselves to whatever they can get their hands on." Kady grasped the girl's skinny arms, heaving her upwards, helping her gather her garment's ragged folds around her exposed chest. "You have a change of clothing, in your abode?"

The girl nodded, her body trembling as Kady guided her by the sprawled bodies. Shrugging herself free, she stood over the nearest one, mesmerised by the pink porridge oozing from the splintered forehead. Flies were already dancing over the moist offal as it steamed faintly.

"Come, girl," murmured Kady. "Think yourself fortunate you evaded death this day. Do not dwell on another's."

The younger female grunted dismissively before spitting into the lifeless eyes. The insects scattered. "Sorry, my little friends," she whispered. "Please, return to your feast. Lay your eggs inside his worthless cunt's skull. These Iceni are fit for nothing else but fodder for your maggots." Shivering, she faced Kady. "Where did you come from? I didn't think there were any other Britons near here. When word spread of the Saxon warbands, our tribe split up. Father ... father refused to run any more. We became like hermits, alone on this beach."

"Nowhere's safe in the West Country. If those Iceni hadn't come across you, West Saxons surely would have."

The girl paused for a moment. "You're not Dobunni. Your accent is southwestern."

"I'm Dumnonii. Saxons drove us from our village."

"You live in the woods? Caves?"

"On an island. The isle of mists."

"Isle of mists? My father used to tell me stories of an island ... where seal people lived ... hidden away behind fog banks in the Hibernian Sea."

"My own father was butchered, by a ... by the Saxons."

"I'm sorry. Hard times, as you said. What brought you *here*?"

"I was heading home, by coracle, but got swept way off course."

"I'm grateful for those currents. You saved my life. What's your name?"

"Kady. You?"

"Edina. Where did you learn to use a slingshot?"

"My father ..." Kady was aware of many hooves pounding along the ground. "Drag your coracle to the shore."

"What of father? We can't leave him."

"He comes with us."

Emerging around the headland were more Iceni riders, perhaps forty. "The coracle!" snapped Kady. Edina rushed to the rear of the shell-encrusted shack. Dragging out the sturdy circular boat, she allowed Kady to take over hauling it towards the waves. While Kady made progress, Edina threw various belongings into a sack that she launched into the boat. Finally she stepped over her father's body, gazing down at him with a broken expression, but the sight of the oncoming horsemen inspiring her to thrust her hands under her oxters and drag him towards the coracle.

Kady glanced along the bay. The nearest horses were scarcely a hundred yards away, their hooves splashing through tidal rivulets. A wave crashed over the coracle.

"Get your father on board!" Kady shrieked, as the pounding surf conspired with the thunder of the cavalry. Edina nodded, lifting his corpse, throwing him over the side. When the next wave broke, Kady steadied the vessel, allowing Edina to clamber aboard. Edina was transfixed by her father's calm expression, imagining him blinking. Mustering all her strength, Kady heaved the little boat through the swell. She was poised to jump in when she fixed Edina with a fearful stare. "The oar, Edina? Where's the oar?"

Edina gaped at her then whipped her head in the direction of the horsemen. "It's still in the hut. Father was painting it."

Kady fought her way through the swirling foam, sprinting back to the shack. She scoured the interior: two beds, a table set with bowls, a fish stew bubbling on the hearth, clothing, a wooden flute. The oar was tucked in a corner where Edina's father had been fashioning it with beautifully intricate designs. Grasping it, she hurried back outside. But the Iceni riders were drawing their horses to a halt between the hopelessly bobbing coracle and the shack. Beyond the grizzled warriors, Kady caught Edina's despairing expression as she cradled her father. A horseman had dismounted and was trudging through the shallows towards the vessel. Kady glanced at the stones strewn around her feet, reaching into her belt to retrieve her scarf.

Goading cries rang in her ears. "That was the vixen who attacked us," one of them sneered. "She hid behind rocks and fired her slingshot."

Another flashed a toothless grin. "Both these fair maidens will pay for the lives they took today. We've not come across women for some days, lads. Don't know about the rest of you cunts, but my balls are heavier than slingshot stones. These two damsels will empty them well. They can drain one of my balls each with their pretty mouths while my sword rests at their throats!"

"Same here," the first one gibed. "Same for all of us."

Edina whooped exultantly. Kady peered towards her, perplexed. The Iceni were drawing their swords. A much larger troop was rounding the headland, rushing along the cliffs to outflank the Celts: she estimated around two hundred.

"Saxons," she hissed. "Somorsaetas."

The frantic Iceni steered their horses, searching for an escape route. Having deployed into a wide semicircle, the Saxons closed in on their prey. An order barked and scores of arrowheads glinted against the sun. The lethal storm felled men and horses, the screams from both drowning out the sound of arrowheads punching into meat. Rearing horses dislodged their riders. Much as Kady despised these Iceni, the one-sided skirmish churned her stomach. The survivors of the barrage struggled to control their pitiful steeds, many with multiple arrow shafts protruding from shoulders or loins. Drawing swords, they resigned themselves to facing the Saxons who broke into a charge. The Britons defended desperately, but numerous assailants surrounded each. No matter how skilfully blows were parried, blades lunged from every direction, hacking them from their saddles.

Kady splashed towards the coracle, grasping Edina's outstretched hand. "I never expected to owe a debt of gratitude to an English warband," she asserted. She scrambled aboard.

Edina cast a withering look towards a Saxon raising an enemy head aloft. Gritting her teeth, she plunged the oar into the churning waves. An arrow tore into the water to their left. The Celts hunkered down as further salvos scythed into the sea all around them. Edina stared straight ahead, her arms working methodically, glancing down at her father's rocking form. "We will not die at Saxon hands, Kady. We must live to consign father to the realm of Manannan."

CHAPTER TWENTY

Bowed over a vat of bubbling liquid, the shaman was stirring the stinking concoction with a dagger.

"Paega! The thane requests your presence."

"Yes, yes. I'll be there. *Shortly.*" Giving a derisory glance in the direction of the irritating interruption, he resumed his fastidious task. Lifting the implement from the putrid broth, he shook droplets onto the straw flooring. Mesmerised by the patterns of steam curling from the toxic mixture, he sniffed warily.

"Paega!"

"Impudent cur!" His voice dipped to a murmur. "We Saxon shamen have dreamt of harnessing the Norse shapeshifting magic for centuries. Allow me to savour my moment ... by all the gods it fucking *reeks*."

"Paega! The thane."

"Yes. I heard you. He requests my presence. I'm coming!"

Scurrying into daylight, he blinked at the stout warrior who had been bellowing so annoyingly at the entrance to his lair. But he focussed on the second armed man, standing respectfully at his hut's doorway.

"Osgar. Ensure no one enters. My ingredients must ferment for a further few hours and must not, under *any* circumstances, be disturbed. Anyone other than myself or the thane making their way in, you have my strict permission to skewer them from arsehole to gob with your javelin, quickly or slowly as you wish."

A smile creasing his features, Osgar nodded.

"That was *not* a joke, Osgar. That was an order. If anyone *does* disturb my precious potion, I'll hold *you* responsible. I'll put your head on the fucking chopping block myself."

Osgar made a curt motion with his head. Although the shaman was older by decades, even the most ferocious warriors in the clan feared his necromancy. Cyneheard's bodyguard indicated for Paega to follow him inside the chieftain's hut. There the shaman bowed to Cyneheard. Beside the thane stood Wilheard, one of the younger soldiers.

"Paega. How go your preparations?" asked Cyneheard.

"Well, my lord. The elixir will soon be ready for the next transformation."

"Excellent news. I have some news of my own. Wilheard?"

The warrior turned to the shaman, his boyish complexion at odds with his grim resolution. "We were patrolling further into the forest, several leagues west of here. We came across large numbers of circling crows. We assumed there had been a battle. We arrived at a clearing. There had, indeed, been a massacre. The bodies appeared to be Britons. Dumnonii, Silures ... or Cymry?"

"Which was it, boy?" Paega snapped. "It is a more ominous portent if any Cymry have been venturing this far into English land. They are usually content to hide in their mountain fortresses."

"Listen to him, Paega."

"They had not died in battle," faltered Wilheard, "their wounds were ... too severe. They had been completely ... mutilated."

Where Cyneheard recoiled from this fresh airing of the details, Paega merely paced up and down. Brow furrowing, he toyed with the animal bones dangling around his neck.

"*Mutilated*, you say? In what way?"

"None of the slain warriors had even had time to engage their enemies with weapons. It was as if demons had fallen on them. They actually looked as if they'd been attacked by wild animals. By wolves?"

At that, Paega fired a glance towards Cyneheard. "Wolves? I suggest only *I* have the power to conjure wolves this far south."

Cyneheard sniggered at this. The scout followed suit, grateful for an easing of the tense atmosphere.

"If not wolves, what would have done this, Paega?" persisted Cyneheard.

"A curious case, my lord. As you know, I've been studying the ways of the druids for some time. Any captured alive in this cursed land, I insist they are brought before me for ... interrogation. Of course, there aren't many of them left, but I have become familiar with some of their customs. For instance, from the information extracted, I have learnt that those further to the north, on their island retreat of Anglesey, still practice human sacrifice. If there *are* druids hiding out in these forests, they might well have performed some mass butchery. Perhaps to appease their gods against the new masters in their land? Whatever. I need to see the evidence at first hand. Wilheard. You must lead me to the sight of your massacre."

CHAPTER TWENTY-ONE

As much as he often dispensed violent death with as much compunction as sneezing, Cyneheard found the scene disturbing. After tethering his horse he made his way among the horrific aftermath of this mass murder. He stepped over a corpse that had been flayed to the ribs. At his passage a black cloud of flies lifted then returned to their grisly feeding. Paega also made his way through the human debris, occasionally stooping to fish a severed hand from the undergrowth, or to prod an eyeless face with his staff. "Not a human sacrifice."

The thane glanced at Wilheard, who was fighting a desperate desire to vomit with an equally impassioned yearning not to lose face before his overlord, or the tribe's shaman. "I'll be damned if I could give a flying fuck who is responsible," barked Cyneheard. "If not a druid sacrifice, what then, medicine man?"

Paega winced at the description, which he always used as a gauge to determine when the chieftain was displaying impatience. Before he could comment he was distracted by motion in the trees. Squinting, he peered into a towering oak.

"Paega?" Cyneheard snapped.

"Sire," said the shaman after drawn out seconds, "I do believe we are being watched."

"What?!"

"Wilheard!" Paega called, ignoring the chieftain. "If you would? Clamber up to the branches. There is a spy up there. Bring him down here."

Grateful for the opportunity to leave the bloated corpses and their overpowering stench, Wilheard hurried through the bushes, stepping up to Paega. Following the direction of the shaman's pointing finger, he set about clambering up the thick trunk. The thane and Paega observed with a mixture of apprehension and curiosity. Wilheard's nimble movements sent him higher. There was a rustling, a thrashing of branches then a muffled cry. A body plummeted to the forest floor, there to wriggle while Cyneheard stomped his full weight on the mysterious voyeur's chest. Although bedraggled, his garments torn and mud-encrusted, he was clearly a Celt.

"What the fuck have we here? How long have you been skulking in the trees, Brit cur? What do you know of what happened to these poor wretches whose ... remains ... lie all around?"

The lad was scarcely a teenager. His wild eyes darted to and fro, not focussing on his tormentor; instead he feverishly sought imagined assailants while jabbering in his native tongue.

"What do you make of this, Paega?" asked the thane.

As Wilheard shinned back to ground level, the shaman paced over to the terrified youth. Listening, Paega nodded. "Cymry, after all. Many words are quite different to the tongue spoken by the local savages in Dumnonia. But he is in complete shock. I fear his mind has cracked. We could torture him for days and he would reveal nothing of consequence. However."

"Paega?" Cyneheard enquired.

The shaman beckoned for his thane to remain silent. He did so, to Wilheard's surprise. Furrowing his flowing robes, Paega crouched to the hapless Briton, touching the palm of his hand to the lad's soaking forehead.

"Hush now, child. Be still. You have nothing to fear from us, I promise."

Now Paega shut his eyes. For minutes the only sounds were the youth's frantic breaths, the shrill cries of birds flitting through the trees and the constant humming of flies. The shaman dragged his hand over the boy's windpipe. Resting it there, he suddenly grasped the throat, his gnarled fingers assuming a fierce strength that took Cyneheard and especially Wilheard by surprise. That ruthless grip remained in place for the minutes it took for the youngster to convulse and cough blood. Moments later his body awaited the attention of the forest's abundant carrion eaters.

"Well?" Cyneheard asked.

"Because his words were not making any sense, even with the smattering of Celt I am familiar with, I probed his memory. This is what I saw. He was a thief who fled his homeland in the valleys of Cymru, drifting south, eventually joining a party of bandits. They had been eking out a living here in these dense trees. They hunted boar. Sometimes they trapped other Celts, cooking and eating them."

At this revelation the others winced. In the pecking order of violence, the razing of villages and the rape, enslavement or murder of their inhabitants were regarded as necessary aspects of conquest. Cannibalism was taboo. The shaman continued. "A few days ago they trapped a young wench who was exploring these glades, alone. But before they could have their way with her, for their bellies, or their pricks, the troop were set upon."

"By who?" Cyneheard gasped. "Not Somersaetas, surely? When an enemy is vanquished there is no need for such defilement. Not even that one-eyed madman Modig would do such rejoicing in blood?"

"Not by men, sire. By wild dogs. Packs of these beasts roam in the deeper regions of these forests. The boy's agility meant he was able to climb this tree, where he could only watch in despair as the others were chased down, killed and dismembered. He has been too terrified to move from this hiding spot and has eaten nought but oak leaves since."

"What of the wench?"

"That is the most interesting aspect. Before she was captured, this redheaded beauty was gathering herbs, flowers, mushrooms and roots. She placed these into a sack. She walked away from this place, unscathed. Apparently the beasts spared her, for a while at least."

"What does this mean, Paega? Why collect such random trophies from the forest? How would she manage to escape the same fate as these other Brits?"

"Because, my sire, that girl is a druid."

"*Another* druid in Wessex? I thought Godric killed the only druid within miles?"

"Godric killed *a* druid. Another matter I've gleaned from my encounters with their kind is that their powers are bequeathed, at the moment of death, to their firstborn. I sense the survivor of this bloodbath to be the daughter of Godric's victim."

"This is *disastrous*. There is a druid at large in the realm of the West Saxons? A virile fox cub, too, not some wizened old crone."

"Don't fret, my lord. By the time we return to our settlement my potion will be ready. We will soon have another wolf warrior to set on this witch's trail."

CHAPTER TWENTY-TWO

Kady's supper was being delayed. Every time she was poised to snap at a crisp chicken morsel, someone else would materialize from the throng to enthusiastically pat her back, congratulating her on her latest exploits before demanding she relive each detail. The herbal remedy she had returned with had already had a marked effect on Mochan's condition, his fever finally breaking. But her rescuing of the Dobunni girl from a terrible fate had truly elevated everyone's spirits. Tannus, in particular, kept fussing over the grateful if bemused-looking teenager Kady had introduced to everyone.

Through the fire's molten tongues, Brice focused on his sister. Although he could only guess at what was being said to her, his eyes stayed rooted to her animated features. He found himself torn between contrasting but equally forceful emotions. On one hand, he was basking in the adulation being lavished on Kady. As her kin, he found himself on the receiving end of just as much backslapping, and because of his gender these blows grew ever more emphatic as drinking horns were replenished. On the other, Brice was stoking a simmering jealousy.

In the aftermath of his father's terrible death, he had inherited nothing. Kady had been elevated to a position where fantastical powers were at her fingertips. Her success consigned him further to the shadows. Where he had once hoped to be known as Brice, son of Kai, a true warrior's epithet, he would now always be Brice, brother of Kady the druid. His peers also treated him differently. Where he had relished the rough and tumble of wrestling or wooden swordfighting, because the druid ways were swathed in secrecy his mates would tell ever more outlandish tales about the fate awaiting all who crossed Kady and her blood. Was this his lot in life: to be continually judged in the context of a family connection he had no control over?

But he did have one thing to thank Kady for, with all his heart. His attention drifted away from his sister to the younger girl she had taken under her wing. The moment Brice set eyes on Edina being assisted from the beached vessel, her slender legs trembling like a newborn foal, he had been smitten. He had edged himself to the front of the villagers gathering on the shore. Most of the others had been chattering excitedly, welcoming Kady back. Brice had stepped over to the frightened girl who looked as if she had been caught stowing away. Smiling at her, he parted the soaking hair matted to her face. The beautiful but fragile features revealed had rendered the normally verbose lad dumbstruck. Impulsively, he leaned towards her and kissed her icy lips, as if this might have been enough to infuse her shocked body with a renewed vitality. Kissing him back, the girl had grinned then sunk to her knees in the shingle. Instantly she was swept off her feet in Tannus' broad arms and carried towards the caves.

Every so often Edina's eyes would harness his own through the fire. And each time this connection was made, Brice felt his heart dancing like the flames between them. He was snapped out of his reverie when Kady gestured for him to join them. Draining his horn, he paced over, grateful for the mead's cloak of courage when his sister shuffled to one side so he could sit between the girls.

"Brice! We thought you looked lonely over there. Come and meet my Dobunni friend."

"We *have* met, Kady."

"Of *course* you have, brother. Why, no sooner were you acquainted than you were trying to seduce her."

Edina guffawed at this. Although furious inside, Brice recognised it would be far more opportune to keep the atmosphere congenial. Instead he turned his back on Kady and peered into Edina's generous eyelashes. "You'll have to get used to living on an island, Edina. How d'you think you'll cope?"

"I'll manage, Brice. I'll *have* to manage. Aside from Cornwall, the south of Britannia belongs to the Germans now. But

I'm Dobunni. We're farmers of the sea. If I can't live on the coast any more, an island's even better. Although. Well. I'll miss father."

"He wasn't killed by Germans, either," Kady interjected. "Iceni raiders."

"Those weasels were going to rape me."

"The bastards," Brice hissed through his teeth. "I wish I'd been there to look after you with my blade."

"It's just been my father and I for so long, I could fall in love with being part of a tribe again."

With that she grasped Brice's hand, squeezing firmly. Brice, his face beaming, uncharacteristically threw an arm around Edina and his sister.

"So you Dobunni are farmers of the sea?" he asked. "What say you take me fishing tomorrow? Perhaps you could teach me a trick or two?"

Kady frowned. "We'll see. As long as you stay close to the shore, Brice. Remember the day Mochan fell? As he dangled on the cliffs the mists parted and he was almost spotted by a Saxon longship, Edina. We may be surrounded by fog banks, but enemy patrols will easily sniff out a coracle that strays too close to the mainland."

Brice kept smiling at the younger Celt. "You know me, sister. I never take risks."

"I know you only too well, little brother, which is why I know that is not true. Not so long ago you announced you were willing to take on a demon wolf."

He reacted angrily, jumping to his feet. The sudden movement drew glances from those seated nearest. "I *still* would, Kady. That is not taking risks. That is just what any warrior of the Dumnonii would have done. If you had been a warrior, perhaps ... perhaps ..."

But the courage of his convictions failed to match his temper. A silence descended on the celebratory feast, all eyes swivelling on the druid's headstrong brother. Kady also stood up, the memories of that terrible night thrust into her face once again. Choleric with rage, she stabbed a finger into Brice's chest. "I think you over-indulge in the Cornish brew, brother. There is no *perhaps*. If any of the village warriors had been with our father that night, the wolf would have gone on a killing spree. Your pride can be admirable, but you must understand the enemy we are facing here. These berserkers, these werewolves, they are a result of dark, dark magic. I don't even know if my powers will be sufficient to protect our people from the next one they send to track us down."

Edina's white eyes darted from Brice, to Kady, then around the company. Her voice wavering, she found the strength to articulate her bewilderment. "What are these demon wolves you speak of? Why are they coming after us?"

CHAPTER TWENTY-THREE

Edina peered away from the shore, over the waves rolling in from the island's vast veils. "Are you sure, Brice? You heard what Kady was saying last night, about Saxon ships ... and demon wolves?"

Brice was still smarting from the encounter. If there had been any truth in his sister's warning, the public belittling simply made him determined to prove her wrong. "Trust me, Edina. We're safe here, on the isle of mists. Look at those grey curtains. They surround us, screening us from the mainland and the open sea. And they are not like normal banks of haar, liable to lift in certain weather conditions. They are *always* there. Something to do with the way the warm currents from the great western ocean strike the cold seas around the coast."

"I've heard of the isle of mists. But I've never been this far north to actually *see* the great fog banks. They truly are a sight to behold. But we'll stick close to landfall, Brice?"

"Of course, my Dobunni friend. Now. If you would care to join me on my trusty vessel?"

With that, Brice gripped the rocking coracle, reaching out his right hand, guiding her aboard. As she took a seat on the crossbeam, grasping its gnarled wood, she noted he had bundled twine and hooks, together with a jar containing a shifting knot of wriggling worms. When Brice clambered aboard, lifting the oar from its resting place, she dug her feet under her seat for further support.

"Hang on, Edina!" Brice yelled. "Until I steer into calmer waters, we'll get sprayed!"

She grinned at this, her adventurous spirit taking hold. Aware of the muscles of Brice's arms flexing while he dug into the water, she reached for the fishing tackle. Gazing overboard she studied the churning waters. "The conditions are perfect for mackerel."

"You don't have to be Dobunni to know that," Brice replied. "These seas are also abundant with herring. But there is one particular creature I'd love to catch today. Truly the most beautiful I've come across so far. And I won't damage her with any hook through her gorgeous mouth when I reel her in."

Edina frowned at this, although this was mostly in pretence. She was flattered to have found herself at the centre of this handsome young man's attention. That he was also the brother of the girl who had saved her life - a druid - made the situation special. Everything had been turned so completely upside-down in such a short period of time she felt any good that might come out of this new twist in her life had to be grasped. And as she gazed towards the towering columns of haar, she pictured her father sinking into the depths after Kady had eased his body overboard while uttering respectful words for Manannan. He would have approved of this clan who had unquestioningly come to her aid. A sense of destiny eased the despair of losing him in such terrible circumstances.

Brice masterfully steered the coracle free of the oncoming waves, into deeper waters. "There!" he cried.

She stared where he was pointing. Twenty feet below, a thick mackerel shoal was spearing through the water, themselves engaged in a hunt for smaller fish. "See how they retract their fins into their bodies to give them extra speed?" she stated.

"I knew they did that."

She humoured his remark. "Of course you did. And here was me thinking the only fish the Dumnonii have ever been renowned for snaring are sticklebacks."

"Sticklebacks can be tricky adversaries, I'll have you know."

Edina chuckled. "I'll load up the bait." Delving into the fetid solution containing the worms, she snatched one. Withdrawing it, she poked it towards a hook. But it slithered from her grasp to writhe around her feet.

"Careful, Edina … you wouldn't want it squirming up your legs!"

But her expression hardened.

"I was joking, Edina."

"No. Look, Brice. It's Kady."

Brice looked back to the island, its shoreline now a hundred yards or more distant. His sister had rushed towards the point where his coracle had been tethered. Now she was waving frantically.

"I won't take us anywhere near the mist," Brice said. "Why can't she just give me some breathing space?"

"She's shouting something. Can you make it out?"

"I can't. Ignore her. Whatever it is, it can wait. I'm hardly about to abandon our fishing trip before we've caught a single fish."

Edina shrugged. "Well. I don't want to get involved in your squabbles." With that, she leaned closer and kissed his cheek. This had the effect of banishing all thoughts of his sister, or the fishing expedition for that matter. Allowing the oar to drop to the base of the boat, he thrust an arm around her. As he gazed into her dreamy expression and glistening lips, a single cry from Kady pierced the clamour of the waves. "*Gwynn!*"

There was a bundle of sackcloth beneath their feet, which Brice usually loaded with fish. But it suddenly squirmed. Both teenagers gaped at the astonishing spectacle. Tiny fingers sought the opening, followed by a tousled mop of red curls. A ten-year-old face blinked at the sunlight.

"Gwynn!" barked Brice. "What in the name of Manannan are you doing hiding in my coracle?"

Edina helped the youngster clamber from her hiding place, assisting her as she edged in between them.

"This, Edina, is my kid sister, Gwynn."

The youngster flashed a mischievous grin then fired a more serious expression at the older girl.

"*Gwynn*," Brice spat in exasperation. "*Why* did you stowaway? No wonder Kady is farting sparks back there!"

"Telling her what you said, Brice!"

"*Please*. Gwynn. Why are you here?"

"Wanted to come fishing with you. I asked Kady first. She said no way."

"And if you'd asked me, young lady, I would've said *no way*," Brice conceded.

"*Exactly*. That's why I decided to be a stowey."

"A stowaway?" Brice corrected her, mirth creasing his lips. Peering back towards their elder sister, still gesticulating, his grin widened. "Why not? As long as you don't mind the worms?"

"Course not! Can't catch fishies without worms."

"Excellent," Edina observed. "I think there's something of the spirit of Boudica in your kid sister, Brice. A little warrior, eh, Gwynn?"

"Of course! Now let's fish!"

Dismissing Kady's distress, Brice searched for their prey again. Listening to Edina and Gwynn chortle as they fixed worms to hooks, he resumed paddling. That was when he discovered the coracle was now riding a deceptively insistent current. They were approaching the mist too quickly for his liking. Thrusting the paddle downwards, he held it there, attempting to bring the coracle round to face the island. The force was too strong.

Edina cottoned on to his alarm. "Everything okay, Brice?"

The boat lurched into a deep trough. Gwynn shrieked as a wall of water smacked into the hull, sending the coracle spinning wildly, wrenching the oar from Brice's fingers to send it into the depths.

CHAPTER TWENTY-FOUR

The three horses stepped warily over the shingle, their hooves dislodging sand fleas that investigated the huge beasts in persistent clouds. Their riders drew their garments tighter: the temperature had dipped and murky clouds were mustering over the sea. Ahead of them, a mass-execution had occurred. Cyneheard dismounted, Wilheard following, both drawing swords. Paega remained where he was, gazing down at the emaciated corpses, not with compassion, but intense curiosity. He counted fifteen in all; naked, severely bruised, the seagulls pecking at their blanched flesh oblivious to the approach of living humans. Iron handcuffs were affixed to each victim's wrists; the other ends of the lengthy chains securing them disappeared beneath large boulders. They had been beaten then abandoned to the tide.

"More dead Brits, Paega," Cyneheard remarked. "A druid sacrifice this time?"

"No, sire. I recognise the technique. I would suggest these natives were captured by the Somorsaetas."

"Modig. The fucking fanatic."

"Indeed. Drowning is one of his favoured methods of dispatching enemies."

"One of many, it has to be said. Of all the West Saxon tribes, the Somorsaetas have pushed furthest into Celtic land. They have slaughtered most of the Brits this side of the Severn. Modig lost an eye to a lucky arrow strike while flushing the last Celts from Somerset. Some say his mind was affected."

"I fear his judgment will be even more impaired at present, sire."

"It will. Some say he has gone completely mad since his son failed to return from a patrol. He fears Oxa fell to an ambush.

Modig will stop at nothing until he has cleansed these conquered lands of Celts."

Turning away from the grisly scene, Wilheard followed the flight of several gulls. The birds plunged beyond an outcrop. The young lad listened to the screeching cacophony coming from that direction. Cyneheard and Paega also noticed. The shaman glared at the congregating birds. "More Brits pegged out for the sea?"

Cyneheard and Wilheard climbed back onto their horses; the three Saxons headed towards the commotion. Disorderly seagulls cawed at the riders splashing through the shallows and rose from their meals. Used to meagre shoreline scraps, they had been gorging themselves on large carcasses sprawled among the rocks.

Paega shook his head. "This is becoming a habit, discovering dead natives."

Cyneheard studied the corpses. "I have nothing against dead natives. I only object that someone else has had all the fun."

Paega eased down from his saddle. Leading his horse by the reins, he crouched to a cadaver, seizing its russet pigtails, forcing the head as far as rigor mortis would allow. The skull was cracked, the hair matted with pinkish matter oozing from a fist-sized dent. "None of these men were drowned. This one was felled by a single shot from a sling."

Cyneheard was checking out another of the slain. "A similar wound. Not the weapon of choice of any Saxons I know, Paega."

The shaman nodded. But instead of adding anything else, his fingers sought his bone necklace. Closing his eyes, he began reciting a muted chant.

Cyneheard frowned towards Wilheard. "The shaman places himself under a trance. He will be asking Tiw to grant a vision of what actually happened here."

Wilheard observed the elderly man's expression altering from bliss to agony, fury to contentment. During these facial contortions his shamanistic verse increased in volume and velocity, before tapering to a whisper. He opened his eyes.

"What did you see, Paega?" demanded Cyneheard.

"These men set upon a defenceless girl."

"Our druid friend?"

"No. Someone younger. But the redheaded witch came to her rescue, bringing down these dogs with a slingshot. The rest of their party were unfortunate to encounter a warband of Somorsaetas. Those surviving the arrows were disarmed, then chained before the waves."

"This witch is leaving her mark, Paega. She should be easy enough to track down. There are always dead men in her trail."

"Alas, her trail has gone cold. However, by the time we return to camp the potion that Osgar was guarding will be ready. The time has come to seek out another champion, sire. Someone with the supernatural strength to pick up that trail, who will bear the title of druidslayer, who will proudly follow Godric to the feast table of Tiw."

CHAPTER TWENTY-FIVE

The warriors faced each other, swords pointing to the ground, but their visors almost touching. Those gathered in the secluded glade observed with tense apprehension. The spectators appreciated neither man would wish to be first to blink, a tiny gesture that would be enough to lose face. But a scarlet tinge was warming the western skies. This stalemate had progressed to a point where these macho theatrics were almost an indulgence.

Presently horses approached. The thane's mount entered the clearing, Paega and Wilheard close behind. The dueling men maintained the intensity of their staring.

"Oswald? Edwig?" the chieftain snapped. "What reason for this?"

Cenric, the gaunt man umpiring, bowed to Cyneheard, murmuring to the swordsmen to relinquish their stances.

"We have covered many miles today," continued the thane, "and already seen more than our fair share of corpses. If I'm about to lose one of my most reliable fighting men, I demand to know why. And quickly."

Oswald turned from his adversary. "My lord, this is down to Edwig's son, Glaedwine. He made unwelcome advances on my daughter, Godiva. When she told him no, the swine ignored her. He took her, like a dog on heat. We hold many Brit captives. The boy could have had his pick of native wenches for his bed. I aim to teach his family a lesson by taking Edwig's head."

Bristling with contempt, Edwig spat to the ground. "I don't believe your daughter, Oswald. I doubt there are many here who do. Her tall tales are nothing new. She is known for her prick teasing. It wouldn't be the first time the strumpet has flashed her beady eyes at me. And her plump tits."

Cyneheard shook his head. Their argument had passed the point when it could be resolved by anything other than iron. Oswald absorbed the enormity of the insult thrown into his face. Then he barged into Edwig with his right shoulder, swinging his sword high over his helm as he did so. "You miserable cunt. I'll have *your* fucking head."

Edwig parried the clumsy blow, sparks spitting from his blade, following on with a deft jab which his opponent only just managed to fend off. Oswald, the bulkier fighter, also had the greater fire in his belly. Each time Edwig recoiled from his swinging sword, his rage grew until he was lashing frantically, sweat spraying from his contorted features. Edwig was a more tactical combatant. Although he appeared to be reeling from being on the receiving end of the relentless barrage, Cyneheard appreciated these defensive strokes were merely about buying time. The thane admired Oswald's brutal approach to the duel, but at the same time he was disdainful of the way the larger man was allowing his strength to be sapped without realising the counter-attack would not only be inevitable, it would more than likely cost him his life.

Oswald grinned after a ferocious swipe grazed Edwig's shoulder, just as the latter had been a second too slow in squirming out of the sword's relentless path. Sensing blood, Oswald thrust his weapon again. This time Edwig was quicker to react, evading contact. Oswald's expression twisted from satisfaction to frustration as the blade sliced into the turf, embedding for crucial moments. Edwig took the opportunity to conserve his strength, waiting as his panting opponent heaved at his sword's hilt. Pulling the blade free, Oswald made no attempt to snatch a rest, pressing on with his vicious but clumsy assault.

In having allowed his resentment to rule his swordplay, Oswald had been growing ever frustrated at Edwig's defensive skills. He began taking risks with his strokes, overstretching, leaving his torso exposed. Edwig finally saw the opening he had been waiting for. He focused on the great iron shaft as it was hoisted high over Oswald's head, glinting against the dying sunlight, then brought his own weapon up to block the downward blow. Oswald aimed his next almighty swipe at Edwig's helm. Although there was a crack as his headgear was launched into the air, Edwig had seen the blow coming a mile off. Despite the ringing in his ears, he thrust his own blade into Oswald's unprotected left oxter. The man gasped as blood flowed over Edwig's sword. Desperately positioning himself to ward off his adversary, Oswald felt the strength seeping from his quivering leg muscles. He raised his weapon, anticipating another thrust towards his upper torso. Instead Edwig hacked into his left shin. Gasping, Oswald slumped to the ground. The injured man felt blood from the first wound leaking into his undershirt, gluing its material to his flesh. Raising his sword again, he blinked at the meagre light filtering through the tree canopy while he prepared to block Edwig's next powerful attack. He was shocked when Edwig simply smacked at his blade, effortlessly driving it aside.

Oswald clenched his teeth. "You fucking weasel," he gasped. "You fight like a fucking Brit."

"Shut up and die like a Saxon," Edwig countered, forcing his tip into the soft skin between neck and jaw. Twisting the sword, glutinous blood bubbled from Oswald's mouth, drowning his final curses. When the death throes had ceased, Edwig bowed over him and murmured a respectful prayer. "Tiw awaits you, Oswald. I swear no more will be said about Godiva. And I swear Glaedwine will do everything in his power to protect her honour in future." Crouching, Edwig dragged his soiled weapon across the undergrowth.

Cyneheard looked to Paega then the victorious fighter. "Well fought, Edwig. You have proved yourself worthy of a task we would now set you."

"Anything, my lord? Name it and it shall be done?"

"In time. The rest of you. See that Oswald is prepared for a noble Saxon burial. Edwig. Come with Paega and myself."

CHAPTER TWENTY-SIX

Paega struggled to make his voice heard above the waves and the rain lashing the swell. "Another storm is brewing," he exclaimed. "It heads this way. The witch's trail was already faint. By sunrise it will have vanished."

As Cyneheard and Edwig drew their horses alongside, the shaman was glowering into the bay's churning waters. When the party had returned, the triumphant swordsman in tow, the chained Celts had been submerged. The fierce currents would be flaying their already damaged corpses.

"Do you think our champion here might fare any better, Paega?"

"I *know* he will, my lord. In wolf form his senses will be magnified a *thousand*-fold. We know how our own hounds can chase down prey, how they can latch onto the scents of fleeing game or natives, even after days have passed, or rainfall such as this has hampered the trails. It will be the same with our wolf warrior. Even *more* so."

Edwig shifted in his saddle. He appreciated the honour of having been selected to go through the shapeshifting. But being referred to as a wolf warrior heightened the sense of foreboding he was doing his best to mask. He turned his attention to the surrounding landscape: above the tossing trees, a scattering of rooks struggled against the relentless wind. "Where do you think the witch has gone, shaman?"

"That is a mystery, Edwig. She may have headed inland, making for the dense forests that clog this country's hinterland. But there are so many dangers there ... for warriors let alone young girls. She may have clambered into one of her kind's sturdy little boats and chanced her luck with the waves ... although given the unpredictable nature of these wild western seas, I fancy she probably did take her chances with Saxon patrols and made her way inland. She is probably heading for the frontier with Cymru. The druids remain strong to the northwest."

Cyneheard recoiled when a gust whipped spume from an oncoming wave over the three Saxons. "Fuck this British weather. It comes straight from the bowels of hell. We do not want this druid of ours joining company with others of her kind. One is bad enough. A coven of the bastards is the *last* thing we need, Paega."

"Which is why we must strike before this storm comes any closer to land. Before the witch gets even further from our clutches."

Edwig swallowed and tasted salt. During their canter across the countryside he had buried his face against his horse's mane, allowing the increasingly inclement weather to dampen his sense of dread. All at once he appreciated the enormity of this situation. Suddenly he craved to be home, a rabbit stew bubbling on the hearth, warming his hands against the dancing flames while Glaedwine regaled him with exaggerated accounts of boar hunting. His knuckles whitened against his reins as Paega approached: the fact that Cyneheard's own right hand was poised over his sword lest gentle persuasion be required did little for his ebbing confidence. Fixing Edwig with an uncompromising stare, Paega fumbled for the sack firmly secured to his saddle. Delving inside, blinking against the rain that had drenched them all to the bone and transformed his own hair to white rat's tails, he withdrew the prized jar.

Against the elements, the sound of urgent hooves drew the attention of the three Saxons. Paega grinned when Wilheard appeared from beyond the headland. Although it was growing ever darker, they could make out he was clutching some object tightly to his left flank, while his right hand struggled with his excitable steed. When he drew closer the others noted, with varying degrees of revulsion, his trophy was a head.

"What is the meaning of this, Wilheard?" the thane articulated, gazing disdainfully at the seaweed-festooned locks.

"I managed to find one, Paega, just as you requested," Wilheard explained, lifting the head towards the shaman.

"Excellent. Consider this poor creature. Look how he died," Paega enthused. He snapped his fingers at the younger man, demanding he hand over the grisly memento. After securing the dead Celt's pigtails, Paega held it aloft, smacking the side of the skull to send it spinning like some child's toy.

"I still don't get it, Paega," mentioned Cyneheard. He fired a glance at Edwig who was horrified by the twisting scalp.

"Here," exclaimed Paega, poking his fingers into a large fissure in the skull, caked in matted blood. "This is the point where the redheaded witch split this fellow's head open with her sling. Look how accurate, how forceful, her strike was?" He clutched at the missile that remained embedded in its victim's bone. Heaving out the stone, he scrutinised it in his palm, using his body to shield it from the rain.

"What do you want of this stone, Paega?" demanded the thane.

"Oh, I don't want anything of it, sire. As I've said, the witch's trail has gone too cold, even for a shaman. But a wolf warrior will be able to catch a scent. Tiny traces of our quarry's fingers will be lodged in this little rock - the sweat of battle, her skin marks - and with the black wolf magic flowing through your veins, Edwig, you just might be able to use the stone to inspire a vision of her current whereabouts."

He handed it to Edwig who held the shard as delicately as sparked tinder being applied to a fire. "I will try my best, Paega."

Steadying his horse, Paega handed the phial across. "Now. The potion. Be warned, my brave warrior. The elixir is not renowned for its pleasant aroma. Take a deep breath, toast Tiw, and knock it back swiftly. Nature will take its course over the next half hour. Or less. Godric seemed barely fifteen minutes. As long as the thane, Wilheard and myself have time to beat a hasty retreat."

Cyneheard paled at the thought of the half-man, half-wolf that would be scrambling around on all-fours, baring its teeth and baying at the full moon rising above the treeline. Paega had described watching Godric speeding off through the thickets, consumed by a bloodlust for the witch's father.

"Edwig," said Cyneheard. "Steady yourself. Drink the shaman's potion. You will become a wolf warrior, a soldier of Tiw. This time tomorrow we will be composing ballads in your name. You will be forever known as Edwig, druidslayer. A fine honour for Glaedwine to live up to."

That Cyneheard made no attempt to describe this adulation in terms other than posthumous sent further pangs of alarm through Edwig. Lightning forked over the darkening seas, followed by a terrific rumble. Edwig tugged the cork free with his teeth. Recoiling from the fetid stench, he touched the container to his mouth. Noxious fumes rose from the concoction, clawing at his throat. Shutting his eyes he fought the urge to vomit. Instead he gripped the phial until his fingers trembled, as if it was something he wished to strangle the life from. "To Tiw," he murmured.

The others repeated the toast. Then Edwig tossed back his head as he gulped the potion down. Tears streamed down his cheeks. His chest was wracked with ferocious coughing fits, each spasm threatening to dislodge the vile mixture from its precarious resting place in his gut. Eventually this passed and he felt a calm descending. As the fingers of his other hand inadvertently dug into the stone, a vision of a red haired teenager flickered into his mind, then was gone. His eyes opened, staring wildly. The others were already several hundred yards away, spurring their horses towards the woods.

CHAPTER TWENTY-SEVEN

Brice relinquished his grip at the rim, slumping into the coracle. Edina was whimpering as she nestled into him. Gwynn trembled with terror, her thin arms wrapped around the older girl.

"You'd be amazed how sturdy these vessels are," Brice cried, struggling to make himself heard above the turbulent waters. "We can't sink. No way. We'll just have to ride out this storm."

Edina peered gravely at the mountainous waves, each rolling beneath their tiny coracle to lift it high, before ploughing onwards.

"Assuming we don't sink, then what, Brice? The mainland belongs to the English. Anywhere we beach will be in the middle of Saxon territory. I would rather we all threw ourselves overboard to drown than become prisoners of the enemy."

This frank confession jolted Brice. "No, Edina. My sister managed to lead you to safety in a vessel such as this, didn't she? I will do the same."

"You're not a druid!" Gwynn piped up.

Brice crawled over the buffeting boat. Scrabbling to the side, he hauled himself up, gasping as spray lashed his face. Blinking, he gazed at the waves crashing onto a distant bay in white explosions. "Land! Within the hour the tide will have carried us ashore. I'll find something to use as an oar. Then we'll find a hiding spot. When the tide turns, we'll make for the mists again."

Edina clambered beside him. She took a few moments to analyse the geography. "My father's hunting ground. Our hut was just beyond that headland. I didn't think I'd ever see it again." Brice was smiling at her, but Edina's expression remained ominous. "Where I once called home now crawls with Saxons."

* * *

Brice kept glancing at Edina's shivering features, at his softly whimpering sister, then at the waves tossing their vessel. While he might have stated it was only a matter of time before the tide transported them to safety, he admitted to himself he had no idea how long this might take. He had been anticipating some relaxing of the tempestuous seas, perhaps cawing seagulls that would indicate proximity to the shore. At least the encroaching darkness was now cloaking the monstrous waves.

He disengaged his aching arms from around the two girls and heaved himself up to the boat's rim. The rain persisted; visibility was reduced to yards. No matter how hard he stared into the murk there was no sight of the bay. The coracle was a slave of the sea, its motion reduced to erratic spinning that made gauging its direction of travel impossible. For the first time since setting out from the isle of mists, the true scale of their predicament rammed home. His male attributes – pride, bravado, obstinacy – had seeped from him, just as surely as if they were now swilling around in the bilge at his feet.

Edina clasped his hand. "Rather Manannan welcomes the three of us into his lair than we fall into the hands of our enemies on the mainland. If anyone was to be my first, I would have wanted it to be you, Brice. Not a bunch of stinking, toothless Iceni, or worse still, Saxons."

Brice was overcome with the moment. Rather than giving her a fitting reply, he felt a great sob funneling up from his ribcage. He buried his face in her shoulder.

Gwynn began tugging at his sodden garments. His hand sought his sister's. But she nudged him more insistently. "Brice! Look!"

"What is it, Gwynn?"

The youngster's eyes were white and she was pointing a trembling hand straight into the storm. Edina peered up, and her expression wavered between astonishment and delight. Brice whipped his head round. Hovering above their stricken vessel were a dozen or so mysterious black birds. Unable to comprehend their sudden appearance, Brice simply gawped at their fluttering wings. "Crows?" he gasped.

"Petrels," replied Edina. "Storm petrels. They live here, on the oceans, only coming to land to breed. But look closer, Brice."

"What?"

"I see it!" Gwynn squealed excitedly. "*Look*, Brice!"

"Look closer at the birds," Edina insisted.

Brice gawked at the petrels, his vision trying to cope with their wavering flight and the ever-rocking boat. Then he could make it out. Except it made no sense whatsoever. These plucky birds were manoeuvring in a rigid formation, their wings skillfully maintaining a position above the coracle as they were jolted by the elements. But the most astonishing aspect was the fact their claws were all poised around a winding length of rope. The closest of the troop suddenly dived towards them, thrusting the end of this coil into Brice's flabbergasted grasp. Edina lunged at it, helping to wrap it securely around his fist. Gwynn, too, leapt up and gamely tugged at this mystical twine. The petrels hovered for further seconds then soared upwards to vanish into the gloom.

The mystery of these last moments was compounded when all three felt a tension engaging with the rope. Fighting against this unseen force, as if they were competing in a tug-of-war contest, Brice fought the urge to simply let go. Instead he found his fingers were clamped tightly, as if the rope itself was controlling him. A panicked glance to the girls told him they were each experiencing this implacable pressure. Except there was nothing threatening about it: Brice felt reassured by the exertion required to keep the twine taut.

"Gwynn! Brice! Are you there? Do you have the rope?"

"Kady!" Gwynn squealed, relief erupting across her features.

"Kady?" Brice cried out, scanning the waves.

There was a jolt as another coracle impacted their boat. They lurched forwards, but such was the supernatural power being exerted by the rope they maintained their grip. Brice had never felt so overwhelmed with joy at the sight of his older sister as she clambered aboard, her own right hand tight round the lifeline, oars strapped to her belt. Although similarly soaked to the skin, she was also beaming.

"My angels!" she whimpered, engulfing Gwynn in her arms then roughly clasping Brice by the scruff of his neck.

"How did you find us?" Brice asked, the incredulity breaking his voice.

"I recited a specific verse to Manannan. Some of his sea-beings guided me to your stricken craft. First, the selkies helped me steer in your wake. Then, when I drew close enough to actually *see* your coracle fighting with the waves, I summoned the storm petrels to help me transfer the lifeline."

For once, Brice had to accept his sister's gifts were something to be cherished rather than coveted. But Kady was in no mood to accept any praise, even if Brice was actually demonstrating signs of having swallowed his obstinate pride.

"Why did you set out, Brice?" she demanded. "With Gwynn?"

"She was hiding in the coracle, Kady," he screeched. "I didn't even know she was there."

"Did you not see me shouting?"

Brice could only gaze down at the rope, now loose across his palms. "I just wanted to take Edina fishing."

"And you, Edina?" Kady continued. "Any Dobunni who has ever harvested the seas must appreciate the signs that a storm is on its way? Well?"

"I suppose I wasn't thinking straight. These past days have been such a nightmare. And I was flattered by the attention of a handsome Celtic warrior." She injected her comment with enough flippancy to embarrass Brice and inspire a theatrical wince from Gwynn.

Kady also found herself chuckling. "Failing to recognise when a storm is brewing on the horizon is one thing, Edina. But falling for the charms of *this* ugly oaf? I worry about you, my Dobunni friend, I really do."

Brice and Edina joined in with Kady's gently goading laughter.

"What's done is done," she concluded. "As long as lessons have been learned." Kady then stood upright, motioning for Brice and Edina to help maintain her balance. "There," the druid remarked, shielding her face. "I sensed we weren't alone. Other vessels on the Hibernian Sea were surprised by the tempest. These coracles are far too easily driven off-course, as well we know. But a sturdier ship lies a mile away. If you help me with the rowing, Brice, we'll make our way to them. If they'll let us climb aboard, we can tether this boat, then shelter until the storm breaks. Tomorrow we'll make our way back to the isle of mists."

"What if they're English?" Edina voiced the question Brice had been about to articulate.

"It is a fishing vessel, not a warship. They are likely of the Dalriati, the tribe scattered along the coasts of Hibernia and Caledonia. They may have been dragged hundreds of miles off-course. Just like the trio I've just rescued."

Despite the alarming lurches into immense troughs, their coracle, vigorously rowed by Kady and Brice, was soon closing on their target. When the larger craft was ten yards distant, Kady studied it more closely. It was a traditional Celtic galley, bulkier than the sleek longboats favoured by the English or Norse; designed for sea harvests rather than piracy.

Kady placed her paddle beneath her legs and cupped her palms. "Hey! Boat coming alongside! Hey, there!"

A heavily bearded face appeared at the prow. Alarm etched into his weatherworn features. Kady watched him barking over his shoulder. When a colleague appeared, a rope was tossed towards the young Britons. Once the coracle was hauled alongside, the hirsute sailor thrust his muscular forearms out to heave Gwynn, Edina, Kady and finally Brice aboard.

His comrade beckoned them inside a cabin at the stern, draped with ox hides. Stepping gingerly over coils of netting, they stooped inside. Moments later the shivering youngsters were huddled around an oil-fired lamp, its quivering flames emanating a welcome heat.

The bearded man spoke in a booming voice. "Welcome aboard. I'm Cormac. This is my brother, Diarmaid."

The other fisherman nodded curtly, before delving into a sack and withdrawing potatoes and salted pork. Each handful passed around the Britons was accepted with appreciative smiles then wolfed down. Diarmaid then handed over a flagon. Kady discovered this to be mead rather than drinking water, but it satiated her thirst and eased her parched throat. Reluctantly, she passed this to Gwynn. The youngster gulped with the enthusiasm of one who had already acquired a taste for the brew: no doubt during surreptitious sampling beneath feast tables. What was important was that the little girl was kept hydrated.

After allowing them time to refresh their appetites, Cormac peered towards Brice. "Do any of you have names, then?"

Although he had felt inclined to address Brice, he remained sheepishly chewing at his meat. Kady swallowed a husk of bread. "I'm Kady. This is my brother Brice, my sister Gwynn, and a friend, Edina."

"Pleased to make your acquaintances," Cormac stated, shaking hands. His taciturn brother did likewise. "So, what on earth brings you four seal pups so far from land in your little tub?" he continued. "And I can tell you are far from home, by your accents."

Kady glanced at Brice before explaining: "Like yourselves, Cormac, we were out fishing, but close to the shore, in our coracle. When the storm struck, we were unprepared. We were driven further out to the Hibernian Sea. You are Dalriati?"

The men nodded in unison. "Aye," affirmed Cormac.

"You Dalriati have a warlike reputation. Some of your kin have settled on the west of Caledonia, where your neighbours are not renowned for their hospitality?"

"Indeed. But the Caledonii are friendly enough when we have much fish to trade with them. We are skilled fishermen, not pirates like the Vikings." Cormac paused, helping himself to a generous slug of mead. "You are Britons. Where is your home? We have heard rumours of our Celtic brethren being driven from the West Country by the savages from Germania. Is this true?"

Although they were miles out at sea and in the company of apparent allies, Kady still felt wary of divulging too much. "Yes, it is true. We are Dobunni, from the Severn estuary. Our clan fled into Cornwall some months ago."

"Terrible," Cormac conceded, stroking his beard. "You think the Germans will eventually take Cornwall? Then Cymru?"

"What if they make their way over the Hibernian Sea?" Diarmaid interjected.

"There are some who are fleeing the invasion," Brice spoke out. "And some who are making a stand. My sister ..."

"His sister is ensuring that our tribe are having plenty to eat," Kady butted in. "The West Saxons have blockaded our normal trade routes."

Cormac frowned, gazing at the billowing hides. "May the gods grant that your homes are still there when this accursed storm runs its course. We shall take you as close to the Severn as we dare. Our own holds are crammed full of iced herring and mackerel: which will be no good to our families if our vessel should be boarded by a Saxon longboat."

A crash of thunder followed a lightning fork. Kady felt Gwynn digging her nails into the back of her own hand. Reassuring the youngster, she took a final mouthful of bread then wrapped her arm around her sister. As a contemplative silence enveloped the Britons, the sea's implacable swell became soporific. Kady felt herself becoming enveloped by fatigue. She glimpsed Cormac's concerned eyes twinkling above his thick beard then clutched Gwynn tightly. Within seconds both girls were snoring.

* * *

When Kady awoke, the rains had ceased, the waves had receded and the dawn's welcome glow was seeping into the shelter. Sensing her sister was coming to she shook her gently. As they yawned and stretched, Brice and Edina disengaged from their curled-up position. Kady felt obliged to aim an irked look at her brother, but quickly focused on Diarmaid who was standing up, flexing his muscles.

"Morning, my little British friends. The storm has headed towards the mainland. Cormac is on watch. I'll find out our position."

They watched him lift a flap of hide aside. Sunlight streamed in, together with a chorus of squawking gulls. But something froze the fisherman in his tracks.

"Diarmaid?" said Kady.

"No!" he bellowed. "Cormac!"

The alarm in his voice triggered the Britons to scramble to their feet. Brice unsheathed his sword. "What is it, Kady?" he hissed.

Ignoring him, Kady stepped behind the fisherman. Peering beyond, her gaze took in the figure near the bow. Cormac was dead, his tunic pierced by scores of arrows that had pinned his corpse to the gunwale. Blood had flowed from so many wounds it looked as if he had been swimming in it.

"Cormac!" Diarmaid repeated, and as he cried out he leaped from the cockpit.

As he jumped nimbly from beam to beam, Kady followed his progress. When his body was poised in mid-air between the final board and Cormac, it suddenly swiveled. Kady gawked at the arrow that had sought his neck with such lethal accuracy. Blood sprayed as he tumbled into the hold.

CHAPTER TWENTY-EIGHT

Edwig writhed across the stones, weeping as searing pain lacerated every muscle, every bone. The broiled rabbit he had broken his fast with rushed up his gullet and splattered before his stinging eyes. His whole body convulsed so violently he felt ribs dislocating. He stared to the black clouds that appeared to be mustering directly overhead. "Tiw ... my god of war ... I beseech you ... welcome me into the ranks of your army ... and deliver me from this torture."

The relentless sleet exacerbated rather than doused his torment, and his body writhed over the rocks until great tears were slashed in his tunic. Rain saturated his screams and blurred his surroundings. When he tried focusing on the absurd stone Paega had given him, he was appalled to discover coarse hair sprouting from his forearms, and talons protruding from his gnarled fingers. The discomfort was so acute he forced himself over onto his belly, to a stance infinitely more bearable. When he pressed his arms and legs onto the pebbles, pushing to rise on all four limbs, the pain in his muscles subsided. A previously undreamt of strength flowed into his hindquarters. A delirious tempest of raw emotion erupted within. All at once he experienced unbridled joy, uncontrollable hunger, and a sense of invincibility. Most overwhelming of all, he felt such hatred for humankind he was fleetingly taken aback before succumbing to the giddy notion of inflicting violence; of not just killing his enemies, but tearing their flesh apart to gorge on the warm, sweet meat, and feel the juicy offal slithering down his throat.

Aware of the bloody rock in his huge fist, his eyes narrowed. Immediately he could see the one with the red hair who posed such a threat to his kind. As the vile magic seeped into his blood, Edwig ceased to be. The beast crouched, snarling at the elements soaking through his coarse fur to his hide. Shaking his entire frame like a drenched dog, he focused on the object in his palm, crushing it to shards with his immense talons. He knew her trail did not snake inland, into the vast forests. Nor had she fled further north along this coastline. Breath rasping, he noticed the moon that was now bathing the storm-battered beach with silver. This stirred the wolf in him furiously, consigning the hint of the Saxon warrior even further to the background. Filling his lungs he howled. The exultant war cry heightened his animal desires. He desperately needed to satiate his hunger. With that notion he could visualise his prey: in a boat, paddling towards a veil of mist. An island lurked beyond, where hundreds of natives were hiding. They would all have to be hunted down.

Allowing the stone to slip from its grasp, the werewolf pointed its long snout towards the horizon, testing the air. Instantly it received a flickering scent: young Celtic flesh. Growling at the black seas, the wolf warrior's immense limbs carried it into the surf. Bracing its broad shoulders against the powerful waves, it smashed its way through, its flaring nostrils snatching at pockets of air. After several minutes of this enraged battling, it surged beyond the point where the waves were breaking. A sleek, dark shape against the grey water, it began swimming. And with each dogged stroke, its appetite mounted.

CHAPTER TWENTY-NINE

Brice unsheathed his sword, gritting his teeth, his muscles taut. Glaring at the entrance he prepared to meet whoever was outside. "Out of my way, sister."

"Stay!" Kady implored, seizing his collar. "They are beyond your help, Brice. Another boat approaches fast. There are archers on-board who will pick you off the moment you break cover."

"What kind of boat, Kady?" he demanded.

"A longship."

"Saxons?" Edina gasped, sinking further into the cabin's gloom.

"I think not, Edina. There is a Viking dragon at its prow ... but it's bigger than a pirate ship. It looks as if it has a hold below deck."

"For *fish?*" Brice was dismissive. "I am a warrior of the Dumnonii ... with nought to fear from fishermen, Norse or otherwise."

"The hold is not for fish, brother. It is for human catches." Closing her eyes to seek her father's words, her concentration was broken by the Viking vessel colliding with the smaller craft. Timbers splintered along the gunwales and the four youngsters were thrown to the floor. As Kady struggled to her feet, through the slit in the doorway she saw grappling hooks twirling, sparking against the morning sunlight, before biting into the deck. Staring into the grain of the beams at her feet, she tried shutting out the cries of the approaching marauders.

Beloved daughter ... the selkies have been following you ... you must ...

A scream destroyed the connection. Edina's hands were flapping towards Gwynn, who had squirmed through the opening.

In an instant, the younger girl had darted outside, squealing: "Where's the dragon?"

Kady followed, unfurling the sling from her belt, priming it with a sharp-edged stone. Ahead of her, Gwynn had stopped dead, mesmerised by the intricately carved beast with its lurid red eyes. Several Vikings were already clambering aboard, barking in their harsh tongue. Doubting these wild seafarers would have any compunction about killing infants, Kady snapped: "Gwynn. Come to me."

Outstretching her left hand, she snapped her fingers. Gwynn, perturbed by these unkempt fighters with braided beards and tattoos imprinted in necks and skulls, stumbled backwards. When she was close enough, Kady grasped her shoulders, forcing her to stand behind. Brice and Edina collaborated in the human shield before the youngster. Kady desperately tapped into her father's voice again. He translated what the Norsemen were bellowing.

Four Dalriati brats, Egil.

Round them up, Rangr. Chain them. Any other adults, slaughter them.

* * *

Brice, Edina and Gwynn seemed involved in a contest as to who could retch with most gusto. The Britons had been dragged aboard the longship, bound, then unceremoniously bundled below deck. Their wretchedness had been compounded upon discovering the Norsemen were traveling with pigs in their hold. As the vessel sailed northwards through the Hibernian Sea, transporting them to an unknown fate, they were cowering in a horrendous bilge of seawater, vomit and swine faeces.

Between bouts of seasickness, Gwynn bawled hysterically. Nothing Kady could say would placate her, and her sister's delirium was also hampering her tapping into her father's words. Brice's face was ashen, gooey saliva trails marking where he had thrown up down his chest. Edina had not fared much better. Worse still, the backdrop of human bellies being emptied was alarming the swine, who would continually squeal and shove, before depositing even more steaming brown sludge from beneath their curled tails. Whenever any snout came too close, a Celtic boot would send the beast squeaking into the murk.

Presently the hatchway opened. The warrior named Egil, the Norse warship's captain, considered his pathetic catch. Briefly wincing at the daylight, Kady stared into his steel blue eyes. Frenetic visions flooded her mind. These pirates had spent several weeks plundering both coasts of the Hibernian Sea. Prior to being blasted off-course, their last landfall had been to sack a Manx village. After massacring most of the inhabitants, they seized the choicest women and bundled them aboard, adding plump swine to their booty to ensure fresh pork for their journey back to the fjords. At some point a dispute had arisen about ownership of one particularly voluptuous slave. A lethal combination of pillaged mead, Viking machismo and sharpened swords provoked a brief but vicious duel. The wounded party, in a devastating display of spitefulness, slunk below deck and slit the throats of all the terrified women. Most of the hapless natives had been tossed overboard. Three bodies had been retained to keep the pigs fattened: the vile soup they were languishing in also contained half-chewed human remains.

But it was the final thought flitting through Egil's mind that truly speared her with alarm. He was considering the prices to place on his prisoners' heads when they were stripped and shackled to the posts of an auction platform. Egil was estimating Edina and herself would fetch a goodly pocketful of coins from their prospective husbands; Brice, who would become some ageing spinster's plaything, less so. But Gwynn's fate was to become a toy for a lone hermit who lived in caves above the Norse village, a gnarled madman who preferred his flesh as young as possible.

The door slammed shut. For the first time since her father's untimely death, Kady succumbed to hopelessness. Her knowledge of the future, the all-pervading stench, the horrid screeching of the pigs, and the noxious solution swilling around her shivering body were the sickly attributes stoking a monumentally black cloud of depression. There was no chance of any redeeming voices from beyond the grave. Her father's spiritual presence was simply too impotent for her current reality. The druidic magic had deserted her. And she no longer cared.

CHAPTER THIRTY

After drifting into fitful sleep, Kady jerked awake when something brushed her fingertips. Her eyes whitened when she saw it was a human jawbone, riven with bite marks itself. She glanced at the others: Brice and Edina were hunched together, heads bowed. Gwynn seemed locked in some troubling dream, her shoulders twitching.

There was a grating noise as the hatch was dragged open again. Egil leered into the gloom below. On this occasion Kady did not require her druidic senses to read his thoughts. In this lawless age, a man's power over property won at swordpoint was absolute. This Viking captain wished to break the voyage's monotony by spending some minutes sweating on top of the eldest Celtic captive. Gloating at her, he placed his great palms on the doorway's rim. She regarded a lavishly tattooed forearm, the green-scaled necks of a multi-headed hydra coiling from his elbow to the back of his hand, where seven purple tongues licked at his tanned flesh. She stared at his cruel mouth, horrified by the way his own darting tongue was moistening his lips. His lascivious grin exposed crooked teeth, weatherworn as sea stacks.

There was a lumbering footfall across the deck. He vanished from view. There was a muffled yell that was cut short when his severed head tumbled down the short ladder to splash at her feet, the blue eyes boring into her shocked features. His headless corpse plummeted, its life fluid spurting from the gaping hole by the serrated spine. Drenched in his blood, Kady screamed; the others soon followed when they were roused by the commotion. Around them, pigs scampered towards the bobbing head. Wondering what new hell was being visited on them Kady threw her arms out to her younger charges. Edina and Gwynn clung to her, while Brice gazed fearfully towards the hatch.

High above the longship, stars twinkled. Several dark shapes leapt over the hatchway. Boots tramped across the deck over their heads. There were cries, guttural obscenities; and screams, shrill as seagulls. A man shrieked hysterically, his agony drawn-out, as if he was being spit-roasted over a furnace. Kady's eyes were drawn to a crack in the flooring where glutinous blood was gathering before oozing down to splatter across the startled pigs.

After each unearthly screech from above, more blood seeped below deck. Kady spotted a pig edging closer to them, its grotesque features seeming to distort, its snout elongating, its eyes glowing red, reminding her of the fire demon that had presaged her father's death. There was a heavy crash. Another body hurtled into the hold. It had been hacked open from throat to pelvis, the innards splattering down the steps as it fell. When the Viking slumped into the bilge, several swine launched themselves at the macabre feast.

Kady snapped out of her trance. The illusion faded as terror stiffened her muscles. Concentrating on the hatchway, she backed further into the pigs' pen, hauling the others with her. They eased themselves through the revolting sewer until they had squirmed into the hold's narrowest point. The dragon's head would now be directly above, staring towards the horizon. With her druid's eye she could visualise the scene behind the figurehead. The Norsemen had been annihilated: all of them. Some had been tossed overboard during the melee. A blizzard of voracious seabirds trailed in the vessel's wake, diving at the impromptu feast. The remainder of Egil's crew was sprawled over the deck, the ferocity of the attack that had dismembered their bodies making it impossible to determine numbers. But Kady knew the tally of vanquished Norsemen to be twenty-three.

Finally her mind's eye tracked the assailant, witnessing the shadowy creature that was stalking across the ghoulish mementos of its attack, randomly plucking heads and tearing strips and devouring the warm meat. When it stood upright and was bathed in the full moonlight it bayed towards, the shapeshifter was exposed in all its terrible glory. This wolf warrior was a quarter the height of the mast, its black fur splattered red, half-masticated tissue glistening in its monstrous teeth. Then she watched its bloodied muzzle testing the air. It thrust the Viking head it was clutching over the ship's side and began pacing towards the hatchway.

"Listen to me," Kady hissed. "We must hide."

"Where can we hide?" Brice barked.

"Shut up, Brice!" Kady implored. "Watch what I do. You too, girls. We must hide ourselves in the shit and blood, leaving only enough space to breathe."

"Why? What is happening up there? Who has attacked the Vikings?"

"An even fiercer enemy, Brice. Now. Into the swamp."

She eased herself backwards into the foul mixture, cringing as the meld of body fluids and filth enveloped her body, seeping into her garments, swirling around her hair. As she became almost fully immersed, even with her lips puckered as tightly as possible, the taste of the hellish cocktail seemed determined to invade her mouth. But she sensed the demonic beast lurking at the hatchway, exploring the fetid murk beneath. She knew it was searching for her. Grasping Brice's tunic, she persuaded him to prostrate himself in the repulsive solution. He did so, pushing Edina and Gwynn down. Feeling ever more confident of her abilities, Kady managed to keep her hysteria under control. Her father sought her again.

My beloved one, blood is a potent shield against demonic forces ... the beast is so consumed by its own bloodlust it is searching for prey it can recognise, breathing the air it breathes ... immerse yourself in the cesspit and you will become invisible to it ... blood is a basic elements of druid magic for protection ... hide in the blood and this monster will not even be able to sense the presence of a druid ... be strong ...

The ever-increasing motion of the boat rendered this operation even more perilous. Remaining rigid, their terrified eyes fixed on the gloom above. They could only snatch at furtive breaths while the swill flowed over them, faeces and body parts slithering across their skin. There was a loud splash. As the terrified pigs jostled into corners, their trotters stomped all over the Britons. Kady raised her face as much as she dared. Blinking through the slime, she peered over the straining backs of the swine. The werewolf was hunched in this confined space, its shaggy face probing among the squealing animals. It kept brushing them aside, its paws swiping at them as if they were toys, flipping them at the wall. Those not killed outright would wail as they floundered in the mire, their backs broken.

Heart in her mouth, Kady sunk backwards. Beneath the excrement and blood her hands sought Gwynn's and Brice's. Brice was already firmly clasping Edina. After an age, the few remaining swine returned to rooting among the bilge. Footsteps bounded towards the gunwale. Then the beast jumped overboard. Kady heaved herself up, dragging the others out of the soup. "Stay here, Brice. Look after your sister and Edina."

"Where are you going?" he pleaded. "You can't leave us here?"

"I'll be back. I need to check the … attacker … has left the ship. I sense he has, but I must see for myself."

Pushing her way through the stinking concoction, Kady pulled herself up the short ladder. Once clearer of the hold's corrupt stench she became aware of the creature's scent. It clung to the air above the decks, mixing with the harshness of all the gore it had so recently opened over the decks. Using the butchered Vikings as stepping-stones, she made her way to the stern. Creeping closer, she grasped the edge, stealing a glance overboard.

Her eyes tracked the beast's silvery wake across the moonlit waves; just ahead, its huge hairy shoulders pushed towards land. But her fear had got the better of her caution. Following its powerful strokes for seconds longer than she should have, she watched in horror as it halted and treaded water, its ugly head staring back. Their eyes locked. The wolf roared ferociously and wheeled around. It began paddling back towards the longship, its glaring eyes keeping her rooted to the spot. Stumbling over a mutilated Norseman, her foot slithered into his intestines and she fell heavily, her head cracking on the beams.

* * *

"Kady!" he cried. Bowed over his sister, Brice shook her desperately. Her eyes remained resolutely shut. Then Edina screamed. Brice glanced towards her. "What is it, Edina?"

"The monster is coming!"

Brice pushed peered over the waves. The werewolf was thirty feet away, closing fast. As it ploughed through the waves it snapped its jaws at them, anticipating its next kills. He turned to Kady. "What would our father have done?" He stared into the dark clouds. "Manannan ... what can I, Brice, son of Kai, do to save the druid?"

Kady's eyelids flickered apart.

"Kady?!" Edina cried. But Kady remained in a stupor.

Brice seized a sword from the bloodied timbers. "I'll show the monster how the Dumnonii meet our destiny."

Almost imperceptibly, Kady's lips moved. Gwynn leant to her, placing her right ear close to her sister's mouth. "Don't understand ... she's saying funny things, Brice ... all foreign."

"The monster!" Edina gasped.

With Kady's incantation growing ever more insistent, the three young Britons crept to the gunwale. The wolf appeared to be struggling to gain any purchase in the waves. A wide circle of white bubbles was forming around it. Something appeared to be moving just below the surface, swimming incredibly fast. Occasionally there would be a glimpse of shiny grey skin breaking the waves. Whatever was encircling the wolf was accelerating all the time. The beast bayed indignantly, its incensed face seeking the spectators on the boat, before its head was whipped away by the momentum of the fantastical currents being generated. The mysterious beings swam faster still, until their trap began inexorably tightening around their target. The sea circular patterns formed an ever-narrowing funnel of water. This maelstrom was roaring as it spun, drowning out the wolf's cries.

The Britons felt the Viking ship rocking wildly as it was dragged towards the vortex. The youngsters were tossed among the hacked corpses on the deck. Brice struggled to his feet, forcing his way back to the vantage point. At that moment Kady's spell ceased. Brice glimpsed the creature flapping its arms in outrage, its final despairing howl cut short as it was sucked into the depths. The whirlpool faded into waves that gently buffeted the longship.

"Girls. Help Kady to her feet. Take her up to the prow, to the dragon. I'll steer us back to the island. But first I'll throw what's left of the crew into the sea."

CHAPTER THIRTY-ONE

The island's shrouds were drifting so close Kady imagined the rest of the world had dissolved. Except she knew it had not: Wessex, where the evil Saxon necromancer was growing in power, was a matter of miles away. Every day she would stare at these mists and anticipate longboats; every night when a full moon basked over their rocky sanctuary her ears would strain for nightmarish howling. Edina approached, munching on an apple, handing another to Kady.

"Thanks, Edina," she said, grateful for the distraction.

"They're *so* juicy, Kady. The orchard here might be small, but the fruit is bountiful."

Kady crunched into the crisp skin. "I've always loved the smell of fresh apples. But inheriting my father's gifts means my eyes are opened to new tastes, new experiences, every day. Just standing here on this headland, I can identify every flower, each plant, all the scuttling insects." She pointed towards a tree stump. "That fungi is delicious when roasted, with nettle seed seasoning. It also makes the diner lightheaded and giggly, but without the hangover that follows a mead binge. Don't screw your nose up, Edina ... it is *especially* delicious with a poached egg dropped on top."

"I'll take your word for it, Kady."

"An almost identical fungus is growing on those rocks over there ... but a few hours after eating *that*, the diner would go blind."

"At least blindness would have saved my eyes from the horrors I've seen these past few days, Kady. But right now I could do with a flagon of that warm Dalriati beer. And I would gladly put up with the hangover."

Kady scowled. "I have enough visions of my own ... sometimes after partaking of druid potions ... sometimes they just flit into my head."

"What has happened to the rest of my own people, the Dobunni?"

Kady paused, listening to a curlew's haunting cry ringing among the rocks. "When the West Saxons swept into the West Country, the surviving Dobunni fled northwards. Your own family were among the last south of the Severn. The Dobunni eventually joined with the Brigantes. They are thriving, Edina, up near the Solway Firth. There they are wary of raiders from the north, but at least the Caledonii only come for their livestock, not their heads. And the only wolves are four-legged.

But in my druidic dreams I've witnessed the fate of British tribes right across our former realms. In most cases, those who have eluded the Germans have used the forest tracks to flee into the wilder parts of the country, into forests or marshes. Other stragglers are making their way to Cornwall, or into the valleys of Cymru. Anglesey remains a druidic fortress, but the Cymri are struggling there, as the English keep sending more men at them, bigger armies. The English send Celtic slaves tunnelling beneath the Cymri fortifications, even women and children. They are easily replaced when the tunnels collapse. The Pennines have become a front line between the beleaguered Carvetii in Cumbria, and the English in North Humberland. Each week a British fort falls."

"Can anything turn the tide against the barbarians, Kady?"

"There is one sign of hope. Deep in the great forests east of here, that straddle the Saxon and Angle kingdoms, a Silures clan is making a last stand, launching guerrilla raids, then disappearing into the trees. I think they could inspire a more widespread revolt against the invaders. Except the English know that, too. They will be determined to root them out."

Edina nodded grimly, tracking a troop of eider ducks emerging from the mists. Glancing to the white flowers scattered around their feet, she sighed. "There is such natural beauty in these islands. It is terrible what the barbarians are doing to it."

"I will do everything in my power to protect these islands, and to protect my people. My father has imprinted all the information I require. I see the forests stretching across Britannia as a haven ... containing potent shrubs, roots and fungi ... all fabulous ingredients for all manner of remedies and potions. And I appreciate their potency can never be underestimated."

"Especially in the wrong hands."

"Exactly, Edina. Saxon medicine men are dabbling in ancient magic, but twisting it for their evil ends, unleashing dark forces."

Edina linked arms with the older Briton. Gannets were dive-bombing the waves a hundred yards-offshore, their sleek white arrows providing another diversion. "Nature is, indeed, beautiful. Let is not dwell too much on these dark forces, Kady. We have a story ripe for a saga, do we not? It begins with a storm. We have good characters, poor Cormac and Diarmaid, the Dalriati fishermen. We have evil characters, the Vikings."

"Egil, the Viking captain, with his serpent tattoos."

"The Viking captain losing his head, wrenched from his shoulders by the Saxon wolf warrior."

Kady glanced over her shoulder. "However choice the tale may be, Edina, we must guard its secrecy. Gwynn will do whatever I tell her. But I know it will be a struggle for me to maintain Brice's confidence. It is enough that our little community has to stay hidden from Saxon patrols. Knowing there are also werewolves intent on hunting me down will cause widespread panic. There are those in my tribe who might well demand my banishment to the mainland, lest I bring these demonic wolves straight to our doorstep. Perhaps they would be right."

"*No*, Kady. Your powers have proved invaluable. You've saved my life, *twice* now. You rescued your siblings. You're a *heroine* to your tribe. They need you. *I* need you."

Kady squeezed the younger girl's arm. The familiar sounds of the village coming to life drifted from the caves. Clucking hens were pestered for eggs. Water vases splashed as they were filled from springs to be taken below to soothe sleep from faces.

"Can you summon the seal people at will, Kady?"

Frowning, she turned to Edina. "Not at will. The selkies are an ancient race, proud to serve both Manannan and his loyal subjects on dry land. They do have immense powers, but they are also extremely vulnerable. As seals they are prey to the orcas that prowl the deeper waters. Some Celts hunt them, for their meat, their skins. But when they shapeshift into seal beings they possess superhuman strength. You saw that when they drowned the werewolf."

"Surely the selkies will always be able to protect this island from invasion?"

"The seal colony basking on our shores numbers several hundred. Of these, only a score or more possess the power to shapeshift. My father was a close friend of the selkies' leader, one called Lugus. But there are thousands of miles of ocean out there, Edina. And in some channels, close by this island even, the sea plunges into vast canyons, miles deep. Our position remains vulnerable."

In the silence that followed Kady pictured her father. Instead of his stern side, brow furrowed while he described swimming with the seal people, she merely saw the kindly face peering over the supper pot, eyes twinkling with love as he prepared his wonderful stews for his family. Again it struck Kady that despite this vision of domesticity her father's position had formed part of a chain stretching back millennia, to the forgotten ages when the tribes had built their stone circles. She was merely the latest link. But the thought that she might prove to be the final one filled her with a renewed dread.

* * *

Kady dipped a shard of grainy bread into her bowl, smothering it in the delicious gravy, wolfing it down. Around her, others were devouring the rabbit soup with a silent fury, the absence of conversation exaggerating their impolite slurping and chewing.

Every so often Torean would cast his eye across the hundreds clustered inside this communal cave. Always quick to display impatience, where he might once have bemoaned this huge cavern's inhospitable nature compared to the comfortably-furnished cabins he had taken for granted, he was grateful his clan could still congregate like this at all. Concluding his meal, he passed his empty plate to his eldest granddaughter, Freya. The teenager added it to the pile she was rinsing in in a large pot of water bubbling above a fire.

Kady handed Freya her own bowl, stared into the flames licking at this pot, then the larger strands of orange and red blazing in the hearth. Seated next to her, Edina followed the direction of her scrutiny.

"The smoke, Kady? What if it was spotted by an eagle-eyed lookout on a passing vessel?"

"We're safe here, Edina. Look. At the centre of the cavern, a natural cavity leads up to the island's surface, three hundred feet above us. When we first settled here, before any fires were lit, Tannus and his brothers constructed tubing from hollowed tree trunks. The rising fumes are coaxed along an elaborate plumbing system, down into the deeper caves that stretch beneath this island and reach far under the sea."

"Fantastic. Only the seals know we're here. And the gulls."

"The sea is a better defence than Hadrian's Wall." Kady took a sip of wine. "My father explained all about this sanctuary to me, in a vision. Lugus once told him about this place. Seemingly it was last visited countless centuries ago, when the Celts had first come from Europe to explore these far-flung islands they assumed were at the edge of the world. No one has ever actually settled here because it is always surrounded by mysterious fog banks and because the offshore currents are so treacherous. These long-forgotten explorers were first to name it the isle of mists."

Kady felt the alcohol impacting her: understandably, with so many recent adrenaline surges. Now she felt light-headed and chatty. Grasping Edina by the hand, she continued. "Our tribe once relied on a steady trade with our neighbours, as well as communities further afield. Now we must make do."

"Not many sagas are ever conceived when a tribe is *making do*," Edina bemoaned.

"Sagas? Did I tell you about the demise of the Saxon patrol? They thought they had captured me when I was ashore gathering ingredients. I lured them into quicksand. I told Torean about the encounter. Even as I was half way through describing the scene, I realised here was another tale destined to be blown out of all proportion as another of his after-dinner stories. Within a matter of months the number of Saxons sucked into the mud will have jumped to at least thirty. I wouldn't put it past the old rascal to throw in a siege catapult for good measure."

As Edina chortled, Kady extracted a handful of mixed berries from a bowl. Chewing them with relish, she stood. "Edina. I feel I have been hogging you for too long. Brice is patiently waiting a chance to invite you for a stroll. I'm heading to the beach myself."

* * *

Kady set off along the path to the narrow inlet. The light was fading; the subdued waves lapping the shoreline were transforming to slate grey. She could make out several seals basking in the twilight after a long day involved in their own struggles, tussling with herring shoals while maintaining a constant vigil for orcas. Breathing evenly, she allowed the tension to seep from her body. The sound of the waves faded. In this calm she could sense the scrutiny of the seals. Concentrating harder, she became aware that the closest of the lounging mammals was a selkie. With this realisation came a vision of the creature's recent experiences.

In Kady's mind these juddered in a frenetic collage. She saw the world through the seal's eyes as it waddled across scree towards the surf. Its awkward land movement transformed the moment it entered Manannan's realm, as it missiled through the murky waters, its flippers whipping myriad bubbles to either side. In the gloom below were glimpses of kelp forests. The seal dived to lurk among these undulating fronds. Ominous black and white shapes prowled overhead: an orca pod. She picked up on the seal's terror as these great beasts powered over the flowing seaweed. Finally the seal broke cover, joining others scything though panicking herring shoals. Then it tracked the seabed rising to a rugged outcrop of submerged rocks, peppered with orange anemones. Crabs scuttled into recesses to avoid its inquisitive snout. Sunlight shimmered across the surface as the seal poked its head to snatch breaths of cool air. More of its kind lolled around rocks fifty yards offshore. When it clambered onto a ledge, feeling the warm sun on its back, mounted men cantered along the beach, jerking their mounts to a halt every so often, using their swords to poke around bushes.

The seals were wary. When one of these men barked a single word – "Oxa!" – the group slithered into the sea again. The seal explored the shallows, uprooting pebbles in a search for molluscs. Suddenly it started. Beyond a green haze of seaweed, a human face loomed, tiny shrimps weaving among the beard's tendrils. The seal retreated. When it broke the surface again it froze: a hundred yards further out, a black dorsal fin punctured the waves.

"Kady!"

The shrill voice released her from the trance. Her eyes snapped open. The seals were also startled and worked their fattened bodies back towards the lapping waves. Her cousin, Artur, was striding towards her. A gangling youth a year older than her, his long legs brought his feet crunching down onto the shale.

"Kady. Torean sends for you. There's a ship, out to sea. Coming this way. We need your crow's eyes."

CHAPTER THIRTY-TWO

Kady followed Artur bounding over the shingle to the grass. Following a path that skirted the feast chamber far below, they arrived at the cliffs on the island's Atlantic coast. Hundreds of feet below, the sea persisted with its ceaseless siege. With the tide near turning, the waves dashing against the rockface were huge, potent enough for their spray to carry to this perilous vantage point.

Kittiwakes, guillemots and puffins huddled into precarious ledges. Kady noticed a fulmar, wings stretched while it rode the air currents. But much as she admired the wildlife sharing their isolated domain, she respected the urgency of Artur's message. Shielding his eyes, his unwavering stare scanned the turbulent waves. The Hibernian Sea was a cauldron of conflicting currents stretching for two hundred miles to Hibernia's jagged east coast. The Dumnonii knew little of that mysterious island, save that its tribes were reputedly wilder than those north of the Roman wall.

"There!" he announced, his right hand stabbing over the procession of ragged grey furrows. "Look there, Kady."

Kady followed the direction of his adamant gesture. At first she found it hard to discern anything beyond the sea's shifting patterns. Murmuring a guttural incantation, she offered a prayer to the goddess Nemain, mistress of the crows and ravens. Stretching her arms aloft, she visualised being one of those great black birds. Instantly, her perspective of the scene transformed, the turbulent waters becoming so close she could practically reach out to touch the curling tips of each wave. The raven navigated high above the swell, riding air currents to avoid being swamped by the water that sometimes churned mere inches below.

Artur recognised the concentration etched into his young cousin's features. He had witnessed this so many times before;

going back to the occasions his father's eldest brother, Kai, had begun tutoring his shy daughter about the ancient ways. In Kady's trance one wave was like a grey mountain range rolling by. Climbing to its summit, she felt the spray lashing the raven's feathers. Then she saw a darker shape. In the constantly billowing furrows, a little boat was tossing. Swivelling her own body to maintain a hovering position, she plunged a hundred or more feet. Although the longboat's prow cleaved the sea, its deck was swamped. From the ornate carvings around its hull she recognised it was Celtic, the principal designs of leaping salmon indicating a fishing community far to the north: Dalriati or Caledonii. The crew had been lost overboard.

Now Kady forced the raven's eyes further into the recesses of this floundering boat. There were deer pelts floating in the stern. The boat subsided, leaving the spying bird suspended above what now resembled some child's toy. A flashback began to unfold. Kady saw the same vessel moored by a sandy beach. Silvery moonlight bathed the scene. Tribespeople were skulking from stone huts, some holding Roman legionnaire shields that were aged and dented. The faces staring towards the boat were smeared with broad stripes of woad dye: Caledonii. Despite the ferocious make-up, the village was well attended, the livestock plump. From what Kady knew of the landscapes inhabited by the northern tribes, she assumed this location lay on the northwest coast, beyond Antonine's Wall.

A leaden beat sounded on a drum. Six women emerged from a large hut at the centre of their village, transporting a boy on a stretcher fashioned from deer pelts. Around twelve or thirteen, his skin was white as snow. There was muted sobbing from onlookers. The bearers lowered their precious load into the vessel. An axe blow severed the mooring rope. The women shoved at the stern, coaxing it through the surf. As the vessel made headway, lit torches were passed along a chain of bodies and tossed into the craft. The fitful drizzle dappling the sea's surface hampered the flames but eventually, as the boat drifted towards a headland, smoke began streaming from the kindling beneath the stretcher. Then there was a lurid flash and a thunderclap. The black skies unleashed torrents of rain. The fire was extinguished and the longship was abandoned to the sea.

Kady felt her legs buckling; Artur threw an arm around her shoulder. "My visions drain my strength at the best of times, cousin," she murmured to him. "Worse still when I receive a vision *within* a vision."

"What did you see, Kady?"

"It is a funeral ship, with no one aboard to steer it away from the walls of mist. It is drifting this way."

"I don't like this, Kady. What sort of omen is it when a funeral ship heads towards our hideout?"

CHAPTER THIRTY-THREE

Although the subterranean village was many yards from the clifftops, the sound of crashing surf carried. The villagers crowded around the fire's wavering tongues, mesmerised by the constantly weaving patterns of red, orange and yellow. Nettle soup had been prepared, spiced with a combination of herbs, laced with succulent mushrooms Kady had harvested that morning.

Bowls were cleared away. Pipes crammed with dry leaves were lit: a peculiar Roman habit that had spread to Britannia centuries before, but which Kady found even more distasteful with her honed druidic sense of smell. Torean was ushering some of the younger village children to cluster before his seat. Kady had always enjoyed the chieftain's storytelling skills. Even as a young adult she found his booming baritone, jovial expressions and mastery of different voices and sound effects irresistible.

"This tale is about my grandfather. Years ago, children, he is the chieftain of our clan. His name is Drest. One day Drest is walking along a cliff path in Dumnonia and as he stares out towards the horizon, he sees ships coming. Three ships. As they draw closer, he can see their sails, painted with a raven, a white bear, and a fox. He can also see that each of their prows is carved with a great dragon head."

At this description there were intakes of breath among his rapt audience. Kady noticed Gwynn among them; her little sister's eyes darted fearfully towards her, so she smiled reassuringly.

"Can anyone guess what kind of ships are sailing towards Dumnonia? This fruit to the first one who does." Torean produced a ripe red apple from the bowl by his side.

"Jutes?" exclaimed Judoc, a plump boy, eyeing the fruit.

"No, Judoc. Nice try."

"Were they Bretons?" piped up his brother Ninian.

"No. I'll give you a clue. You're heading in the wrong direction."

"Dalriati?!" Judoc blurted out.

"Not Dalriati either, Judoc."

Gwynn thrust her hand up.

"Ah, our druid's sister. What say you, young Gwynn?"

"Norse longboats!"

"Excellent, Gwynn!" roared Torean, tossing the apple towards her. That she caught her prize effortlessly filled Kady with even more pride. "Norse longboats. *Pirates*. As soon as Drest realises pirates are coming to raid the Dumnonii villages, he blows his ox horn, three times." Here he filled his lungs and convincingly approximated the sound, inspiring giggles among the children. "Cadeyrn the druid is first on the scene. Gwynn, Cadeyrn is your *great*-grandfather."

"Kady has told me about him."

"That's good, Gwynn. When Cadeyrn realises the danger facing the village, he runs to the shore. You see, children, druids can speak to certain creatures; creatures no one else can see. And Cadeyrn knows that among the seals lying on the shore, there are some who can change, into creatures who look very like humans. Cadeyrn goes to speak to these seal people. He can talk to them in the own language."

At this twist, some listeners glanced over at Kady, who responded by winking. "At Cadeyrn's request, several seal people, *selkies*, swim out towards the Black Needles. These are rocks that the longships have to sail past, on their way to land. The selkies swim then climb onto the rocks. Here they change into human form, or as the druids would have it, they *shapeshift*. At the same time, the sea god, Manannan, is in one of his moods. He decides to make black clouds gather and he whips up the waves. Soon a mighty storm is tossing the Viking ships, up and down, up and down, and their crews must keep a close eye out for hidden rocks. As the longboats approach the shore, their lookouts spy the Black Needles, and shriek at their oarsmen to steer away from them. But the selkies haven't just shapeshifted into people. As they cling to those rocks, with their strong, webbed hands, they have shapeshifted into *beautiful* women, their long hair flowing with the wild winds. They begin singing to these Norse sailors, and despite the storm, their voices carry, sweet as birds.

The Norsemen immediately fall in love with them. The storm dies. The rocks alter into an island, with trees and flowers of every colour they have ever seen, and some they have never seen before. Golden pheasants scuttle across the grass. The Norsemen abandon their oars and the man at the helm of their ship steers straight towards these naked women, who are singing and enticing them to join them on their island, laughing as the waves continue to crash over them, only to leave them where they are, sticking there, like limpets. The moment the ship draws close enough for the sailors to cast their anchor onto land and the men prepare to jump overboard to join these beautiful women, the selkies shapeshift again, changing back to seals. The spell is broken. Now the Norsemen realise the peril they are in, but it is too late. Their wooden ship is dragged onto the Black Needles. Its keel is split into a million pieces and the sea bursts over them while they scream. In seconds, all that remains of their longship are splinters of wood and the dragonhead that slowly sinks.

The second ship is following close behind. They don't even notice what has happened, because the selkies have shapeshifted into beautiful maidens *again* and the Black Needles have turned into a paradise, *again*. The same thing happens. As soon as they draw alongside, the spell breaks."

"*Again!*" chirped Gwynn.

"Yes, little one. *Again*. The ship is destroyed, *again*. This is repeated for the third and last of the Viking vessels.

"*Again!*" chorused all the children.

Torean chuckled. "Watching from the cliffs, all that Caderyn sees is three wooden ships sailing straight into the Black Needles, one after the other. Such is Manannan's fury, not one of the Norse pirates is swept ashore. All are dragged to the bottom of the sea."

Kady giggled at the awestruck faces gazing up at the storyteller. Perhaps one or two of his younger charges might have nightmares about selkies and shipwrecks. But she appreciated

Gwynn had stories of her own that would likely induce sleepless nights among most adult listeners. Kady's attention was diverted when Ardal weaved through the throng, clutching two goblets, offering her one. She smiled then patted the ox hide on the flooring. He sat cross-legged beside her, instantly nuzzling close enough for her to rest her head on his shoulder. She sipped at the rich cider.

Kady regarded Ardal as her best friend and over the years an unspoken bond had evolved between them. Quiet and conscientious, much as he hated to be singled out, Ardal's reserved nature was at odds with most of the clan's male teenagers who were forever goading one another, more often than not coming to blows. Her brother, Brice, was one of the chief culprits, seizing any opportunity to poke fun at Ardal.

Kady relished Ardal's reliability. She found the antics of Brice and his boorish clique tiresome, his nature the polar opposite to her friend's. When it became exhausting fending off Brice's self-obsession and jealousy, Ardal was always a breath of fresh air. And, for all his diffidence, he possessed a razor-sharp wit that could leave her helpless with laughter. The only other person who had been able to make her guffaw that way had been her father. She felt privileged to count Ardal a confidante. One reason Brice had never warmed to him was that Ardal was not Dumnonii. He had been a foundling, discovered as a bleating bundle in the aftermath of a Norse attack on a Durotriges village eighteen years previously. The pirates had been repulsed when Torean and her father had mustered the neighbouring clans to rout them. The baby had been discovered among abandoned booty, concealed in a bundle of clothing. The mother who had placed him there had fallen to the sword.

Torean had adopted Ardal as his own son, giving him a name that translated as 'courageous.' Despite his tender years, he had proved himself worthy of this handle on several occasions as a boy: fighting off wild dogs armed with only a poker one time; on another occasion leaping into a burning barn to save the screaming children who had inadvertently set the building alight while playing with a torch. When Kady shuddered at the thought of a building engulfed with flames, like the homes of their village on the mainland, Ardal placed a reassuring arm around her shoulder.

"I love father's stories," he murmured to her. "Especially the ones about drowning Norsemen."

Kady grinned, noting his bleary eyes. Ardal was fond of his father's cider; something she gently teased him about, but which she found herself keeping a watchful eye on. The only occasions she ever had cause to chastise her friend were when he over-indulged and became uncharacteristically maudlin.

"You'll probably have a head on you in the morning, Ardal, like one of those Viking sailors after he launched himself at a raving beauty but ended up headbutting the Black Needles."

He sniggered and drained his goblet. Eventually his head lolled onto her shoulder. Within a minute he was snoring gently into her ear. Mesmerized by the flickering fire, her mind drifted. When she shut her eyes, she received another vision of the mysterious vessel, closer this time, drifting towards jagged rocks. Her heart sunk as she watched the Caledonian's body being tossed by the waves. She could see his face, the white skin accentuated by the tribal ink flourishing over his neck and cheeks. Suddenly his eyes flickered open.

CHAPTER THIRTY-FOUR

Prising herself away from Ardal, she bounded towards the cave entrance. Everyone else was so engrossed in Torean's next saga no one noticed when she tugged the deer hide blanket at the doorway to one side. When the wind rushed in, tossing the fire and ruffling hair, onlookers were only concerned that she hoisted it back again as quickly as possible, assuming she was braving the elements to visit the latrine.

An easterly wind was lashing the island, bringing water with it: an icy combination of sleet and salty spume lifted from the churning waves. She could sense the boat's presence. Where her earlier vision had implanted an image of a bundled body, she now saw a face contorted with terror, screaming as each wave engulfed the decks, clutching desperately to the splintered wood that was all that remained of the mast.

Bowing into the gale, she struggled towards the shore. Ahead of her, the new moon cast the palest flicker of light onto the rocks and the seals she knew would be huddled among them. Where these mammals would normally have backed off the moment they were aware of her approach, they remained where they were. Kady began singing an ancient song she had never heard before, but which her father was conveying telepathically.

> *Children of the sea, hear me, hear me ...*
> *From Manannan's realm your strength I seek ...*
> *Oh wondrous selkies, beautiful and free ...*
> *Come breath with me, in human form ...*
> *For I am Kady, a druid's firstborn ...*
> *Our paths are shared, our true course is one ...*

Although it was the gentlest of lilting melodies, a magical force projected it over the waves smashing onto the beach. The silhouettes of the slumbering seals altered, as if the deep shadows were being sculpted by the elements. Presently there were several taller figures moving towards her. Her heart pattered. The first selkie came close enough for her to glimpse its features. It was male and although she knew it was a seal that had altered shape, it was outwardly as human as any of the villagers she had just left behind. The being was naked, seaweed encrusting its pale and hairless skin like a shawl. He smiled graciously.

I am Lugus.

His lips remained still but Kady heard his words inside her head.

You have summoned us from the realm of Manannan, lord of the oceans. We appreciate your need to bridge the realm of the land dwellers and those who make their home in the sea. We acknowledge your mystical powers, Kady, daughter of Kai, for we have met your kin before. Kai was a good friend to the selkies. Tell us how we may help?

Reaching out, she opened both her palms. Lugus clutched them with his webbed hands. Once she felt their fingers entwining, she projected her own message.

Thank you for answering my call, Lugus, of my father's great friends, the seal people. There is a boat heading for this island, from the northwest, from the great sea. There is someone aboard who is in grave danger. He will be dashed to pieces on the reefs and will surely drown and fade into Manannan's kingdom, instead of his own. The storm is too strong for me to climb into my coracle to assist. I would be grateful if the seal people could rescue him?

Lugus squeezed her hands.

Consider it done, Kady.

"Kady! Are you all right?!"

As the harsh voice rang out again, she twisted round. Ardal was clambering over the rocks towards her. When she turned back to Lugus, he had gone and the selkies had reverted to seals.

"I was worried about you. Someone said they saw you rushing outside, in a panic."

"I'm fine, Ardal."

"I saw you with the seals. Were you ... were you talking to them?"

"Yes. The boat I was telling you about. It's changed direction. I know there's someone on board."

"On a funeral ship?"

"Someone's alive. The selkies are going to try and save him."

"I see. But it's freezing out here, Kady. They're dishing out bread, still warm from Sulian's oven. And refills of your delicious nettle soup to dip it into!"

They linked arms and returned to the caves. After warming themselves by the fire, they strolled over to a table where platters of bread had been laid out. Ardal handed her a slice then grasped one himself. The bread was grainy with crispy husks and mouth-watering. Ardal grinned and Kady mirrored his smile. But he remained distracted. "If an abandoned ship could drift towards our hideaway, Kady, what is there to stop a determined Saxon navigator?"

"I was pondering that myself. But worse than that, Ardal. Now we know the enemy are hunting druids, what will stop the next wolf warrior from swimming from the mainland?"

CHAPTER THIRTY-FIVE

Malcolm cursed as his fingers toyed with the agonising swelling around his right eye. As a Celtic chieftain he had long been accustomed to honour and dignity, and to commanding respect. Now he was shackled in the mud behind an enemy hut, wrists bound, cowering from the arbitrary lunges of his guards' spear butts. The way of life enjoyed by his people for countless summers had ended.

His clan were from the Belgae tribe and they had enjoyed prosperity during the decades since the Romans had left Britannia. Working their farms and orchards for the common good, freed from the obligation of surrendering exorbitant tributes to their Latin governors, they had bartered over crops, meat and poultry with their neighbours – the Artebates, the Durotriges, the Catuvellauni. They had furnished their dwellings with fine pottery and dressed in decorous tunics, bedecked with bronze necklaces and jewels.

Hostile tribesman had begun attacking the trading parties: fierce warriors with lank blond hair, who screamed their war cries in some alien tongue. These were not isolated bandit attacks. Soon the English barbarians were swarming into Belgae territory, plundering livestock, razing homesteads, their superiority in numbers inevitably prevailing. Malcolm had hoped his own village might remain untroubled if he dissuaded his own men from encroaching into the territory where whole communities of these Saxons had now settled. He could only wince at his gullibility.

Three weeks before, a thousand-strong Saxon warband had emerged from the dawn mist like wraiths, overcoming his sentries as the wind scattered seeds. Those villagers who had not been summarily butchered had been rounded up with netting, or by snarling hounds. The pitiful survivors had been marched westwards, deep into West Saxon territory in a snaking column, each manacled to the uncertain gait of the prisoner in front. The destitute procession had taken them by English homesteads, where the women and children always took great pleasure in hurrying out to greet their passage with rotten fruit, earth clods, pebbles, lungfuls of spittle, or the contents of latrine buckets.

Three weeks, Malcolm mused as he gazed around the remnants of his clan. Many of their women had not even made the lengthy journey into servitude and had last been seen screaming while burly Saxon soldiers dragged them off to the clearings where they had once been courted. The English bastards had stripped Malcolm and his warriors of all their finery, the unkempt bastards delighting in kicking their captives so they could rejoice at them scrabbling around in the mire like swine.

These nights would only grow longer. Many among his depleted company were wracked with ferocious coughs. The Germanic tribes had not only transported iron weapons with them in their longships, they had brought all manner of infections. Malcolm wondered how long it would be before the older villagers gave up the fight for what was left of their wretched lives.

Against the flickering torches from sentries on the stockade high above them, he watched the faces of his kinfolk dissolve in shadow. The time had come. He would raise everyone's spirits with tales his own father had told him in more pleasant circumstances by the campfires of his youth: stories that had been handed down for generations. He was grateful the gloom created a cloak for his bruised features, masking his shame. When he began, his voice barely rose above a whisper for fear of antagonising passing guards. This added gravitas. Within seconds the other prisoners were hanging on his every word.

"I'm taking you back five hundred years, to the fiercest battle ever fought on this island. The hero of my story is my forefather, Malcolm, who I'm named after. He is around the age I am now, thirty-one. Long, long before the Romans built the great wall to protect Britannia from the wild Caledonians, Malcolm is marching in a Roman army, far, far to the north. He serves with one of their elite legions, the Ninth Hispanic. Many Celts are proud to serve in the Imperial Roman army. Today they are marching through Elsick Mounth, the great pass through the Cairngorm mountains, hunting for Caledonii and Picts.

When Roman scouts discover the location of the enemy granaries, filled with recent harvests, the legionnaires march towards them. To lose these stores would mean winter starvation, so the Romans manage to coax the savages from the forests and glens where they've been hiding.

The enemy muster around a mountain, known to the Romans as Mons Graupius. A party from the Imperial army make for the snow-capped peak, including two senior centurions, to parley with the enemy general, Calcagus. After all, the natives have been persuaded to see the benefits of making peace with the Romans in Britannia. Might windswept Caledonia not benefit from civilization? Might these savages not be tempted by descriptions of hot baths, lavish feasts and slave girls to warm their beds?" The appreciative sniggers rippling through Malcolm's audience were short-lived. "The Caledonii reply is swift. A catapult fires ten severed heads towards the Roman lines, where they dash against rocks like eggs. Malcolm and the many other veterans curse their cohort's Tribune. Augustus Marcellus is thin as a whip, a blond-curled, twenty-six year old son of a nobleman, who is treating this northern campaign as colourful chapters for his scribes to include in his biography. He knows nothing of warfare, even less of warfare against barbarians at the edge of the world.

Now hooves thunder. A chariot races towards the legions, wheels whirring, rider and pillion warrior crouching behind its wicker frame. The brazen, wild-eyed young chieftain suddenly jumps astride the frantic horses, accustoming to their uneven gallop, raising a spear above his head. He screams Celtic obscenities, spittle flecking his face like a rabid dog, snarling at the invaders. A decurian screams: '*Pila!*' Javelins fill the air. The Caledonian waits, his bare feet rooted to the backs of his steeds. Then he executes a backwards-somersault to land behind them. His pilot steers the chariot clear as the weapons embed in the soil. Reaching down, the taunting tribesman plucks at one of the Roman heads, brandishing it by its ear. Glancing over his shoulder, he swings the trophy until the ear and a portion of skin tear away from the skull. When the pilot halts the chariot, the pagan thrusts the ear into his mouth, jaws grinding. Eventually the chariot disappears over the prow of the hill.

Malcolm concentrates on the impending battle. Mustered along the lower slopes of Mons Graupius the savages number thirty thousand. Calgacus has marshalled his infantry above the slope, his charioteers on the plain. Facing them, Britannia's Imperial governor, Gnaeus Julius Agricola, has placed eight thousand auxiliary footsoldiers in two equal lines. His light horsemen flank this main body, with legionnaires held in reserve. Staring at the enemy hordes, Malcolm's heartbeat drums. The savages are so densely packed they assume the appearance of some vast monster, twitching and quivering throughout the length of its shadowy body. Trumpets blast. The command executed, a host of javelins soar into the savages. Some missiles are hewn aside; others find their mark, skewering torsos, transforming battle roars into death gargles. Then Agricola orders his elite fighters at these mountain people: four cohorts of Batavians from the Rhine and two of Tungrians: forged from natives into disciplined warriors by the might of Rome. Their short swords and regimented battle drill quickly have the pagans falling back in disorder. Incisive jabs rupture bellies, hack stomachs open ..."

As ever with his tales, Malcolm augmented descriptions of combat by miming the actions, invoking winces and sniggers among his audience. In the shadows his outstretched right arm approximated the twisting motion that would disembowel an adversary. "Steaming guts pour over still screaming clansmen. Thrashing limbs bring down their comrades. Celtic, German or Spanish soldiers plunge metal into rib cages, until the iron stench of blood hangs in the air. In such close quarters the Highland chariots are useless and soon the armoured soldiers overwhelm them, their horses slaughtered, their smashed wooden frames hindering retreat. Hundreds of savages stumble to the mire, but are trapped in a scrum. So begins a massacre, as legionnaires are consumed by bloodlust, any orders to stand down ignored in the frenzied swinging of swords.

From his vantage point high on the hillside, Calcagus can only watch in despair as Agricola orders his reserve mounted brigades, the *alae*, in from the flanks. The barbarians' will to fight fades like the dying embers of a fire. Hemmed together in their shivering painted nudity, they form into unruly knots, cowering as thousands of cavalrymen encircle them, slicing into their ranks at will. While the horses bellow, their white-eyed stares as demons, the riders work their pitiless way around the defeated men. The scene becomes a harvest from hell. Instead of corn, the skulls of men are being sliced apart, their blue corpses the abandoned chaff.

Malcolm's cohort sweeps into the fray. A lone Caledonian chariot thunders towards him, the same chieftain who desecrated the centurion's heads. The barbarian launches a heavy spear. Its blade grazes Malcolm's cheek. A legionnaire anticipates the advance and lies down. When the horse is above him, rearing its legs, he draws his *gladius* down the length of its abdomen. Its guts spill, swamping him in fluid. He rolls out of the way as the horse continues; but only as far as it takes for its uncoiling intestines to entangle its legs and cause it to tumble, the chariot colliding with the thrashing beast.

Malcolm leaps atop the wooden structure, seizing the co-driver and slicing his throat, then engaging the warrior. His adversary is a tall individual, a man of noble bearing. Unlike the tattooed peasants forming the bulk of this ill disciplined but fearsome army, its captains are semi-civilized. In different circumstances, Malcolm might have admired the intricate designs carved into the six-sided shield. But the Caledonian's youth is his undoing. Where a more battle-hardened chieftain would have continued with the engagement in a bid to wear out the opponent, this headstrong lad takes one chance too many. He overstretches a lunge at what has only been a feint by Malcolm. Realising his costly error, he tries to bring his shield up but Malcolm, a veteran of this merciless northeastern front, would never miss such an opportunity. He thrusts at the enemy's head, catching his left temple, the tip puncturing the skull to half a sword length. The mind that spent hours carving his shield is reduced to red clots oozing down the shaft. His final gasp bears the name of his god.

Malcolm rallies his comrades as they press home the victory, following in the wake of the cavalry stampede, isolating stragglers, butchering them where they beg for mercy. At the head of a group of panting legionnaires, each one emitting the satisfied yelps of victory, Malcolm stops. The Romans in front are nervous. They stall, rather than continue the attack. Forcing his way to the front, he realises the soldiers are all repeating one word: 'Berserker.'

These are the barbarian fighters most dreaded. They are from Norse tribes allied to the Caledonians, who have settled in the most northerly British islands, the Shetlands. Berserkers are warriors who not only fight to the death, they intend taking as many of the enemy with them as possible. Before battle, their medicine men supply them with potions that drive them insane and transform their minds into those of beasts. For the duration of any fight they have superhuman strength."

Here Malcolm's voice dropped to a whisper. His listeners craned to hear but he paused until a Saxon's lumbering footfall passed nearby then faded. "There are rumours a few Norse shamen possess potions *so* potent they enable their subjects to fully shapeshift into wild animals." His speech resumed its urgency. "The legionnaires form a circle. The savage is seven feet tall, built like an ox. Malcolm studies the brute. His torso glistens with sweat. Tattoos spiral across his huge chest muscles. In his right hand he clutches a double-headed axe, the blades dripping red. His left clutches a Tungrian head by its pigtails. Malcolm counts seventeen slain around his feet. This enemy is contorted with the rage of a man preparing to enter hell. So many have died at his hands that his head and shoulders appear to have been dipped in red paint with only the obscenely bulging eye whites protruding. He goads his enemies, raising his head to the heavens to utter a soul-curdling scream then shakes his foul trophy so crimson drops spray his terrified audience.

Malcolm steps out from the ring, turns his back on this monster. He exclaims: 'Men of Britannia. Soldiers of Rome. *This* is Rome.' He sweeps his sword to include the land as far as the grey Firth to their right. 'All of this is the Roman Empire. This cursed savage is an affront to your wives, your children, your comrades, to Emperor Domitian and to Mars himself! Well?!' Those still bearing javelins lower their weapons towards the berserker. A missile is thrown. The savage uses his axe blade to splinter the wood. Then a second. But he has insufficient time to counter the third which pierces his right shoulder, the impact sending him spinning into the path of a fourth and fifth. These strike his stomach and thigh. But he ducks suddenly, casting the head at his onlookers, lunging at the wooden shafts to heave them out. With an enraged howl he throws himself at the nearest Romans, impaling two men with the first spear, using the second to whip the legs from under another three. Wielding his axe he slices each of these men across their throats. Next he decapitates a petrified auxiliary who has been playing dead in the moor, praying to the gods he remain unnoticed. The men back off again. Malcolm throws himself to the ground. Legionnaires cry out as they fall over him in their desperation to escape. He feels the brute's full weight. It squeezes the air from his lungs. The soles of the berserker's feet are sticky with human fluid. Malcolm knows if he makes a sound he will lose his life. The agony is unbearable. He is close to blacking out. The weight lifts. Metal clashes overhead. More Romans are screaming their dying breaths, their corpses littering the moor. Malcolm heaves himself to his feet. He is directly behind the savage. He watches how all the legionnaires in front react to his unexpected manoeuvre. Unfortunately the berserker notices too, halting his progress, swivelling round, his lethal axe high above his head, his face so close that Malcolm can smell the stench of his furious breath. The Roman auxiliary raises his own weapon and thrusts it towards one of the tattooed spirals; one that forms a convenient blue target centred on his heart. But the fiend summons further reserves from his unlimited well of strength, twisting his lumbering body to one side, sneering as Malcolm's sword gouges a neat furrow across his pectoral muscles. The crimson weeping seems more like a provocative embellishment to his tattoos. Malcolm assumes he is staring into his destiny. The clamour of battle fades, leaving only this superman's snorting and his own harsh, shallow sucking at the pitiless northern wind. A curious sensation overcomes him, his body weight seeming to sink down to his torn sandals, leaving him floating. When the maniac's talons close around his neck, it is as if it is all happening to someone else. Even as he is raised five feet into the air, his muscles slackening as he prepares to receive the final blow, he feels devoid of fear.

Somewhere there is an anguished groan, a punching. The sound is repeated. Gradually the outside world begins trickling back, like waking from a nightmare. The vice-like grip at his throat loosens. Malcolm's feeble eyes are drawn to the berserker's chest. Among the whirling designs are punctuating studs, forming the shape of Orion's belt. At first Malcolm can't comprehend why their metal tips are dripping red. Then there is more pronounced gasping from behind the Titan. The javelin tips gouge even further, the supreme effort of a dozen legionnaires, inspired by Malcolm's bravery, forcing their enemy away from the soil where so many of their comrades have fallen. With a final, feeble cry, life departs the Caledonian champion's body, freezing him in this position. There is a loud splintering of wooden shafts as he collapses, face forward, his steaming shit erupting from his arse."

The lavatorial conclusion brought a welcome respite after Malcolm's grisly account of the Caledonian defeat. His audience remained introspective for a while longer, until the downpour outside distracted them. The rain that had been dappling against the Saxon village's sturdy wooden structures all morning had transformed to relentless silver spears. Dogs were skulking beneath the opposite buildings, jostling for position with noisily protesting pigs in the gloom.

Saxons stared from windows, grateful for the waterproof pitch liberally applied to roofs. Excused from foraging for food or tilling the outlying fields, the menfolk were grateful for this opportunity to take shelter. Soon tankards were being refilled and bawdy hunting songs were filling the smoky atmosphere. Feasts were prepared, their drifting aromas adding to the misery of the Celtic prisoners who were also chilled to the bone. As they huddled closer for meagre warmth, Malcolm's tales of ancestral bravery were forgotten.

Presently the door to the nearest hut swung open and a woman lunged the contents of a wicker bucket towards them. Chopped carrots, potato peelings and pork offcuts peppered the muddy ground. The woman lingered, waiting for these natives to scramble for the debris like the pigs they were. Malcolm calmly leaned towards the scattered food, his shackled neighbour moving with him to allow maximum reach. Gathering the food into a small pile, covering it as best he could with his trembling hands, he offered the rations around the company.

"Eat up, dogs!" the woman cried out. "For tomorrow you are going to your new homes, the menfolk to the Cymru front as tunnelers, the women and children to brothels." The hut door slammed, muffling the laughter that greeted her outburst.

"What did she say, Malcolm?" one of the females enquired of their chieftain.

"My ancestor Malcolm served with Batavians who spoke a similar tongue to these Saxon bastards. I can but guess. Perhaps she taunts us about our fates? It is a pointless speculation." He shovelled a handful of potatoes and meat scraps into his mouth, staring at the torrents flowing through the village.

After some time their monotony was broken by approaching horses. The gates to the stockade clattered open. A dozen riders cantered in, their hooves digging muddy clods, scattering these in all directions. The hapless Britons cowered. The two Saxons towards the rear were hauling a pair of riderless horses. Somewhere a harsh voice bawled: "The chieftain returns!"

Scores of warriors stumbled merrily from their beer hall, greeting the dismounting horsemen. As the bellicose troop passed the manacled prisoners, several lashed their filthy boots under the hut. Malcolm received a heavy blow to the small of his back and pitched forwards into the mud. This provoked gruff laughter.

"Thane!" called the tallest of the drunken Saxons. "Good to see you, Modig. We made sure to leave plenty ale for you and the others! Any news of Oxa? Or Torr? Where did you come across their steeds?"

Raising his face to the slate grey skies, the Saxon chieftain glowered, allowing the rain to splatter his scarred cheeks and leather eye patch. His men watched warily, for their thane was prone to bouts of silence, sometimes ending in laughter, but invariably explosions of temper. There was relief when he merely sighed, glancing at the soldier who had spoken. "The horses were down by the shore, Cuthbert, fifteen miles hence. There was no sign of my son, or our other comrade. We've been searching all afternoon, but had to give up when the skies opened. Frige is in a mood with us, for some reason! Not butchering enough of these accursed blueskins!"

Modig stomped his foot into a deep puddle, showering the prisoners with black water. "At first light we go back with the hounds. We'll find out what happened to our blood brothers. Whatever the mystery, I sense a few dead natives by the time we've solved it. We must continue purging these islands until every last fucking blueskin is enslaved or dead."

With that he strode over to the captives. Selecting a victim randomly, he fumbled in the darkness, seized the nape of a neck and dragged a man outwards.

"That one was their chieftain, my lord," Cuthbert explained. "He likes to tell them all bedtime stories."

"Is that so. I know of someone he could try lulling to sleep."

Cajoling the Celt to his feet, Modig shoved him in the direction of the large pit excavated in the centre of the Saxon encampment. Malcolm halted when he reached the crater's lip, gazing downwards uncertainly. Modig's men fanned outwards, trudging around the perimeter, while other Saxons emerged from huts, braving a soaking in order to enjoy Modig's sport. Presently Malcolm discerned movement down there. A darker patch stirred among the shadows: matted brown fur shifted and an angry grunt boomed. Malcolm's eyes widened with horror when the creature rose onto its hind legs, its snout testing the array of scents tantalizing its reddened muzzle from ground level. When the bear slashed a paw towards its audience, the necklace of chains coiled around its thick neck muscles jangling, it stretched to almost eleven feet.

"Proud British chieftain ... meet Bee-Wolf. He belongs to my son, Oxa. He loves his pet bear. He found Bee-Wolf when he was an orphaned cub, near drowned, by the River Oder. Oxa has raised him, ensuring the beast has never grown out of his wild streak. Hence the chains. Since Oxa has been missing, Bee-Wolf's temper has been growing. Perhaps you could soothe him with one of your stories, soothsayer?"

Modig concluded his spiel, cruelly awaiting a reply from the Celt who simply shrugged, casting his fearful eyes towards the monster's bared teeth. Modig clapped his hands on Malcolm's shoulders. "The sooner you native curs learn to speak English, the quicker you'll jump to your masters' orders." His blows to Malcolm's shoulders grew more insistent, until the Celt was forced to dig his heels into the mud to prevent himself being pushed forwards. Modig's fists persisted; one decisive blow sending his prisoner teetering to the edge. With the bear fixing him in its sights, Malcolm's arms grasped at the air as he plummeted. He landed with a snapping of bones, his bleary eyes focussing on the light of the world above, before the swiftly lunging silhouette blotted it out.

CHAPTER THIRTY-SIX

As the first robins trilled, Angle soldiers began hauling the captives into the open, overcoming reluctance with spear butts or boots. The painstaking procession to the south coast had now been on the open road for several hours, the guards listening out for any sounds more disturbing than birdsong. Even this far from the remaining British territories in the West Country, the dense trees either side of their snaking pathway still harboured hostile Celts. Some even believed the forests to be haunted.

The edginess among their escorts went unnoticed by the pitiful prisoners. They concentrated on walking, because if they paused to rest they would be beaten. The mouthfuls of rotting boar meat and cups of rancid water they had received earlier had been to fortify them for a hundred mile forced march. Their destination was Portus Adurni, formerly the site of a large Roman fort, now an English market town on the south coast. Here they would be bartered for a diverse range of goods.

"Keep them native dogs on their feet!" Octric bellowed, grunting with the effort of heaving his thickset frame from his saddle to crane over his shoulder. Shielding his eyes against the drizzle, the overseer frowned at the human chain. The prisoners mutely trudging in his wake were roped together, heads bowed, clothing tattered, struggling to cope with the sodden earth slithering at their bare feet. As he watched them, a figure stumbled, jerking those in front to a halt. The nearest soldier reacted swiftly.

"Up, Brit, up! Or I'll run ye through where ye lie!" The Angle jabbed at his victim's backside with his spear shaft. Octric was about to urge his horse onwards, but his furtive eyes were drawn to the prisoner. She was a female and as two compatriots helped her back up, his attention roved over her figure. He reckoned this maiden was around fifteen or sixteen in summers. Despite incarceration in a stockade, the rain had washed her hair, exposing its vibrant chestnut colour and highlighting skin as white as statuary in a Roman temple. The elements had also soaked into her thin garments to reveal generous curves. The overseer was faced with a dilemma. Tomorrow this beautiful Briton would be placed on a platform and become another's property. By the evening she could be heading to the Jutish fortresses on the Isle of Wight, or to the fens of East Anglia. As he peered down at her, he noticed the way she glared back at him, radiating defiance from her steel-blue eyes. He cursed the fact he had never noticed her before. Then again, he had lost count of the number of these Celtic wretches who had been hauled into his village to fester in a makeshift prison before being escorted to auction. In that instant his decision was made: he had to have her between his thighs. When he considered the slave market, he appreciated the price she would fetch if left unsullied. He would ensure she was not damaged down there. "Untie that 'un, Aldagund," he snapped. "Brings her to Octric."

The soldier worked at the knot, twisting the twine, digging it away from her wrists while sniggering at her pained expression. Then he clawed fingers into her bare shoulders and dragged her to the corpulent chargehand.

"Name, bitch?" Octric barked. When she peered up blankly, he recalled the smattering of local phrases he had overheard. "Beth yw eich enw?"

"Aerona," she mumbled, her insolence wilting as she trembled before him, rubbing at her bruised skin.

"Aerona. Pretty. Octric wishes to take Aerona aside, for a while." He smirked at his underling. "Octric'll see this fine vixen has a last look at her homeland afore she gets whisked off to be wedded to some fat old Saxon oaf, who'll fuck her every night then collapse onto her, snorin', fartin' and stinkin' of mead and sweat!"

If the younger Angle thought Octric had just provided an uncannily accurate self-portrait, he kept the notion to himself. Instead he gave the prisoner a further nudge in Octric's direction. The overseer held his right hand out to her. She hesitated, glancing back to the other prisoners. Most were staring into the ground by their filthy feet.

"Octric's not goin' to eat you. Unless you asks us nicely," he leered, ogling her breasts. He snapped his fingers at the soldier who grasped her about the midriff, forcing her up onto Octric's lap. When she was draped over the front of his saddle, he smacked her backside. "Go on, now," he rasped, and his horse cantered towards the treeline, Aerona squealing as the motion dunted her up and down.

Aldagund watched until the horse's white tail had been swallowed by the trees. Shrugging, he swung his arm. The slave convoy continued the long march.

Deftly steering his horse, Octric gazed down at his booty. "Tells you what, Aerona? Don't think Octric'll send you to Portus Adurni after all. Reckon you'll make a fine slave for my *own* bed. That way Octric can fuck you *anytime* he wants. He'll fuck you ... *thousands* of times. Can you imagine that, Aerona? Do you Brit cunts even learn how to count? Not *one*. Not a *hundred*. *Thousands*. Can you even imagine such a number, bitch? *Thousands* ..."

His rambling ceased so abruptly that Aerona swivelled round. His head had whipped backwards, the momentum lifting him from his saddle and pitching him several yards behind his horse, arms flailing. When he collapsed into bracken, growling in consternation, her eyes drifted to the point of impact: a length of twine had been secured at neck-height. Warriors erupted from the undergrowth on all sides, mostly females. One grasped the horse's reins, soothing the nervous beast. Hands lifted towards her; gratefully she listened to cocky Celtic voices while she was lifted down.

"Where did you come from?" she gasped. "You've saved my life."

"*We live here*," answered a Celt, her voice hissing behind a mask of black cloth. "We live in the forest and we kill fucking Germans." This tall fighter stepped lithely over to the dazed overseer who had enough wits about him to fumble for his sword. The Briton got there first, easing it from its scabbard. With a lightning-quick movement, she aimed the point into Octric's chest, centring on his solar plexus.

"Did you really plan on raping a Celtic child, you fucking English worm?" the warrior challenged.

The man squirmed, his rudimentary grasp of the local dialects evaporating. "Coins," he stammered, "in pouch, in saddle?"

"Did you plan on fucking that child?" the woman demanded, her finger stabbing towards Aerona.

"Gold", he muttered, then recalling the Roman, he spat out: "*Aurum! Aurum!*"

"Your fucking *aurum* is worthless here, English dog," she castigated. Her head whipped round. "What is your name, beautiful one?"

"Aerona."

"Aerona. You realise the fate this worm had in store for you? The fate the English have in store for all of the British?"

"I've seen it happen to my loved ones, so many times, dragged from the stockade and into the trees. Sometimes when they're drunk the bastards just barge in and help themselves while their mates laugh and drink mead and wait their turn."

"*Aurum!*" squealed the overseer.

The fighter slammed a boot hard into his jaw. "Silence, worm. Aerona. Do what you have wanted to do for so long." She handed her sword towards the timid teenager, who gazed fearfully at the intricate patterns carved into its blade. Glancing at the Angle's shifty eyes, listening to his muffled whimpers, she clenched her fingers around it, testing its weight. Becoming accustomed to the feel of it, Aerona studied the sunlight burnishing along its length. Twisting it to and fro, she blinked away tears before turning to the overweight slaver.

"Quickly," the bandit ordered. Lifting her boot from his face she stepped back two paces. Octric's eyes flickered from her to Aerona before he sucked a lungful of air, ready to shriek for help. Picturing the faces of every member of her tribe who had died so brutally by English hands Aerona raised the sword, its silver blur sweeping down across the overseer's neck. So keenly was the sword sharpened, the impact of the blow carried on into the soil beneath. Trailing blood, the head rolled into the undergrowth.

"Was that your first kill?" the older woman asked, reaching for the weapon, extracting it from the ground as Aerona relinquished her grip.

"Yes."

"You struck like a veteran. The spirit of vengeance is strong in you, beautiful one."

"Where have you come from? I thought the Angles had driven any remaining Celts into the West Country?"

The woman squinted through the trees, noting the position of sunlight glinting from an Angle helm. "I am Fia, chieftain of the Silures. My clan choose to stay. We hide in these forests, and we strike the English whenever they venture too close."

Aerona nodded. "The Angles are herding the rest of my people to Portus Adurni."

"Not any more," the Celt replied, wiping the bloodied weapon in the corpse's tunic. "Come with me."

Aerona followed the camouflaged fighter until her band had reached the edge of the trees. The slave train was already a hundred yards ahead, struggling over the mud-encrusted remains of the Roman road. The Celtic leader cupped her hands to her mouth, approximating the harsh chirrup of a peregrine falcon. A second later a hailstorm of arrows whistled through the air. Scores of Angles slumped from their saddles. Although curtains of drizzle were cloaking the carnage, Aerona noticed figures launching into the confusion, darting through the corpses to home in on wailing or twitching men, each axe or sword blow filling her with a grim satisfaction.

The ambush was over in minutes. The Celtic warriors released the ropes from their countrymen then led them all back into the trees. Aerona watched the riderless horses cantering into the murky distance then followed the others into the forest shadows, using the headless cadaver as a stepping-stone.

CHAPTER THIRTY-SEVEN

Gazing into the clouds, Angwen had thought this was one the most pleasurable methods of travelling he had experienced. A more uncomfortable aspect was the water seeping through cracks in the floating log, sticking his garments to his backside as he contemplated the drifting scenery.

The river's flow had already carried him several miles from the Atrebates village. Aside from a brief spell when its course had threaded over a small waterfall, forcing him to grasp the bark, his transit had been pleasant. As he watched the treetops gliding by, he tallied the birds he could differentiate in the background: coots, woodpigeons, herons, bitterns, warblers and a dipper.

His flight had been much less traumatic than most. Celtic villagers in the path of the rampaging English warbands were usually forced to flee for the trees with whatever valuables they could thrust into a sack. The warriors hunting them on agile horses often found suitable tracts to outflank their quarry. Then the forest floor would run red with blood. As a druid, Angwen's life was particularly precious. But he was over a hundred years old, and while in remarkable overall physical condition for one of so many summers, his legs would never have coped with the rigours of escaping over land. His brethren had carried him to this hollowed log and cast him adrift.

Observing rooks soaring across the clouds, Angwen mused how this familiar world had been transformed. The English had seized the lion's share of the territory his tribe once called their homeland. Pockets of Celtic settlement remained within the vast new kingdom of East Anglia, but it was only a matter of time before these were ethnically cleansed. At least his escape plan was straightforward. He had been advised to lie still until the log floated into choppier waters. That would indicate the estuary where the river flowed into the German Sea. At this point he should clamber out of this makeshift canoe. There was a sheltered elm grove to the north of the inlet where he could eke sustenance from the abundance of nuts, mushrooms and berries. Eventually a rescue coracle would be sent to wind its way through the channels patrolled by Angle craft. Until then - and assuming there would be any survivors left to search for him - he would have to live off the land. It would not be a perfect existence for a once-proud druid, but preferable to lingering torture at the hands of sadistic captors. Angwen had reluctantly complied. He had no desire to desert his community; although he appreciated he would only have slowed them down. While he could recall many of his potions and spells, his ageing mind diminished their power.

Suddenly the log was juddering. With a laboured groan, he lifted his hands to either side of the hollowed-out portion, grasped the bark then heaved himself into a sitting position. He was puzzled; he could see no sign of the open sea. Dipping fingers into the river, he touched the drips to his mouth: no hint of brackishness. The log remained meandering along the river's course. On either side, banks of earth were clogged with weeds. The trees forming a canopy overhead were denser than ever. The waterway was so calm the only ripples were coming from water boatmen skimming along its surface. Yet the log was clearly jolting. And there was something else, a muffled yet insistent noise above the soporific gurgling. Then a furious snarl lacerated the tranquil atmosphere. His heart leapt.

Twisting his stiff torso around with considerable effort, his eyes whitened. A huge dog was swimming alongside, thrusting its jaws at the bark. From the wake churning behind, Angwen guessed there was another taking up the rear. He appreciated there were feral beasts roaming these forests, but when a head thrashed above the surface he noticed a leather collar, encrusted with polished metal studs. These were war dogs. With that realisation his heart sank. He scanned the riverbanks for any sign of their masters.

Something flashed through the air, clattering onto the log. He saw the grappling hook, a grubby rope tightening. Presently men with unkempt blond hair materialised among the bracken on both sides. Angwen's body quivered. Had he enough wits to remember the appropriate spell that might cause a diversion, he doubted it would be potent enough to last. As the log was hauled towards the banks, he gazed up into a youthful face, given the illusion of maturity by a straggly beard, fingers grasping an axe. Angwen focussed on the boy's calm expression before he raised the weapon; flipping the blade towards himself he brought the shaft crashing into the Celt's forehead.

* * *

Angwen came to, discovering himself naked, wrists and ankles secured by ropes. Blood had matted to his face and his head was pulverised with pain. Realising he had awoken, a warrior approached. The elderly man had no fight left in him; certainly no magic to salvage the situation. But the armed man still approached him with caution, aware that while he might have been ancient and apparently defenceless, there was also a strong likelihood this solitary evacuee was a druid.

Turning to other Angles watching from a distance, the soldier barked in his own tongue. A female emerged from the throng, her lustrous hair tied in extravagant pleats. Tall and curvaceous, she wielded a twisted cane. Despite her tender years Angwen sensed this woman possessed a modicum of shamanistic ability. But he was more aware of his nudity and squirmed self-consciously as she approached.

"Old man. Your tongue I speak. Once I sailed the coastlines of Europe with my father, trade in many things. We visit Celts of Brittany, we barter for weapons. They spoke like you savages. What is your name, druid?"

"Angwen."

"Angwen. Hild of the North Folk am I, daughter of Linn, king of East Anglia. We know of a village, deep in these forests, a hideout for the enemy. Foolish are they. They do not run, nor surrender … they stand … their new masters they fight. Know you of this village?"

"I don't. My own village is far. My people set me adrift, thinking I would have a better chance of escaping. If there are Britons defying you, I hope they create many English orphans."

"Such anger from old man. *If* there are Britons? Britons, there are. We know about their forest stronghold for time. They raid our positions then vanish to the trees ... like mist. When patrols search, never come back. I need to know where village is. A local druid you are, so you must know this. You give me the secret?"

"If I knew, you would be the *last* person on Earth I would share with this."

"I think we persuade you."

"I won't be wasting any more breath on you."

Hild flicked a glance over her shoulder, snapping her fingers. Two soldiers stomped towards her, dragging something through the undergrowth. Whatever it was, it was struggling, making whimpering noises. One of the guards launched a ferocious kick at whatever was being hauled. A muffled scream was cut short by another heavy booted stomp.

"On your feet, you fucking Brit bitch!" the protagonist snapped, tugging at the thick leash. The other end was wrapped around the neck of a slender girl. As she tried standing, her legs wobbled. The gag that was thrust inside her mouth reduced her cries and sobs to pitiful sounds more reminiscent of a cat. Her legs looked to be on the verge of giving way again; her guard seized her long hair and kept her pinned there, forcing her head right back.

Angwen struggled to his own feet, his manacled hands covering his crotch but a modicum of strength returning to his stature. He stared at the other prisoner. "Keelin? Is that you?"

An almost imperceptible squeak emanated from her. The warrior pulled her hair even tighter, his knuckles whitening.

"What have these unspeakable barbarians done to you?"

The other guard's gums drew back in a horrid grin. He drew his tongue across his lips then stroked the youngster's backside.

"You *bastards*!"

"I thought you not wasting breaths, druid?"

"She is only a child! Have you none your own, German? Have mercy on her. Take my life, if you must, but please spare the girl."

Hild gazed at him scornfully. "I have four. We Angles many children, for next generation of warriors. I think ... Keelin ... one of eighteen teenage girls we keep alive after last village we torched ... is not a child."

"She most certainly *is*. I was present at her birth. Thirteen summers ago."

"I don't see Celtic *children* ... only *rats*. They are vermin who infest our new country."

"Bastards!"

"Perhaps not rats. *Pets*. Yes. These Celtic beauties now *playthings* for our young warriors. Their bastards will join our armies." She nodded towards the girl's captors. The one who had smoothed the prisoner's rear now used that hand to draw a dagger from his belt. He placed this at the youngster's throat.

"This plaything has been over used. She has difficulty walking."

With that remark an ugly sniggering filtered through the assembly of warriors.

"Hild?" implored Angwen. "You are a mother ... you must have a heart? Please, spare the girl. I know where there is a vast deposit of gold and jewels, the produce of many years gathering from decaying Roman towns by our villagers. I know where it is stashed, deep in the forests. I'll tell you exactly where to find this treasure. If you let Keelin go."

"One piece of information to release her, druid."

"I'll even lead you to this Roman treasure myself, though my bones are old and weary."

"I do not give two fucks about Roman trinkets. I want to know where is hideout. Tell me and I spare girl. We will put you both in your log again."

Tears flowed down Angwen's cheeks. "Thank you, Hild. You *do* have a heart."

"I have heart, but not patience. Location of village?"

Angwen's glance darted towards Keelin, whose eyes were wide, beseeching him not to reveal this information. When she shook her head vehemently the guard clutching the long, dank strands merely hauled her scalp even further backwards, so she ended up staring into the tree canopy.

"The quickest way is to follow the course of the river where your men found me, back upstream. After about four miles you'll come across a small tributary. It is hard to spot, but an immense oak tree highlights its position. This was used by my brethren to execute criminals in our ranks, especially those who violated our women and children." At that remark he allowed his gaze to pointedly take in the surrounding warriors. "This macabre signpost should strike a chord with you English."

"To point!"

"The oak I'm referring to will be easy enough to locate. The corpse of the last victim of these trials will still be hanging from it, albeit as a carcass stripped of its flesh by crows. There are no other visible paths or clearings that will make your journey straightforward. The undergrowth is harsh, often mile after mile of twisting thorns. The stream eventually cascades over a waterfall into a deep ravine. Dense trees hide the glen below. That is where the village lies."

Hild nodded. "Not so difficult?"

"Might I have some clothes now? And could you remove the gag and shackles from Keelin?"

"Atelic. Bring the girl to me."

Angwen expelled a sigh of relief, sinking to his knees. Where the sun had been striking the grass it created a welcome warm cushion for his trembling knees. "Keelin. I'm just glad I could help."

He regarded the men standing either side of the trembling girl. The one who had been holding a dagger to her throat suddenly drew it across her windpipe, keeping the blade lodged there while blood erupted over his ringed fingers. Staring straight at Angwen he proceeded to jerk his weapon back and forth, sawing through muscle and bone, until he cleaved the girl's head from her neck. When the body fell away, his companion kicked it aside. A scream lodged in the druid's throat as the shock rendered him mute. He focussed on the terror frozen on the girl's face. The thug paced over to Hild and passed her the gruesome trophy. Hild grasped her hair, holding the object at arm's length so the dripping blood missed her boot and splattered over clusters of bluebells.

"Would you like to take Keelin with you, when we set you free?"

"Unspeakable monsters ... unspeakable ..."

"Is that a yes or a no, druid?"

"N-no."

"No, don't want to take her? Or no, don't wish to be set free?"

This female warrior was so many decades younger than him; articulate for a barbarian, yet so pitiless. At that moment he realised hope was lost and he had witnessed far too much cruelty than his ageing mind could bear. Closing his eyes, he willed some long-forgotten druidic words to flow back to his feeble mind. He felt the touch of a blade against his own throat. Phrases began drifting from his sub-conscious, verses that slowly began slotting into position. The blade dug in, sharper; the evolving pain felt like the sunlight was striking a single point around his Adam's Apple. The English bitch was deliberately prolonging the moment. This had the effect of sharpening his resolve, focussing his recall. The lines of the spell altered from vague hints to words he instinctively recognised. The blade was piercing his skin, probing relentlessly. He felt his blood trickling, slithering around his skin in warm trails. Still he concentrated. Now he began reciting the words.

"Too late for prayers, old rat."

Hild thrust her knife deeper into his throat, hacking into his windpipe, vigorously enough to sever flesh and muscle, but deliberately maintaining control of the motion, allowing her victim to keep breathing for as long as possible. Angwen found a smile creasing his lips as her sadism granted him time to conclude the ancient spell.

"What the fuck is funny, druid?" She increased the pressure, slicing through the spinal chord. She grinned when the

Celt's body flopped to the ground. "Did we all hear the old fool's ramblings? Pass the word. Seek out this hanging tree."

"What shall we do with the savages, my thane?" asked Atelic, lifting the druid's head as casually as if it was some large vegetable destined for a cooking pot.

"The druid wanted to be with her, didn't he? Stick them side-by-side on poles, near the entrance to our fortress. They can replace the pair that have been there for several weeks now. They're starting to really stink." Gazing at her underling, she was struck by how distracted he had become. "Well, Atelic? I presume you value you *own* head enough that you'll obey my orders with a bit more urgency?"

His eyes were staring at the ground next to her. Her rising indignation gave way to curiosity when something began caressing her bare calf, just above the fur-trimmed rim of her boot. Glancing down, her expression altered from irritation to terror. She was aware of Atelic backing off, dropping the druid's head.

Curling around her leg, slithering in methodical circles, was a snake. Although it was striped like an adder, its scale was grotesque, extending some thirty feet, resembling creatures she had once seen in a Roman fresco. Transfixed with horror, Hild moved tentatively, lest she provoke it. Atelic summoned more resolve and waved his bloodied blade at the monstrous beast. Fixing him with pitiless red eyes, it lunged its massive fangs, the movement occurring within the blink of an eye. Atelic staggered backwards, blood oozing from twin points at his neck. Hild watched him writhing and convulsing, his flesh transforming to deep purple, foam erupting from his mouth to gag his shrieking death throes.

Hild gripped her own knife and made to jab at the creature's head. But it merely wrapped itself tighter around her leg and torso. Eyes bulging from their sockets, she stared around the clearing. The others had fled, abandoning her to her fate. The pressure continued, equally as methodically as when she had been administered the *coup de grâce* to the druid. Only then did it truly occur to her that this snake was not native to these conquered lands and could only have emanated from the medicine man's latent powers: powers he had only summoned the strength to exert with her extreme provocation.

The grip tightened at her neck until she found it difficult to inhale. The fantastical reptile had dragged her down until she was prostrate on the forest floor. In this position her vision centred on the druid's lifeless form. Remorselessly the creature he had conjured positioned itself so its huge head was edging ever closer to hers. Its massive forked tongue flickered, darting out to lick her cheeks, leaving a foetid trail. When the snake released pressure, allowing her to snatch a breath, she was engulfed by the realisation of the true horror about to unfold. As she was hauled ever closer towards that widening maw, dripping with green mucus and blood, its rancid breath distracted her from the agony of her splintering ribs. Angwen's serpent began the painstaking process of swallowing her alive.

CHAPTER THIRTY-EIGHT

Parting the branches, Fia observed a trio of swans soaring above the meadows, following the course of the Thames towards the salt marshes many miles to the east. "Such beautiful creatures they are." Directly below the majestic birds, the morning sunlight glinted from helms and sharpened blades. "Such evil creatures." Easing the foliage back into position, she turned to her comrades-in-arms. "The Angle warband numbers four hundred. Not the usual slavers and their henchmen, either."

"Those oafs are usually too drunk on plundered mead to make an entertaining fight," a voice sneered from higher in the tree. "They assume Britons are all as docile as the ones they keep as slaves."

Fia sought her sword's pommel. "These are battle-hardened men, among them housecarls of Linn of the North Folk. Their blades are crusted with blood after years of driving Vikings from the coast."

"And razing British villages." The female voice came from behind: Aerona, her features caked black with mud, her knuckles tight around her bow. Fia's smile flashed beneath her own warpaint. The girl liberated from the English overseer had been an eager recruit to her fighters. Having been a hunter of wildfowl, Aerona was an adept archer and Fia had no doubt the youth would be equally skilled at felling larger targets. "They assume their numbers will make us easy prey," added the youngster.

Fia nodded. "Their thanes will be boasting of the one-sided battle awaiting them in these trees."

"English dogs," chipped in another concealed lookout. "They'll already be licking their lips in anticipation of the mead they will be downing tonight to toast their great victory,"

"And the prisoners they will either slaughter, enslave or fuck." Fia cupped her hands and approximated a jackdaw's hoarse cry. This was echoed by the others clambering from their viewpoints.

Moving fluidly through the dense woods, their noses eventually picked up the stink of the corpse hanging from the oak. Here their progress was improved: for several days beforehand an advance party of pioneers had painstakingly worked through the thorns clogging the riverbanks, hacking a path towards the waterfall, maintaining stealth by slicing through the dense vegetation with knives rather than axes. Fia's patrols had observed them the whole time, sometimes lurking in undergrowth mere yards distant. Although this activity had indicated the enemy had discovered the location of the Celtic retreat, undoubtedly by torture, Fia had ordered no enemy lives were to be taken. She had wanted their trail unimpeded so that as many English warriors as possible could make their way towards the point where battle would commence.

* * *

The vanguard arrived at the gully, their scouts surveying the falls plunging hundreds of feet. The ravine was sheer, its sides glistening with precipitation. But Angles had fought in similar terrain for centuries. How else had their forefathers destroyed the Roman legions that had trespassed into their forest realm in Germania?

The thane leading the assault, Ro, was tall and muscular, known for his rapacious taste for native girls. But he also relished despatching their menfolk. Peering through the tree canopy, he sniffed, anticipating the smoke from campfires. There were none. "If it turns out the druid lied about this hideout, I'll have the heads of all the Brits in our slave compound," he growled.

Another soldier crouched. "If they *are* down there, my thane, there will be no escape. The housecarls have formed a wide circle, out in the trees, surrounding all possible escape routes."

"Like hunting wild boar armed with swords rather than tusks! Except they will be much slower when cornered. The only issue now is climbing down. Fetch the ropes. When we have dropped enough men into this fucking hole, we'll scatter these Celtic bastards like foxes invading a coop!"

A young warrior strode over. "Sire. Some good news."

"What is it?"

"I can show you."

Ro followed, irritated at the interruption but confident he would not have been lightly troubled. The lad hunkered down, grasping at ivy flowing over the lip of the ravine.

"Well?"

"Look at this, sire."

As the leaves were parted, Ro studied the wiry entanglement. At first he could see nothing, but not wishing to appear foolish before his men he squinted. There. The ivy was concealing steps. Ro followed their direction. Perfectly carved from the limestone rockface they marched downwards, disappearing from sight beyond further curtains of clinging leaves. Ro placed his weight onto the first step, averting his eyes from the sheer drop. He crept further on, easing his way past the verdant walls screening this passageway from above. Pausing to examine the extent of the stairwell, he about turned. "This path will lead us all the way to our quarry. My dick senses plenty of Celtic strumpets waiting for us all." Ro sprang back to the top. "Here, boy. Now."

The warrior approached warily. Ro slapped him across his shoulder blades; although the lad winced with pain he appreciated the honour of being singled-out for the thane's jovial violence. "My boy, your eagle eyes have swung the battle even more in our favour. All we have to do is stroll down to the natives. You will have your choice of their maidens tonight, I promise you." More generally, he bragged: "The British encampment is within our grasp. I want all their males mutilated, and all their women stripped, bound and brought before me before any of the housecarls take their pick. I will have first choice." He unsheathed his sword, raising it high. "But there will be enough prime British cunt to go around. There's nothing worse than having to queue for a fuck when we overrun their villages. Angles. Forward."

Ro clambered onto the first step, swiftly finding his stride. His men followed, their zeal for the impending slaughter and rape translating into barely-suppressed growls. After several minutes progress, the thane peered back over his shoulder, estimating close to a hundred Angle warriors were negotiating this shortcut. Facing the front, his eyes noted the staircase alighting on a pathway of scree that wound into the trees, its stones recently disturbed.

"Look below, lads," he derided. "See how they have been scurrying to and from their lair, these Celtic rats."

When he spat out the final syllable, a disturbed woodpigeon flapped overhead. Startled himself, he tracked the grey shape melting into the canopy. Moments of tense anticipation followed as his soldiers waited for him to continue.

Aerona heard the bird, but her attention remained riveted to the brash Englishman resuming his hike, his muscles tautening when he arrived at the final step. Here he paused, preparing to launch himself to ground level. Aerona primed her weapon, drawing the string. The moment the chieftain threw himself forward her fingers parted. Judging his motion to perfection, her arrow whistled, striking between the eyes, sending his lifeless body crashing to the shingle. This incited a hail of arrows, aimed with similarly devastating precision. Bodies collided as the lethal archery instigated a human avalanche. Warriors either sprawled over the stair or were pitched into oblivion, and shrieks echoed around the chasm. For those cowering from the arrows, there was nowhere to hide. The steps were awash with blood. Boots slithered uselessly while struggling back up the stairwell, only to be blocked by packed bodies being driven forward by the momentum of the advance. The arrows continued until the last Angle standing threw his sword aside. Aerona transformed his pleas for mercy into a squeal with an arrow to his crotch then silenced him with another to his forehead.

"Good shooting, Aerona," Fia noted. "None remain on the stairs. But there are still scores at the lip of the canyon, near the point where I tugged aside enough ivy for the fools to see the steps, and many hundred mustering beyond. They must also be welcomed to our forest domain. Aerona, stay here and guard the stairs."

Fia beckoned her warriors to follow her away from the carnage. Skirting the Celtic encampment's timber ramparts, they dipped through a sea of ferns until they had arrived at the foot of the ravine, fifty yards from the limestone steps. Here a fissure in the rocks allowed enough room for a supple body to enter. Fia eased her way through. Thirty feet inside, the crevice funnelled into a wider tunnel. After a brisk ascent, slushing through a subterranean stream, the tunnel opened into a large cavern. Fia listened to her comrades following as she climbed higher, her boots seeking the well-worn holds in the rockface. Within ten minutes the patrol had reached the narrow chimney dappled by daylight.

Easing outside, Fia crawled through the sedge until she could make out shifting helms. Dismissing them, her eyes scanned the undergrowth until she came across the brushwood that had been meticulously woven around the shrubs. Another Silures fighter squirmed alongside. Fia slapped his shoulderblades and he sped on. While he began striking a flint against stone, Fia and the others masked the sound with jackdaw cries. There were sparks, a flash, and then the kindling caught alight. Voracious flames engulfed the tinder snaking around the perimeter of the gorge; within minutes vast plumes of smoke were billowing over the men poised at the cliffs.

* * *

The housecarls had listened to the familiar sounds of a furious battle ensuing but could only toy impatiently with their weapons. Linn had issued strict orders for them to hold the line.

"Steady, lads," barked their sergeant: a squat thug, one eye bruised from an encounter with an annoyingly resistant slave girl. "Plenty fuckin' blueskin cunts will be headin' this way ... any fuckin' minute by sounds o' it ... great sport it'll be ... makin' my dick fatter just fuckin' thinkin' about choppin' the cunts with us blades." Confirming his loathing of their prey, he hacked and gobbed onto a tree bark.

Fia heard the rasping English voice and although the words meant nothing, she deciphered its contempt. Gazing to the treetops, she puckered her lips and whistled the triplet cry of a Long Tailed Tit. The responses sounded around a wide circuit.

The housecarls shifted nervously, the sergeant scanning the foliage. "Wish them fuckin' birds would shut the fuck up. They's doin' me fuckin' head in."

* * *

Smoke flowed over the Angle warband, blotting out the meagre daylight filtering through the forest canopy. Beyond, the scrub crackled, and flames cast a sinister glow. Eyes bulging, the soldiers bunched into an ever-tightening scrum. When some tried forcing a path through the conflagration, they were forced back, their comrades having to beat at their tabards. Others scampered down the stairwell, only to be slaughtered by arrows immediately. In-between coughing and spluttering, scores of men were now howling in terror. Enveloped by black fumes, knots of the English warriors found themselves hemmed at the edge of the void. Panic surged through the ranks, the men ebbing and flowing like a human current. There were screams as the ground suddenly yawned beneath boots that kicked desperately at thin air before bones smashed into the base of the ravine, or crumpled against the walls as they plummeted.

Dozens more Celts had taken the secret passageway to this level. Camouflaged figures continually emerged from strategic gaps among the dried branches, bludgeoning blinded Englishmen before vanishing. The repeated onslaughts left twitching mounds of corpses. After each attack an eerie silence descended. Breathing harshly, the Angles scanned the smoke, imaging thousands of enemies on all sides. Periodically, Celts hurtled through this wilderness, features daubed with mud, limbs mottled with blue woad, bellowing blood-curdling gibes. To the hapless defenders these antagonists were indeed wraiths, and the stories about this haunted forest had proved to be all too true.

There were cries of a path discovered through the inferno. The survivors of the depleted English warband scattered, tossing weapons away. The undergrowth hindered their sluggish stampede, while the Celts persisted with targeted strikes, funnelling their enemies towards another precipice. Here the forest floor suddenly gave way, loosely bunched branches collapsing beneath heavy boots, pitching men into a pit lined with timber spikes. Pitiful stragglers blundered beyond these traps, until light began filtering from the forest edge. There was a sense of relief, for they also knew the housecarls' ring of steel would be a matter of yards ahead.

Thirty-three Angles halted. Before them, a Celtic warrior stood brazenly, next to butchered housecarls whose arrow-ridden bodies had been piled high. Removing her helm, her chestnut hair cascaded over the shoulders of her bloodied mail. Between vivid stripes of woad, her eyes blazed hatred.

The nearest swordsmen summoned their final reserves of energy and charged, determined to hack her out of the way so they could break out of these cursed woods. Fia waited until they were ten feet away, then leapt upwards, seizing a branch, levering her body into a large beech. The moment she had vanished from sight, scores of archers sprung into view from where they had been skulking behind bushes, their arrows scything into flesh.

CHAPTER THIRTY-NINE

His eyes intent on the ominous shape, Wacian's knuckles whitened around his spear shaft. "We have him cornered," he thundered.

When one of his men swept a torch, eyes flared in the undergrowth. "It looks like we've trapped a devil," he gasped, his breath wheezing after the frantic chase.

Wacian scowled, but as he grew accustomed to the murk he received a clearer impression of the darker bulk shifting among the shadows. They had spent many hours stalking this gargantuan boar. Several times it had doubled back, turning on its pursuers, transforming hunters to hunted. Its razor-sharp tusks had eviscerated three of his finest fighting men, leaving them screaming on the forest floor. But the ebb and flow of the long night's dogged hunt had eventually gone in their favour; a dozen arrows had embedded in the monster's shanks, sapping it of strength. Now, with less than an hour until daybreak, it had stumbled into a bog.

His boots testing the springy turf, Wacian raised his weapon. "A devil? No, lad. A hairy pig, nothing more. And soon to be sliced up to break our fasts." Fixing the animal's gleaming yellow orbs in his sights, an urgent roar escaped his barrel-like diaphragm. His javelin hissed through the air, piercing the huge skull between those terrible eyes. The spasm that coursed through its powerful muscles brought blossom cascading like snow from overhanging branches.

"He will feed us for days," Wacian concluded. "Now. Strap him to poles, take him back to the village. Wyot the butcher will have his work cut out."

* * *

The Jute hunting party tramped through the woods in an extended column, Wacian striding at its head. Always puffed-up with self-importance, his slaying of the ferocious boar, and the thought of adulation and a mead-soaked feast sent him swaggering onwards. His russet locks flowed as he swigged cider from an ox horn.

Behind him, four bearers struggled with the immense carcass. Between mouthfuls of his beloved sweet alcohol he would swivel round to marvel at his prize, before nagging the carriers to keep up. When he arrived at the point where patrols normally crossed a winding river by a ford, the chieftain lifted his right hand. "Stop, lads." He scrutinised the glade on the far side, where the shadows beneath the oaks and ashes were fading with the dawn. "Where the fuck are the sentries? I expected to be sharing news of our success with someone from the village by now."

Thrusting the horn into his belt, he drew his sword from its scabbard. Pacing down the narrow embankment, he pitched into the ice-cold shallows. Although he could feel sizeable fish slithering by, he paid scant attention. He was intent on what might have drawn the sentries back to the village. There had been no hostile Celts this far south for decades, but a constant threat came from further afield. Ever more frequently were Norse warships plundering English settlements on the eastern and southern seaboards. Marauders had attacked the Isle of Wight twice in recent months, and repelling them had cost many of his bravest warriors.

"My thane. The river!"

He had been listening keenly, anticipating the piercing horn blasts that would signal the sighting of longships on the horizon. Instead he considered the creatures bumping against his shins. "Its waters are fair swollen with fish. Had we not already captured the boar, the river could have provided a fine harvest." He dragged his attention from the distant treeline. But it took further seconds before his immediate surroundings made sense. The flowing water was stained red, as if he was wading through blood. He felt more slithering fish, invisible in the crimson gloom. There was a flicker of movement closer to the surface, white flesh darting by. Then a human hand materialised down there, momentarily latching onto his right leg. "What the fuck?!" Rooted to the spot, he stared down, expecting the fingers to grip tighter. As quickly as it had inexplicably appeared, the mysterious hand vanished.

"Thane? What do you see?"

"I thought there was someone ... someone in the water."

"There!" proclaimed one of his bodyguards, Wulfric, jerking his sword tip towards the river. "And there!"

"What the fuck do you see, Wulfric?"

"There *are* people in the water, my lord. Look!"

Wacian's eyes roved over the torrents. Every so often there would be a glimpse of pale objects emerging from the red waters before sinking again. There was another hand, then what resembled ragged sackcloth: flesh serrated from an upper arm, unfurling in the meagre daylight. The sight of a severed child's head, the terror of her demise etched into her delicate features, finally spurned Wacian into action.

"There has been slaughter upstream. The village has been attacked. With me."

The boar was unceremoniously dumped by the wayside. Swords were drawn, and the hunting party plunged down the embankment, splashing over the crossing, weapons glinting against the pale light filtering through the foliage. As they weaved between trees and vaulted over storm-blasted trunks, droplets of rain began providing muted background percussion. By the time they were nearing the edge of the woods, the cloudburst had gathered strength, and lashing rainfall had transformed day to night again.

Wacian led the way, instinctively following the trail back towards their homes. Heart hammering in his chest, he anticipated the clashing of arms and the roars of battle. Instead an eerie tranquillity hung over the huts looming through the downpour. Wacian gestured for his men to fan out on either side, this pincer formation swiftly encircling the homesteads. The chieftain crouched, eyes darting left and right, poised for the first screaming Norseman to lunge from the gloom.

"Thane. Quickly."

Creeping by the blacksmith's forge, Wacian noted tools scattered over the ground. The voice had carried from the far side of the clustered huts. "Quickly!" it pleaded again, and he registered the despair. Halting, he swept his sword behind, lest enemies were skulking close by. All he could see were empty huts, rain cascading from their roofs to sluice into puddles. Rounding a corner, he could make out a knot of his warriors in the distance, silhouetted against the storm, their sodden capes and furs clinging to their bodies. The closer he drew, he realised they were staring intently at the ground. So many questions demanded answers.

"What the *fuck* is going on? Has there been a raid? Where the fuck *is* everyone? Well? What have you found?"

Further words lodged in his throat. When he drew level, he discovered several of his battle-hardened soldiers spewing into the swirling mud. His wavering eyes sought the source of their alarm. Here was a pile of human corpses. But the swordsmen who had slain the villagers had done so with such unremitting savagery that no single body had been left intact. The aftermath of this one-sided butchery was random anatomy: heads, feet, fingers, forearm stumps, torsos, rib cages and scalps, clustered in an unearthly heap. Viscera slithered among the tissue and bones, pooling beneath nightmarish lumps of meat mutilated beyond recognition. Although diluted by the elements, gallons of blood meandered towards the river that skirted the village.

"My lord."

Wacian followed the direction of Wulfric's stabbing finger. A figure was emerging hesitantly from the treeline, pallid as a ghost. "Survivors?" the thane choked. "Praise the gods."

Wulfric recognised his wife, Milburga. She stumbled, barely managing to right herself. Immediately he sheathed his sword and ran to her, locking her in a furious embrace. "What happened, wife? How many Norse longboats? Why did the sentries not sound the alarm? How many escaped into the woods?"

Wacian stepped over, prising Wulfric away from her. Shock had rendered her expressionless. The chieftain gripped her shoulders and gazed into her dull eyes. "Milburga ... *Milburga*. None of us has ever witnessed such bloodshed. How many Norse overpowered the sentries, then marched everyone here to be massacred in such a way?"

Her eyes wavered into his, creases forming in her forehead. With an effort, a whisper escaped her lips. "*One.*"

"What?" Wacian's incredulous tone echoed. "*One* warrior did all this?"

The thane had to concentrate to take in her tentative reply. "After the sun had gone ... he came from the shore ... he ... he appeared from the shadows ... no soldiers could withstand him ... during the fighting, a few of us managed to slip into the woods with Judd ... we thought the enemy would surely follow."

"You make no sense, wife," Wulfric berated her.

"*Quiet*, Wulfric," Wacian admonished. "Take your time, Milburga. What do you mean *one* warrior crept ashore ... one warrior did all *this*?"

Milburga's eyes began wavering, the lashes fluttering like moths before a flame. She swooned into Wulfric's arms. She struggled to speak, so Wulfric leant closer, pressing his ear to her quivering lips. His forehead furrowed.

"Take her inside, Wulfric," said Wacian. "She needs rest. But what did she say to you?"

"She makes no sense."

"What the fuck did she say, Wulfric?"

"She said it wasn't a warrior."

"What then?"

"She said ... a *wolf*."

CHAPTER FORTY

All were hooked on the shaman's words. Despite his lank white hair and sinewy frame, his voice was strident, and as he considered the flames his eyes glared chillingly red. "The battle in the haunted forest is like a storm. The sky darkens. Arrows fall like rain. The ground thunders with charging warriors ... then warriors scream, their boots sliding through the swill of blood and entrails ... then warriors die. The *aftermath* is a terrible limbo, belonging to those who are neither living *nor* dead. The air becomes thick with the cries of these *almost* dead: the damaged, the maimed, the mortally wounded, writhing on the ground, clutching at wounds, wailing dementedly, begging to be released from the misery of this limbo so they can join their fallen comrades around Tiw's feast table ... so much screaming ... *screaming*. But after *this* battle in the heart of the haunted forest there are no *almost* dead. Aside from the cawing of the crows mustering on treetops, preparing to feed on rotting flesh, there are no human sounds. The reason? There *are* no wounded, no *almost* dead warriors. Only *dead* warriors."

Paega opened his eyes and drew them from the flames where he had so clearly witnessed the slaughter. As ever, the vision had left him drained of energy. Inside the cavernous hall, the fire cast shadows that danced across the crossbeams. Plumes of smoke drifted around the central vent, black and threatening as an imminent blizzard.

Upwards of fifty chieftains and their escorts were mustered. For days prior to this gathering, messengers had been criss-crossing the English kingdoms to arrange this rare council. Although historically the fraught relationships between Angles, Saxons and Jutes had frequently spiralled into bloodletting, kings and eorls were honour-bound to invite their thanes to muster warbands to support rivals in times of common danger. This was an ancient Germanic tradition, known as a blood truce. The thanes who had ridden into the East Anglian capital of Elmham represented West, East and South Saxons, Jutes of Wight and Kent, North Humberland Angles, Middle English and Mercians.

English towns, villages and farming communities were flourishing throughout the east and south of the island. But stories were spreading about wild Celtic clans sheltering in the vast forests in the hinterland, hindering any attempts to settle there. Whenever Englishmen attempted hacking a path into the dense woodland to make way for villages, savages in blue warpaint would attack. Repeated guerrilla attacks were being launched from the forest's impenetrable depths, their targets spanning an ever-widening perimeter. The very nature of these lightning strikes – the sacking of settlements, the razing of crops, the routing of slave convoys – meant the true numbers of the enemy was open to conjecture. Some argued thousands of native Celts were holding out among the square miles of trees. Others claimed mere hundreds was a truer reckoning: was it not equally likely the insurgency might be centred on a single warlike clan? One thing was certain. Whenever English warriors entered the forest in numbers, they did not return.

Because the Germanic tribes had grown used to vanquishing Britons, myths began to spread. Chieftains refused to accept mere British warriors were defeating their men: surely their druids had raised the dead. In time these vast tracts of hostile woodland came to be known as the haunted forest. The recent annihilation of an Angle warband had fuelled this illusion. No English settler would be safe until a blood truce had been called, and the forest clans destroyed, whether supernatural or not.

Paega sat down again. Many of the warriors present regarded this particular shaman with suspicion, pondering the significance of the weird trinkets he draped around his neck. But his thane seated beside him, Cyneheard of the West Saxons, was highly respected. Cyneheard stood, thrusting his chair backwards. Background murmuring ceased. "What Paega saw in his mind's eye occurred two moons ago. Simply sending in further patrols to root out these devils will do no good at all."

"We should forget about the haunted forest!" a voice clamoured from the throng. "We can't defeat the undead. The Celts of the forest have powers we can scarcely imagine!"

Cyneheard glowered over the sea of helmets, throwing his arms into the air. "Nonsense! Since crossing the River Stour this morning and entering the realm of the East Anglians, my tribe's shaman, Paega, has spent some time receiving visions. He has assured me there are no druids among the natives hiding in the great forest, only a few Celts. Plucky fighters, yes, but vastly outnumbered. I appreciate the trees in the forest are dense, the terrain wild and inhospitable. And the natives know every inch of ground, every glade and clearing. But there are no demons facing us.

However, the enemy can set ambushes as effortlessly as breathing. There have now been two incursions by my Angle brethren, and one by a warband of East Saxons. Those brave men now dine with Tiw. These Brit bastards continue harassing farmers and slavers using the Roman roads nearest their forest. They pillage at will, help themselves to livestock. They free prisoners. And butcher the gaolers. This has become a matter of honour. We might have established strong kingdoms on this island, but the fact even one village remains holding out against the new rulers is untenable. Aside from the forest being a safe haven for Celtic raiding parties, the very existence of these renegades will become symbolic for those who would wish to fight back against the occupation. This forest stronghold is a poisonous wound. It must be amputated before the disease spreads.

In order to overcome these defiant curs, separate war parties are, to use a Saxon saying, as much use as farting against the north wind. We need to declare all-out war. This is why eorls and thanes right across the land, of Angles, Saxons and Jutes, have agreed to pool our resources. Rivalries have to be put to one side for the greater good. Before our host, King Linn of the East Anglians, addresses us, I would ask you all to show your respect for his daughter, Hild, who fell in battle at the hands of the accursed natives."

Cyncheard resumed sitting, seizing a wine goblet and quaffing generously. A thunderous tattoo echoed beneath the rafters as pommels rapped against shields, and boots stomped the ground. Rumours of Hild's horrific demise had filtered across the English communities, the details ranging from her having been stabbed in the back by a captured druid, to falling victim to some magical forest entity possessing several heads. Whatever the truth might have been, one aspect many present would agree on was the fact that Celtic magic had played a part.

This was what was truly feared – more so than the guerrillas – although none would admit as much. All these warriors appreciated the cult of the druids had to be stamped out, just as the Romans had once attempted. Only superstition got in the way of a more open discussion of the fact. Some feared to even mention the druids by name, such was their dread of invoking primeval forces. But a more common consensus was that trusting in the ability of swords or axes to split heads was preferable to fretting over isolated displays of sorcery. The tactic had been working well since the first longboats had sailed westwards over the German Sea. English battle prowess would surely prevail.

As the respectful acclaim died, Cyneheard's eyes darted from face to face. For all his defiant rhetoric, this hall remained steeped in suspicion. Eorls and thanes who had ordered the raiding of territories of men standing a matter of yards away on numerous occasions, continued exchanging pleasantries; staring threateningly the moment backs were turned. The assembly's focal point remained the empty seat on the raised dais in the centre of the hall.

After a suitably melodramatic delay, Linn marched through the company, flanked on either side by columns of bodyguards. These warriors wore Roman legionnaire breastplates that had continued to be fastidiously polished; when they passed the fire its great flames reflected through their ranks, as if they were wreathed in flames themselves. The soldiers heading each column were brandishing banners emblazoned with the pouncing red kite of the

North and South Folk of East Anglia, the talons of this bird of prey grasping two white doves.

The Angles claimed more territory than any of their Germanic cousins, having established homesteads for much longer, and had developed an extensive trading network. This meant the kingdom ruled by Linn, together with his cousin Aart's realm of Mercia, his half-brother Eadwulf's North Humberland, and the Middle English territories governed by their cousin Quenna, were also far more affluent. All present could see Linn was immaculately dressed, his blue cloak fastened to his breastplate by an ostentatious jewelled brooch. His torc was gold, and he wore thick bracelets on either wrist. Cyneheard knew full well that Linn's reasons for tackling the Celts had less to do with defending the overall position of the English occupation than maintaining safe passage for Angle traders and slave convoys.

When he stood up, Linn attempted to mask his disdain at these unkempt Saxons and Jutes enjoying the less-prized contents of his wine cellars. He was a wiry man, with a habit of stroking his manicured black beard and toying with his jewellery. He was also known for the way he continually clicked his fingers at underlings to replenish his goblet. His crooked nose, hooded eyes and gaunt cheekbones gave him a cruel appearance. Cyneheard could not fail to notice the resemblance between the Angle chieftain and the hawk adorning his coat of arms.

Acknowledging the greetings, if hardly unanimously delivered, Linn swept his majestic cloak behind him and eased into his chair. Although his guests were waiting for his opening speech, he glowered over his shoulder and grunted to a slave girl. A beautiful Iceni maiden bowed then presented him with a fruit platter. Selecting a pear, he bit into its skin, snapping his fingers at the slave. She immediately presented a cloth for him to dab at the juice trickling into his whiskers. Finally he deigned to acknowledge his guests.

"I thank Cyneheard of Wessex for his kind words about my beloved Hild. May she be enjoying her place at Tiw's banqueting table." Sympathetic murmurs greeted this remark. "I thank you all for respecting the blood truce, and for taking up my invitation to join me here in Elmham. I know it will have been a hard ride for many of you. A lot of the Roman roads are impassable now, especially for those of you who journeyed from the south ... some parties will have had to cut across rough country."

Cyneheard nodded graciously. Sipping wine, he exaggerated a grimace. If Linn was offended by the Saxon's apparent lack of taste, he ignored it for the time being. "To the point. The Britons. These accursed natives cut down too many of our proud footsoldiers. The longer they defy us, the greater the degree of insult. Make no mistake, these cursed dogs will pay. In blood. *Rivers* of blood."

This raised the attention level of many of the otherwise sceptical onlookers. Several enthusiastically struck their shields again.

"Tomorrow night our warbands will congregate by the forest. We will enter then follow the native trails through the trees until we arrive at their hideout in the ravine. Then we lay siege. We will set fire to their homes. We will round them all up. Their heads will decorate the spikes around our homesteads as a warning to any other natives who would defy our might."

The acclaim became widespread. The tumult of weapons smiting shields rose in intensity, thundering around the hall's confines, echoing beneath the wooden beams. A sliver of a smile creased Linn's features. He lifted his goblet towards the Celtic girl who deftly refilled it from a skin. His gaze lingered on her ample cleavage and he licked his lips. Again, he gestured for her to apply the cloth to his face.

Cyneheard gritted his teeth. Linn's enthusiastic rhetoric was clearly at odds with how disinterested he actually was. The king seemed torn between the difficult questions of how many of his young warriors' lives to commit to this bloody campaign, and how much wine to ration himself to if he was to remain capable of satisfying himself with the slave girl later. Cyneheard's misgivings went equally unheeded. The mood was degenerating into warmongering: blood-curdling yells echoed through the hall, and mead was tossed into the air to shower over upturned faces. He faced Paega, shaking his head. "You would think the Brits already defeated."

Paega nodded, but his attention was diverted. Cyneheard faced him. "What is it, Paega?"

"Look, sire. Seems we have a late guest."

The Saxon thane about turned. A heavyset redhaired warrior was barging his way to the front, his gait blundering, his booming belches reeking of mead. Mirth faded in his wake as he elbowed all from his path. Tattoos flourished over his massive upper arms, and his russet beard was cut into forks.

"Wacian", commented Paega. "The Jutish Thane will drink anyone here under the table."

"A champion boar hunter, Paega. And also the biggest drunken bore any of us here is likely to meet."

Once the newcomer had negotiated a prime position before the gathering, he swivelled on his heels, raising both arms high into the air. His right hand clenched a large axe, its blade discoloured with layers of clotting blood. Linn's bodyguards bristled, lifting their own weapons, training them on this usurper whose defiant gesture had drawn a veil of silence over the assembly. All eyes rooted on this menacing intruder.

Linn heaved himself from his seat, his haughty demeanour replaced by red-faced anger. "What do you mean by interrupting my war council when I am still making my introductions? Introduce yourself properly to the company before my bodyguards see to it that your miserable corpse is reduced to crow fodder!"

Instead of replying, the latecomer dismissively flicked his cloak over his shoulder. Caked mud from his horse journey flecked the king's table, adding further degrees of choleric rage to the Angle chieftain's features. Wacian turned to the table immediately to his right, snatching the drinking horn from a flummoxed East Saxon.

"No offence, my friend. You would not begrudge a comrade the chance to wet his throat after a long ride from the south coast? A blood truce is always a fine excuse for the draining of flagons."

The man shook his head, clearly grateful to have been seen as being hospitable, avoiding any need to challenge this character's brazen intimidation. The redhead quaffed generously, swept the back of his hand over his beard then burped like a walrus. "I am Wacian," he proclaimed. "I am of the Jutes."

"We were wondering when you would show up," Linn sneered. "Always with the dramatic entrances."

Ignoring the remark, Wacian repeated. "I am of the Jutes, the first German tribe to settle in Britain. Never forget, all you Saxons and Angles, the Jutes of Wight, the Wihtware, are descended from *foederati*, mercenaries hired by the Romans to guard Britannia's southern coasts against pirates, *centuries* ago, when *your* ancestors were still crawling around in caves in the Harz Mountains." Disapproving growls rose, forcing Wacian to clamour above the din: "The Isle of Wight was the first territory to be seized from the native dogs, long before any Saxons or Angles had plucked up the courage to venture inland. When we conquered the island, slaughtering the Celts we captured, the fortress of Wihtgarabyrig was built on their graves. Jutes have guarded the Solent for decades. Few are the Vikings who dare raid our lands. And the only druids you will come across on the isle are the rotting heads we keep as trophies on spikes."

Wacian's bragging certainly demanded his audience's attention, if not their approval. "I have travelled several days and nights to Elmham. I have questions for you all. First. We have heard much talk of the dangers of the haunted forest, where British demons are supposed to lurk, overcoming any soldiers sent to root them out. We don't even know the strength of this enemy, do we? They strike and then melt into the forest depths, evading our patrols, skulking in the darkness like fucking bats in a cave. But how do we know sending even greater numbers of warriors is the answer? I suggest the more you stoke a fire, the bigger the flames. So let me tell you this, Angles and Saxons. I am not willing to sacrifice *one* Jutish warrior, let alone the several hundred Linn proposes each of us to conscript for his war party."

Throughout the hall, voices raised in anger. But others nodded in agreement, particularly among the Saxons and Kentish

Jutes. If disrespect was being shown to Linn, it was hardly surprising: of all the commanders present he was the least likely to have ever been seen fermenting English unity, unless there was something to be gained for the East Anglians. Squirming in his seat behind Wacian, he could scarcely contain his fury. For several moments he appeared to simmer, the muscles around his neck straining. Finally he erupted. "What *outrage* is this? Are the Wihtware cowards?"

This retort caused the whites of Wacian's eyes to flare. The word was rarely used, unless the person uttering the supreme insult was resigned to backing this up with cold metal. Wacian turned slowly, the remorseless swivel of his muscular frame more menacing than if he had reacted within the blink of an adder's strike.

"Linn, my Angle *friend*." Wacian pronounced the word like a synonym for something he had trod into while exercising his hounds. "If you and your armed toads would care to test my valour, I would willingly step outside, along with any other of your Angles who would care to tag along. But that is a separate matter. All I am saying is this, Linn. I disagree a frontal assault into the heart of a vast forest will work. Consider the Battle of the Teutoburg Forest, when our glorious forefathers ambushed three Roman legions who dared to try and conquer our people." This reference prompted an approving roar to reverberate through the hall.

Linn scowled over the assembly, outraged at the power shift occurring before him. "I recall well the stories of our glorious victory," he agreed, at least acknowledging this historic Germanic triumph. Five centuries before, three heavily armed Roman legions and their auxiliary regiments, amounting to over twenty thousand men, had marched over the Rhine and into the dense Teutoburg realm in a concerted effort to finally subdue the rebellious German tribes. Using their knowledge of the inhospitable terrain, the natives had waited until the Romans were all hacking their way through the undergrowth in a line that drew out for miles and miles, and then launched a series of concerted ambushes. These had continued throughout the long days and dark nights, until the Romans, bewildered and disorientated, had split up in their ever-growing desperation. They had been slaughtered to a man. The victory of the forests had entered Germanic folklore as the defining moment that epitomised their spirited independence. Invoking this feat had been a masterstroke. Wacian had not only demanded the floor from Linn, he now commanded it.

Dejected, Linn sat back down. He attempted to save face. "I'm willing to concede there may be other strategies we should consider. But these Brits must be flushed out or they'll remain a thorn in our side for generations. If not a full frontal assault, what is the alternative, my Jutish friend?"

This time the emphasis on the final word remained literal. The assembled chieftains recognised a thawing in the bristly relationship between the Angle and Jute.

"I was getting to that, Linn, my friend. I have come across a solution that will solve our little problem without the cost of a single English life."

Modig heaved his corpulent frame upright, his one eye focussing on the Jute. "I agree with Wacian. We need not waste any more fighting men on the blueskins. I say we set their haunted forest on fire. It has not rained for some days and the woods will be dry. Flush them out with fire, I say."

Linn looked perplexed. "Modig. The Somorsaetas may have become renowned for their burning down of Celtic villages. But setting the very forest alight? This would be impossible. The trees cover an area that spreads from east to west coasts. Such an inferno would be impossible to control. It could damage as many of our own homesteads."

Wacian shook his head. "I was not thinking of sword or fire to flush out these native rogues."

"What, then?" demanded Linn.

"I was thinking of teeth."

"Teeth?"

"Let us unleash the wolves of hell on these bastards."

The spirit of optimism appeared to fade for a moment. The chieftains glanced at one another nervously, unsure of what to make of this turn of events. Cyneheard caught Paega's eye; a curious look passed between them.

Wacian continued. "My comrades. I think the time has come for my demonstration. Please. Follow me."

After his grandiose statement he paced towards the doorway. The others followed in his wake, like so many incongruously brawny ducklings. In the courtyard outside Linn's headquarters was a large object draped with a woollen blanket. This box shape was resting on a litter that had been pulled by a train of horses. Savouring the theatricality of the moment, Wacian paced around this mysterious item.

"Gather around, please. Gather around. Don't be nervous."

With a sweeping gesture of both hands, he invited his audience to form an orderly circle. The mystery was exacerbated by the uncanny noise filtering from within. It was a low growling, although it was like no wolf or hound that any of the assembly had ever heard before. Or at least, the majority of them. Cyneheard eased his way to the front of the curious throng, dragging Paega alongside. Again, they exchanged sly expressions that betrayed the fact that they were experiencing a hint of *deja vu*.

Linn shuffled his way before the strutting Jutish warrior. "What is this, Wacian? What are you hiding from us? Have the Wihtware bred some particularly bloodthirsty hounds, that will track these Brits to their lair?"

The flippancy in his voice was lost on the rest of the assembly. Wacian did not respond. Instead he turned, lifting his right hand towards the covering. Grasping folds of the cloth in his powerful fist he twisted, and began dragging the blanket away. A wooden cage was revealed. It was fashioned from the thickest oak, in three overlapping rows. Whatever was trapped inside obviously required stringent imprisonment.

Cyneheard noticed Paega stifling a grin. The thane murmured: "'I'll say one thing. The Jutes favour more elaborate cages than we do.'"

Paega sniggered under his breath. If anyone within earshot noticed, this was quickly superseded by Wacian's booming voice:

"Behold, our saviour." Lunging his arms, he tossed the blanket aside. This had the effect of arousing the shadowy mass lurking in the recesses. The cage's inhabitant erupted, issuing a blood-curdling howl. Huge clawed hands grasped the innermost bars, seizing them, attempting to prise them apart. When this failed it snarled, spraying those closest with spittle. Instinctively the spectators drew back.

"What devilment is this, Wacian?" Linn's features crinkled in horror. "Is it a wolf, shaped like a man? Or a man, shaped like a wolf?"

All eyes were rooted on the cage. The Jute chieftain snapped a finger and one of his cohorts shuffled closer, bearing a torch, passing it to him. Wacian held the flames towards the metal enclosure. This sudden spotlighting had the effect of causing the creature inside to growl with renewed savagery. The whole cage shuddered as it forced its full weight against the bars, barging its body against the sides, its talons poking through gaps.

Linn plucked up the courage to stride closer. His bodyguards followed closely, swords drawn. Inside this cage the beast temporarily ceased its demented struggling. Instead it regarded these onlookers with red eyes that smouldered with hatred.

"This," snapped Wacian, his voice gloating, "is a Norse werewolf. A berserker. Wodin's Men, as they call themselves. When the moon is full, their medicine men feed mystical potions to their warriors. This alters their minds until they believe themselves to possess the power and battle savagery of wolves. When the mixture takes full effect, a shapeshifting occurs. The warriors actually change shape and size, transforming into huge wolves ... *werewolves*. I believe this black magic can also turn Viking warriors into bears."

Linn was awestruck. "Where in Tiw's name did you come upon this ... *werewolf*? And how did you capture such a savage monster?"

"A story for you, Linn. But first, more of your fine Anglian mead."

The king clicked his fingers, summoning slaves from the hall. Laden with drinking horns, the Celtic maidens passed them around the company, none daring to cast their eyes in the direction of the mysterious construction. Wacian drained a horn then launched the empty container at the cage. As mead flecked the creature its hairy fists shook the bars.

"At the last full moon, my warriors and I had embarked on a boar hunt. When we returned to our village, we discovered the aftermath of an attack. By a shapeshifter." His melodramatic tones ensured his audience's attention was rapt. "The morning after the raid, we discovered the Viking vessel had run aground, caught in the treacherous currents between the island and The Solent. Its keel had been cleaved in two over submerged rocks. But as my men scoured the shoreline for drowned pirates, they came across one cowering in the brush. His clothing was reduced to rags, but they were dry – it seemed he had not even made it back to the craft. There was blood caked around his mouth. We had come across the fucking shapeshifter ... although with the rising sun, the magic wanes and shapeshifter becomes man again. What we saw before us now was an old man, near naked, shivering with fear. Naturally my men wanted to drag him away and hack him to pieces with their swords, such was the carnage he had inflicted while possessed with the black magic ... but I knew he would be of more use to us alive ... if only for a little while longer. So I summoned my shaman, Judd."

Relishing the extent to which the other chieftains were hanging on his every word, he paused. "Judd is wise, but ancient and virtually blind. Although he accompanied my entourage here, the journey has sapped his strength. He rests."

"Well? What did Judd do ... when you summoned him?" Linn demanded, flexing his fingers with impatience.

"First of all, he cast a basic spell, one that enabled him to communicate with the Viking. Judd asked him if any of the shapeshifting potion was left? At first the cur denied all knowledge of any potion. The cunt just shook his head, cursing Judd with Norse words. So Judd asked if one of my soldiers would fetch a copper bowl from his hut, and if someone else could capture some rats ... alive." Wacian grinned at this, aware of the inquisitive glances darting around. "We produced the rats quicker than the bowl ... so many were skulking around our huts, drawn by the stench of offal, I merely had to cast a basket onto the ground to catch a dozen.

Judd asked my warriors to spreadeagle the Viking, while he placed the bowl on his stomach. Then he asked me to force the rats underneath it. And when Judd snapped his fingers, Wulfric lit a torch then held it to the bowl. That got the rats scrabbling for the nearest exit ... the cunt's guts. Strangely, all the bile seemed to freeze in his throat at that point."

As the audience gasped collectively, Cyneheard raised his brows towards Paega. "By the time the fat drunkard finishes his story, the beast in the cage will have shed its fur again."

Wacian continued. "The Viking was screaming now, begging Judd to remove the rats ... those furiously scratching claws certainly loosened his tongue ... he told Judd what remained of the potion was contained in a phial, hidden in his garments ... Judd groped around in the rags and found the container. The Viking cur now screeched at us to release him. Judd told Wulfric to keep the torch where it was. Of course the rats were soon clawing deeper into flesh and muscle ... I'll wager none of you have ever heard anything like the screams someone makes when rats are burrowing and gnawing their way up through their gullet. After the Viking had breathed his last, Judd took the potion away. He has spent several days analysing its contents ... casting spells that allowed him to decipher the ingredients."

Linn smacked his palms together. "By the beard of Tiw! Has Judd uncovered the shapeshifting secrets?"

"He has been accumulating all the necessary ingredients. I believe the recipe is almost within his grasp."

"What of the potion recovered from the Viking?"

"Enough for two more transformations, Linn."

"Who lurks in the cage, Wacian?"

"Among the flotsam and broken timbers from the longboat, my men came across several corpses. One of the pirates was still breathing. I pumped at the cur's chest, squeezing The Solent from his lungs. Judd offered him some monkswood soup. He quickly revived. We chained him. We kept him fed and watered. We give him a bed and watched him gain strength. Our special captive accompanied us all the way to Elmham. I locked him inside the cage the moment we arrived outside your great hall, Linn. Then I forced him to take mouthfuls of the elixir, so I could reveal the potency of this black magic to my comrades-in-arms. I fear this Norse scum will be at death's door by the morn."

"You said *two* more transformations, Wacian," Linn pointed out.

"Yes. This first was by way of demonstration. The second will be prior to battle. I'll flush the Celtic dogs out of the forest. *I* will become the next wolf man."

This announcement provoked waves of cheering and shield rattling. Paega leant towards Cyneheard until his gnarled lips were almost brushing his chieftain's ear. "I must compare recipes with my Jutish friend, Judd."

"Please do," Cyneheard whispered. "The ability to shapeshift is such a potent weapon. Presuming Judd does manage to uncover the potion's secrets, Wacian will want to share them with all present at the blood truce ... so the Brits can be consigned to history, just like the Romans."

CHAPTER FORTY-ONE

Wacian glowered into the cage. For all the alarming baying and snarling that had carried across the encampment throughout the night, and the fierce clawing that had left the wooden bars raked with marks, the naked figure revealed by the dawn light was indeed a pathetic specimen. The ancient man had curled into a foetal ball, his gnarled knees tucked beneath his wizened chin. A rancid puddle of liquefied shit rippling beneath his quivering form completed his degradation.

"Your dark powers have drained you, Norseman. And you are a wolf warrior no more." Wacian growled. Turning to the soldier behind him, the thane snapped his fingers. "Tolan, your spear."

The younger warrior handed the shaft towards him. Wacian swung the tip to eye-level, then fed its lethal point between the bars. The Norseman cowered, too weak to skulk out of the way, his wild eyes fixating on the metal barb homing in on his flank. When the tip finally touched his skin, puckering the flesh, he winced. Wacian smacked his lips together and grunted, forcing more of his weight against the obstruction. He was aware of others making their way over to the cage to observe this sport. There were cries of encouragement.

"Come on, Viking. Fight back, you old cunt!"

"I'd heard you were pirates and cutthroats. Your longships are feared from the Baltic Sea to the edge of the world! Instead you squeal like a little girl."

An ugly grin creased Wacian's features. Gritting his teeth, he thrust the spear deeper still, watching with malevolent satisfaction as blood oozed from the wound, running down the wretch's white flesh to mingle with the excrement. His victim's lips opened and shut dumbly as a fish, while his eyes wavered towards the clouds. Wacian forced the weapon onwards until the metal tip was buried in flesh. Now the momentum of the thrusting spear heaved the Norseman from his position on the floor of the case, prising him off the ground, until he was impaled against the cage's bars on the far side. Wacian held him there, studying the spasms coursing through his dying body.

"Tolan. I'm tired of this. I have a thirst to quench. Finish him." Wacian relinquished the weapon.

His underling stepped forward and accepted the wooden shaft, puffing as he exerted pressure against the violently twitching body. "He wriggles like a stuck boar!"

Wacian nodded grimly. "Where is Judd?"

"He breaks his fast in his tent, sire," Tolan gasped, sweat trickling beneath his lank fringe as he jerked the spear backwards and forwards, until a purple balloon of guts slithered from the fissure like some horrid eel.

"Fucking hell," Wacian concluded. "It worries me to think I may end up drained of my life force like this poor Norse cunt. But I swore to the other chieftains I would take the last of the potion. I will fight against the wolf magic when my time comes to face the morning after."

CHAPTER FORTY-TWO

Wacian smelled his destination long before he saw it, the stench of rotting flesh guiding him closer. Drawing level with the tree, he gave a cursory glance at the atrophied cadaver. A solitary rat was suspended from the right foot, gnawing at the remaining shards of blackened skin hanging from its toes. The maggots squirming inside the eye sockets of the man's mummified face gave the illusion of movement, as if the corpse was tracking Wacian's approach. He hacked and spat a mouthful of thick phlegm towards the rat. Startled, it dropped to the forest floor and scuttled from sight.

Wacian delved into his tunic and grasped the phial. "Well, Celtic dog. I know not what crime you were guilty of. But I *do* know the native hideaway is not far. I think it is high time I toasted Tiw." He lifted the container. "Such an insignificant nightcap. A few mouthfuls, scarcely enough to wet a warrior's whistle. Yet this is all that stands between victory and failure." He gripped the cork stopper. "I hold in my hand the fate of, who knows, several hundred Brit bastards. I would not wish to be one of them after the moon has risen. I will be bringing Hell into their midst."

Unplugging the lid, he winced at the noxious odour then swiftly thrust the beaker to his mouth.

* * *

Moonbeams dappled the river as Wacian skulked along its banks, his nose testing the air. Fifteen minutes after having drained the flask, he was marching more purposefully, tingling with excitement. A bewildering array of scents assailed his nostrils: wild garlic, elderflower and lilies. The noises surrounding him in this wondrous arboreal landscape rose in intensity. A magpie cawed from its vantage point at the top of a yew tree; goldfinches chirruped from their lofty perches, their sweet melodies heartbreakingly beautiful. His hearing became even more finely tuned. Half a mile to the south he was aware of badgers rooting through the earth, grunting as they probed for worms to devour. Another mile further into the forest, he could hear a river, swollen by recent rains, crashing over a waterfall. He knew this to be the waterway that decanted into the ravine. With this realisation came the first pangs of agony. Pain speared through his body, commencing inside his rib cage, then spreading out to the tips of his toes and fingers. His muscles convulsed then stretched, as if his frame had been placed inside a large rack. His head involuntarily jerked backwards and in that moment, as his panicked eyes stared straight upwards, the ragged black clouds parted to give him his first clear sighting of the full moon. The transformation intensified.

His whole body arched as his shape contorted from man to beast, biped to four-legged canine. Coarse hair sprouted from his back to his face. He found the more animal he became the less the human pain concerned him and he could cope with the traumas of his body lapsing into this predator. Within ten minutes he was completely werewolf, his lurid red eyes gleaming. Gazing to the sky once more the moon cast its aura over his huge, muscular body, bathing him in intense silver light. This had the effect of increasing his bestial potency to even greater levels. Filling his lungs he tossed his head back and howled like the alpha male of a ravenous wolf pack.

Outside the forest, the English warriors huddled around campfires gripped their weapons when the piercing cries shattered the calm. Wacian had informed them the effects of the transformation were severe and unpredictable. There was no guarantee he would be able to focus on his original mission at all and was just as likely to head back in the direction he had travelled in, following the scent trail that would lead him back here. None of these warriors dared contemplate what it would be like to fend off such a crazed adversary.

But Wacian was entirely focussed on the Celtic village. He was now so acutely animalistic he was engulfed with a desire to snap his vicious teeth around the necks of these renegades, to savagely twist his jaws and guzzle their glutinous life juices. The notion of preying on these natives stoked an overwhelming bloodlust. The moon illuminated the clearing ahead of him before vanishing behind clouds. Despite the sudden absence of light his nocturnal vision was bringing him a lucid picture of the scene. His long snout testing the air, he bounded in the direction of the hidden fort. Although his way was constantly barred with fallen trunks, entanglements of thick bramble and many other obstacles, he moved with lightning speed, effortlessly manoeuvring around every barrier. He even ensured his huge paws avoided dry branches to ensure his progress remained as stealthy as possible. He also resisted the urge to bay further war cries.

The clouds drifted apart again and revealed the trees thinning into a long expanse of trampled grass, cleared of thorns by the Angles prior to their ill-fated assault. Wacian leapt over the river then skirted the opposite side leading to the waterfall. The ground here was marshier, but far less exposed. To his left he was aware of a pike picking at the remains of a dead beaver pup. Further upstream a shoal of tench cruised lugubriously. He thought of sweeping them onto the banks with his claws before sinking his massive teeth into their fat bodies while they struggled, feeling delicious hot guts sliding down his throat. But he resisted this urge. In no time at all he would be able to satiate himself with human flesh. Moving tentatively across the swamp, he tested the ground ahead, his paws sensitive to points where the mossy cover was insufficiently knitted to cope with his immense strength and weight. Progress was tedious but within half an hour of stalking he could hear the strident roaring of the falls.

He caught human scent. The natives moved through these glades freely. He knew a large party had passed here during the previous days, no doubt heading out to launch a cowardly attack on his brethren. His tongue flicked between his enormous canine teeth and felt a globule of thick saliva slithering from his tongue as he considered sinking his fangs into their throats, drinking the blood gushing from jugular veins.

He plunged into the river. Although it was ice-cold and its currents rapid, immersing his fur made him feel alive. He swam, using his strength to steer himself around rocks. It was laborious work but within ten minutes he had skirted the swampy terrain. Hauling himself up the banks, he shook his pelt then clambered back into the forest. Pausing for breath he listened intently. Close by, a leveret had been eviscerated by a weasel. Although this ambush had occurred several days ago he could still inhale the tantalising remnants of the kill. The thought of the tiny furry thing being ripped apart, its pink tubing and warm blood seeping into the soil carpeting the forest floor, was almost too much to bear. Vague though it was, the aroma of butchery invaded his senses, revitalising his pressing hunger.

As he made his way around trees and leapt over thickets, he was aware of smaller creatures scuttling out of his way: rabbits, voles, hedgehogs. But they need not have bothered. Much as he craved fresh meat, this monstrous wolf was not interested in prey that could be devoured in a few urgent swallows. He reached a place on the riverbank where the Celts fished regularly. Fish scales and dried black blood caked the vegetation. The thought of so many vulnerable humans was intoxicating. Longing to taste their young, his mouth filled with saliva. He stooped right down until his muzzle almost touched the forest floor. He snorted at the bewildering abundance of scents: pine needles, rotting leaves, the dung of many creatures. There was a powerful stench of rotting tissue after the recent battle. He fought hard not to dwell on this.

He was already becoming expert at balancing his human and animal sides. With sufficient will power he was able to tap into the latent powers of either facet, depending on the circumstances. He could concentrate on bringing his own self to the fore to think tactically, considering his mission in terms of the numbers and varieties of weapons that would be wielded against him. It was easy to lapse into the base instincts of the carnivorous monster, although giving free rein to these animal instincts and purely lusting after blood hampered his decision-making. Much as he was eager to fight as a wolf warrior, he appreciated there was more to shapeshifting than just transforming into a wild beast for a few hours. If this magic could be controlled, it would be a truly devastating war weapon.

The ravine yawned before the wolf. Crawling to the point where the ground plunged into gloom, he skulked over, his nose testing the air. None of the Angle war party had survived to describe this location but it was well signposted to him: an intoxicating aroma of congealed blood lingered in the air, trailing down over a staircase. Although this was cloaked in darkness, the stench of violence enticed him to follow the steps. Launching himself downwards he alighted at ground level. The notion of human prey invaded his senses. It took considerable effort to suppress a triumphant howl. Squatting behind an elm's thick trunk his eyes homed-in on his target. Between the tangled branches his razor-sharp vision noted helmeted silhouettes guarding battlements. His lips drew back into a demonic leer. He almost felt pity for these natives. Each one was breathing his final minutes on this earth prior to being torn limb from limb.

CHAPTER FORTY-THREE

Fearful of being near their chieftain when the shapeshifting elixir began coursing through him, the thane's bodyguards crept from the trees. Judd had insisted joining Wacian when he took the potion; now he was squeezing his scrawny frame through the tangled undergrowth, his shaft poking at the pathway ahead, barking when the escorting soldiers fussed over him.

Eventually they returned to the rise where hundreds of torches and campfires stretching as far as the men could see, mirroring the night sky. In his mind's eye, Judd received a similar vision. Judd was steered to his own tent among the Jute contingent. Parting the ox hide flaps, he stooped inside, feeling around the floor, re-emerging with two sacks. Sparking dried kindling, he blew into a small fire, despite the effort provoking furious coughing. Eventually flames licked around a cauldron and smoke billowed. Once bubbles formed in the murky water, he groped into the sacks and spread their bizarre contents over the ground, his deft fingers identifying the items he had demanded his men seek out these past days: plants, flowers, fungi, a selection of dead or dying animals, and the severed head of a wolf cub.

He focussed on the latter object. "Wolf blood," he whispered, "the most vital ingredient of all. I believe you were snared in woods a mere thirty or so miles away ... very fortuitous ... considering how scarce are your packs this far south ... although not so lucky for you, young wolf."

Touching a finger inside water now close to the boil, he winced before lifting the head by a tattered ear and dropping it into the frothing cauldron. Stirring with a wooden spoon, he patted the ground until he found the vellum sheet. He had inked a complicated list of ingredients, his handwriting remarkably fastidious for one so afflicted, although the fact he was one of the few literate members of his tribe rendered the point moot. It was merely important to preserve this record for the other tribal shamen. Wacian had demanded it with his customary blunder, barking into his ears with his mead-soaked breath.

Judd's gnarled fingers delved through the ingredients strewn before him, to snatch at flower petals, or fistfuls of leaves, each of which he could identify by touch far more accurately than any of the soldiers who had harvested them would have been able to by sight. At one point his fingertips sought the newt that had been playing dead on the grass and now tried to slither free of his grasp. Poking its tiny head inside his mouth, he snapped his teeth around its neck. Spitting out the head, he held the shaking body while dark green blood seeped into the vile soup.

Presently he was aware of footfall. "Who's there?" he rasped, his frail voice breaking. His eyes remained rooted in the direction of his concoction.

Another elderly figure emerged from the gloom, squatting beside him. "Such a stench, Judd. And I'd heard that Jutland was renowned for its cuisine!"

"Is that you, Paega?! My Saxon friend! What brings you to the Jutish camp?"

"Shamanic curiosity, you might say, Judd. Wacian's story of capturing a Norse medicine man, and of your mission to uncover the potion's secret recipe was ... *remarkable*. I wanted to see if the Saxons could benefit from this dark magic?"

"Of course, Paega. I've spent hours working it out and I believe I'm almost there. I had to cast a series of spells, inhaling the foul-smelling substance, analysing its constituents. In a trance, I was able to visualise every ingredient. I am sure I have mastered it. It will be distributed to the shamen of all of the tribes, of course, together with copies of *this*." He fumbled for the vellum. "I've been compiling the recipe. Kentishmen, Angles, Saxons, we will *all* have our wolf warriors. There will be no more haunted forests to stand in the way of Britannia's new masters."

Paega nodded, licking his lips despite the aroma being acrid enough to draw tears. "Have any other shamen visited, Judd?"

"None yet, Paega. You are the first." He rubbed his fingers together excitedly.

"I see. Once the elixir is prepared for its slow cooking, I would suggest you and I go for a walk, Judd. This infernal fucking stink would make lesser men retch!"

"Of course, Paega. We can go for a stroll. The stars must be splendid tonight, are they not? Thunor's cloak will be glistening?"

"They are, Judd. A fitting backdrop for your magic. I do feel privileged to be the first shaman to witness this truly momentous recipe you have been slaving over, Judd. Although. The Norse sail right around the islands. There is always the possibility the Celts might capture phials hidden in the longships?"

"Doubtful, Paega. I believe few are the Norse shamen who practice these spells, so the chances would be remote. The potions allow warriors to become wolves, but they die very soon afterwards. The magic is used sparingly. In any case, if the Norse think their secrets are in any danger of falling into enemy hands, English or Celt, I believe they will toss the phials overboard. It was an incredible stroke of luck that the weather prevented our Viking returning to his ship ... so we came across the shapeshifter as a dying man, too slow-witted to hide the evidence."

Paega smiled with his lips; but the eyes rooted on Judd seemed dead as the newt's head that fleetingly popped to the surface of the putrid stew. "You realise you are the only shaman amongst the Germanic tribes who would have been capable of extracting the recipe, by casting spells?"

"I think not, Paega. I am well aware of your own powers, my West Saxon friend. I would suggest the *two* of us are the only ones befitting your description. We may be in our autumn years, but we are far more powerful than any of the others, are we not? Modig's medicine man simply hacks open the occasional chicken and claims all manner of visions by staring at the poor beast's gizzard. The same goes for most of the other Saxon shamen. As for the Angles ... they think themselves too civilized to be dabbling in black magic."

Paega sniggered at this. "Modig only hears what he wants to hear, that tomorrow he will be killing more *blueskins*."

"Just so, Paega. But I know you would have been equally capable of coming up with the solution, had you come across a shapeshifter ... in the flesh?"

"Fortunately I will no longer need to do that as you have beaten me to it, have you not? I think the time has come for you to sample the potion, Judd."

"*Me?* The shapeshifting would *kill* me, Paega. No, one of our young warriors will claim that honour. Anyway, there are still several one or two additives required." The Jute stabbed a finger at the vellum.

"No, Judd. I *insist*. It is time to sample the potion."

Judd peered warily in the direction of his Saxon counterpart. "Paega. I'd rather you didn't interfere with what is happening here. You are too impatient. Perhaps it would be best if you returned to your own encampment?"

Paega's eyelids lowered fractionally; although Judd could not see the sinister expression, he was aware of the rising tension. With the stealth of an adder strike, Paega's hands shot out to Judd's cascading white curls. Before a scream could escape the blind man's lips, Paega had forced his head into the cauldron. Even as boiling water lapped over the back of his hands to scald his flesh, he gnawed at his lips while he kept Judd's face immersed. The turbulent liquid drowned out his victim's agonised shrieks. Judd's writhing limbs juddered to a tremulous halt so quickly Paega suspected the shock had proved too much for Judd's geriatric heart. When he wrenched the head from the potion, Judd's features were purple, and his lifeless eyes seemed even whiter. The Saxon shaman emptied the cauldron, twisting the corpse over into the steaming puddle.

"You were an old man, Judd. Fucking *ancient*. Fumbling your way through what little was left of your life. Your sentries will assume a heart attack took you to Tiw's banquet." Seizing the vellum, he gave the list a cursory glance. "I can concur with most of this, Judd of the Wihtware, give or take a few minor ingredients which are merely refinements to the speed of the shapeshifting. But you can rest assured, your secret is safe with me."

Thrusting the sheet into the fire, he watched its ends curling inwards and blackening. Then he skulked away, the night quickly enveloping him, its cool breath caressing his blistered hands.

CHAPTER FORTY-FOUR

Heart hammering inside his chest, Maxwell squinted into the darkness. He blurted out: "I saw a light!" The young Kentishman knew everyone was on edge and false alarms would inspire an unceremonious blow to the back of his head from the irritable thane, Nerian. His eyes swept the land again. The task of justifying his outburst was rendered more perilous by layers of mist shifting over the pre-dawn landscape.

"What kind of light, Maxwell? Torches? From one of the other patrols, perhaps?" growled Nerian, following the direction of the sentry's intent stare.

"No, sire. Just for a moment, something flickered against the moonlight. Spears ... or swords?"

The thane peered into the night before swivelling his head to fix the intensity of his expression on the nervous youth. "Well? What was it, Maxwell? Was it spears? Or was it swords? Or was it a vision conjured from a dream? Are you admitting to me you were *dreaming*, that you were *sleeping* during sentry duty? I would have you stripped and sent off into the shadows where I would use your *screams* to notify me of the presence of any cursed Brits. Well, Maxwell?"

"No, sire. I saw it, too. Weapons," another warrior interjected.

Nerian shoved both from his path and craned into the distance. A wry smile etched into his features. This was no vision from a sleepy guard. For a fleeting moment the moon edged free of encroaching clouds, its silver beams splashing the undulating countryside. Just before they vanished into a dip Nerian caught sight of helmets.

"If soldiers are crossing the moor without torches, that can only mean one thing. Fucking Brits. Pass the word. The Celtic bastards are mounting a raid."

As if on cue, an unearthly howl emanated from the depths of the forest. Despite their shaggy beards and battle-scarred faces, the warriors exchanged shifty glances.

"Wacian, of the Wihtware," remarked Nerian. "Any Brits out roaming tonight are in for a surprise when they return to their hideout."

With that grim observation Nerian strode over to the horses, grasping the mane of his own steed. As its ears remained alert for further wolf cries he whispered reassuringly. Then he mounted the large beast and unsheathed his sword.

"With me, Jutes of Kent. We'll corner these rats as they scurry over the moors."

* * *

Nerian's grip was white-knuckled around the reins. His focus remained the crest of the hill where he had glimpsed the enemy. The panicked Britons would surely scatter to either side, forming into disorganised knots that would make the easiest of targets for English swords. The thought of impending battle sent adrenalin coursing through his lean physique. This was what his race excelled at: punishing the weak; exerting the authority of the strong. His lieutenants were well trained in the art of ambush. At his signal, riders would peel off, their horses thundering to either wing. They would make a wide detour, closing-in several miles further on to cut-off any escape. This particular enemy had done so much damage to the occupying forces they had to be destroyed to a man.

Nerian urged his horse to the crest. At that moment the moon gleamed through cloud cover again, reflecting myriad pools across the glen below. Instinctively he tugged the reins, slowing his headstrong stallion. Raising his sword aloft he urged his men to a halt. Their horses snorting excitedly, the riders glowered into the gloom. Curtains of mist eddied above marshland, swirling with the night breeze. An unnatural heat emanated from underground springs, stirring the vapour clouds. The boggy landscape rose towards limestone crags. But there was no sign of any fleeing enemy soldiers among the constantly churning soup.

"Where the fuck *are* they?" Nerian rasped. "They can't have got far. Wherever they're skulking in this fog, we'll track them down before they reach those cliffs. With me, Kentishmen."

After the heady rush the warriors resigned themselves to this more dogged pursuit. They spurred their horses on, splashing into the marsh, in places knee-deep in murky water. Those brandishing torches were urged to the fore; with sweeping gestures they highlighted the backdrop of swaying reed beds. Nerian led the way, digging his heels in, imploring his horse further into the tall fronds. It was reluctant to obey. The springy moss that lurked below the surface was treacherous to navigate and the mists curtailed visibility to mere feet ahead. Every so often there would be a stirring among the surrounding wetlands, splashing as a horse stumbled, or a warrior aimlessly lunged his sword into bushes.

The thane felt his frustration conspiring with a niggling pain along the stiff muscles of his sword arm. All around him, beyond the drifting banks of vapour, he could make out the muted sounds of this dogged manhunt. Horses would stumble into deeper pools, instigating irritated grunts. There was a constant sweeping of weapons as warriors slashed into clumps of reeds. Hacking phlegm from the back of his throat he spat into the bog. Nerian froze, eyes rooted to the point of impact, the circles widening before dissolving against plants. The warrior to his rear was wielding a torch: a fierce red glow played across the rippling surface. The mist and uncanny heat were working mischief with his eyesight.

"Your torch, lad. Point it ahead of us. Just there," Nerian barked, his sword's tip wavering towards the waters. He squinted. This trick of the light seemed so outlandish he could scarcely comprehend what he imagined he was seeing. There appeared to be men lurking down there, suspended just below the surface: scores of them. Their bodies shimmered with the currents, refusing to cohere for more than a fleeting moment. Were they staring up at him? The light was extinguished. Nerian whipped his head round. Where the torch had struck, the all-pervading fog devoured a hissing wisp of smoke. The chieftain found his tongue refusing to co-operate with the barrage of curses spewing from his awestruck mind. An upsurge in the wind cleaved a corridor in the mists. It lasted long enough for him to glimpse his immediate surroundings. The riderless horse behind him was making off in the direction of all the other abandoned horses.

The ground seemed to come alive. Everywhere he stared, men were heaving themselves free from the warm waters, tugging hollow reed stems from their mouths. Nerian felt hands grasping his legs, hauling him from his saddle; vice-like fingers tugged his blond pleats, forcing him into the murky water. White-eyed, he watched an imposing figure rise from the marsh before him, her long black hair matting to her chest. Her features were patterned with woad, a thick blue band running across the bridge of her nose, accentuating the contemptuous glare in her eyes.

"German dog. Your men are already waiting for you in Hell."

Nerian had no idea what the Celtic warrior had said. But she translated all too lucidly by raising a sword already dripping with Jutish blood, then swinging it across his neck.

CHAPTER FORTY-FIVE

The Angle soldiers shifted, hands wavering over their campfire. Every so often a blood-curdling cry emanated from the trees. Most had been sceptical about the rumours of shapeshifting demons. But these unearthly howls would faze the most battle-hardened warrior.

This band had travelled all the way from Bernicia in the kingdom of North Humberland, ordered south from their farmlands to fulfil their tribe's duty to the blood truce. The younger among them were spoiling for a fight with the Britons who were resisting the occupation. But their more mature brethren accepted their presence here was down to expediency and secretly hoped other patrols would deal with the natives, allowing a swift return to their homesteads. This reluctance to be here was exacerbated by another widely held supposition: the werewolf fighters that were supposed to sway the fight against the Celts were equally partial to English flesh.

One by one the Angles became aware of approaching warriors. Immediately weapons were grasped and the men spread out, presenting sharpened blades to any natives foolhardy enough to tackle such an organised force. Although the only Brits these Bernicians had ever clapped eyes on were furtive slaves, their heads bowed in market squares, all were acquainted with the folklore. When the blueskins went into battle they invariably did so with blood-curdling screams, their wild eyes staring from broad smears of woad. Apparently they strapped the decapitated heads of their enemies around their midriffs; or use them as missiles. Thankfully, the men pacing towards their line were devoid of decorative body parts.

"Stand down, lads," ordered the sentry furthest in front. "They're Jutes." Relief flowed through the ranks as the nearest swordsmen emerged from the night's shadows. "Kentishmen," the sentry emphasised. Thrusting his sword into its scabbard, he raised his right fist towards the man fast advancing on him. "Comrades," continued the Angle, warming to a theme, "what brings you onto the moors this night? We're from the north. Well. Not the *north* north. We don't look like sheep-fucking Picts from the other side of the wall, do we? Under the blood truce, we were sent by our eorl, Osmund, to bolster Linn's forces. Apparently you southerners needed help to flush out a few rebellious Brits."

His mates chuckled along with his jovial bantering, glancing towards the opposing soldiers. But these Jutes appeared less inclined to humorous exchanges. The Angle conceded the newcomers might well have crossed swords that night: certainly the closer they drew he could make out splashes of blood across many tunics. In fact, as they stepped towards the fire's shifting light, he noticed every man bore the stains of grisly encounters.

"Excuse my ill-placed remarks, Jutish brethren. No harm was intended, I assure you. Tell me. Have many Brits have you vanquished on the moors?"

Awaiting an answer from the impassive warrior before him, he failed to notice the stealth with which the other bloodied men were fanning out to outflank the Angles. The sentry became preoccupied with his own welling irritation. "I appreciate you and your men may have been through tough fighting, but that is no excuse to forsake our hospitality."

Displaying even less patience, a comrade butted in: "Especially at this time. Violating the blood truce is deeply dishonourable, and you must know this, men of Kent?"

The sentry raised a placatory hand. "Hold fast, Saewine. These men must be fatigued. I see it in their eyes. Pray introduce yourselves prior to warming yourselves at our fire, Jute, if you will."

The warrior strode up to him; so close the Angle could feel the breath filtering through the thick visor. Without deigning to reply, the soldier lifted the helm and cast it aside, shaking her head, allowing her tresses to cascade over her ill-fitting uniform. Just as the sentry registered the blue stripes across her features, she spat into his flabbergasted face. In the moment that followed, the fire's crackling seemed to intensify. Instinctively the Angle reached for his sword. Pre-empting this, the female fighter seized a dirk from her belt, thrusting it deep into her opponent's guts. Stumbling forwards, coughing blood, the Angle gasped as the moor rushed towards him.

Taking their warlord's attack as their cue, the others in Jutish garb launched themselves at the Angles, the element of surprise ensuring initial blade thrusts were rarely countered. Within minutes the moor was strewn with more butchered men.

CHAPTER FORTY-SIX

His enhanced vision swept across the stockade walls, noting the position of each sentry's helm glinting in the moonlight. A dog began barking. The wolf swiftly rolled around, grinding his hide into wild garlic and clusters of berries. His scent obscured, the yelping faded. Jaws dripping silver globules, he prowled over the short distance between the treeline and the fortress. The thought of so much meat just yards away intensified his hunger.

A timber wall wound its way around the Celtic homesteads for over a mile, each trunk carved into a spike. Even to a lithe half-man, half-wolf, it seemed impregnable. There were watchtowers at intervals. His red eyes scanned the defences, musing that torches would normally flutter from these silhouetted structures. These wretches had no option but to skulk in the shadows, like fucking toadstools. And in the darkness they would die.

With his lupine senses, he could now make out individual faces among the guards. To a man they were locked in concentration, motionless as they stared outwards. He was impressed with the strength of the British defence. But there was a weak point. A true wolf would not have known it. But a werewolf, retaining a glimmer of human memory, appreciated fortified settlements required a waste outlet, a tunnel excavated in the soil beneath the walls for channelling sewage into the forest. His snout traced the source of the pungent stench. Squirming into the narrow fissure, he clawed through the slimy earth and excrement, dragging himself beneath the gap below the wooden barriers.

He inhaled the cocktail of enticing aromas - dried fish suspended over the remains of fires, barrels of honey mead, the pungent tang of fabric dyes – but above all, human flesh, rancid with the sweat of fear. The wolf warrior wondered if there was a druid here, although the natives tended to evacuate their medicine men when under threat. The fact he had progressed this far made him suspect any druid had long been spirited into the countryside. With his victims so tantalisingly close his bloodlust was becoming feverish. His great paws testing the hard ground inside, his lurid eyes counted the sentries: eighteen in total. There were no other villagers to be seen, although he could sense tribespeople lying in the huts, their scent particularly potent. These natives had been hiding from the outside world for so long their stench was ranker than bats in a cave. The notion excited him: whether succulently fresh or spiced with sweat and grime, their meat would soon be warming his belly.

He crept towards a ladder leading to the upper walkway. Alighting on the level, he pushed his body close to the walls, focussing on his first meal. The Celt was tall, but disappointingly lean due to months of frugal dieting. The wolf's sinews tensed, preparing to spring. Savouring the acrid stench of the soldier's long-unwashed garments, his tongue flecked. He sprang from the shadows. Before the guard could stifle a scream the beast's huge jaws had closed, twisting violently, tearing through his neck. In seconds the wolf serrated strips of soft flesh. The meat was cold and stringy after long hours of sentry duty, but delicious. Muzzle dripping red, he bounded on. Such was his speed, each victim was powerless to resist. Most looked frozen with fear, their eyes staring into the skies to implore their Celtic gods for mercy while this slaughter continued at breakneck speed. He had completed his grisly task within minutes. All the guards had been butchered; he listened to heads rolling from the walkway, tumbling to the ground below.

The werewolf leapt from the walls to the encampment. His foul breath rasping, he heard the dogs. They came rushing from beneath huts: four of them, snarling. When they caught sight of him they halted. He growled, baring his own fangs. They charged him in a frenetic mass of fur and teeth. His razor sharp teeth reduced them to horrible entanglement of limbs and viscera.

He turned towards the largest hut: the chieftain's. Hauling himself onto two feet, he paced to the door, easing it open. All were so deep in sleep none had been wakened by the brief commotion. His keen eyes surveyed various figures under blankets. But his prize was the head of this insolent Celtic clan, a man slumbering beneath deerskin blankets in the bed at the centre of the chamber. The wolf padded over. Delving under the covers, his claws closed around the man's windpipe, savouring the moment. He thrust his talons deep into the neck, piercing the flesh, the power in his forearm wrenching the skull from the mooring of its spinal chord. Clutching their chieftain's head in his left hand, he proceeded to fall upon the unsuspecting family members and bodyguards sprawled among the straw bedding, severing more heads. His bloodlust increasing, his attacks became ever more frenetic until he began swinging his grisly trophies around and lashing them against the walls, growling with satisfaction as each pulped like an enormous egg. Tempering his heavy breathing, still clutching the chieftain's head by its lank strands, he made his way to the next hut.

CHAPTER FORTY-SEVEN

Wacian stumbled from the forest, his legs faltering as he neared the edge of the trees. It was daybreak; a meagre sun had climbed above the rolling hills to the east. A cockerel crowing in a distant farmstead briefly interrupted the crisp silence.

The Jutes gathering kindling for breakfast fires watched him warily. Their warlord was barely recognisable, his back stooped, his eyes haggard and surrounded by deep lines. Most striking of all, his characteristic russet hair was matted and grey as slush, although flecked with crimson. Grubby rags protected his modesty.

"Wacian? What happened?" one of his astonished aides managed to blurt out. "Did your shape ... *shift*? We thought we heard a wolf howling ... and it was unlike any beast we've ever heard."

Wacian appeared too weak to confirm their suspicions. "Water ... *please*. Get me some water ... I'll try and tell you as much as I can remember."

His men assisted him towards the welcome glow coming from the campfire. Simmering eggs clicked against the sides of a pot. After some moments one of the Jutes fished them out and cracked them into a bowl, mushing them with a knob of fat he extracted from a slab wrapped in dried leaves. He passed it to his thane. Wacian shovelled a spoon into the food but winced. "My guts ache ... by Tiw, how they fucking *ache*."

Face contorting, he tossed the bowl aside, the violent movement inspiring those nearest to step aside. "Wacian? Are you all right?" one of them called out.

Eyes clamming, he shook his head. Without warning, his mouth opened and he vomited onto the ground. All were transfixed by the vile cocktail that doused their campfire: a meld of blood and half-chewed lumps of pink muscle that steamed in the cool air, the fetid aroma inspiring several among them to expunge their own stomach contents. Wacian himself stared aghast at the object swirling centremost: a ragged human nose.

"The Norse magic worked," he whispered, gulping for breath. "I believe I became a wolf, just like the caged beast we showed off to the other thanes. My memory isn't exactly clear. I recall ... *fragments* ... like trying to remember a dream. Or the hours lost after too much honey mead!" Wacian sniggered at this, but his brow furrowed again and he spat a purple globule into the weeds. "I saw guards on the walls of a stockade. In my wolf form I fell on them, one by one, silencing them, biting their throats, tearing chunks from their flesh ... swallowing chunks of meat ... of *men* ... there were no survivors. The Brits are vanquished. I used up the last of the potion, too. I don't think I could go through *that* again. My strength has ebbed. I must look a shadow of my former self, lads?"

Given the wild expression lingering in their chieftain's eyes, the men nodded at the understatement: in truth he appeared not far removed from death. Wacian was aware of their furtive glances. "Is something the matter?" he demanded. "Tolan? You seem ... *agitated?*"

The weasel-faced warrior absently scraped a knife against the sole of his boots. "It's Judd, sire."

"Judd? What about him? Where is the old buzzard? I thought he would've been keen to check on the results of the foul recipe?"

Tolan took a breath. "Judd is dead, sire."

"What?! What happened to him?"

"I went to his tent this morning, as I always do, to check if he wished to break his fast with us. I found him face down. He'd been boiling a wolf's head."

"He was concocting the shapeshifting elixir."

Tolan nodded grimly. "Alas, he seems to have fallen forward, into his cauldron. We suspect old age has caught him."

"Was his recipe to hand? I watched him list each ingredient as it was brought to him."

"No, sire. When he fell into the cauldron, he disturbed the fire beneath. There were fragments of vellum, charred beyond recognition."

Wacian peered around the company. "Alas, Tiw gives pride of place at his table to our shaman. We must accept the will of our gods. As for the haunted forest, it is but a forest, containing dead Brits. We will rely on English blades rather than demon wolves to root out any lingering enemies."

* * *

Wacian doused himself in a stream, cupping handfuls of the water over his filthy features. He caught his face in the rippling reflection, his beard white as the clouds drifting by. This victory had come at great personal cost. He turned to his soldiers. "Let's saddle up, men. We've earned ourselves a flagon or ten of ale."

His horse was untethered and brought to him. Where he would normally have climbed up with gusto, he had to rely on Tolan crouching on all-fours so he could clamber on. Once secure in his saddle, the large company dug their spurs in and set off. The Jutes had progressed for a mile when they heard a horse galloping towards them. Swords were unsheathed. A rider approached, right hand aloft to signal he meant no threat. "Wacian of the Wihtware?" he yelled.

"Over here!"

The messenger drew up his frothing horse with a frantic tug of the reins. The Jutes could see from his sweating mount he had covered many miles with whatever bulletin he carried.

"Good day, Wacian."

"Good day, warrior."

"My name is Rand. I serve Modig of the Somorsaetas."

"Wacian, from the men of the Isle of Wight. The blood truce can be considered over. Concluded successfully, I should add. Victory was secured over the rebellious British last night. We return to our homesteads."

The Saxon eyed him but tactfully masked his surprise. Obviously the man before him bore no resemblance to the description he had been given.

"I bring ... *uncertain* tidings."

"What do you mean, Rand?"

"Last night there was fighting in the marshes, west of the great forest. A large Celtic war party harried our allies."

"Impossible. The natives were destroyed last night. I should know. I drank the potion that allowed me to do the fucking destroying." His men colluded with their thane, cheering and punching the air.

Rand remained impassive. "Modig and the other chieftains will be pleased to learn of the ... success ... of your shapeshifting mission. Nevertheless, considerable blood was spilt on the moors. A Bernician patrol was slaughtered."

"What?!" Wacian's voice rose with incredulity. His imploring eyes darted around his men for any elaboration. All were equally sceptical.

Rand continued. "And a Kentish thane, Nerian, was found dead in the marshes, along with hundreds of his kin. All had been stripped naked."

"Nerian? By all the gods, what treachery?! But this makes no sense, Rand."

"When news spread that the blood truce had been broken, there were widespread skirmishes. Jutish and Angle patrols clashed in several places around the forest. War almost broke out between the Angles and your people."

Wacian's right hand caressed his sword's hilt. "Tolan? Were you aware of any fighting last night?"

"We stayed close to the forest in case you needed us, my thane," his soldier explained. "It seems we missed ... the excitement."

The chieftain scowled. "So the Angles break the blood truce? After all I've been through avenging their defeat in the haunted forest? The East Saxons will rally to Linn. We Jutes would join with our neighbours, the South Saxons. But there is never love lost between the men of Sussex and Wessex. Where stand the West Saxons in this war, Rand?"

The messenger shook his head vigorously. "No, no, Wacian. The Angles and Jutes were duped."

"Explain, Rand?"

"A Kentishman survived the massacre of the marshes. A Saxon patrol came across him this morning, in a reed bed, bleeding from a head wound. Although this man was dying, he was able to tell them what he'd witnessed. Nerian's troops were ambushed by Brits who'd been hiding in the swamp. This Jute described the way these Brits then stripped Nerian's men of their clothing, before donning the outfits. Disguised as Jutes, they wiped out the patrol of Angles from North Humberland, then melted into the countryside ... here they watched stupid Englishmen setting upon stupid Englishmen ... here they watched all these fools who had assumed the blood truce violated."

"By the beard of Tiw. How was this resolved, Rand?"

"As soon as we received this intelligence we sent messengers, carrying news of this cowardly deception, ensuring the feuding would stop, ensuring the blood truce would prevail."

Wacian gazed towards the skies then contemplated the Saxon's pained expression. "But these Brits must have been small in number? They must have used the element of surprise to overcome the Kentishmen?"

"No. They were part of a larger group."

"That can't be so?"

"Our scouts have been hunting them down all morning, Wacian. We came across tracks, to the west. They indicated a warband, heavily armed, several hundred strong."

"They *cannot* have come from the forest hideaway, Rand. The men in that Celtic fortress fell to a wolf warrior. *All* of them. *None* survived to slip across the moors and begin attacking my comrades-in-arms."

"Modig does not doubt your courage in falling upon the Brit stronghold, single-handed. But it appears most of the renegades slipped out of the village under the cover of darkness *before* your attack. Judging by the tracks, there were also considerable camp followers. Women. Children. Their warriors have been harassing the English occupation for months and now they roam freely."

"I can assure you, Rand, the Brits hiding in the haunted forest were slaughtered to a man. I can still fucking *taste* them."

"I repeat. There are close to a thousand enemy warriors roaming over English lands. They came from the forest."

Tiring of this exchange, Wacian was on the verge of dismissing the Saxon and his impudent inferences. But a sense of honour weighed heavily. It was his duty to prove to Modig and the other chieftains the extent of his victory the night before. Failure to do so would be an admission that his shapeshifting escapades had been blown out of all proportion. This would be inexcusable enough in front of this Saxon; before his own men it was unthinkable.

"There must be some explanation, Rand. But first of all, I would like you to accompany me to the defeated fortress. I wish Modig to know the Jutes played their part in destroying the Brits. I cannot believe the thousand native warriors you speak of escaped from the village in the ravine. I repeat. *None* escaped."

Rand was diplomatic enough to offer a gracious smile. But this masked his growing contempt at a chieftain whose boastfulness far outweighed his actual courage.

CHAPTER FORTY-EIGHT

Having covered many miles on horseback, the opportunity for Rand to stretch his legs had been welcome. But he had spent hours trekking across wild forest terrain, and the only time Wacian's bragging halted were the frequent occasions he drew the convoy to a halt so he could throw up among the undergrowth. Now Rand was confronted with stairs hacked into the sheer rockface. He had no great head for heights, but it would be unthinkable to admit as much to the Jutish buffoon.

The descent was laborious because Wacian insisted on taking the lead, and for all his gruff embellishment of his attack on the Celtic encampment, he would huff and puff and sit down on every sixth step. Here he would lean into the cliff, eyelids wavering shut. On more than one occasion Tolan had to nudge him awake. Eventually the party arrived at the base of the stairwell. Wacian found more of a spring in his step when he caught sight of the battlements and ushered the others onwards.

An eerie stillness hung over the trees. None spoke; insects buzzed while scabbards clanged and heavy boots trod through the brush. Finally the tall wooden wall presented itself. Wacian proudly strode to the front, eager to show off the gruesome results of his handiwork to Modig's man. After his crazed butchery the night before, he had removed the long pole bolting the stockade, launching it to one side before kicking his way out. The great doors opened to reveal a charnel house of human devastation. Corpses were sprawled all over the encampment's interior, limbs twisted or smashed. None had their heads attached; these had been cast into a corner, forming a macabre heap of faces gaping through matted hair. All present were veteran fighters, but this remained a difficult sight to absorb.

"Behold, the Brit chieftain!" Wacian cried, his finger jabbing at the head he had thrust atop a lance, planting this centremost. They peered up at this grisly battle memento.

Frowning, Rand stepped over to the ghoulish standard.

"Don't be so cautious, my Saxon friend," mused Wacian. "I don't think he's got much fight left in him!"

Grateful for the incongruous brevity, his men guffawed.

"My Jute friend," stated Rand. "Do many native chieftains have such blond hair?"

"What?"

"I recognise this man. I was drinking with him at the feast to seal the blood truce. He is Sighard. A sergeant of Linn's housecarls."

"Impossible!" roared Wacian.

"Look at the heads," ventured the Saxon. "These men are not Celts. They are Angles."

"No!"

His anger growing, Rand stomped over to the nearest body. "Angle tunics, arms of the North Folk and South Folk. Although their heads are severed, the blood at the neck hasn't flowed. It was already clotted dry. And see the great sword wounds in this one's chest? Over there, you still see an arrow protruding? By the gods, the crows have already had a good bellyful of most of these unfortunate fellows. They were not killed last night, Wacian."

"I don't understand," Wacian pleaded, his bluster evaporating.

"I understand *perfectly*, my friend. The natives are nowhere near as stupid as many of we Englishmen like to delude ourselves. These men were already dead, casualties of the battle of the ravine, propped up to man these battlements."

"Why the fuck would the Brits do that?"

"To buy time. The assumption would be that our scouts would report the fort still heavily defended. That would keep hundreds of our soldiers occupied here. As it goes, it looks like the garrison and their families sneaked out under cover of darkness. They didn't even need their decoys."

"That might explain the guards on the walls. But why place corpses inside the huts?"

"The Brits have a twisted sense of humour?"

"I see little humour in what they have done." Wacian gazed up at the butchered head of the man once known as Sighard.

"I would choose my words when it comes to explaining this to Linn," the Saxon continued. "But the more pressing issue is the Celtic army. We need you Jutes to muster with all the warbands from your Angle and Saxon brethren, to find these native dogs and crush them once and for all. We suspect they are heading southwestwards. They will be making for the lands beyond Wessex, known to these curs as Dumnonia. The blood truce remains until we catch them. And kill them."

CHAPTER FORTY-NINE

Their horses resting within the shelter of a beech copse, the warriors were replenishing skins by a fast-flowing stream, ever attentive for news from outriders. But the Celts seemed to have vanished as swiftly as the dissipating morning mists. Dousing his face in cooling water, Wacian looked to Rand. "What will you say of the assault on the fortress when you have Modig's ear, or indeed any of the other chieftains?"

"I saw the aftermath of the wolf warrior attack. It was bloody. There were slaughtered men everywhere. *Pieces* of slaughtered men. I was reminded of a chicken coop after a fox has filled his belly. That is all that Modig will hear from me, Wacian, you have my word on that."

The Jutish thane glowered across the rolling heathland. "Yes, your word, Rand. And your pockets lined with pieces of gold from the Isle of Wight ... with more to follow. A fair exchange during this fragile blood truce between our tribes."

* * *

After another day riding, the Jutes eventually passed gangs of surly Saxon sentries, cantering into Modig's settlement as the sun was sinking. A huge force had already mustered, the smoke from hundreds of campfires smudging the darkening skies while suppers turned on spits. Wacian's troop sought the other Jute warriors who had gathered for the blood truce, although the numbers already huddled around their fires had been depleted during the skirmishes. After they had set up camp, enthusiastically downing mead flagons and wine skins, Rand approached again.

"Men of the Isle of Wight. A council of war is requested," he stated. "Modig would be honoured if you would join the other

Saxon and Anglian thanes. We will be discussing the best tactics to employ when the Brits are discovered."

In Modig's chamber the representatives of the various English tribes huddled together, gorging on roughly hewn cuts of beef, washed down with honey ale. The atmosphere remained good-natured, even when talk turned to the most appropriate methods of hacking down Celtic children in flight. A hush fell on the assembly when Modig clambered on top of a table, stomping his boots down several times until he achieved order.

"Greetings, brethren," his voice booming beneath the rafters. "We have gathered here in the West Country in order to cut off the renegades before the rats scurry to the sea. This is a personal quest for myself. My son Oxa is missing. I fear he was set upon by blueskins. I wish revenge to be most brutal." His good eye took in the forest of silhouetted heads nodding in approval. "And this native warband that has become such a thorn in our side ... these blueskins might well inspire other pockets of resistance. Wiping every last blueskin off the face of our new country is in all our interests. That is why we honour the blood truce."

Wacian weighed-up Modig's impassioned words. That he had been so deceived by the Britons in their forest lair made revenge equally personal to him. The warrior in him was inspired, although he had never felt so fatigued. The long ride into the Saxon territories had taken its toll on his already embattled physique. Every so often he winced in agony as mysterious pains lanced through random part of his anatomy. He wondered if he had poisoned himself during the night raid: in wolf form he had been gorging himself on dead flesh. But he insisted on maintaining standards befitting his thane status. He could ensure a few days of bellyaches, even if it meant casting as much unchewed beef as ribs beneath the tables for Modig's hounds.

"My lord, you should rest," Tolan whispered.

Wacian waved his hand at his underling. "This could be the Brits' last stand in the south. The Wihtware will not miss out on such a historic victory. Epic sagas will be written about the events that occur these next few days. Do we really want the sagas to record the Jutes of Wight did not attend because their warlord went to fucking bed?!"

"My shaman has consulted chicken blood," continued Modig. "He assures me the Brits will be spotted before the next full moon. So we will ride after the last blueskins and destroy them. I do not think it would be wise to take any more for your slave pens. They would only become a focus for attempts to free them by their countrymen. We must drive the blueskin dogs into the sea ... and drown every last fucking one of them."

This warmongering bravado was lapped up. The whole gathering cheered, rapped weapons against shields, and then swigged more beer. By midnight the throng were so fired-up with ale and wine, Linn had to use his utmost powers of persuasion to stop many of the Saxons from attempting to clamber aboard horses to seek out their enemies there and then.

Wacian sipped at his mead. He was prepared to await the sunrise: none of the other chieftains had been through what he had in order to rid their territories of natives. But he also appreciated how much it had taken out of him. He felt unbelievably weary. Although a man in his thirty-fourth year, he felt as if he was double that tally. Despite all the revelry as his colleagues toasted the impending day with its promise of slaughter, he desired only to return to The Solent, to sink into layers of soft wolf pelts and sleep for a month.

Wacian stood, swaying. Those closest cheered; Tolan thrust his arms towards him, while roaring at his apparent drunkenness. "Steady yourself, my thane! You took on a village of Silures scum on your own! Methinks you should put up more of a fight against this West Saxon mead!"

Wacian would once have broken Tolan's nose for such public insolence. But the chieftain was in no mood to banter. Craving fresh air before retiring, he pushed his way out of the chamber. After five minutes of stumbling he arrived at a headland, the Hibernian Sea unfolding before him in an endless pool of ink he could imagine plunging over the edge of the world. Far below waves were crashing into rocks. As he watched the encroaching tide, he speculated about the fate of Modig's son. In his mind's eye he visualised a shoreline where seals were basking on shingle. Soon there would be more seals than Britons on this island. When they eventually flushed-out the guerrillas, justice would indeed be served. If this corner of Britannia was to be the site of a Celtic last stand, it would certainly be passed down through the generations in boastful sagas. But what was destined to unfold could scarcely be dignified with the title of a battle, he mused. It was going to be as one-sided as slaughtering pigs in a pen with an axe.

Then he started. He realised he had never seen this bay where seals wallowed, yet it was strikingly familiar. It dawned on him it must have something to do with the shapeshifting potion. Was a portion of the wolf medicine's sinister power lingering in his bloodstream, giving some mysterious insight? He wondered what else he might be able to see. Shutting his eyes, he relaxed, allowing his thoughts to wander freely. The crashing waves, cawing seagulls and occasional drunken braying of men receded to a background burr. Now he could visualise enemy soldiers prowling through a long gulley, scouts skulking along the crest and scanning the horizon for pursuers. They marched in silence, their boots smothered with docking leaves. Hundreds upon hundreds of swords and axes glinted against the moonlight. They presented a fearsome picture with their wild locks and staring eyes, their faces obscured by thick warpaint. At their head strode a female warrior. Wacian marvelled at the cruel beauty of her flowing hair and alluring green eyes.

The picture segued into another. This time he saw a younger Celtic maiden, a pretty redhead, in a forest clearing. She was lying on a tree branch, observing someone gathering plants. He had no idea how he could possibly know this, but he got the impression the hooded figure in this tranquil scene was her father. But the calm was shattered when a wolf warrior burst into the picture.

"Godric," he gasped, although he was dumbfounded to know the name of the man who had shifted shape. He felt a spark of sadistic pleasure as his vision revealed the monster savaging the man then escaping, while the girl remained hidden in the tree canopy. "Kady ... of the Dumnonii." Again, realising he had developed some fantastical sixth sense quickened his heartbeat. He followed the progress of the wolf as it retreated. He watched the beast transform into human form. After a tortuous journey Godric staggered towards an encampment. "A Dorseatas fort on the southern coast. Cyneheard's stronghold."

Heart hammering, he headed back to the encampment. He barged his way past Modig's guards and into his chamber. Such was the ferocity of the door's reverberation against its frame the atmosphere of effusive merrymaking dwindled. Among the tables, warriors were alternating between pawing topless harem girls draped over their laps, and waving empty drinking horns at slaves poised with ale flagons. Linn was snoring, his forehead slumped over a puddle of wine that had ruined his embroidered shirt.

"The Jutish wolf!" roared Modig. "I saw you skulk out an age ago ... that was one long fucking piss? All the more room for more of my fine ale! Most of your Jutes have passed out ... all the more blueskin bitches ... they'll serve you mead until it seeps out your ears before fucking you to within an inch of your Jutish life!"

Wacian marched to the head table where several of the English leaders had rolled under it in drunken stupors. Atop the table, a bard was in mid-verse, an island of sobriety among the debauchery as he extolled a Bernician victory over Picts. The stocky man raised an eyebrow when the Jutish thane blustered nearer. Wacian grasped his heels and pitched him to the floor.

"Brothers!" he bellowed, "I have seen the Brit war party."

This pronouncement raised some of the inebriated faces. Eyes sought him. Taking a deep breath, Wacian savoured his moment. He felt he had never been able to see the world so lucidly. Considering the assembly, all impatiently awaiting his next sentence, he gazed below the tables, roving over the naked flesh. Inexplicably, he realised he knew the names of all those girls down there: Genofeva, of the Silures; Luigsech, an Iceni; Afiic, from the Artebates tribe; Brietta, of the Brigantes. This incomprehensible knowledge prompted his throat to dry. More visions seeped into his mind, so vivid they blotted out his immediate surrounds. The Celtic warband were in coracles, pushing out to sea. But the Dumnonii girl was the key. The warriors in the boats were going to take shelter in her sanctuary, on an island. It was close by. At that moment it dawned on him: the redhead was a druid.

He could see Modig's lips working furiously, demanding some explanation, but everything had muted. Then a bitter voice resonated inside his head. The room seemed to freeze, leaving Paega's eyes boring into his.

Yes, I know you can hear me, Wacian. Only you can hear me. You've taken an ancient potion, but the magic you chose to swallow comes with a heavy price. You've entered a dark and dangerous world. You're a slave of the demonic wolf, Fenrir. You've discovered fantastical new abilities. You've managed to work out that my comrade Godric killed a druid, and that the druid's offspring lives. She is growing in power. She will be far more of a thorn in our side than the Silures. But you will not reveal any of this to Modig and the others. Because when you swallow the dark potion without casting the appropriate counter spells, you poison yourself. Vikings or Englishmen, Woden's men or Tiw's men, you live for one night as wolves, then you die withered old men. I can see inside you, Jute. Your guts are slowly dissolving.

Impaled by fear, Wacian stared into the ground. Now he could discern an ancient burial site many feet below: the skeletons of a man, woman, three children, four dogs. This dated from the Stone Age, before the Celts had even been native to these islands. Time was unravelling and a terrible fire had kindled inside his ribcage. Somewhere in the far-off distance he was aware of his name being repeated. But he was inside a wolf's body again. He was running freely across thick grass, enjoying the sensation of it whipping against his snout. Suddenly he came across a mountain of brown fur. He halted, whining. Staring up, he saw a monstrous creature, armed with twin tusks. It flicked his head towards him, its razor sharp horn piercing his chest. Wacian clutched the molten shaft being forged inside his chest and tumbled backwards.

CHAPTER FIFTY

Kady gauged all the variables: the stone's size and shape, the wind strength and direction, the distance to the Saxon. Priming the sling's pouch, she orientated her body slightly to the right, her arm commencing a vertical rotation around her head. Concentrating on her target, she felt every aspect of her motion channelling into her missile: her torso, her shoulders, her waist, her arms, her elbows, and her wrist. The sling now emitting its deadly whistle, she sucked air into her lungs, and once her projectile was almost at the peak of its swing, she shrieked "Dumnonii!" and released it. There was scarcely a hint of the stone's flight, until it pulped the skull, sending shards of mush across the sand.

"Excellent shot, Kady!"

Swiveling round, she smiled at Ardal emerging from the trees.

"Hi, Ardal," she called, waving the now innocuous cord in his direction.

He hurried alongside while she stepped towards the downed man. Both studied the warrior Kady had fabricated for her practice: its body, garments stuffed with leaves, the head a rotting turnip.

"I would ask you to teach me the fine art of the slingshot, but I prefer fighting with swords. Throwing stones is for girls, Kady."

Long used to his wind-ups, she poked a friendly elbow into his midriff. "Girls? If an English warband was to row right up to this beach, Ardal, I could smash all their heads before they'd even poked a toe into the water. And before you'd unsheathed your sword."

Ardal nodded at this, picturing the trail of destruction his friend could accomplish with her simple weapon. But as he stared out over the waves, he suddenly bristled.

"What is it, Ardal?"

"English warbands?" Panic raised his voice an octave. "Did you sense one approaching?"

"What?!"

"*Look*, Kady. A boat approaches. Look. Coming through the mist. More following!"

"No, Ardal. Please. No need for panic!"

"Kady! If the Saxons have discovered our hiding place, you can't take them on single-handed, druid or not." Without another word, he thrust his thumb and forefinger to his mouth and emitted a prolonged, piercing whistle. It echoed across the island; within minutes villagers began congregating hurriedly.

Kady glanced at the crowds stepping across the pebbles, shielding their eyes from the mid-day glare as they peered towards the sea. Tannus gripped his forge hammer, fingers flexing. Torean unsheathed his great broadsword, drawing its blade to his lips and kissing the metal. Emulating this, her brother Brice caressed his own weapon. Surrounding them, a fearsome array of swords, axes and cudgels blazed against the sunlight. Shaking her head, Kady faced the approaching flotilla.

"We're here to back you up, Kady," Tannus blustered.

"I don't need any back up," she protested.

"Nonsense."

"I really don't. I *invited* them."

"What?" Tannus was incredulous. "You invited Saxons to our hideout?"

Kady grinned, looking back to the nearest boat. Its rowers were now negotiating the breakers, the warriors being rocked by the swell clutching their own weapons tightly.

"Not Saxons, Tannus. These are our Celtic brethren. They are Silures."

Torean elbowed his way to the front. "Explain, Kady?"

"The Silures fled into Cymru some time ago, but one clan remained in their ancient lands, where the great forests sprawl towards the lands the enemy call East Anglia, where they have been launching guerrilla raids against the English. When their hideout was discovered, they escaped westwards across the moors, heading to the Hibernian Sea."

"And how have they ended up here? You *knew* about them, Kady?"

"My father's spirit explained they were on their way."

"How did they know where *we* were?"

"Their druid was named Bradan. My father knew him. Bradan was very old. He died some months ago, without an heir. With his dying breaths, he sketched a map onto parchment, showing the isle of mists, in case his people was ever driven from the forest. Their chieftain, Fia, consigned his map to memory, then destroyed it."

Torean frowned at the line of approaching coracles, with still more materialising from the shifting grey curtains. "They have a female leading them? Interesting. But you might have warned us, Kady. Ardal's alarm call was not good for the pressure of my blood!"

"Enemy patrols have been scouring the West Country, searching for them, from all the German tribes, Angles and Jutes, as well as our accursed Saxon neighbours. They have an unfortunate habit of joining forces when they share a common enemy. I sensed they were approaching, but did not care to announce this until they actually *did*, for fear of raising false hopes. The seas beyond the mists are treacherous today. Seeing their coracles now has taken *me* by surprise!"

The newcomers began disembarking, splashing into the shallows. Their tunics were similarly brightly chequered to the Dumnonii who were now rushing to meet them, vigorously shaking hands, assisting with baggage. As well as warriors clambering from the boats, there were elderly villagers, children, and women clutching infants; Aerona and many other Celts liberated from slavers swelled their ranks.

A young woman alighted from the vessel bringing up the rear of the convoy. Her long, bare legs, flamboyantly tattooed with dark whirls, steadied her against the waves, and as she surged through the surf she drew her wolf pelt tight to her ample curves. The wind was tossing her wild hair; the sunlight transformed it to flames. But her beautiful, green-eyed and high cheek-boned face was her most captivating feature. Her striking eyes were offset with thick bands of blue woad. Many of the Dumnonii menfolk studied her progress somewhat too intently, receiving cuffs around the ear from their partners. But as this warrior's gaze darted over the islanders, she smiled warmly. Kady stepped into the tide towards her.

"Fia?"

"And you must be Kady? Daughter of Kai?"

"Yes. My father fell to a wolf warrior."

"I'm sorry, Kady. You did great honour to his memory, leading the Dumnonii to the isle of mists."

"And I'm Torean, chieftain of this clan of the Dumnonii," Torean interrupted, pacing up to Fia, offering his hand. When she returned the handshake, he found himself forced to stifle a pained gasp.

"Pleased to meet you both. Pleased to meet all of you. I can assure you we went to great lengths to ensure our flight from the mainland went unnoticed. Even although the English patrols are thicker than wasps. And ten times more irritating!"

CHAPTER FIFTY-ONE

The yelping of the hunting dogs scattered the gulls that had been picking among the seaweed. "Easy, boys, easy," Modig hissed through his wizened teeth, his good eye studying the barren shoreline. Earlier that morning he had given the hounds another scent of Oxa's saddle. The search party had been led to this beach where the dogs were now tugging at their leashes. His men had scoured parts of this rocky landscape before, but its crags and crevasses stretched for miles. Modig knew his son lay wounded somewhere among the rock pools.

One of his soldiers gestured into the distance. "My thane. I see something. Over there. Something was moving."

"My loyal dogs have keener eyes that any of us. Let's see if they can flush out any sign of my boy."

The Saxon chieftain let go the chains. They clattered as the four hounds sped across the uneven ground, the excitable rasp of their breaths carrying, fifty Saxons following in their wake. When the dogs arrived at their quarry, chasing crows and jackdaws, all realised what had been discovered. The others kept a respectful distance as their thane stepped closer to the body. Clapping his hands, he drove the dogs from where they continued sniffing and nuzzling. The man was face down, his matted hair a haven for clawing things: crabs, shrimps and sand fleas. Heart drilling, Modig crouched. Grasping the long hair he wrenched the head around. The corpse's expression looked deceptively calm, the eyes shut. If the warrior had suffered in his dying breaths the waves had erased any evidence of it.

"Torr. Keep looking for my son," Modig ordered.

They all began poking among the boulders. Modig pulled open Torr's top, searching for evidence of wounding in the skin that had stretched like white parchment across his rib cage. Having spent such time as a prisoner of the tides, the smell of death was nauseating. The dogs continued to root around the vicinity. Modig peered to the grey horizon. "Why did my son dismount at this accursed spot? How did he drown, he and Torr? There are no blueskins around here any more. We Somersaetas torched the last of their villages months ago. Outlaws? None would dare. Any Saxon warrior would eat those drunken inbreds to break their fasts. In any case, Torr was not slain by sword."

"Tis a mystery, my thane," replied a soldier.

"It is. Save for the cesspits of Cymru, Cornwall and the lakelands west of the Pennines, what used to be Britannia is now English land." Inspired by his own rhetoric his gruff voice gathered volume until it boomed over the bleak shore, lest any stray Celts remained skulking in the undergrowth. "We fucking *own* your land now, from here to the Roman wall." Halting in mid-flow his bravado diminished to a guttural whisper. "Apart from the mysterious army that has been eluding our allies ... the blueskinned cunts no one ever sees before they vanish into thin air ... who drove my sword brother Wacian mad."

The hounds had resumed their fretful barking. He turned to the nearest warrior. "Take Torr. Strap him across your saddle. Tonight we grant him an honourable Saxon burial."

The soldier bowed, heaving the body, its clothing weighted with seawater. Modig trudged across the scree. "What have the beasts discovered now?"

"You'd better come and have a look, Modig," came a hoarse reply.

Again, he felt the apprehension rising. The dogs had worked their way across the rocks, drawing up at the foot of a towering cliff. The warriors milled around, searching among tall weeds. Whatever scent had attracted the noses of these bloodhounds, they were growing ever more agitated.

"Can you see anything, Atol?"

The gangly lad nearest the cliffs bent down, taking a few seconds longer to acknowledge the thane's testy question than his immediate comrades-in-arms felt to be healthy.

"It's a cave," Atol finally remarked, poking his broadsword into the tangled undergrowth.

Modig marched up, barging past Atol, ducking down to investigate. "A cave, it is. Well, Atol. Would you care to crawl inside for a closer look?"

"But, my lord ... I *fear* caves. There are trolls in these caves in Britain, are there not?"

Modig smiled, especially when the other warriors also chuckled at Atol's awestruck expression. "You *fear* caves? Well now, Atol. Can you explain to me ... no. To *all* of us. Which do you fear the most? Celtic cave trolls, which not one single Saxon warrior has ever clapped eyes upon? Or *this* fucking blade. Which you can *easily* clap your eyes upon ... before I drive it up your fucking arse!"

With that, Modig unsheathed his sword, holding the blade unwaveringly towards the young man's reddening face. Atol threw himself onto his knees, squirming against the weeds, derisive laughter ringing in his ears. The ground below his hands was slimy with seaweed. The further into the darkness he crept, the greater the stench assailing his nostrils. Eventually this became so overpowering he was forced to tug his tunic up to smother his nose and mouth. Wriggling over damp pebbles, he winced when centipedes scuttled over his hands. Finally the tunnel opened into a chamber where he was able to stand. A draft cooled his face and when he gazed towards the cave's roof, a funnel led directly to the clifftops, allowing meagre sunlight to filter into the gloom. His gaze returning to his immediate surroundings, he took in the walls, glistening with moss and bat shit then peered around his feet. Stagnant puddles remained from the last high tide. He froze: a hand protruded from a larger pool. Heart in his mouth, he stepped over, stooping below a limestone buttress. Fearfully he gazed into the waters that had filled a wide fissure in the floor. Below the surface, like a white stone fringed with swaying seaweed, was the petrified face and beard of his chieftain's beloved son. Atol bowed to the Saxon warrior. "You dine with Tiw now, Oxa. I'll take you to your father."

He heaved the corpse from its submerged position, reacting to the putrid reek. As he fought to jerk the stiff figure upright, as if struggling against a superior wrestling adversary, his eyes flicked to the cave walls, noticing elaborate drawings etched into the walls. Shifting position in an attempt to get the best purchase on the dead warrior, his gaze lingered on this primitive sketch. A familiar gruff voice called from the cavern's entrance. "Atol! Hurry up in there! If you take much longer the tide will fucking seal you in!"

"It's Oxa," Atol gasped. He returned to his grim task. "Fucking hell, Oxa," he groaned, painstakingly heaving him along the tunnel. "Your father will be organising *three* funerals at this rate."

Blinking against the light at the cave entrance, Atol felt the young man's weight slip from his trembling hands as Modig embraced his son. The battle-hardened chieftain sunk to his knees, burying his face in the seaweed forming a ragged scarf around the lad's white skin. His shoulders heaved while he stifled his sobbing against Oxa's lifeless features. Presently Modig felt a flicker of movement at the point where his own skin touched ice-cold flesh. Astounded, he drew back, cradling the face with his palms. The others watched nervously.

"My son? Oxa?" Modig uttered in disbelief. He peered up at his men. "I felt his lips ... quivering." When he stared back at Oxa, a black slit appeared at the mouth, a fissure that seemed to smile. "He lives! My son lives! Oxa!"

But Modig's astonished expression twisted with horror. Tiny skeletal legs prised a gap through the puckered blue lips, wriggling urgently, pausing to test the change in environment. As the warriors gasped, a green crab worked its way free of its entombment, brandishing its pincers, a sliver of pink flesh dangling from its chewing mouthparts. The beast crawled into Oxa's beard, swiftly followed by several more. Outraged, Modig snatched at them, wincing as their claws jabbed into his fingers. Blustering, he tossed the creatures aside. His men watched them scurry into the wild grass. When the ruddy-faced chieftain noticed one lingering, its claws raised, he smashed his right boot down. The crab was reduced to a pulp of shell fragments and purple innards.

"When I get my hands on the blueskins responsible for my son's murder, they will be treated with even less mercy. I swear by Tiw."

Scraping his sole against the pebbles he pointed towards the tethered horses. "Secure Oxa and Torr. We will give them heroes' burials. Then we will toast them on their journey to join Tiw's army."

The riders were sullen during the canter back to camp. The thane's knuckles were white around his horse's reins. There had been no evidence of a fight, no slain enemies to act as Oxa and Torr's servants as they travelled to the underworld. And worse than the crawling things that had so defiled his son? Those whom he would wreak vengeance upon had vanished.

Much as Modig was staring ahead, the others appreciated his brooding silence could rupture as suddenly as a lightning strike. The cave bear would likely be gorging on fresh meat before the day was done.

* * *

Gathered by the shore, the tribespeople watched the sombre procession. The two warriors were carried to their respective boats, each dressed in battle armour burnished for hours by Celtic slaves. Mildgyd's head was bowed, shoulders quivering as she bravely attempted to mute her tears for her lost husband. When the torches were applied to transform the wooden hulls into blazing infernos, Modig about turned, whispering a prayer to Tiw for the departed. He threw a conciliatory arm around his daughter-in-law and kissed her flowing blond hair.

Atol's head was respectfully bowed. Eventually he watched the twin vessels drifting further into the bay, collapsing in on themselves as the fires began devouring their blackened husks. His gaze wavered beyond the funeral boats, noticing the way the keen breeze seemed to be herding the waves from the point where sea and sky merged in a grey blur. Instantly his eyes blinked wide. He turned to his chieftain.

"Sire. I've just realised something."

"What is it, Atol?" Modig made no attempt to disguise his irritation.

Atol saw how his chieftain's eyes were red-rimmed but persisted. "The cave where I discovered Oxa."

"What about it?"

"I've just remembered. I noticed drawings on the walls."

"And what of it, Atol? These natives love to decorate their surroundings. The heathens on the far side of the great Roman wall actually paint their own *skins* head to toe."

"I know. But what I saw ... I've realised it wasn't just decoration. It was a map."

"A map? And what was this map of?"

"It was a map of the bay where we found Torr. It's dawned on me. The lines were describing the location of the cave, at the foot of the cliffs. The beach was long, horseshoe shaped."

"So there was a map of the beach inside the cave?"

"But. There was also a circle. I thought it was the sun, or the moon, this big object in the sky. There were figures around this sun. But they were also *on* it. When I first glanced at it I assumed them mythical beings. Fire nymphs or moon sprites?"

"Atol. If you don't get to the point, I'll see you served to Bee-Wolf, just like the blueskins he enjoyed last night."

"Now I realise this circle wasn't in the sky at all. It was an *island*. And this island was encircled by a great shaded ring ... mist ... like the fog banks just beyond the horizon. This island must lurk there, a mere few miles out. And these figures weren't supernatural beings. They were people. There's an island out there, among the mysterious mists, far enough from the coast to be hid from prying eyes. Perhaps the dwellers in the cave picture are long gone ... but it proves the island is large enough for people to live there."

Modig's annoyance switched to an intense stare. He gripped Atol's shoulder so hard it made the younger Saxon flinch. "Atol. By all the gods, have you unearthed the key to the mysterious death of my son and Torr? As well as a hiding place that could swallow up an army of blueskins from right under our noses? Forget Wacian's ale-fuelled ramblings the other night, now we have the answer. *Now we have the fucking answer!*" The rising excitement in his voice attracted curious glances from other mourners. "There are no natives for hundreds of miles here on the mainland. But there's an island, out to sea. And where there are islands, there are islanders. By all the gods, Atol, they will sing sagas about you, my fine friend!"

Modig's voice became a roar. "After the funeral feast tonight, we will hold a council of war. Send messengers to all the other English thanes who have gathered for the blood truce. Tell them the Somorsaetas have unearthed the location of the renegade hideaway. We must make ready a fleet of longboats. Tomorrow morning we will sail to this island. And I swear on the soul of my son Oxa, I will see the Brit scum die in excruciating agony, every last fucking one of the blueskins … men, women and children."

CHAPTER FIFTY-TWO

Kady picked her way through the rock pools. Clambering around a headland she sighted scores of wallowing seals, immediately sensing the selkies among them. While most tensed upon her approach, the one she knew to be Lugus remained calm, tilting his whiskered face as she crouched and stroked his head. She felt a tingling sensation at her fingertips and she closed her eyes when this intensified, knowing this to be the precursor to him shapeshifting again. When she opened them, a shimmering mist had descended: the sea-being stood before her, his features exuding warmth which she reciprocated.

Thank you for coming to my assistance, friends of the druids.

We are pleased to serve Kady, Kai's druid daughter. The seal people have always been pleased to serve the Dumnonii."

Good. Were you able to save the person aboard the ship?

We swam to the vessel. I climbed aboard myself, and steered it past the reefs that lie northwest of this isle of mists, eventually beaching the boat on the next headland. The boy was safe. He remains there, in a deep sleep. I thought it best he rested there until help arrived from land.

I thank you, Lugus. I am at your service.

And I yours, Kady.

The mist dissipated, revealing the selkie had returned to his natural state, although she could perceive Lugus' intelligent spirit in the seal's limpid eyes. Negotiating boulders, she headed to the shipwreck. Its shattered timber put her in mind of the skeleton of some long-beached whale. A gaping hole had been breached in its hull and she stooped through the aperture. Strewn around the deck's buckled frame were fragments of kindling. Kicking the charred branches aside, she came across the bundle of rags she had visualised through her crow's eyes. Delving inside she discovered the passenger: a boy of around eleven or twelve. His face was dusted with freckles but his cheeks and neck were tattooed with extravagant whirls, in the manner of the tribes beyond the wall. Delicately, she touched his neck. There was a faint pulse. But as she made contact with his skin she also received a potent message. This boy's veins coursed with druid blood.

Kady watched his long lashes flickering, but just as his bleary eyes sought hers, the lids closed. She shook his shoulders, fearful his ordeal had sapped his strength and he might never recover, druid or not. Grasping his sodden garments, she tried heaving him. He was a dead weight. She was aware of footsteps. Ardal had been following her, keeping a respectful distance while she had communed with Lugus. Now he was hovering close by.

"Ardal," she called. "I need a hand."

"I thought so, Kady."

Ardal ducked inside, then heaved the lad up and over his shoulders. Although the journey back to the caves was painstaking, Ardal managed to negotiate the boulder-strewn obstacle course, finally transporting the fragile bundle into their subterranean lair. The boy was placed on a bed of animal hides in the small cavern that served as the community's sick bay. When Kady applied a goblet of water to his lips, he sipped fitfully before succumbing to sleep again. Dismissing Ardal, she spent long hours rooted to the gentle rise and fall of the youngster's chest, watching for signs of him stirring, listening for traces of his own telepathic powers.

∥∥∥

Ardal rushed into the bedchamber, his urgency jerking the candles, startling her. "Kady. *Kady!* Torean demands everyone's presence."

"Ardal, please. Remind him this boy is a druid, who must be revived with great care. If this isn't done properly, there is every chance his powers will wane, if not fade completely. If he doesn't die first, of course. Tell Torean *that*."

"Kady. Torean has something he wants to show us."

"How important?"

"Life and death."

Casting a lingering glance at her patient, she muttered under her breath, but followed him. All the villagers were streaming along the paths leading from the caves, mustering around the clifftops on the island's eastern shore. Several hundred Celts filed out and looked in the direction of the mainland. Beyond the horizon, the towering clouds were discoloured by trails of black smoke.

Torean pointed towards the skies. "I spotted this when I was walking my hounds. Campfires. Judging by the smoke, *thousands* of campfires. The moment we have been dreading has arrived. The enemy have discovered us."

Fia scowled. "As you know, Torean, my clan went to great efforts to sow discontent among the English, setting warbands against another. When the dogs lived in Germania they were always at war. Perhaps those are not the campfires of an army facing this way, but *two* armies facing each other on a battle's eve. Perhaps Saxons against Angles?"

Kady faced Fia. "I'll find out the truth."

* * *

Hurtling across the bay, her soles jousting with the slime-covered stones, she made her way to the point where the seals remained basking in the sunshine. Scampering over to Lugus again, she caressed his leathery hide.

Lugus. I need your help.

There is great urgency in your voice, Kady.

My people face a terrible peril, from the mainland. Can you show me what the seals can see, Lugus, where the great land is closest to the isle of mists?

It will be done.

Kady observed the seal wriggling awkwardly from his position on the rocks, but after launching into the churning waves, transforming instantly. Closing her eyes she could see the underwater vista through Lugus' eyes. As his head darted left and right, she glimpsed kelp beds below flickering fish shoals. The seabed unfolded at a dizzying pace, flounders and plaice flapping off into the murk in puffs of sand. Presently the dappling sunlight increased in intensity until Lugus broke the surface. What Kady could see left her gasping for breath. The shore was seething with warriors and their horses, numbering in the thousands, the shields they bore and their brandished banners emblazoned with the arms of Angle, Saxon and Jute eorls, all standing together. The Germanic tribes that had settled throughout the east and south of the former realms of the British Celts had mustered an army. Its sole purpose was to destroy her people.

CHAPTER FIFTY-THREE

After she had related her vision, a silence descended. For moments the only sounds were kittiwake cries and the sea's relentless churning.

"It is just as I feared, Kady," Torean finally conceded. "The English have discovered our hideout."

She nodded. "They await the turning of the tides."

"That means they will launch their assault three hours' hence," stated Fia.

The brief exchange instigated panic. Torean raised placatory hands but felt despair: after having made a good fist of surviving on this rock and evading the enemy, was their fate to be sealed in such a short space of time?

"I need to rouse the young druid," Kady concluded.

"Why, Kady?" demanded Ardal. Instead of answering, she strode towards the entrance to the tunnels, going straight to the bed where the stranger was still showing little signs of recuperation. Regarding his boyish features, serene and at odds with the warlike stripes daubed over the skin, she lifted the goblet by his bed and emptied it over his face. His eyes opened. Touching a finger to his lips, she projected her thoughts.

Listen to me. I am Kady, a druid of the Dumnonii. You're on the isle of mists, off the coast of Dumnonia. You've been shipwrecked. You were sailing in a funeral ship.

The boy yawned and stretched feebly, blinking at the unfamiliar surroundings, but nodding at the source of the internal voice.

Kady? A beautiful name. I'm Anwell, of the Caledonii.
You're a druid?
Just like you, Kady.
And the funeral ship?

My people thought me dead. I had cast a spell to save the lives of many of my tribe who had succumbed to plague ... the magic was potent. It cured them of the terrible illness but drained the life from me. I could see and hear but no longer speak or move ... in this near coma they assumed me dead ... I felt them place me in a boat. Kindling was tossed all around me. I listened to them singing their dirges, heard my sisters weeping ... then felt the boat being pushed out. After the rocking started I felt the impact of the fiery arrows. Were it not for the rain I would have been turned to charcoal.

We must give thanks to Manannan for raining tears down on you!

Smiling at him, she lifted the cup. This time she tipped a few droplets into it from a phial chained around her neck. The mysterious liquid was purple, with a rancid smell. She touched it to his trembling lips.

Wolfsbane?

Yes, Anwell ... mixed with crushed foxglove petals and oyster juice. This would revive a weary horse.

After swallowing the mouthful the improvement was remarkable. Within minutes his skin was tinged with colour. His appetite was next to be restored and when Kady propped him up with pillows, he gratefully wolfed down a hunk of bread. Presently the cloth draped over the bedchamber entrance ruffled and Torean entered.

"Kady? How fares your young charge?"

"He is doing well, Torean. Thanks to one of my father's favourite prescriptions."

"Good, Kady." But the chieftain lowered his voice and leant closer to her. "A shame this revival seems destined to be so short lived."

Anwell looked to Kady. *What does he mean?*

I'll explain.

"I've called a council of war with the elders of the Dumnonii, and with Fia and her cohorts. We don't have long to make our plans."

Kady nodded, then nudged the boy. "Anwell. I'd like to introduce you to our chieftain. Torean."

"Torean? I'm honoured. Your druid saved my life."

Kady delighted at the way his juvenile voice rolled around the Caledonian syllables. Torean reached out and shook the boy's hand, pleasantly taken aback by the strength of his grip. Anwell smiled when an imposing woman materialised in the doorway. Although struck by her vivacious beauty, Anwell noticed a faint scar running across her chin. He knew whoever had inflicted that wound would not have lived to boast about it.

Kady explained. "Fia, of the Silures."

"Pleased to make your acquaintance, Fia," said Anwell.

Fia pretended to frown. "Your tattoos? I took you for one of the painted people, the Picts. But your tongue is Celtic, like us, although from much further to the north."

"I'm Caledonii, from the west coast. The Picts we give a wide berth. We never venture over the Cairngorms."

"I'd heard *everyone* north of the wall was ferocious, liable to take the heads of anyone straying into their glens? Yet you seem a well-mannered young boy."

"If I may be so bold, you look as if you would not flinch from a swordfight yourself?"

"That would be an accurate assumption, Anwell," Torean butted in. "The Silures of the great forest have been holding out against the Germans, for months."

Fia nodded grimly. "When we realised the bastards had discovered the location of our fortress, we slipped by their patrols."

Torean, never one to miss an opportunity to boast, butted in: "They didn't just slip by the English patrols, Anwell. The Silures caused mayhem."

Fia slapped Torean affectionately across his shoulder blades; as much to shut him up, Kady speculated. "Although we have always lived among the trees, we had heard of the isle of mists, making good our escape here. It seems Celts from all the corners of the land are gathering on his little island."

I can thank the selkies for bringing Fia's people here safely, Anwell ... and yourself.

I would like to meet these selkies, Kady. There are seal people out on the islands near my own village.

Kady articulated herself. "Anwell. Despite our best efforts to keep our sanctuary hidden from the English, an army is readying to attack us."

"The English? They are that strong, even out here, by the Hibernian Sea?"

"Alas, yes. I've had visions of their various tribes, amalgamating, sending warbands out to the west ... normally Saxons and Angles guard the boundaries of their separate kingdoms, but they have united, with the Jutes also, to drive the last Celts out of their realm. They refer to this union as the blood truce. Their longships will surround us long before nightfall. I don't have enough druidic powers on my own to stop them. You must accompany us to the council of war, Anwell. We'll discuss what we could do. If anything."

CHAPTER FIFTY-FOUR

Brice clung to a precarious perch on the tallest elm, its trunk bowed by decades of easterly gales. Here he stared intently into the vast veils of mist shielding the islet from the mainland, watching for the first sails. Below, the hectoring voices had become intense enough for Torean to crack his sword hilt against his shield to restore order.

Studying all these strangers, Anwell shivered. Most appeared sympathetic when they caught his eye. But he was wary of the Dumnonii druid's brother. Occasionally Brice would interrupt his lookout duties to fire him a contemptuous glare. For all that the Germanic barbarians posed the gravest threat to all present, Anwell had noticed the older lad glowering enviously at the extravagant tribal marking adorning his neck and cheeks. Kady had warned him Brice's jealousy of her own druidic skills was only outweighed by his dislike of outsiders.

Although frail from his nightmarish journey on the Hibernian Sea, Anwell appreciated his mystical skills had not completely waned. But a close-quarters telepathic conversation with another druid was one thing. The complicated spells required for wielding magic seemed far more elusive.

Kady found herself increasingly distant from the debate, and instead focussed her attention on Anwell. Attempting to tap into his thoughts, she found her probing was falling on the psychic equivalent of deaf ears. She sensed the boy's powers were still weak, his mental as well as physical strength ebbing and flowing.

Now Fia stood. The legacy of her clan's fearless actions guaranteed her words would carry considerable weight. Conversation faded as everyone focussed on her piercing eyes and angular cheekbones freshly daubed with warpaint. "I propose boarding coracles with my warriors. We will row further down the coast, then slip ashore, striking the English curs from behind. If we hit them hard enough, they will panic. In the confusion, the rest of you take coracles to Cymru."

Tannus shook his head. "Not one of us doubt the courage of our Silures brethren, Fia," he declared, "but even if you caught the rats completely by surprise, there are just too many of them. When a wasp stings a charging bear, it still charges."

"Can you think of a better suggestion?" Fia snapped. "Either we take the fight to them, or else we simply wait here to die."

Torean patted the blacksmith across his shoulders. "I would echo Tannus' sentiments, Fia. The Silures battle prowess is legendary. But Cymru is sealed off from the south. Saxon longboats blockade the Severn and the Somorsaetas are thick in the forests, hunting down Britons as if we are nought but boars."

"What then, Torean? What course of action?" demanded Fia.

"You don't need to send your fighters ashore, Fia," Torean replied. "I say we make a stand. We can defend this island well. We're prepared for it. We can roll rocks down the slopes. We have enough arrows to keep their ships at bay ... for days. Yes. We can stand and fight. Taking the fight to the English would be suicidal."

Fia shook her head. "Keep their ships at bay for days? How many days? The English could simply encircle us, stop us from fishing. They could aim arrows of flame into these apple trees. They could starve us."

Exasperated by the stalemate, Ardal peered to the clouds, carrying traces of the smoke plumes from the mainland high above the haar, only to dissipate into wisps. If only the soldiers stoking those campfires could be so readily dispersed. His eye caught a fulmar riding the currents, blissfully unaware of the human catastrophes unfolding far below. He regarded the chieftain, who was now offering a graphic description of the effect a boulder would have on any English warrior when dropped from height, punching his opened left palm with his right fist, adding a gruesome sound effect that reminded Ardal of a snail being trod upon.

Jerking his attention back to the knoll his eyes sought Kady. It was only a matter of time before the Dumnonii elders deferred to their druid's counsel, although he suspected there would be little she could offer in the face of such insurmountable odds. But the position she had occupied was empty. As the minutes dragged, a sense of unease grew, until his natural protectiveness came to the fore. Excusing himself from the council, he paced down the winding path that led to the isle's eastern shore.

Crunching over the shingle, he disturbed scores of seals that slithered off rocks into the sea. He wondered if any might be this Lugus that Kady spoke of. Following their sleek grey shapes propelling further into the surf, he noticed the fading wake of some craft. Squinting, he tracked this to its source a hundred yards offshore: a coracle, a flailing oar, and red hair cascading in the wind.

"*Kady?!* What the fuck are you doing? *Kady?*"

Rushing into the swell, he pitched himself forwards, each broadside of water sapping his strength, filling his mouth with salt. For futile minutes he expended as much effort hacking up spume as stroking through the waves: like most of the young Dumnonii men, his swimming skills amounted to ungainly floundering. His locks wrapped over his dejected expression in a freezing mask. Tugging the hair away he could no longer see the coracle. His heart hammering, he shrieked: "Help! *Help!*"

He caught sight of Kady's boat again, fleetingly, before the mists swallowed it.

CHAPTER FIFTY-FIVE

Torean glowered towards his son, motionless, staring towards the walls of mist. "Ardal? What has happened?" he barked. "And where is Kady? Where is our druid?"

Ardal shrugged before bunching a fist and driving it into the water swirling around his waist. "Manannan! Bring her back to me!"

"What do you mean, Ardal?"

Anguish contorting his features, the lad jerked a finger into the distance. "She's in a coracle, heading straight towards the English. Alone."

Fia squinted over the swell. "She is but a girl. I salute her courage. Not even my most ferocious warrior would go so willingly to certain death."

Brice jostled to the front of the congregating crowd. "I warned you about this. Kady thinks she has the magic to take on a thousand warriors?" But the enormity of the situation overwhelmed him. Instead of continuing a tirade, he pictured his sister struggling to steer her little coracle towards a beach where enemy soldiers would laugh and jeer, her imagined powers condemning her to violent death. Tears streamed down his cheeks.

Ardal glanced at him then faced Torean. "Why would she do it, father? She has always been the one to urge caution. *Why?*"

"Perhaps she thinks she can win us some time, son."

"I don't care whether or not she would ever have been as powerful a druid as Kai. I only ever saw Kady for what she was. The woman I love."

After sharing this with the others, he sunk to his knees, his shoulders juddering as he wept. Brice waded towards him, grasping his sodden shirt and hauling him up. Throwing an arm around him, he steered him back to the others.

"I know why she did this." Anwell's hoarse Caledonii tones boomed across the gathering.

"Why?" demanded Ardal.

"She is trying to tell me."

Brice stomped over the shingle to the boy, seizing him by the scruff of his tunic. "What?! What do *you* know that no one else does, you northern savage?"

Anwell ignored him, instead closing his eyes, breathing deeply.

"*Answer me!*" Brice shrieked.

Fia snapped. "Silence, Brice, for your sister's sake! Silence everyone. Kady now communicates with this druid by thought."

Brice clammed, glaring into the intricate patterns curling over the Caledonian's features. Anwell's lips parted but all were startled to hear Kady's voice projecting.

I slipped away during the council. I knew you would only try and stop me if I divulged my plan, Anwell, you and all the others. The English now know many Celtic fighters make sanctuary on this island. They have declared a blood truce, and rivals have sent warbands from all their kingdoms, Saxon, Angle and Jute. But there is more to it than that. I have sensed a powerful shaman in their midst. He has been hunting me. It is he who has been conjuring the wolf warriors. He has tracked me here. I am the one whose powers he fears, no one else. I will surrender to him, offer myself as a sacrifice. While the enemy are so distracted, you must insist to Torean that everyone boards the coracles and makes for Cymru.

Anwell's eyes snapped open. The effort of being Kady's conduit having drained him of energy, his body sagged. Tannus paced over to steady him.

Fia faced Torean. "That young girl has more courage than us all put together." Stepping closer, she whispered: "I pray that when her end comes it is swift, rather than the lingering torture so often favoured by the German bastards." When Torean nodded, she raised her voice again. "My fighters would provide the more effective distraction. We resort to my original plan. My warriors will take to the coracles and beach a mile further down the coast from the German dogs. Then we strike."

Torean gazed into the mists. "For all her caution, always the impetuous streak. Kai was the same. She had the makings of a fine druid. One of the best."

Ardal's features hardened. "I'm going after her. I'm going to bring her back."

"She has too much of a head start, Ardal," cautioned Torean.

"If I row hard, father, I might head her off."

He selected a coracle, hastily untying it from its mooring. "Tannus. Place Anwell inside. When he comes to, perhaps he can reach her thoughts and try reasoning with her."

Heaving the boat into the surf, Ardal clambered aboard. Tannus waded towards him, placing the senseless Caledonian into the wicker chamber. With a nod to the others, Ardal pushed out to sea.

"May Manannan guide you," Torean cried. As he watched the craft battling the waves, he caressed his sword. If druids or sea gods failed them, there would only be steel.

CHAPTER FIFTY-SIX

The colours of their kingdoms were strident in the wind: East Anglia's eagles, the golden wyvern of Wessex, Mercia's blue and gold, North Humberland's yellow and red stripes. Gathered on the headland, bolstered from the keen sea breeze by flagons of mulled wine, the eorls and thanes surveyed the army. This alliance of so many men from England's four corners was momentous.

At the outset of the blood truce, many were the voices pondering the wisdom of mustering such a force, given there were more potent enemies who might take advantage of any slackening of defences. Viking longships continued sacking villages on the eastern and southern seaboards. As the forest leaves withered, raids on North Humberland were increasing, with Caledonii and Picts greedy to fill their own larders with stolen livestock. Gazing towards the grey horizon, some of these English commanders had questioned why crude marks etched into a cave had been seized upon as irrefutable evidence of some native hideout. Modig of the Somorsaetas was scarcely known for his perception – most of the Angles and Jutes, and several of his Saxon brethren, considered him a madman. But Angles, Jutes and Saxons had all suffered at the hands of the natives these last few months. The trail of the forest rebels led to this coastline, so if some seal-shit infested rock was sheltering a few hundred half-starved British, then all these Englishmen of rank wished to be able to boast they had witnessed the severing of the last Celtic head between Wessex and Cymru.

Linn passed his goblet to one of his bodyguards. With a click of his finger, a cloth was summoned from the king's favourite Iceni. After she had curtsied and passed it to him, he patted his mouth. To the eorl next to him, he murmured: "A fine body of warriors, although I must say the Saxons and Jutes never dress appropriately for battle."

"They do not, sire. It would not be the first time our men have mistaken them for Celtic savages in the heat of battle."

"Just so. I hope these incidents can be kept to a minimum when the Brits come at them with their blue warpaint and their tree-felling axes."

Overhearing the latter part of the king's conversation, Modig peered over. "These are not woodsmen we face today, Linn. These blueskins are skilled fighters, possibly the very ones who gave your housecarls such a bloody nose."

"We shall see, my Saxon friend," Linn replied with a gracious nod. To his eolderman he murmured: "Perhaps we should just remind our sergeants their men should only hack at the savages who have blue stripes across their faces."

Modig dismissed the imperious Angle. Although the respect for the blood truce was ingrained, he was relieved it would only last until the last Celtic head was rolling into these murky waters. Then all these warlords could return to their respective kingdoms and get back to stoking animosities.

He studied the pendants planted at regular intervals towards the point where the waves were dashing. At dawn he had ordered scouts to navigate a path over the miles of treacherous mudflats so the longboats could be dragged into position without waiting hours for the tide. Then he noticed something further out, perhaps a mile offshore. A coracle was bobbing towards land.

"What gives, Modig?" called Linn. Modig faced the East Anglian, again glowering at the man's robes, more befitting a wedding than warfare.

"Fuck knows," he grunted.

"They say some of these natives have magical powers. But even one of their gods himself wouldn't dare to take on so many warriors?"

"I don't like it, Linn," replied Modig. "You're right about the special powers."

A lean horse cantered towards the Saxon chieftain, its rider tugging the reins. "Sire," he reported, "lookouts send word a Brit is approaching."

"A champion warrior, perhaps? Is the blueskin the size of a Viking shithouse?"

"No, sire. Just a girl. A redheaded girl."

Linn sniggered. "Inclement conditions at sea, Modig. Perhaps this native fool is hopelessly caught in a current?"

"Then let the current bring the blueskin to us, so I can hack her red head from her shoulders. Sound the order to advance."

CHAPTER FIFTY-SEVEN

Battling against the swell had taken its toll. Kady was exhausted, her muscles serrated with pain, her limbs trembling as she relinquished her grip on the oar and collapsed. A white-capped wave smacked into the hull; wrenched from her seat, her skull cracked against the keel. The last thing she was aware of was an imploring voice inside her head, its burr Caledonian, but this seemed to be coming from some unimaginable distance and the words made no sense. Her father's sub-conscious tones, always so diluted whenever she was in shock, had abandoned her. Her quivering vision traced the smoke trails high above the rocking craft before she sunk into a stupor.

When she came to, she felt the boat being jerked from side to side. Eyes flickering open, she spied white fingertips clutching the boat's rim. Reaching out, she brushed against clammy flesh, cold as the surrounding seas. Webbed fingers grasped her own.

Kady.

Her name flowed into her sub-consciousness, transmitted in the melodic language of the seal people.

It is I, Lugus. You must go no further. There is danger. My people have already suffered at your enemies' hands. There is a mystic among them who has dark powers. He would go to great lengths to destroy you and this sacrifice will do nothing to spare your people. You must flee from this place. Your friends approach. You should go back with them, back to the isle of mists.

Her strength returning, she felt the sea-being relinquishing his grip. She heaved herself to the side of the coracle. Gazing down, she saw Lugus peering towards her with intense emerald eyes.

Thank you, Lugus.

She was aware of other voices. Ardal was shrieking at her from a fast approaching coracle. Cowering next to him, Anwell's features were pallid and he was watching the tossing waves nervously.

My strength is weak, Kady. But he insisted I came along ... to rescue you.

As their vessel drew closer, Kady smiled at them. "A blow to my head and a word from my selkie friend have drawn me to my senses. I admit Fia's plan has the most merit."

"Her warband are setting off to outflank the English," explained Ardal. Thrusting his oar into the water, he drew his craft alongside. Poised against the sea's erratic motion, he judged a moment to leap into Kady's boat. When he threw himself aboard, she grasped him, joy sweeping over her. Soaked to the bone and trembling with cold, they embraced like limpets. Relief banishing his usual reticence, Ardal's lips sought hers. Kady peered into his brown eyes, returning the kiss, pressing her mouth tighter into his, their weight a bolster against the coracle's motion. They broke off when their uninhibited reunion was disturbed by a heavy splash. Kady stared overboard.

Lugus!

Among an explosion of bubbles, she glimpsed his metamorphosis, limbs shrinking to flippers, the sleek humanoid torso fattening into a seal's bulk. The selkie gave a final gasp and a forlorn air pocket billowed upwards, its silver lining revolving. After it dissipated, Kady saw red clouds seeping around dappled grey skin. The lifeless body slipped into the murk, blood seeping from the dirk buried handle-deep in his skull.

There was a violent crack beside her. Ardal pitched forwards, a crimson gash lacerating his forehead. Dumbfounded, Kady peered behind her. The tattooed boy was clutching an oar, blood dripping from its flat edge. She tried entering his mind.

Why, Anwell?

There was no response. For a fleeting moment she felt a connection but its source was unrecognisable and so unbelievably evil it took her breath away. Then the Caledonian lunged his weapon again, catching the older druid squarely across the side of her head. She felt a vast whale open its monstrous maw to swallow her whole. Anwell then crouched, the oar dropping from his limp fingers into the sea. He gazed at the other boat, his dull eyes rooted to its wake as it drifted ever shorewards. He did not blink.

CHAPTER FIFTY-EIGHT

The agony persisted. Then fitful dreams would take hold and the pain would fade, replaced by a sensation of rocking, as if she was in her mother's arms again. During a period of deeper unconsciousness, a vision came.

A hundred or more seals were powering across open seas, their twisting and spiralling through the clear waters as co-ordinated as a starling flock. Among the streamlined shapes were several shapeshifters, Lugus at the forefront, the myriad bubbles in his silvery wake the guide for the others to follow. Kady sensed their collective glee at latching onto a vivid scent. Soon the sea was rich with the overpowering stench of seatrout. Kady could make them out, their bodies dark against the dappling sunlight, their bellies swollen after the voracious feeding that preceded them migrating upstream to spawn.

The seals plunged into the lugubriously shifting kelp forest so their silhouettes would not betray their presence. The shoal was directly above, so bloated with sprats and sand eels they scarcely seemed to be swimming, merely content to drift landward with the currents. As one the colony paddled upwards, ravenous jaws scything into their docile prey. But Kady started. These fish were already dismembered, their motion solely down to their bodies being buffeted by the shock waves of the hunt. Kady's stomach churned at the sight of all the fish entrails, the slowly sinking purple matter that had transformed the sea into a vile soup. But the seals circled, gorging themselves; even the selkies were slave to their animal instincts as the feeding frenzy churned the water, transforming their undersea realm a sickly red. Minute fish scales swirled all around; Kady imagined being trapped in some nightmarish galaxy. Seeking the light struggling to penetrate this murk, she could make out unnatural textures forming walls on all sides. Nets were closing in on the underwater feast, hands dragging this web into position. Above the surface there were muted voices, commands snapping: in English. The seals continued satiating their hunger until Lugus screamed a warning, extricating himself from the trap, twisting his body downwards into the kelp. The others swam in hysterical circles, blinded by the scraps of their abandoned meal, colliding heavily. Terror-stricken wails filled the seas. As they were hemmed closer together, their panic increased. The first arrow struck home. A seal whirled into its brethren, a missile embedded in its neck. Soon the waters were recoiling with repeated volleys, those arrows failing to secure an immediate target lashing downwards in trails of bubbles, like ravenous gannets. When the nets hauled the survivors closer to the surface, axe heads began bearing down. The hunt was over in minutes.

The vision faded, leaving Kady acutely aware of the blow to her head. On the periphery of her eyesight her jaw seemed grotesquely swollen. The lulling quality of the boat had been replaced by a violent shaking. A wave dashed against the coracle, its spray lashing her face. She grasped Ardal by the scruff of his neck, shaking him. "Ardal! Wake up!"

His eyelids parted. He mustered enough strength to emit a gruff moan. "What happened?"

"Anwell attacked us. He killed Lugus."

"*What? Why?*"

"I don't know, Ardal. But my druidic powers granted me a terrible vision of the last moments of Lugus' life."

"What did you see?"

"I saw the selkies ... ambushed."

"*Ambushed?*"

"They were massacred, by Saxons. I think only Lugus escaped."

"And Anwell killed him? Is he a traitor, Kady? Does he carry German gold in his pockets?"

"I haven't figured that out, Ardal. It makes no sense. The selkies saved his life, so I don't know why he would betray them ... or us."

Kady grasped the boat's rim. She hoped the prevailing offshore current would have carried them some way back towards the mists. Anticipating open seas she appreciated they could just as easily skirt the island and drift westwards into the great ocean. She raised herself and looked over. "By the gods. No."

Their coracle lurched, crashing against rocks, spilling them into the surf. Coughing out the salty water, Kady managed to stand, assisting Ardal. The nearest English soldiers regarded them with a mixture of curiosity and mirth. Among the ranks of bristling swords and spears, her eyes were drawn to a squad of cursing warriors, their mail gauntlets tight around a quivering leash, struggling with some deranged beast. At first glance she thought the horrific creature one of their werewolves, somehow impervious to daylight. But when the hulk of dark brown fur raised itself on hind legs, she realised it was a cave bear.

"*Look*, Kady!"

"I see it." Kady grasped his hand. "Help me retrieve the coracle, Ardal."

"We'd never make it. We're in range of their archers."

"*Ardal ... just fucking help me!* Help me drag it onto land."

Forcing his way towards the jolting boat, he seized it and hauled it towards her. Beyond Kady an order was barked: the men striving to keep the lumbering animal at bay dropped their chains. The bear remained still for seconds. Its nose deciphered the array of scents until it focused on the two humans in its immediate path. With a booming roar, it bounded towards them. Kady crouched, beckoning Ardal to follow. Kady eased the coracle over them, like a great tortoise shell. Panting with adrenaline, she murmured a verse then brushed her fingers against Ardal's taut arms.

"I can't move! My muscles have turned to stone!"

"That's because there's a thousand pounds of meat eater heading straight towards our wicker shelter. You'll be able to hold it in position a bit longer." The bear slammed into the hull, the barrier splintering. Ardal's muscular form kept the coracle rooted although the beast pawed furiously, its bellowing increasing each moment its prey remained elusive.

"I caught Anwell's expression, Ardal," she gasped, eyes darting around.

"What about him?"

"He didn't know what he was doing. He was in a trance."

"Fuck him, Kady. You and I are here; he is not. You think this is how it ends for us?"

"Perhaps. I've been through so much ... I don't really care any more. I only care you're here with me, to share my final moments, in our beautiful Celtic land." She embraced him. "I've always kept you at arm's length. I suppose I didn't want you to become too attached to me. A druid's life can be short."

"*Can be?*" he snorted. "But I know all that, Kady. I'm not that naïve."

Huge incisors gnawing into the hull destroyed their moment. Ardal lashed his right foot towards the snarling monster's snout. The bear yelped and drew back. Kady snatched a look through the cavity. Her eyes whitened. Horn blasts pierced the air. Hundreds of English footsoldiers began advancing across the bay. The bear shoved its face through the breach, eyes glaring. As it shook its huge head, sticky froth sprayed the cowering Celts. Kady glanced at the ground. Her fingers clawed at an exposed rock. A snapping jaw came so close she could feel the fetid breath against her cheek. Feverishly her fingernails clawed into the wet shingle. The bear squeezed its shoulders into the fissure, its neck muscles straining as it judged it had enough space to seize the nearest prey. Kady felt the earth relinquishing the buried stone. Snatching it free, she balled her fist around it. The monster reacted to her sudden movement and bellowed with rage. Kady smashed the rock into its skull, the splintering bone horribly magnified by the hull's upturned curve. She rained four more concentrated blows into her target until its brown eyes rolled upwards and blood matted its fur.

The enemy had increased pace, the nearest of their warriors yards away, close enough to make out individual faces peering beneath helms. Kady could see how fervently knuckles were gripping weapons and banners.

"I lost my sword when we crashed ashore, Kady. But you prime your lethal slingshot, my love. Take as many of these German bastards with us as you can. Brighid is ready to welcome us with open arms. Our parents await."

Kady studied his handsome face, her fingers brushing at his tears. In their final moments, she had never seen her laconic friend so brimming with life. "I love you, Ardal."

"I love you, Kady."

She rubbed Ardal's shoulder and his muscles relaxed. He heaved the coracle aside. They stood together, thrusting themselves clear of the coracle, both shouting: "For the Dumnonii!"

The moment the wicker boat clattered to one side, a host of spear points lunged towards their horrified faces. Warriors encircled them; beyond, archers trained arrows. There was a cantering of hooves. A chieftain drew up, steadying his mount. "What flotsam has our sea god, Wade, spat onto our English land? Nought but a couple of Celtic dogs. I would've simply taken your heads, but you took the life of a loved one. Bee-Wolf. The bear was my son's. For that reason a special fate awaits you. In your final moments, look at me, blueskins. I am Modig of the Somorsaetas, a Saxon warlord. Today we to row to your island to slaughter all who live there, down to the last babe, except for the girls we take as slaves for our young warriors."

Ardal had understood nothing of his foreign speech; Kady merely pretended this to be the case. Without taking his eyes off them, the Saxon snapped his fingers. The soldiers parted, allowing the Celts to see what was lurking in the background. Four thick wooden lances had been swiftly impaled in the mud, their shafts crossed and lashed with ropes into twin X-shaped structures. Modig clicked his fingers again. Kady and Ardal felt their backsides booted as they were persuaded towards their crucifixes.

Men crowded, hacking and gobbing at them, poking with spear butts. One corpulent Saxon waddled closer and seized Kady's tunic, tearing it, leaving her clutching desperately as its loose folds flapped from her exposed breasts. This was greeted with a ribald roar. Ardal squirmed free of the men dragging him towards the lances, smacking his forehead into the antagonist's skull. There was a crack, a spurt of blood and the fellow staggered backwards, sending a further three soldiers tumbling in his wake. Those flanking Ardal heaved him downwards and rained punches and hilt blows at his face. Spluttering, the Celt spat mouthfuls of blood and teeth at the furious Saxons.

"Enough!" bawled Modig. "I want this sideshow finished. I want the boats launched. Lash these blueskin dogs to the spears."

Kady smarted as a large palm slapped her full in the face. Blinking stars away, her arms were hauled to the opposite beams, her wrists secured so tightly a pulse insisted beneath the twine. Turning to her right, she watched Ardal being trussed.

"Bring branches," barked Modig. "The stink of roasting Brits will be an entertaining distraction as we drag our armada down to the sea."

In the corner of her vision, Kady saw men approaching, laden with kindling that they proceeded to stack around the structures. From her elevated position she watched hundreds of English soldiers trudging across the puddled shore, some trundling longboats over logs. When they passed the Celts they gazed distractedly, so familiar with casual violence meted out to prisoners the spectacle had become banal. Her body trembled, digging her shackles into her skin.

"It will be a draw-out death, Celtic bitch," Modig's taunted. "I see much of the wood is still green, or damp from last night's rain, so the flames will be most reluctant to finish you. You'll most likely choke long before your tattoos start peeling."

Kady closed her eyes, seeking her father's wisdom. But it was impossible to focus in her distressed state. Passing men rained curses on her in their ugly Germanic voices. The first boats were already being pushed through the waves and soldiers were clambering aboard. Her heart flipped when she caught a whiff of burning wood. In the corner of her eye Modig dismounted. A hunched lackey passed him a flaming torch. The Saxon chieftain bowed to Ardal, touching the flare to the bundle of branches.

"I would've fed your cooked carcass to Bee-Wolf, you blueskin cunt. I'll feed you to my hounds instead. This time tomorrow you'll be dog shit."

Once flames began licking, he paced over to Kady. When he was close enough, he tossed the torch. It sparked and flashed; heat nipped her feet when the fire started devouring the brittle kindling beneath the damper branches. Perhaps it would not be as lingering a death as he had predicted. The thane raised his hand and an underling fetched his horse. He clambered aboard, just as Kady's father passed a message from the underworld.

The bear belonged to the German chieftain's son ... Oxa ... he was one of the two men you enticed into the sucking sands ... now think of the words you would use to tell him this ... you already have the power to switch from our native tongue to that of the invaders ...

Snatching a breath among the smoke plumes, she addressed the Saxon in his own language: "I am Kady of the Dumnonii people. I am a druid of the British Celts. We are close to the spot where I took Oxa's life."

Some of the colour drained from Modig's cheeks, alarm overriding his sadistic taunts. "You can speak the German tongue? And a druid? What do you mean you killed my son, you fucking witch? How do you know his name?"

"I drowned the Saxon bastard in quicksand. No glorious warrior's death for Oxa, no injuries of war that would entitle him to sit with your god, Tiw. He died a slow, agonising death, his lungs slowly filling with sand and worms and crab shit."

"You fucking *liar*. Oxa sits with Tiw, vanquished by a dozen Celts in battle."

"I do not lie. I was close enough to see the fear in his face."

"You *lie*."

"I was close enough to see the red skull on his neck."

Modig's knuckles whitened around his horse's reins. Gawking at Kady, his jaw dropped, as if her words had struck him dumb. Digging his heels into his horse, he drew up as close to the flames as he could without distressing his beast then dismounted again. He unsheathed his sword. But he paused. Although there were no darker hints in the blue skies above, an intense thunder was rumbling from the horizon. Modig gazed upwards for a moment; hundreds of Englishmen did likewise, glancing curiously at one another as the tumult rose to an ear-splitting crescendo. The ground was quaking. Loose stones cascaded from larger boulders. Some lost their footing. Horses whinnied in terror. Modig turned to Kady. Although the flames had begun stinging her feet, she was grinning. Taking in her mystifying expression, he raised an eyebrow but prepared to lunge his sword into her belly. That was when the screaming began. He swivelled round. All along the shore, those soldiers who had made it furthest into the sea were leaping from their boats, casting weapons aside, pounding through the shallows towards land. Beyond, an immense wall of water, thirty feet high, was hurtling inwards, plumes of foam flecking from its curling crest. A mirror image of this tidal surge flowed from the bay's opposite side.

Kady sucked a deep breath as the sea rushed on, sweeping men in its wake, immersing Modig and adding him to the human harvest that writhed in its swirling vortices before they were sucked from sight. The water struck, dousing the fires, wrenching the lances from their mooring, the impact splintering the shafts. Kady's arms flapped freely again but she spiralled down into a nightmarish underworld, where soldiers whirled all around her, limbs thrashing as they mouthed silent screams. Bubbles rushed past her face, myriad silver air pockets that cruelly taunted her agonised lungs. Among the gloom, more purposeful shapes were darting around, weaving around the drowning soldiers. One flashed closer. It was a selkie. She felt its webbed hand reaching to her. Although her ribcage was on the verge of exploding, relief coursed through her as she was guided to the surface. When she breeched the waves, she gasped greedily snatching sweet air into her lungs. She glimpsed the sea-being's serene smile before it plunged into the deep. She wondered how many others from its clan had survived the hunt. Her instinctive relief was short lived; as she treaded water she peered among scores of thrashing limbs. "Ardal!" she shrieked. "Ardal! *Where are you?!*"

Something brushed against her kicking legs. Gazing down she saw another selkie, rising from the depths, hauling a body. He stroked the last few yards to the surface himself; his seal guardian relinquished its grip and melted into the churning waters. Ardal similarly gulped air. "What happened?" he managed to blurt out. "Druid magic?"

"No, Ardal. Not even the most powerful druid could cast a spell to interfere with Manannan! We can thank the weather. At certain times of the year, Rhiannon, the moon goddess, creates freak tides. They turn this bay into a whirlpool, with massive waves that rush towards land. The invaders picked the wrong time to tackle the Dumnonii!"

"Kady. I don't know what I'd do if anything ever happened to you."

She whispered into his ear. "And I don't know what would happen to our people if anything ever happened to me. Our people will always need a druid. So I will need an heir."

They grinned together at that, and as an empty Saxon vessel drifted by, the thought inspired the urgency of their stroking towards it.

CHAPTER FIFTY-NINE

In the dusk they emerged from the trees surrounding the headland. Hundreds of Saxon fighters now made their way towards the beach, singing and swigging from horns of mead. Their revelry was at odds with the horrific scenario that greeted the haphazard arcs of their torches. Many squinted, their drunken vision blurring the true extent of the massacre. Their flames flickered over innumerable corpses, each bloated by watery death and either floating like driftwood, or being unceremoniously dumped onto the shore. Silhouetted against the moon's glow, two figures strolled towards the shoreline.

"So the sea prevailed, thane."

"Just as you predicted, shaman."

"The great waves rolled across the English army exactly as they did in my vision ... I've seen something similar, my lord, years ago, around the Frisian islands. When the moon goddess Mona reaches a certain point in her cycle, low-lying lands are lashed with freak tides."

"Perhaps we should have shared this with the others?"

"Indeed," the shaman observed, a wry smile spreading across his crinkled features. "But we didn't tell them about Edwig, either. So the others knew nothing about how we were trailing the redheaded witch."

"Exactly, Paega. You suspected this island retreat *long* before that puffed-up, one-eyed cockerel Modig's boasts about cave drawings."

"Under the influence of magic, I have seen glimpses. I also knew there were supernatural elements among the seals, conspiring with the witch. By striking when the sea-beings were at their most vulnerable we have also eliminated them as a threat."

"And the seal hunt provided the necessary delay, keeping us away from the battlefield. I did not want our tribe to become part of the vision you described, of an army reduced to flotsam, of proud warriors turned fodder for crows and seagulls and rats. As for the fucking natives, their celebrations will be short lived."

"Indeed, my lord."

"But what is *far* more important is the knowledge that you, Paega, *only* you, possess."

"And I must thank Judd's unfortunate accident for keeping it that way."

"Yes, Paega. Because of your potion, and because of the loss of so many of our potential rivals, we are now the most powerful tribe in the west. This new land will be *ours*." Despite the fact he was now gazing down at a drowned man, the head wrapped in a gruesome bandage of kelp and digging crabs, Cyneheard smiled. "Look at this one, Paega. See the hooked fish emblem on his tabard? A Jute of the Wihtware. One of Wacian's bodyguards. And look further along the shore."

Grasping the old man's collar he coaxed him over the shingle. When they both felt the sting of freezing water against their shins, Paega squinted in the direction his chieftain was pointing. All he could make out were scores of corpses, some lodged together in absurd embraces, others jerking as the oncoming waves tugged at their inert limbs. Among the soldiers were war hounds and horses that had succumbed to the ferocity of the tidal rush. Cyneheard halted. "Look at this fine Jutish warlord, still sitting astride his mount as if he is the proudest chieftain to ever lead his men onto the field."

Paega scowled at the bizarre spectacle. "Wacian! Impossible. We watched him collapse onto the floor among the scraps and bones from the feast. Like his shaman, Judd, he sits at Tiw's banqueting table. Wacian was dead *before* the sea rose."

"His bodyguards insisted the drunken pig still lead them into battle, Paega. So his body was propped up in the saddle, his legs lashed to his horse. The fucking Wihtware and their weird customs."

Paega said nothing. Instead his eyelids were clenched. Cyneheard squinted into the shaman's gaunt features. "What is it, Paega? You look as if you've seen a ghost. Although you have so many to choose from." He laughed sarcastically.

"It's seeing Wacian again."

"He *is* quite ... disturbing. Look at him. I remember a fierce warlord, a hunter of boars, and an even fiercer drinker. The shapeshifting potion turned him into an old man. Like Godric."

"No, sire. What I meant was ... I *felt* something."

"What the fuck are you talking about, Paega?"

"The witch among the Celts, the firstborn of the druid slaughtered by Godric, the girl Modig was about to burn alive without even appreciating who she was ... I sense her life force. I fear she survived the tempest."

"You could use your mind controlling spell again, to attack her?"

"That can be employed on another who shares the gift, but *only* if their will is weak. As we watched from the cliffs I knew the young boy in the coracle was a druid. And I sensed he had recently emerged from the type of deep slumber that follows the casting of strong spells. He was a *perfect* subject. But this mind control *only* works if my target is close enough that I can actually *see* them. Then I can get inside an enemy's thoughts, especially if they are of tender years. They can become my puppet. That is just what I did with the boy when I made him turn on his allies. The cur is adrift at the moment. When he falls into their hands again, the Celts will have his head for what I made him do. Whatever. He was expendable."

Cyneheard grinned, his sparse teeth catching the moonlight. "Puppets or not, your wolf warriors will eventually sweep across their island."

With that the Saxon chieftain crouched to Wacian's body. A dull sheen flashing from his sword, he lunged, slicing across the corpse's neck. The head flopped into the surf, its long white hair trailing like seaweed. Cyneheard bowed to the mutilated chieftain, seizing the wet locks, heaving them from the water. With mock reverence, he held this macabre trophy high, drawing the attention of the other beachcombing warriors. Their pouches laden with precious gems or jewellery looted from drowned men, they slowly gathered around their thane.

"This is Wacian. His Jutes lost many warriors to the waves, as did the Angles, the Saxons of Sussex and Essex, and some of our own brethren ... Somorsaetas ... Wilseatas. The blood truce is over and the only enemy still standing in our path, those accursed Brits, will be vanquished soon enough. All the remaining West Saxon thanes will pledge their allegiance to my sect once word of my wolf warriors spreads. The throne of Wessex will be mine. The West Country is ours. At the next moon, my fighting wolves will roar over Dumnonia and into Cornwall; at the next again, Cymru, until all that is left of the Celts are rivers of their blood. I will then turn to Mercia, to East Anglia, to North Humberland ... then the lands over the wall. We will be masters of these islands."

"Shall we select a warrior tonight, my lord?" asked Paega. "Under cover of darkness, row him out to the island, let him slip unnoticed onto the rocks, there to take my potion? Why not select *ten* wolf warriors?"

At this statement, scores of the Saxon soldiers thrust their weapons towards the black skies, imploring they be selected for the shapeshifting: it meant premature death for any warrior but joining the ranks of Tiw's men was a truly heroic end. Nodding proudly, Cyneheard beckoned everyone into silence. "I shall be choosing my next wolf warriors soon. But the natives aren't going anywhere. The fools don't realise they've taken refuge in their own tomb." With that the Saxon chieftain roared then tossed the severed head towards the stars.

Made in the USA
Charleston, SC
12 November 2015